Love Me Anyway

J.P. Grider

Published by Fated Hearts Publishing, 2017.

Love Me Anyway
Published by
Fated Hearts Publishing
Naked and Far From Home Copyright 2015

2nd Edition Love Me Anyway Copyright 2017
ISBN: 978-0-9997834-0-5[1]

Cover design by Indie Solutions by Murphy Rae

This is a work of fiction. Any similarity to any person, place, thing, or event is purely coincidental and a result of the author's imagination. Any references to historical events, real people, or real places are used fictitiously.

Copyright © 2017 by J.P. Grider

---

1. https://www.myidentifiers.com/myaccount_manageisbns_titlereg?isbn=978-0-9997834-0-5&icon_type=errors

Love Me Anyway

A Description

Tia Mercury was a freshman in high school and had her first serious crush—on a senior who wouldn't touch her. At least not until she turned eighteen.

Clinton Daniels was not your everyday teenage boy, and because his tougher-than-nails father wouldn't let him forget it, Clinton became a loner. And learned to distrust everyone.

Until he met Tia. She was sweet, she was funny, and she knew nothing about good music. It was the nineteen-eighties for goodness sake—time to turn off that AM radio crap. So while Tia drooled over Clinton, he was busy making her mix-tapes. She was falling in love. He was ignoring his heart. See, Clinton had a secret. But sharing it could cost him their friendship, and he was not willing to risk losing the only person he ever loved.

Love Me Anyway is a serious story that spans a decade. A tale about unconditional love and what two people are willing to look past to prove that love.

Also By J.P. Grider

The Hunter Hill University Series
Calling California
Mending Michael
Reaching Rose

Young Adult Books
Sacrifices (A Paranormal Romance)
The Memorial (A Short Story)

New Adult Books
When Glass Shatters
Don't Look at Me (coming in Spring 2018)

DEDICATION

"We Will Rock You"

This book is dedicated, not to a person, but to a decade. A decade that, for better or worse, was defined by significant and serious moments, such as the fall of the Berlin Wall, the unfortunate disaster of the Space Shuttle *Challenger*, and John Lennon's shocking assassination, as equally as it was defined by frivolous and trendy moments, such as its big hair, wacky neon clothing, and some of the greatest movies to date (think *Back to the Future, E.T., Pretty in Pink, Sixteen Candles, The Breakfast Club* to name a few). But to me, a teenager who grew up in The Eighties, the decade was defined by its music— the good and the bad. As a fourteen year old on August first, 1981, I became glued to the television the moment Mark Goodman appeared on the screen introducing the innovative new concept that he coined "the best of TV combined with the best of radio"—MTV Music Television. A concept that rocked my world by introducing new faces, such as Madonna, Bon Jovi, and Duran Duran and gave a face to already well-known bands, such as The Rolling Stones, Led Zeppelin, and Queen. MTV may not be the 24-hour music video channel that once held the teenage world captive, but to me, it helped define the greatest decade ever—The 1980s.

CHAPTER ONE

"It's a Kind of Magic"

Present Day
CLINTON

Her face made me smile. It was a sweet face. A kind face. Soft. Plump. Pleasant. And her heart matched. It was full of love and of life. The effect she had on me took me by surprise, and I may not have known it then, but Tia Mercury would become the most important person in my entire life. She helped me become the person I am today. Tia helped me to see the truth about myself, whether she intended to or not, whether she truly accepted that truth or not.

This is *our* love story, and though I am inclined to tell it, I will let her do so. For her version is a much different love story from my own.

CHAPTER TWO

"Crazy Little Thing Called Love"

September, 1980
TIA

The first time I met Clinton, I fell head over heels. He had this long, thick, almost-curly brown hair that made a girl jealous, and the right amount of muscle to make a girl feel safe in his arms. Not that I'd had the opportunity at the time to be in his arms, but it wasn't hard to imagine. Plus, he was a senior in high school. I was only a freshman, so his being older was another source of my infatuation. But honestly, Clinton was beautiful. And not just on the outside.

The day I met him, though, I had just bought a fifty-cent bag of red Swedish fish from the Campus Sweet Shoppe. Fifty fish in a small brown bag—Heaven. He was talking to my best friend Najia, who happened to be Clinton's next-door neighbor. Najia and I had plans to walk around town, and the usual routine was to meet each other halfway between our homes and then start our trek from there. But that day, Najia hadn't been at the designated spot—the campus—so I continued on toward her house, where I found her talking to the hunky, scruffy, beautiful boy.

"Oh, Tia. I'm so sorry," Najia said, then looked at her friend and said, "Clinton, I gotta go."

As Najia walked toward me, Clinton waved. "Okay, Naj. See ya." But he looked at me and winked.

Najia, her back to Clinton, waved a hand over her shoulder. It was hard for me to turn around and head back the other way with Najia, because my eyes were glued to the boy who was now walking up the stairs to his house.

"Oh my God, Naj, who was that?" I asked, the pathetic dreaminess in my voice floating off my tongue.

"Who? Clinton?" she asked, almost sounding disgusted that I'd asked.

"Yeah." I rolled my eyes and fluttered my eyelids as I thought about him again.

"Oh my God, he's such a dork, Tee. Besides, he's eighteen. It's against the law."

"Ew. I'm not talking about sex, Naj. I'm only thirteen, well, almost fourteen, but still."

"Exactly. He's eighteen and probably used to fooling around with... Scratch that. It's Clinton. Probably not." She laughed.

"Really?" I asked in a whisper, as if anyone else could hear us talking on the busy avenue. "You don't think he's ever done it?" I said softly, still afraid to be heard.

"I don't know, Tee. I barely talk to the guy. Today he just wanted to know how Tasha was doing."

"Oh yeah. How *is* your new puppy?"

"Adorable. Later, come back to my house. We'll play with her."

"Okay."

As Najia and I continued our walk, all I could think about was getting back to her house to see Tasha.

Well...

Really to see Clinton.

Oh my God, I'd never been so attracted to someone in my life—well, besides Shaun Cassidy that is. But I felt bad for Najia at that moment because all I wanted to do was ask her about Clinton. I didn't want to annoy her, though, so I managed to concentrate enough to focus on her and our walk. And sharing my fifty red fish. I just don't know how I did it. The image of Clinton was impossible to swipe from my mind.

When we arrived back at Najia's house, I was disappointed to find out that Clinton wasn't home. "His car isn't in the driveway," Najia pointed out, "so cool yourself down."

"I didn't even ask."

"You didn't have to. You were straining your neck so much I thought I'd see your head pop off."

"Naj." I rolled my eyes, but she was right. I could not keep my eyes off his house, just hoping for a sighting.

When we opened the door to Najia's, Tasha's little legs pattered quickly toward her and she jumped onto Najia's lap. "Hey, pretty pretty. Hey, pretty pretty," Najia cooed and picked up Tasha to carry her to her bedroom.

"So, why Clinton?" she asked me, catching me off guard with her question. "You really think he's cute?"

I felt myself blushing. "Yeah. You don't?"

"Eh. He's not my type. I guess he's okay, but—" she laughed "—I watch him with his brothers and they, like, tear him apart."

"Why?"

"I don't know. I guess that's what siblings do. He just, he never fights back. They're older than him, and I've watched them for years torture him."

"Poor Clinton," I mused, mostly to myself but loud enough for Najia to hear.

"That's why I think he's a dork. Fight back, for goodness' sake."

"He looks strong," I said, recalling his thick frame. "Plus, what is he? At least six feet tall?"

"I heard his dad telling my mom he's six-three."

"Holy crow."

"Still, Tee. It's Clinton. He's a dork."

I shrugged. I wasn't going to convince her differently. Besides, he was eighteen. All I could do was dream about him anyway. Like I did Shaun Cassidy.

LYING IN BED LISTENING to my favorite radio station, I couldn't get my mind off Clinton. Najia had said he was a dork, but I didn't think so. I mean, what did a freshman in high school really know? But to me, Clinton seemed cool, and I would have loved to get the chance to know him.

Before leaving my best friend's house, I got Najia to tell me a little more about him, of course without me sounding pathetic and all. So I found out that he worked for the local food market. *Who knew?* All those times my mom had asked me to go with her, I should have gone. Well, now I would.

At some point, I fell asleep, and I know the last thing I thought about was how to get Clinton's attention. The first thought I woke up to was, *Clinton's eighteen*. He might still have been in high school. Maybe he went to *my* high school. Boy was I excited now. I couldn't wait to get to school to ask Najia if he did.

HE DID.

Clinton went to my high school.

Since it was only mid-September, I had nearly nine months to grab his attention before he graduated. But *could* I catch his attention? In his eyes, I was a mere child, the best friend of his next-door neighbor (if he even knew *that* much). And he was an adult. A senior in high school. Forget about my mom finding out. She'd whip my behind.

I'd just have to hide it from her.

But I was getting ahead of myself. First, I had to get Clinton to notice me. And hopefully, he liked girls with flaming-red hair and a few freckles, because unfortunately, God had graced me with Raggedy-Ann looks.

During lunch, sitting at my usual table with Najia, Val, and Christie, I scanned the room to see if Clinton shared this lunch period too. But there were too many kids, and the cafeteria was too large for me to pick him out without making myself conspicuous. And then it occurred to me that seniors didn't usually stay in for lunch. Darn it.

Later on in Algebra, since I had no idea what the teacher was talking about anyway, I found myself doodling Clinton's name all over my notebook. Now, had I found out his last name, I could have scrawled my first name in front of it, but since I didn't know, I settled for drawing his name inside my fancy arrow-adorned hearts. And sometimes...I would put his name above mine with a heart in between. When the bell rang, I raced to the door to see if I'd pass Clinton in the hallway, but though I'd done this after every class, I never did run into him that day. So after school, I threw open the front door and told my mother I was going to the market and would she mind giving me money so I could pick up dinner.

"Pick up dinner, Tia? Since when are you concerned about picking up dinner?"

"Since now. I'm hungry." I turned from her stare, since she knew me better than anyone. I didn't want her to see my lying eyes.

"Then you're in luck, because dinner's in the oven. All you need to do is wait an hour and a half."

"I can't wait that long, Mom. How 'bout I go get a snack?"

"In the cabinet."

I stomped my foot like the thirteen-year-old I was and said, "Mom, please. Can I just have a couple bucks to go to the market? Please," I begged.

She shook her head, and I knew she knew this wasn't about needing a snack, but Mom was too kind to say anything. "My wallet's in my purse."

From our Mickey Mouse phone in the den, I quickly dialed Najia to see if she could meet halfway and come with me. "You're crazy, Tee, but yeah, I'll come."

"Thank you, Naj. Meet you at the campus in ten minutes."

I hurried up to my room and put on my cutest denim mini-skirt and my red ankle boots, keeping on the ivory sweater tank that I had worn to school. Then I ran a curling iron through my hair and fingered the curls to keep them loose. I couldn't wait to see Clinton...Clinton what? Darn it, I needed to find out his last name.

So the first thing I asked Najia when she met me at the Campus Sweet Shoppe was, "What the heck is Clinton's last name?"

"Daniels." Then she cracked up. "I can't believe you want to go see Clinton at the food store. You're crazy, Tee. You haven't even had your first kiss, and suddenly you're looney over an eighteen-year-old. And notice I said looney."

I knocked her in the arm with my elbow. "Stop. I just wanna see him."

"Looney, I tell ya. Looney."

I didn't care how looney Najia thought I was; seeing Clinton at the market was worth it. The first thing we did when we got there was look for him. We found him at register three. That meant if I wanted to see him close up at all, I'd have to buy something and go to his register. Lucky for me, Mom let me take her two-dollar bill. I talked Najia into buying a couple chocolate bars and a pack of bubble gum. Najia just shook her head at my lunacy.

My hands shook as I put the candy on the conveyor belt. It was my turn next.

"Hey, girls," Clinton said to us after his last customer left. "So, Najia, you never did tell me your friend's name," he said, winking at me.

Oh my God, I think I'm gonna faint.

"Clinton," Najia said coolly. Not as in The Fonz cool, but as in indifferent cool. "This is Tia. My best friend."

"Hi, Tia. Nice to meet you."

I wanted to giggle. I wanted to giggle so bad it hurt. But he was eighteen years old, and if I wanted him to like me, I had to act more mature. So I held back my laugh and smiled. "Hi. Nice to meet you too."

And right after I said it, Najia cracked up, holding her belly.

Clinton shook his head, and I wondered if he thought I was a dork too. He put my stuff in a bag, and my hand shook as I handed him my two-dollar bill. I was so nervous, I took the bag and left without my change. I walked so fast out of the store that I hadn't even realized that Najia wasn't with me.

"Nice move, Tee," she said, still laughing at me when she caught up with me outside.

"Naj." I sat my butt down on the brick ledge of the store and whined. "He's never gonna like me now."

"Tee. He's eighteen. You are nowhere near that. Like him from afar. He's too old for you."

Just then, Bobby Bennett was walking by with Todd Adams and they stopped. "Hey, what's up?"

"Hey," we both said at the same time.

"What are ya doin' hanging out by the food store?" Bobby asked.

"Getting candy," I said, not afraid to talk to the boys who were actually my age.

"We're going for pizza. Wanna come?"

"Sure," Najia said.

I'd rather have stayed on the food store's brick ledge trying to catch a glimpse of Clinton through the front window.

But just as we started walking with Bobby and Todd to the pizza place next to the food store, Clinton came out of the store and stopped us. "Tia, you left without your change." He held out my dollar and ten cents change for me to take.

"Oh. I, uh, didn't, uh... Thank you." Najia was right—I was such a child.

"Well, you're very welcome."

I took the money from his hand, and when my fingers grazed his palm, I thought my heart was going to hop right out of my chest. It was on fire. Like burning up a million degrees. So were my fingers where I had touched him.

Then he winked at me.

If I had a fainting problem, that's when I would have found out, because I felt all the blood draining from my face, and I thought I was about to pass out. God must have felt bad for me, because he kept me on my feet.

Clinton went back into the store, and Bobby, Todd, Najia, and I headed for the pizza place, much to my dismay.

As we followed the boys, Najia whispered in my ear, "How come you don't like Bobby anymore?"

I shrugged. "I don't know. I just don't," I whispered back. But really, did a thirteen-year-old girl have to have a reason why she didn't like a boy anymore, after pining over him for nearly a year? I didn't think so.

Since Najia didn't have any money, we only had enough for two slices of pizza and no drink or one slice of pizza and a small Coke. We decided we would eat our chocolate bars and order two small cokes.

"So, Tia, you seein' anybody?" Bobby asked me.

"Yeah. I'm seeing everybody. I ain't blind," I joked.

"Ha ha. Very funny. I thought you liked *me*."

"Old news," Najia told him. "She likes *older* men now."

I snapped my head in her direction. "Naj."

She laughed. "I'm not gonna say anything."

I roll my eyes.

"Who you like, Tee?" Bobby asked. "C'mon, I won't tell."

"Just leave it alone."

"Ah, c'mon, tell us," Todd chimed in.

"Let's go, Naj," I said, crumpling up my chocolate wrapper and grabbing my soda cup.

"No. Wait for us," Bobby said. "We'll walk you home."

They tossed their pizza and followed us out, lighting cigarettes when they reached the street.

"If you're gonna smoke, don't bother walking us home."

Najia hated cigarette smoke. I didn't mind; I actually enjoyed the smell of it.

"Oh, don't be such a goody-goody," Bobby said to Najia.

"She's not a goody-goody. She'd just like to keep her lungs clear for a while longer."

"Eh. Who gives a shit," Todd said.

"*This* is why Tee is going for the older guys. 'Cause you're all stupid as shit."

"Who is he, Tee?" Bobby wouldn't let up.

"No one you know."

"I'll figure it out, you know. Then I'll kick his ass."

"Uh, yeah right. He's like six foot three and huge." Najia continued with, "You're what, four foot five?"

"Oh. You kill me, Naj," he said.

The walk home was a painful game of twenty questions. Bobby asked the questions. I evaded the answers.

It's true, I really had liked Bobby...a lot. He had been my first crush, albeit a puppy crush. It was sixth grade when I'd first become aware of him. At that time though, I had been too afraid to talk to boys, and he had the reputation of getting underneath girls' clothes. He was not for me. Certainly not. But rumor had it he had the hots for me regardless.

But then eighth grade came around, I'd hit puberty, and stupidity set in. I was then madly in like with Bobby Bennett. And he couldn't have cared less.

Secrets were few and far between in the town of Haledon, and it was no secret that since eighth grade, my heart had been beating for Bobby. He knew it too. But up until today, he had shown no interest. Not until he found out I had set my attentions on someone else.

With Najia, Bobby, and Todd long gone off to their respective homes, I pondered my sudden interest in Clinton Daniels. I thought about him through dinner, through scrubbing dishes, through showering. And then I went to bed and thought about him some more before falling asleep and dreaming about him.

My crush on Clinton became as huge as my crush on Shaun Cassidy, whose poster was currently hanging on my wall. And because of Clinton's real-live status in my town, he would become far more of an obsession than the bubble gum pop star in the leather pants.

CHAPTER THREE

"You're My Best Friend"

TIA

Walking to school without Najia was boring. She'd called me that morning—she was sick.

But as I headed up Zabriskie Street, a brown 1970-something Grand Prix pulled up, on the wrong side of the road, alongside me. For a tenth of a second, I startled, until I realized that the car was the same one that had been parked in Clinton's driveway the other day.

My stomach fluttered and my chest pounded like it had that day when I touched his hand.

Music was blaring when he rolled down his window. "Need a ride?" he asked, his elbow hanging out the window, his music suddenly lowered.

"Uh."

"I won't bite. I promise."

"Suuu...sure?" I was such an idiot.

I slid into the front seat. *Nice car*, I was thinking, but I couldn't say it out loud.

"Tia, right?"

"Yeah." Thank God *that* came out.

Clinton turned the knob on his stereo, and an orchestra-type song blasted from the speakers. *Scaramouch, Scarawhat?*

When the song ended, I found the courage to ask, "So, you like orchestra music?" Of course, my words were too soft and probably barely heard.

Clinton belly-laughed. "Orchestra music? Don't tell me you never heard of Queen."

"Of England?"

He laughed even harder. "What kind of music do you listen to, Tia?" Obviously, he wasn't talking about the Queen of England.

"Uh, seventy-seven?" I *asked*, as if I didn't listen to the station every chance I got.

"Seventy-seven WABC? You listen to AM radio?"

I sucked in my lips, embarrassed at his reaction.

He chuckled and turned down the start of the next song. "That was the *band* Queen."

"Oh."

"You ever hear 'We Will Rock You' and 'We Are The Champions'?"

"Yeah."

"That's Queen. That's the man—Freddie Mercury."

"Mercury? That's *my* last name." Like he cared.

"No shit? That's the coolest last name in the world. You know people say Elvis is the King of Rock, but I disagree. Freddie's voice blows his away."

"Yeah?"

"Hell yeah." He reached over and patted my knee. "Don't worry. I'll get you listening to good music in no time."

And that was how Clinton and I became friends.

CHAPTER FOUR

"Funny How Love Is"

TIA

"Tia. There you are," Clinton said when I met him at his locker two days later. I had found out where his locker was the morning he drove me to school and we walked in together. "I looked for you and Najia this morning. I wanted to give you a ride."

"She's still sick. Chicken pox."

"Ouch."

"Yeah."

"Well, where were *you*?"

"I was running late, so my mom drove me."

"Cool. Here." Clinton handed me three cassette tapes. "Queen's first two albums are on the one cassette. *Sheer Heart Attack* and *A Night at the Opera* are separate. I figure that should tide you over until I record the others."

"Wow. That's so nice of you. Thank you." My heart was racing a hundred times faster than usual, because Clinton had actually *made* me something. I had to have at least been on his mind a little for him to even *think* of making me copies of Queen albums. *Holy Shit.*

"Now you have no excuse for listening to AM radio. By the way, it's WPLJ you want to listen to. Ninety-five-point-five on *FM*." He accentuated FM.

I laughed. Well, giggled was more like it, but I was trying. Eventually, I would stop being a giddy little girl around him.

The homeroom bell rang while I was laughing, and now I was late. "Crap."

"Oops. Sorry about that, Tia."

"See ya later. Thanks again, Clinton."

It didn't matter that I raced to my homeroom on the other side of the school. It didn't matter that I was panting and out of breath. Because when I got to homeroom two-sixteen, Mr. Ritter wouldn't allow me to enter his classroom.

"This is not a good way to start off your freshman year of high school, Ms. Mercury," he said. "Please go get a late pass from the main office."

"But..."

"No excuses, Ms. Mercury."

And that was that. He turned his attention from me and began roll call. *Shoot.* I hoped my mom wouldn't find out about this. I'm sure she'd say that my being the daughter of a teacher meant that I should always show respect to other teachers. And being late for any class, including homeroom, was showing *dis*respect.

AFTER SCHOOL, I WENT home, and the first thing I did was grab my little pink boom box—not much boom, but at least it had speakers—from my room and take it with me to the front porch to do my homework. The first cassette tape

I put in was the one with that "Bohemian Rhapsody" song Clinton had on in his car. Right away, I was hooked. I loved the lead singer's voice—it was like this crazy opera, pop, rock, angelic sound. I'd never heard anything like it.

By the time I got to my homework, I was finished listening to *A Night at the Opera* and I put in one of the other cassettes. Still loving Freddie Mercury's voice, I was not as into the songs as I had been before, so I was able to complete my assignments. But not without taking a few involuntary breaks to think about Clinton. *He actually made* me *cassette tapes. That's gotta mean something, right?*

THE NEXT MORNING, CLINTON was actually parked on the corner of Zabriskie Street.

"Hey," I said to him, noticing how cool he looked with his elbow leaning out his open window, his thick bicep straining through his white tee shirt. "What are you doing?"

"Waiting for you."

"Me? Why?"

He held up a cassette tape. "Got another one. Their most recent."

"Wow. Thanks." I reached for the tape, but he pulled it back.

"Oh no. Gotta get in first."

I could not contain my smile, so I covered my mouth.

He laughed and said, "Come on. You don't want to be late again."

I got in, and he handed me the cassette. "Did you get a chance to listen to any of the others?"

"I did. I *love* that guy's *voice*. Oh my God, it's, like, amazing."

Clinton laughed again. "Yeah, Freddie Mercury is definitely one of a kind. And lucky you, you share his last name."

"That's cool, right?"

"Very cool. Though, it's not his *real* name. His real name is Farrokh Bulsara."

"That doesn't sound like the name of a lead singer of a rock band."

"Hence the name change."

While the conversation flowed, I decided to take a deep breath and blurt, "Why you being nice to me?"

"What kind of question is that? Would you rather me be mean to you?" He, of course, was chuckling between his words.

"No. I just don't know why you're, like, being nice, like waiting for me here today. Making me tapes." I shrugged, quickly losing my confidence.

His laughing stopped and his face went serious. "I like you. You're, well, you're nice." Then after a moment's pause, he smiled and said, "And you listen to AM radio. I feel it's my mission to rescue you from that bubblegum music before you fry your brain."

That cracked me up. "Thanks."

He nodded and kept his eyes on the road, but I saw his lip quirk, and I could have sworn the color of his skin turned a red tinge.

When we got to school, instead of going in through the bottom door—closest to Clinton's locker—we walked in through the main entrance. "You shouldn't be late again. I'll walk you to your locker."

"Then *you'll* be late."

"Eh. My homeroom teacher doesn't care."

"Oh. Well, thanks."

That heart pounding started again. *He's walking me to my locker now.*

"You're by the history wing, right?"

"Yeah. By Mr. Ritter's room."

"Right. I have him for U.S. History."

"I just have him for homeroom, but he doesn't like me very much."

"How can anyone not like *you?*" Clinton smiled. And then...then, he took my hand.

That heart of mine? Yeah. I looked down to make sure, but I could have sworn it had just tunneled its way out of my chest. It hadn't, thank God, but boy did it feel like it had.

As we neared my locker, Clinton squeezed my hand. "So, if I don't see you beforehand, I'll be at the corner of Zabriskie in the morning?"

Oh my gosh. "Sure. Okay."

At my locker, Clinton just stood there. He let go of my hand, but he didn't move. So we stared at each other for a couple seconds before he leaned in, nodded, and said, "Okay. See you tomorrow." Then he let go of my hand and walked away. *I think he was going to kiss me. I wonder what stopped him.*

AS PROMISED, THE NEXT two weeks, Clinton's brown Grand Prix was parked at the corner of Zabriskie Street, and for the next two weeks, Clinton drove me to school. We talked Queen every morning, and Clinton walked me to my locker each day. He still held my hand, but he had yet to kiss me. I was quickly falling in love with both Freddie Mercury and Clinton Daniels. Freddie for his beyond amazing voice, and Clinton for just being Clinton. He was adorable, sweet, and fast becoming my very best friend in the whole wide world.

Once Najia's chicken pox cleared up and she was back in school, Clinton's car was no longer waiting at the corner in the morning. And I didn't see him at my locker in school. His car was in the lot, but he was nowhere to be found. And I had no idea why.

"Hey, Naj, have you seen Clinton lately?" I asked on the way home from school the fourth day of not seeing him anywhere.

"Uh. I guess. When?"

"At all."

"Oh. Well, yeah. He was pulling out of his driveway in the morning before school my first day going back."

I shrugged. "Have you seen him at school?"

"Here and there. Why? What's going on?"

"I don't know. It's just, I haven't seen him, so I was wondering."

Najia's hand landed on my shoulder. "Tee, I found out that he's going to be nineteen in December. You *can't* like him for sure now."

"Nineteen? Really?"

"Yeah. Nineteen."

"Still. I'm going to be fourteen on the thirteenth. We could at least be friends."

"Tee, what nineteen-year-old boy wants to be friends with a thirteen-going-on-fourteen,-year-old girl? Mostly, they want to be *friends*," she said, using air quotes, "with other eighteen- or nineteen-year-old girls."

I shrugged again, dropping the subject and keeping the rest of my thoughts to myself. *Why would he just stop waiting for me? And why haven't I seen him at school? Is he avoiding me?*

I was so anxious to see Clinton that I asked my mom if I could have money to run to the store to get chocolate. I ate a lot of chocolate.

"Sure," she said. "Just pick up some aspirin while you're there. I have a headache." She reached in her wallet and pulled out a five-dollar bill. "Do *not* use it all."

"Thanks, Mom."

"Bring back the change," she reiterated.

I ran out the door without responding to her.

Bobby was hanging out at the food store again. "Hey, good-lookin'," he said to me as I walked into the store, Bobby close on my heels.

"Hi, Bobby." Last month, I would have been blushing over his calling me good-looking.

"So who's that kid I saw you drivin' in to school with last week and holding hands with in the halls?" Bobby asked, following me through the store.

"A friend."

"And *who* is your friend?"

"Najia's neighbor."

"So he's the older guy you like?"

I picked up the aspirin on my way to the candy aisle, but I really wished I could lose Bobby, because I'd never be able to talk to Clinton if Bobby was there. "So, Bob, are you here for a reason?" I asked, anxious to get him off my back.

"Just saw you. Thought I'd follow you in."

"I'm not that exciting."

"Sure you are."

I grabbed a bag of Hershey's Kisses and a big bag of M&Ms and then said, "Okay. See ya at school tomorrow."

"Hang out with me."

God, I would have died for him to say that before I met Clinton.

"I can't." I headed to the registers, trying hard to get away from Bobby, but he wouldn't leave my side.

"Come on, Tee. We can make out."

Coming to a dead stop, I turned and faced him. "What kind of thing is that to say?"

"You know you want to."

"God."

"You can call me that if you'd like."

In line for Clinton's register, my stomach was fluttering and my chest was pounding—mostly due to seeing Clinton, partly due to Bobby's make-out offer. I'd heard he was an awesome kisser.

Clinton was done with the customer in front of me. "Hi, Tia," he said quietly, not as excited to see me as I was him.

"Hi."

He rang up my order and bagged it without saying anything more. I was too nervous to ask him what I'd done wrong, so I just said bye and walked out.

"Isn't that the kid who was driving you to school last week?"

I'd forgotten Bobby was still behind me.

"Yeah."

"Doesn't seem like a good friend to me. He hardly talked to you."

I ignored Bobby.

He rubbed his hand on my back. "Come on, Tee. Come to my house."

"No, Bob, I can't."

His hand moved down my back until it stopped on my butt.

I turned to face him and punched him in the gut.

"Ow. What'd you do that for?"

"Go home, Bobby. By yourself."

As I walked away from him, I heard him still whining about my punch to his gut. I just laughed it off and headed home.

IT WASN'T UNTIL THANKSGIVING break that I saw Clinton again. And that was by accident. The Friday after Thanksgiving, Najia and I decided to hang out at the local soda shop. Tuffy's was the last of the fifties leftover malt-style shops. They had fountain drinks, penny candy, and the best ice cream in the world. There were metal tables, a tin roof, and pinball machines. Most recently, they had added two arcade games—Asteroids and Pac-Man. With this addition, Tuffy's had reinvented themselves as the local teen hangout. It was mostly freshmen and sophomores hanging out, but occasionally, the middle-schoolers came in to play.

The first thing I saw when Najia and I walked in that day was the guy behind the counter. It was Clinton.

"Naj, did you know he was working here?"

"No. I haven't seen him lately."

"Should I leave?" I whispered.

"Of course not." She tugged me by the sleeve. "Come on. Let's put our quarters down to hold a spot. I'm dying to play Pac-Man. I heard it's awesome."

I wasn't dying to play anything, so I just stood in the corner beside Najia and watched the boys who were already playing the arcade games.

"Well, well, look who's here." Bobby and Todd now crowded the corner.

"Hey," Najia and I both said as Bobby put his quarter behind Najia's at the edge of the screen.

"Get your quarters off the game," Matthew, the kid currently playing Pac-Man, said. "You're blocking my screen."

"Geez," Najia said.

"Put them on top of the game," I suggested.

"I don't think she can reach," Bobby said, referring to Najia's height.

"Go to hell," she told him, and stood up on her toes to put the quarters on top of the arcade game.

"So what's up, good-lookin'?" Bobby said, purposely brushing his arm against mine.

"Nothing." I wasn't really in the mood for him today. I was too nervous thinking about Clinton standing behind the counter.

"So your *guy* works here now?" Bobby continued talking to me.

"He's not my guy."

"Yeah, well, people are talkin'."

"What?"

Bobby shrugged. "At school. I heard some guys teasin' him 'bout going out with some freshman."

"Oh my God. When?"

"All different days. I've been following him."

"What the hell you following him for?" Najia asked.

Bobby didn't answer her; he just stared at me. Then he stepped closer and touched my face. "I wanted to get a handle on my competition."

Shoving his hand away, I pushed myself out of the corner and walked out of the store, stopping on the sidewalk out front to calm down. *The teasing. Of course that would make Clinton stop talking to me.*

"Tia?"

When I turned around, Clinton was standing outside the door.

"You okay?"

"I'm fine."

Clinton stuck his hands in his pockets and jutted his chin. "That kid Bobby bothering you?"

"No. He's just, um, being himself. I can handle him."

"If you need me to kick his ass, I wouldn't mind."

"Thanks," I said, now able to smile.

"Come back in. I'll buy you a soda." He kept his voice quiet, as if he was unsure of his invitation.

Clinton held the door open for me, and then he patted the first stool at the counter. I sat.

"So, I can make you any flavor soda you want." He tapped the silver knobs behind the counter. "We got cherry, grape, strawberry, orange, maple, cream, root beer, and cola. I can give you any combination you want."

"Really? You can do that?"

"Sure. They're syrups. I add the seltzer to it."

"Oh."

"It's how they did it in the fifties, I guess."

"Wow. Okay. I'll have, um, strawberry and...actually, can I just have the strawberry?"

"Sure. That's my favorite, too."

I watched him squirt syrup into a glass filled with ice.

"Like it sweet?"

"Very."

"Thought so." He squirted more syrup into the glass then sprayed in the seltzer.

"Try it," he said, sliding the glass across the counter.

I brought the straw to my lips immediately. "Oh my God, this is so good."

"Right? I don't know why they ever switched to bottled soda," he joked.

He stepped back to lean against the stainless steel freezer behind him and looked around the store.

I continued sipping my soda.

His arms were crossed in front of him, his butt against the freezer, when he said, "Tia," quietly.

"Yeah?"

"I'm sorry. I'm sorry I've been avoiding you the past few weeks."

He was *avoiding me. I knew it.*

"It's just." He stepped forward and took a rag out of his back pocket and started wiping down the counter in front of him. "You're young. And, well, some people started talking and, well, I, not that I really give a shit what people say. Lord knows they talk about me anyway, but..."

I just stared at him, not knowing what to say.

"You're young. I'm gonna be nineteen on the twenty-first of December." He smiled. I didn't. "I like you. A lot. But I shouldn't."

Clinton Daniels likes me? A lot?

"Do you understand?"

Truthfully, the answer was no, but I smiled and nodded anyway.

"That's why I stopped picking you up for school. I'm really sorry."

"It's okay," I lied, fighting back tears. This felt like my first break-up.

"Anyway, I still made you a few more tapes. They're in my car."

"Oh. More Queen?" I spoke, even though it was hurting my throat to do so.

"No. A bunch of different stuff. Boston. Styx. Kansas. Just some of my favorite songs, not entire albums."

"Thank you," I coughed out, still holding back my urge to cry.

He pulled his keys out of his front pocket. "Here." He tossed them at me. "Car's parked around the corner."

"Really? I can just go in your car like that?"

"Yeah, Tia. You can go in my car like that. The tapes are in the center console. I labeled them 'FOR TIA.'"

"Okay," I said, jumping off my stool. "Thanks."

At that very moment, happiness seeped in. Clinton had done something special for me. And I had to remember he'd said he liked me a lot. I just wish he didn't think I was too young.

I grabbed the tapes from Clinton's console and inhaled the car's scent before locking it back up.

"Ya find them?" he asked when I came back in and hopped on the stool.

"Yup. Thank you so much." I was in a better mood now.

"Stop thanking me. I like doing it."

"Hey, Clinton, can I have a Coke?" Najia plopped on the stool next to me.

"Sure. Can or fountain?"

"Fountain," I suggested. "It's better."

"Okay. Fountain. So, how long have you been working here, Clint?"

"Since Wednesday. Pays more than the grocery store, plus it's more fun."

"All you need is one of them old-timey hats and aprons," she said, causing us all to laugh.

"Shh. Don't give Karl any ideas."

All of a sudden, Clinton's smile dropped into a frown as two hands squeezed the space between my neck and shoulders. Without thinking, I closed my eyes, knowing exactly who it was. But I didn't like him anymore—I liked Clinton—so I leaned forward and elbowed Bobby in the ribs.

"Ow. Whatchya do that for?"

"Keep your hands to yourself."

"Geez. What turned you into a bitch?"

I rolled my eyes, but only Clinton could see me do so, since my back was still turned to Bobby.

But again, Bobby's hands were on me. This time, he wrapped his arms around my chest from behind. Before I could elbow him again, Clinton's mouth opened. "Get your goddamn hands off her. Now." Clinton wasn't fooling around. He was angry—I could tell by his red cheeks and his enlarged pupils.

"What's it to you?" Bobby said, though his arms were no longer on me. "She ain't your girlfriend."

"She ain't yours either, and she already told you to keep your hands off her."

"You're what, eighteen, nineteen years old? You get your rocks off on little girls? Last I checked, that's still against the law."

"Get the hell out of my store."

"This ain't your store, soda boy."

"But I have the right to kick your ass out. Now get out."

"Fine, ya infant-chasing pansy."

Clinton's whole demeanor changed after Bobby left, and he barely said two words to me the rest of the day.

Nor did he say much to me the rest of that school year either. Every time I'd go to Tuffy's with Najia, or Val and Christie, Clinton was polite, and he always had a sweet strawberry soda waiting for me, but there was no more conversation. No more talk about music. No more cassette tapes. No more anything. So, for the rest of my freshman year, I was sad.

But instead of letting the world, or at least the town of Haledon, know, I kind of started going out with Bobby Bennett.

CHAPTER FIVE

"Someday One Day"

TIA

Najia, Valeri, and Christie were all on vacation with their families the first week in July, and I was bored. I hadn't gone to Tuffy's in two months, and I was dying to see Clinton, but I couldn't bring myself to go alone. Instead, I reread *Persuasion*. Thank God for my front porch, where I did my reading, otherwise I wouldn't have even gone outside.

"Come on, Tia. It's time to go."

"I'd rather not."

"Tee, I don't want you home alone on the Fourth of July. You're coming with me."

"Mom, I'm fourteen. I can stay home by myself."

"Yes, but you've done nothing but sulk all week, and I won't let you sulk alone today. Besides, you'll have fun. It's up on Greenwood Lake."

"Why do we have to go all the way up there?"

"Because that's where my coworker lives, and that's where her barbecue is." My mother brushed her long hair behind her ear. "Come on. I'm not feeling up to it either, but I think it'll do us both some good."

"Fine. But I'm bringing my book."

"That's fine. You may want to grab a swimsuit. She lives on the lake."

FORTUNATELY, THERE were several docks on the woman's property, and I was able to read my Jane Austen book while dangling my feet off the edge and into the cool water. It was a good day.

What I hadn't expected was the day to turn great. For a while.

About an hour after my mom and I got there, some of her friend's cousins showed up. I would have never guessed that one of those cousins would make my day a little brighter.

His long strides made it to the end of the dock before I had a chance to slow my racing heart. "I thought that was you," he said when he reached me. His bare legs were right in front of my face, sexy as hell.

When I attempted to stand and greet him, my foot got caught under my other leg and I fell forward onto the deck, landing on my hands and knees—not a graceful move at all. And especially not one I wanted to make in front of Clinton Daniels.

He squatted down. "You okay?"

Mortified, I said nothing and just sat my butt back down.

Clinton stood back up, kicked off his boat shoes, and sat down next to me, both our feet now covered up to our ankles in lake water.

"I wasn't expecting to see you here today," he said, his heart evidently calmer than mine, according to the composed tone of his voice.

"My mom works with Lydia."

"Oh. My dad and Lydia are cousins."

"Oh."

"So, how've you been, Tia?"

I nodded. "Okay. How 'bout you?"

"Eh. Not bad. Working a little extra at the store."

Again, I just nodded, afraid to speak.

"You haven't come in in a long time."

Looking down at the water, I said, "Why bother?"

"Why bother?"

I just shook my head, too inexperienced in dealing with boys to come across cool.

"Tia? You know it wasn't a good idea to talk with you too much when you were at the store. Bobby was there every day."

Swallowing back my fear, I decided to just blurt, "And you're afraid of a fifteen-year-old punk?"

"No. I'm not. But it does worry me about what he said."

"Talking to a minor is not illegal, Clinton." I was doing a good job of tamping down my fear of speaking my mind.

"No, it's not. Tia, don't be naive. You know we're talking about more than *talking*."

Okay. Now I was back to not knowing what to say.

"When I first met you, I didn't know you were a freshman. I thought, maybe, there was something there, between us. I *wanted* there to be. Actually, I was surprised that I even *had* those feelings for you."

"What?" *What kind of comment was that?*

"I don't feel things for people, Tia. I never cared enough for *anyone,* even my family. And I *trust* no one. No one worth trusting. But when I picked you up that first morning, well, it was a strange experience for me. It's been hard for me to be away from you."

"Oh." *Really?* Oh my goodness, my heart was screaming to get out and hug this boy. Actually, *I* wanted to move closer and hug this boy, not just my heart.

"Anyway, the morning Najia went back to school, remember, she had chicken pox?"

I nodded. Of course I remembered. It was the day Clinton stopped waiting for me on the corner.

"I asked her what year you were in. When she laughed and said you were a freshman, I thought, well, maybe that's not so bad. But then I asked her how old you were, thinking, hoping, maybe you were fifteen, like I was when I started high school."

"You were fifteen when you started high school?"

"Yeah. My negligent father was too lazy to register me for school at the normal age. If it weren't for my cousin reminding him it was against the law not to register your children for school, he probably wouldn't have even registered me when he did. Anyway, when she told me you were still *thirteen*, and you wouldn't be fourteen until October thirteenth, well, that was just way too young, sweetheart. I'm actually embarrassed I felt that way about someone so young."

The urge to cry was consuming me. It was just like that day he told me all this at Tuffy's. I didn't want to cry, though—that would only confirm he was right and I was too young. I couldn't just run away, because that would be childish too. So, I kicked at the water and started singing "Carry on My Wayward Son" in my head.

"Tia? Please don't be upset."

"I'm not," I said way too quickly.

"I'm sorry about avoiding you again too. I was trying to...get a grasp on all these weird emotions I got going on."

I still kept my mouth shut, in order not to cry.

"I don't like seeing you with Bobby either."

I cast my eyes in his direction; he was staring down at me.

"I noticed the last few times you were at Tuffy's, he was hanging on you. And you *let* him."

"Sorry."

"Don't apologize. He's your age. I don't like him, though." There were a few seconds of silence, and then, "Are you going out with him?"

"A little."

"A little? What does that mean?"

"He asked me out. I said I don't know. He said until I know, he'll treat me as if I am."

"He's a jerk, Tia."

"Yeah, well, I like him," I lied. Because I didn't like him. Not like I liked Clinton.

"Okay. Well, unfortunately, I don't have a say in the matter. But—" he paused "—maybe one day, when we're both older, maybe you and I could..."

I snapped my head in his direction.

He laughed.

"Maybe when you're eighteen?"

I closed my eyes and sighed.

"You'll be starting college; I'll be hopefully graduated. What do you think?"

I think I'm gonna throw up, was what I thought. What I said was, "Okay."

He smiled. So did I.

Then he switched the subject.

"So, what are you listening to these days?"

I was apprehensive to talk at first, but I ended up saying, "Those tapes you made me. Plus, I bought two Styx tapes and a Boston tape from the music and poster store by Fancy Cleaners."

"Wow. I'm impressed."

"I've also been listening to WPLJ."

"Gave up AM radio, huh?"

"Yeah." I blushed. I still missed my corny music, but I was trying hard to learn all I could about Clinton's type of music so I'd have more in common with him.

"Then my job here is done," he joked, but it made me feel sad. I didn't want his job with me to be done.

He must have seen disappointment scattered all over my face, because then he said, "Tia," and patted my knee. "I was teasing. Listen, Tuffy's has been slow since school let out. Why don't you come back? I'll have a strawberry soda waiting for you." He wiggled his eyebrows up and down, which gave me goosebumps all over.

Still splashing the water with my feet and hoping Clinton couldn't see the goosebumps standing at attention up and down my arms and legs, I said, "Maybe."

"Don't bring Bobby, though." Clinton nudged me with his shoulder.

"He's not so bad," I said, defending my immature non-boyfriend.

"You're too good for him, Tia. But if he's who you like, then I can't stand in your way."

Again, I didn't know what to say that wouldn't sound childish, so I said nothing.

He patted my knee once. "Did you eat yet?"

"No."

"Think I can pull you away from your book?" He took it out of my hands to look at it. "To get a burger with me?"

"Sure." Clinton handed me back my book and helped me up.

"So, you're a Jane Austen fan?"

"Yeah. She's not all though. I like to read mostly everything."

"Me too. Ever read J.D. Salinger?"

"Yes. You kidding? *Catcher in the Rye* is one of my favorites."

"Hey, mine, too."

"Holden's cool."

"For a whiner," he said.

"Clinton," Mom's coworker called as we approached the deck, where most of her guests were gathered.

"Hey, Lydia." Clinton greeted Lydia with a kiss on the cheek. Lucky Lydia.

"You and Tia know each other?"

"Yeah. We go to the same school." Clinton looked over at me and winked.

"Oh. Yeah. That's right." Lydia looked around, and when she spotted my mom, she said, "Tammy," while waving her arm in the air.

Mom walked over and put her hand on my back.

"Tammy, I forgot you lived in Haledon. Do you know my cousin Bill Daniels?"

"No, I don't think I do," Mom said, looking at Clinton.

"This is his youngest, Clinton. Clinton, this is my friend Tammy."

"My mom," I added.

"Oh," Mom said, confused, looking from me to Clinton and back. "Hello."

"Hello, Mrs. Mercury."

"Hello, Clinton."

"*Ms.* Mercury," I whispered to Clinton.

"Tammy," Mom corrected.

"Tammy," Clinton said. "Hi." He cocked his head toward me. "Tia and I go to school together."

"Ah. Okay. So, you're in high school?"

"Well, I graduated this year. I start college in the fall."

"Oh." Mom tensed up again. "Where are you going?"

"William Paterson."

"That's where I went. Though it was Paterson State Teacher's College when I went."

"You're a teacher?"

"Yes."

"She teaches with me in Ringwood."

"Oh."

"So, Clinton, Tia, help yourselves to food. Burgers and dogs are by the grill. Salads and chips are on the table." Lydia pointed to her serving table at the side of her house.

"Thank you," we said.

While we were walking away, I heard Lydia say, "Sure, Tammy, the aspirin's in the kitchen. Cabinet next to the sink."

"So, that was awkward," Clinton said before I did.

"Heck yeah. Did you see her tense up when you told her you graduated?" I laughed.

"Yeah." Clinton sighed.

When I looked at his face, he was biting the side of his lip. *Damn.* That was going to push him even further away.

Clinton got a hamburger for both of us and filled both our plates with mac and potato salads.

"I can help myself, you know," I said on a chuckle.

"I know. I *want* to, though." Again, another wink.

"Thank you." And another blush for me.

With both plates in his hands, he said, "Wanna go back to the dock?"

"Sure, but I can get us sodas first."

"Ah. Good idea."

After I poured us two Cokes, I followed him to the dock, falling more in love with him by the minute. How was I going to wait another three and a half years before I was old enough to date him?

While we ate our hamburgers and salads, we touched upon a bunch of different topics—one of them being our family situations.

Clinton brought it up first. "Tia." Clinton never called me Tee like the rest of my friends. "You said to call your mom *Ms.* She's not married?"

"No. She's divorced. My dad left us when I was, like, five."

"Oh. Do you see him?"

"No. Never. He moved to Oklahoma. Haven't seen him since."

"Since you were five?"

"Yup. Nice, right? Guess I meant a lot to him, huh?"

"I guess as much as I meant to my mom."

"What? Your mom's not around?" It's one thing having your father leave. I've never heard of a mother leaving. And Clinton implied...

"Nope. She left us about two months after I was born."

"Oh, Clinton," I said with more condolence than I intended.

"Eh. I don't remember her."

"You've never had contact with her?"

"Nope."

"Where's she live?"

"I have no idea."

"Wow. How can a mother just leave their kids? I couldn't live without my..." I stopped, not wanting to make things worse for him.

He raised his eyebrows. "I've never talked about my mother with anyone."

"Oh. That's okay. You don't have to."

"No. It's okay. I want to." After a pause, he said, "Who does that, Tia? What kind of mother leaves her newborn baby? She left me to a man who doesn't have an ounce of paternal instinct or compassion, not to mention he's violent as hell."

"Bill's not your dad?"

"Yeah, he's my dad. But he sucks as a father. Thank God for Lydia. She helped us a lot. Until they moved up here. Then we had to fend for ourselves."

"You have three brothers?" I thought that's what I remembered Najia telling me.

"Yeah. They have as much empathy and refinement as my father." His sarcasm was crystal clear.

I also remembered Najia saying that his brothers weren't very nice to Clinton. "Do you like your brothers?"

"Honestly? They're not my favorite people. Dad either."

"Really?"

"The only reason I'm here with him today is because Lydia asked me to come. Plus my father's a drunk and needs someone to drive him home."

"I'm sorry."

"Please. Don't be. I'm long past over it."

"Still. You got *anyone* on your side?"

He laughed. "Not really, Tia."

I found the words *I'm sorry* stuck in my throat. If I had spoken, I would have cried.

"Don't be sad for me, sweetheart. I told you, I don't care much for people, so I'm not bothered by it. Not anymore."

"You don't care for *anyone*?"

Clinton looked at me for several long seconds and shook his head. "Present company excluded, no. I don't. I do what I have to do to survive. I work to pay for my car. I earned scholarships that will hopefully get me through most of college. And when I graduate, I'll make my way through life without them."

"That's...so sad."

"It's my life, Tia. It's just the way things are. *I'm* not sad, so please don't *you* be."

"Okay," I said to agree with him, but there was no way I *couldn't* be sad. Not when the boy I liked so much was virtually alone in the world.

"Tia. I'm fine. Really." Nodding his head, he said, "So, I saw you at the awards ceremony the last day of school."

"That's changing the subject fast."

"It needed to be changed. So, what were you doing there? Underclassmen had no school that day."

"It was optional whether we went or not." I blushed. How could I tell him I went to school because I knew the seniors would be there? "*Some* underclassmen were there," I said defensively.

"But you were sitting on the bleachers alone."

I had trouble responding.

"Did I embarrass you?"

Again, silence.

"I'm sorry. I didn't realize you were..."

There for him? Yes, I was totally embarrassed. "Congratulations, though. I didn't know you were that smart."

"Eh. Not really."

"Not really? Doesn't valedictorian mean you were the smartest in the class?"

"My grades were good. Doesn't mean I'm not stupid from time to time."

"So, how come you're not going to Harvard or Yale or something like that?"

"No extra-curricular activities. Plus, I'm a coward, Tia. I don't do well with change."

"How's Harvard change?"

"I'd have to go away. This town's all I know."

"Yeah. I guess that'd be hard to do. I always thought when I got older, I'd leave. But...who knows?"

"I hope you *are* strong enough to leave, Tia. It's important to be able to do what you want to do. Maybe one day, I'll find the courage. Maybe one day, *you'll* be the one to..."

He just stopped talking.

"What? I'll be the one to what?"

"Nothing. I'm sorry."

"What though? I really don't know what you're talking about."

On an exhale, Clinton said, "I wanted to say, maybe you'll be the one to give me that courage, but that'd be unfair. Because I just told you you were too young for me. I don't know, Tia. I shouldn't even be talking to you now. I'm a freak. I'm 19. You're 14. It's just inappropriate."

I bowed my head in disappointment. "You know, age shouldn't matter. Not if you have feelings for someone." Now *that* had taken courage for me to say.

His sigh was that of exasperation.

"Well, it shouldn't," I repeated.

"But it does."

We watched the soft waves lap over our feet for the next twenty minutes or so, neither one of us knowing what to say after that. Finally, Clinton asked if I wanted to join the rest of the party in the game of volleyball they were starting.

So I said yes, even though it looked like he wasn't really wanting to play at all. He probably just suggested it because it was getting awkward sitting in silence.

We were put on the same team, and throughout the game, I couldn't keep my eyes off Clinton. But I got some satisfaction watching him avert his eyes every time I caught him looking at me too.

At the end of the game, Clinton went off with some of the guys who were chatting him up while we were playing, and I went to find my mom. *I wish I had cousins to hang with.*

My mother was standing amongst a group of other adults. "Hey, Mom," I said, walking up to the group.

"Tia," she said, smiling ridiculously.

"Hey. Can we go?" I whispered so only she could hear.

She looked awkwardly to the group, but she smiled at me and said, "Sure. Let me go say goodbye to Lydia first." To the group, she said, "Listen, we're going to get going. It was nice seeing you all."

"Bye," the bunch said back.

"Take it easy, Lydia."

"Bye, Sam," she said. Then to me, "You okay, babe?"

"Yeah. Just tired."

In the car, I said, "Thanks, Mom, for leaving early."

"Eh, you did me a favor. The sun was giving me a headache anyway. There was no shade out there at all."

"I know, right?"

"So, how well do you know that boy Clayton?"

"Clinton."

"Clinton."

"Um." *Did I really want to tell Mom I had a crush on him?* "Not very. He works at Tuffy's."

"Oh. I love how they redid that place. Reminds me of when I was young."

"It's cute."

"What's the matter, Tee? You have a frown on your face."

"No I don't. I'm just tired," I said quickly. Too quickly to sound believable.

"Okay." Fortunately, my mother didn't press the issue.

I turned on the radio and sighed. "Why can't you get a new radio with FM?" I asked irritably. I'd never learn what songs Clinton liked if I had to continue listening to AM music.

"Watch your tone, Tia. You may be tired, but that's no excuse to talk fresh."

Ugh. I turned the radio back off and sulked the rest of the way home. *I wish I'd said goodbye to Clinton.*

When we got home, I sat on the porch with my book and my flashlight and continued reading *Persuasion*, wishing I'd stayed and watched fireworks on the lake, because I figured Clinton probably had.

IT WASN'T UNTIL TWO weeks later that I rode my bike down to Tuffy's to meet Christie. Najia was still in Jordan with her family.

"How come you haven't been here?" Christie asked while we were locking up our bikes.

"Been busy doing things with my mom," I lied.

"Oh. They have this new jukebox and oh my God, they have this new ice cream. It's chopped up Oreos in vanilla ice cream. Tee, you gotta try it. It's awesome."

"Oreos? In ice cream?"

"Yeah. Genius, right?"

"Right. I'll have to try it."

"Clinton said it's called cookies and cream."

"Hmmm." *Clinton.* I was too nervous to eat.

There were only a few kids inside the ice cream shop, and "Little Jeanie" was playing on the new jukebox.

"Hey, girls," Clinton said when he saw us.

"Hi, Clinton. What's up?" Christie said.

"Hi," was all I said.

Christie sat down at the counter, but I continued to the back of the store. No one was playing Asteroids, so I lined up a few quarters on the edge of the screen and put one in the slot. Having never played the game before, I was going through my quarters quickly. When I ran out, I figured it was time to sit at the counter. I could get change for a dollar, but that would mean talking to Clinton anyway, and I really didn't want to play the game.

And though I was scared to talk to him, I also really wanted to.

"Hi, Tia," Clinton said right away, before I even chose on which side of Christie to sit.

"Hi," I said, sitting to Christie's left, closest to the arcade games.

"Wanna try the new ice cream?" Clinton asked. "It has crushed Oreos in it."

"You should, Tee," Christie said, holding up her over-flowing spoon.

"Sure. Just a small, please."

"Cup or cone?"

"Cone, please."

"Wow, you're so formal," Christie pointed out, not in the loop about my feelings for Clinton.

"Just being polite." I attempted indifference, just in case Clinton was listening.

"Since when?" she joked.

"Since...it's polite to say please, that's all."

"Here you go, Tia. Tell me how you like it."

I nodded, but Clinton wouldn't leave until I took a lick. I did not want to lick an ice cream cone in front of Clinton.

"You gonna hold it all day or eat it?" He laughed.

With all my thoughts on how stupid I was going to look licking the ice cream, I took a taste then quickly wiped my lips with the back of my hand.

"Good?"

"Good."

Then he tossed me a napkin. "So, you like our new juke-box?"

"Yeah. It's nice having music on in here." I tried my best to keep cool. I liked this boy so much. *If only I were older.*

"Karl thought it would add to the authenticity of the place."

"It does," Christie and I said at the same time.

"Jinx," Christie called first.

I rolled my eyes. *Did I really want to play this baby game in front of Clinton?*

But then Clinton stole whatever was left of my heart when he said, "Tia Mercury. What a pretty name," and added a wink afterward.

"You're not supposed to say her name that quickly, Clinton," Christie complained. "You're supposed to let her not talk for a while."

"But Tia's voice is too pretty not to be heard."

"Thank you," I told him.

I looked at Christie. Her jaw was dropped.

And Clinton's face was red. I noticed that before he all of a sudden walked away and went to the front counter where the penny candy case was.

"Holy crow, Tee," Christie whispered. "Clinton *likes* you."

"He does not," I lied. I couldn't tell Christie what Clinton had told me on the Fourth of July before I'd even had a chance to tell Najia. I wished Jordan wasn't so far away. I didn't even have an address where I could send a letter. I missed her so much.

"Tee, he likes you. Why else would he do that?"

"Do what? Say my name to unjinx me? He probably felt bad."

"He said you have a pretty name, and then he said you have a pretty voice. Boys don't do that unless they like you."

I took a big lick of my ice cream, since Clinton wasn't looking. "If you haven't noticed, he's not a boy. He's, like, nineteen."

"Whoa. Really?"

"Yup."

"Oh. Then does he know you're not even fifteen yet?"

"I don't know," I said, agitated.

"I bet he thinks you're older." She nudges my side. "Look at the way he's looking over at you right now."

I looked but regretted it right away. He *was* looking, but when he saw me notice, he snapped his head toward the front window.

"See what I mean?"

I ignored her that time and finished my ice cream, since it really was delicious, and Clinton was, again, not watching me.

"Wanna play Pac-Man?" Christie asked.

"Nah, I only have a dollar left, and I have to pay for my ice cream."

"That leaves you with fifty cents. Come on."

"I'll just watch."

"Clinton," Christie called. "I wanna pay for my ice cream."

"Sure," he said and walked over to us.

He took Christie's fifty cents. Then she walked over to the games. I handed him my dollar, and he rung me up and gave me two quarters.

"Sorry if I embarrassed you," he said, referring to unjinx-ing me. I think.

"It's okay." Was it? I didn't know. He kept giving me mixed signals.

He liked me.

He didn't want me near him.

He *flirted* with me.

I had no idea *what* to think.

"Good. Here's a quarter. Go play some cool music in the jukebox."

I grinned like an idiot and took his quarter. But then I felt pressured. Secretly, I still liked KC & the Sunshine Band

and Abba, but I didn't dare play AM music in Clinton's vicinity.

Dropping the quarter in the slot, I was filled with anxiety that I wouldn't pick good music. I knew how important music was for Clinton. It was always important to me too, but more because of the fun tempo or the cute guy dancing in tight satin pants than for the phenomenal voice ranges or superior lead guitar-playing.

Due to my limited music knowledge, many of the choices in the jukebox I had never heard of. Fortunately, "Another One Bites the Dust" caught my eye, so I pressed its numbers. Two more choices to go. When I saw Boston's "More Than a Feeling," I got excited. This song was on one of the tapes Clinton had made for me. So I chose that.

The last song wasn't as easy. I saw bands like Van Halen and Led Zeppelin, but those names were just vaguely familiar. I saw The Partridge Family's "I Think I Love You," which I was dying to play, but I wouldn't. On the last page of music choices, I saw Styx, but it was "Babe," and I knew that was more of an AM song than an FM song, but I decided to play it. Clinton would approve, I thought.

With a huge grin on my face, I turned around.

And saw Kristen Jacobs standing at the opening of the counter, her hands on Clinton's chest and her lips close to his face. Clinton wasn't backing away. It actually looked like he was enjoying her touches.

Why shouldn't he be?

Kristen had won Homecoming Queen this past year. Head cheerleader and all. Worst of all, she was Clinton's age.

I turned toward the arcade games and kept to the corner after that, trying hard to dispel the tears.

Tuffy's was not on my to-do list the rest of that summer. I know it was childish, but I really didn't want to see anyone else flirting with Clinton. And besides, Bobby was usually there, and I really wanted to avoid him too. He was always trying to get up my shirt, and I didn't want him to.

Eventually, Bobby realized I wasn't his girlfriend anymore. Not that I ever had been, since I'd never *really* agreed to be.

My bicycle became my best friend for the week, until Najia returned from Jordan. Then I talked her into hanging at the Campus Sweet Shoppe instead of Tuffy's. They didn't have arcade games, but they had tons of teen magazines, so we would sit and read up on Scott Baio, Willie Aames, Rick Springfield, and every other teen idol of 1981.

THEN...

On August first, nineteen hundred and eighty one, watching television became an event.

MTV, Music Television, was born.

And I was *re*-born.

Najia and I put a halt on any outside activities, instead opting to stay in and watch video after video of awesome rock music.

"This is the coolest, coolest thing," I said to Najia while watching Martha Quinn announce The Who's "You Better You Bet." All I could think about was running down to Tuffy's to tell Clinton. But I refrained and let the music, and bags of Hershey's Kisses and M&M's, placate my urge.

I did make it a point, however, to learn everything I could about every music group and every song. The next time I saw Clinton, I would impress him with my music knowledge.

CHAPTER SIX

"Somebody to Love"

September, 1981

TIA

When my purple Converse sneakers hit the marble floor on the first day of sophomore year, the halls were missing Clinton Daniels. He was at college now. This school year, I was going to focus on everything or anything else besides the nineteen-year-old boy who had possession of my heart.

Najia and I had no classes together. Not even lunch. After checking my schedule with my other friends, I found out none of them had sixth period lunch either. So, I sat at a table where a cute, little, harmless-looking blonde girl sat.

"You mind?" I asked, motioning toward the empty seat across from her.

"No. Go 'head."

When I sat, I realized she looked familiar. "Aren't you in my first period English class?"

"Yeah. Miss Bogdanfy."

"Yup. I'm Tia."

"I'm Maxine. Or Maxx."

"I think I remember you walking the halls last year. You're one of the cheerleaders, right?"

"JV. Yeah." Maxine unwrapped her sandwich and said, "I can't believe we're doing Shakespeare again."

"I know. I thought we were done with that last year."

"I've never even heard of *A Midsummer Night's Dream*. Have you?"

"Well, yeah, but not because I'm a fan. Maybe if he didn't write his stories as plays, I'd like reading him." After swallowing a bite of my cheese sandwich, I changed the subject. "So, who do you hang out with?" She was a cheerleader, but I never saw her hanging with them.

"My boyfriend. That's pretty much it."

"Who's your boyfriend?"

"Chris Jackie."

"I don't know him. Does he go to this school?"

"No. He goes to Newman Prep. He's from North Haledon though. We went to middle school together. Been dating since seventh grade."

"Wow. That's a long time. What do you guys do when you hang out? You don't, like, *kiss* the whole time, do you?"

Maxine laughed. "No. We play pool. Watch MTV."

"I *love* MTV."

"Me too. I can't believe no one thought of it sooner."

"Right?"

"Hey, if you wanna ever come over and watch it together, we can."

"Sure."

THAT FOLLOWING WEEKEND, we did just that. Najia came too. Turns out, she and Maxine had several classes together and knew each other from freshman year.

"Pizza's here," Chris announced, walking in with a tall, dark, really cute friend and another boy I barely looked at.

Maxine jumped up. "Ooh. Yay." She took the pizza from Chris's hand then kissed him hello. It made me wish I could just walk up to Clinton and kiss him like that.

"Eric, Don, these are Tia and Najia," Maxx introduced us. "And this is Chris," she added with a cutesy smile.

Eric. He was the tall, dark one.

"Hi," both boys said, but again, I still couldn't tell you what color hair the other one had. I was too immersed in Eric's slate-blue eyes, which made my brain start humming that "Sexy Eyes" song by Dr. Hook.

After the boys plowed into the pizza box, we more reserved girls got our slices and sat on the floor around the coffee table. Maxine and Chris were a little over the top with their canoodling, but I couldn't lie—I would have loved to be cuddling with someone right now. I'd have *loved* it to be Clinton, but at the moment, with my eyes unable to sway from Eric, I wouldn't mind canoodling with him.

"You go to school with Maxx?" he asked me.

I nodded, afraid of stumbling over my words.

"Cool. I go to Newman Prep."

"In Wayne?" I managed to spit out.

"Yeah. I go with Chris and Don."

Feeling a teensy bit more courageous, I said, "No wonder I haven't seen you guys around."

He grinned. Sideways. It was adorable. He could definitely be a model. "I haven't seen you around either. How long you guys been friends?" he asked of Maxx and me.

"We just met this school year."

"I hope that means we'll be seeing more of each other."

What a smooth talker. I tried not to blush, I really did, but I couldn't help it. "Maybe." *Maybe? I couldn't think of anything better to say?*

That crooked grin of his appeared again. "You play any sports?" he had the nerve to ask.

"No. Not really the athletic type."

"So, what *do* you do?" He raised an eyebrow, and I thought he was too much of a smooth talker for a fifteen-year-old.

"Are you a sophomore?" I asked, just in case he was older than fifteen.

"I am," he said confidently, continuing with, "I look a lot older though, don't I?"

"Oh." *Where do guys like this come from?*

He lifted those thick eyebrows again. "So, what do you do when you're not in school, if you're not into sports?"

"I, uh, listen to music, read, watch MTV."

"*Watch* MTV?"

His condescending tone confused me. "Yeah," I said slowly. "It's this new channel that only plays music videos." I thought, well, maybe he'd never heard of MTV and that was why he asked like that.

"I *know* what MTV is. I just didn't know people actually sat and watched it as an activity."

Stuck-up snob. Cute *stuck-up snob.*

"Hey, don't knock it," Chris said. "It's great for making out."

"Oh," Eric said. "So, you make out to it?" he asked me, even though I had a feeling he knew the answer to that already.

"No. I just watch it."

"Maybe we can watch it together one day," he said, raising those eyebrows again.

Who does this guy think he is? Casanova?

I nodded despite my apprehensions toward this boy.

"Eric, stop trying to make a date with my friend," Maxine scolded. "She's too good for you."

Everyone laughed. Except Eric. He didn't look too pleased with Maxine's comments.

Since I now felt bad for him, for God knows why, I said, "I'd like that." *Stupid girl.*

Eric's smile was back, and this time, he actually looked humbled. "You play pool?"

"No."

"Maxx has a pool table. I can teach you."

"Smooth, Eric," Chris said. Don laughed.

Eric frowned.

"Okay," I said.

Now *everyone's* eyes bulged.

After the initial shock wore off, Eric got up and held out his hand for me to take.

It surprised no one more than it did me that I took it.

As cliché as it sounded, Eric taught me how to play pool by standing behind me and guiding the pool stick. His lips a breath away from my ear, his hips pressed into my back, his hands on top of mine on the stick.

Although originally turning me off with his cocky charm, his nearness was surprisingly effective in making me forget Clinton, even if it *was* just until I got home that night.

Eric and I exchanged phone numbers—something I hadn't even done with Bobby—and he told me he'd call me the next day.

He did.

He asked me out.

I said yes.

I'M SO EXCITED," MAXINE said as we headed down to Tuffy's.

Najia's idea. Not mine. I still hadn't entered Tuffy's since that day I saw Kristen Jacobs hanging on Clinton.

"Wow. It's the little things, isn't it?" Najia said in response to Maxine's excitement.

"You don't know. In North Haledon, we don't get to hang out like you guys do. We have no sidewalks. No center of town."

"Yeah, why *is* that?" I asked, curious as to why the town right next to us had mailboxes on the side of the road when ours were attached to the front of the house.

"Who knows?" Maxine had no clue either. "So, I heard about Tuffy's. I hear it's like an old 1950s ice cream shop."

"Yeah. It's cute," I told her.

"And Tee likes the guy who works there."

"Naj."

"What?" Maxine asked. "I thought you and Eric were a thing now."

"We are."

"She just has a crush on Clinton. He's too old anyway. He's, like, twenty."

"He is not," I said defensively. "He's only nineteen."

"Oh, I thought he was twenty already, not that a year makes a difference. He's a college guy."

I shook my head and remained quiet. I wasn't going to admit that he would turn twenty in two and a half months, forever being five years older than me.

"So, you like a nineteen-year-old?" Maxine asked.

"No. He's just a friend. I like Eric."

I thought they had bought it. At least it seemed like Maxine had anyway.

When we walked into Tuffy's, of course the first thing I did was look to see who was behind the counter. It wasn't Clinton. It was Nick, a senior at Manchester Regional.

Needless to say, I was now relaxed and not at all worried about Eric and Chris meeting us here like Maxx had planned. I had no idea what my reaction would be to seeing Clinton. I did not want Eric to figure anything out.

However, Bobby *was* here. And I'd soon learn that he would cause my nerves to start firing all over again.

"Hey, girls. What can I get for you?" Nick said when we sat at the table by the front window.

"I'll have a root beer float," I started.

"Ooh, I'll have the same," Maxine said.

"And you, Naj?"

"Hot fudge sundae."

"Cool. Be right back."

Just then, Eric and Chris walked in. "Hey."

"Hey," we all said back to them.

Eric sat next to me and kissed me on the cheek.

Chris sat at the end of the table and slid his chair close to Maxx.

"So, look who decided to grace us with her presence today." Bobby suddenly appeared at our table.

"Go away," I told him.

"This your new boyfriend?" he asked, eying Eric and ignoring my request.

"She said go away, Bob," Najia spoke up.

"You're not gonna get anywhere with her, you know," Bobby said, looking directly at Eric, whose arm was resting possessively on the back of my chair. "Not even second base. She's saving herself for soda boy over there."

I jerked my head to look behind me. With my back to the counter, I hadn't seen Clinton walk in. He must have come from the back door, because I'm sure I would have seen him walk in through the front.

It looked like Clinton had heard Bobby. Either that, or he was fuming about something else.

"Who *is* this guy?" Eric's voice brought my attention back to the table.

"Nobody." I sneered. "Just some jerk."

"Nice. I'm her ex-boyfriend...and she wouldn't even let me get up her shirt. So you might as well dump her now. I'm telling you. She likes soda boy."

"That's enough." Clinton's tone was firm, yet even. "Unless you want me to kick you out again."

"I'm not in this relationship for that," Eric said to Bobby.

"Yeah. Tell me that in a month," Bobby spat and walked out of the store.

"I gather *you* broke up with *him*?" Eric asked.

"Kinda neither. I just avoided him." I was answering Eric, but my attention was on Clinton, who was also looking at me, which made my heart hurt.

What will it take for me to get over him?

"Tee? You okay?" Najia asked.

"Hmm? Oh yeah. Sorry." I forced myself to stay focused on Eric and the friends I had come in with. "Yeah, sorry about Bobby. He was kind of mad at me for ignoring him the past couple months."

"Understood. No need to apologize." Eric's fingers grazed the back of my neck. "Besides, with me, things will be different. He's immature. I'm not."

I had no idea what Eric meant by that.

His fingers, still drawing circles on my neck, were bothering me, and I was very conscious of the fact that Clinton was watching.

Nick brought us our ice cream and told us his shift was over and Clinton would be serving us. "Karl's in the back if it gets busy," he added.

"So, why does Bobby say you like soda boy?" Chris asked.

"His name is Clinton, not soda boy," I clipped.

Eric's fingers stilled.

"He's just jealous of Clinton," Najia said, covering for my defensiveness.

Maxine was squinting her eyes, trying to figure things out.

"What's he jealous of?" Eric jeered. "He looks like a loser anyway. I mean, who still works in an ice cream shop at twenty-five?"

I was shocked and pissed that he had said that.

"He doesn't look twenty-five, Eric," Chris pointed out innocently.

"No," Maxine said. "I saw him in school last year. And didn't you just say he was nineteen?" Maxx asked me.

"Yeah." This conversation was making me sad. I felt like we were talking about Clinton behind his back, and I didn't like it.

"Still looks like a loser, and why isn't he in college?" Eric continued with his disparaging comments.

"He. Is. He goes to William Paterson. And he's not a loser."

Eric scoffed. "It's not Harvard. *That's* where I'm going."

What am I doing with him? "You're a douche." I slid my chair away from him and closer to Chris.

He raised an eyebrow at me, but I'm sure he was more upset about anyone noticing his bruised ego, so he shrugged it off and started joking with Chris.

While I sulked.

When we were done with our ice cream, Clinton brought our check. Eric grabbed it from him, but Clinton just turned and walked away.

We all divided up the bill, and when they got up to go play the games in the back, I took the money and went to the counter to pay.

"I see you got yourself another winner of a boyfriend, Tia," Clinton said when he took my check and the money.

I shrugged half-heartedly, partly annoyed at Clinton for having anything to say about my choice of boyfriends. *He* could have been my boyfriend and kept me from going out with jerks.

"You staying?" he asked me after he rang me up.

"Yeah. My friends are still here."

"Can I buy you a strawberry soda?"

The root beer float had filled me, but I wasn't strong enough to say no to Clinton. "Sure."

I took my spot—the first stool at the counter—and watched Clinton make me my soda.

"So whatchya been up to, Tia?" Tia. He still didn't shorten my name.

"Not much. Sophomore stuff. Learning about Shakespeare."

He put the red-liquid-filled glass in front of me. It almost looked like carbonated blood.

"Thanks."

"So, sophomore Shakespeare at Manchester Regional. *Midsummer Night's Dream*, right?"

"Right."

"What part are you up to?"

"Who knows?" I'm just gonna buy the CliffsNotes anyway."

"Tia, it's a good story. Don't gyp yourself."

"I'd rather read *anything* else."

"Not a Shakespeare fan?"

"No, not at all. You?"

"Yeah. I enjoyed him."

"So how's college?"

"It's okay. It's a lot of work." He picked up books that were hidden behind the counter. "I even have to study here at work."

"What are you majoring in?"

"Computer programming and..."

"What? That's a thing?" I interrupted him.

He laughed. "Of course it's a *thing.*"

"What is it?"

"Well, computers run machines. *Someone* has to program the computer to run it."

"Oh. Hmmm. I thought smart people majored in Engineering."

"Well, yeah. I'm holding a double major. Computer engineering's the other."

"Wow."

"Do you have plans for what you want to study in college?"

"I don't even know if I'm *going* to college."

"Why not?"

"My mom doesn't have money to send me."

"You can get financial aid and loans, Tia. Don't gyp yourself."

"There you go again with that gyp word."

"It means don't cheat yourself."

"I know what it means. I just don't get why you're using it on me."

"Never mind, Tia." He shook his head. "I just want what's best for you."

"Really?"

"Really."

"Then if you really want what's best for me, *you'll* be my boyfriend, and I don't have to go out with jerks anymore."

With a sigh, Clinton frowned. "Stop, Tia. Please." Pulling a stool up behind the counter, Clinton sat across from me.

I shrugged, embarrassed I had said anything.

"You know how I feel. I just...we can't right now," he whispered, leaning in toward me.

"No one has to know. I won't tell anybody."

"No. We can be friends, okay?"

Who the heck needs more friends?

He took my half-empty glass and squirted more strawberry syrup and seltzer in it, and then took a quick look around the shop before leaning in towards me. "Tia. Every time we have this conversation, you stay away."

"What? You're the one who avoids *me*."

"Okay. Fair enough. In the beginning..." He stopped talking. Instead of finishing, he took the guest check pad that was lying on the counter and slid the pencil out from atop his ear. "Give me your phone number," he whispered, sliding the pad and pencil in front of me. "I can't talk here."

"You want my number?" I whispered in shock.

He chuckled. "Yes. If that's okay with you."

I must have smiled like I'd never smiled before, because Clinton said, "Tia. To talk. About being friends."

Still. It was a start, right?

Clinton hopped off the stool and set it aside. Then he got out his rag and wiped things down. "Go hang with your friends, Tia. You have a boyfriend. He's gonna start asking questions."

"He's a douche."

"Then break up with him."

"I think by calling him that to his face, I already did."

Clinton laughed. "You didn't."

"I did."

He shook his head and chuckled.

"I think I'm gonna go play some songs on the jukebox."

"You'll like it. There's some new stuff on it."

I jumped down and headed directly to the jukebox.

In flipping through, I noticed a whole bunch of new songs. Songs I knew, too, thanks to MTV. I played "The Breakup Song" by Greg Kihn Band and "Take it on the Run" by REO Speedwagon, just in case Eric hadn't taken the hint when I called him a douche. Then I played "Love Stinks" by J. Geils Band—just because it does.

"The Breakup Song" was first to play. It came on when I was already standing next to Najia in the corner.

"Nice, Tee. You played this?"

I smirked.

She shook her head. "That's gutsy."

"Yeah, well."

"Who played this song?" Eric asked.

"Me. You like it?" I asked with a straight face.

I had to laugh at the way he crunched his eyebrows. "You trying to tell me something?"

"You called my friend a loser. I didn't like that."

"So you're breaking up with me? Via a song?"

I laughed. "Via calling you a douche."

Eric gritted his teeth but didn't walk away.

"Would it help if I apologized?"

Okay. This threw me. "What?"

"I'm sorry. I didn't realize you were that good of friends with the guy. If he heard me, I'll apologize."

"Really?"

"Really."

"Why?"

"Because I like you. I don't want to break up with you."

"Oh." *Maybe he's* not *a class one jerkamabob.*

"So...does sorry cut it?"

I shrugged. I was so indecisive.

"Please, Tia." Eric took my hands and pulled me in for a kiss. "I'm sorry. I am."

"You can't talk about my friends like that."

"I promise. No more."

I sighed when he hugged me.

"Let me guess," Eric said, mid-hug. "You picked *this* song too."

"You don't like REO Speedwagon?"

"I don't like that you picked these songs for me, but I guess I can be flattered that I meant that much to you to even be worth the effort."

He was soooo not worth the effort.

I think I played those songs more for Clinton's benefit. To reiterate the fact that I didn't have a boyfriend.

Pulling away quickly, I said, "You know what, Eric? I think we *should* take a break from each other."

"But we've only been together for three weeks."

"I know. I just...I have a lot of homework and stuff, you know." I wanted to be mean, I did, but he was, like, sometimes nice, sometimes not, and I just found it easier to be kind.

"No, I don't know."

"Okay, well, I'm sorry." I looked at Najia and said, "I gotta go, Naj."

"What? Why?"

"Um, just, I have to get to my homework. I can't fail Algebra again."

"Be right back," she said to Maxine, but Maxx followed us out anyway.

"What's going on?" Maxx asked.

"I broke up with Eric, and I just wanted to get out of there."

"You don't like him?"

"I'm sorry, Maxx. I know he's your friend, but I really don't. I'm sorry."

"He's not *my* friend, he's Chris's. And he's not gonna care."

"Really?"

"You want us to go home with you?" Najia asked.

"No. You guys go back in. I really do have algebra homework."

"Okay," they both said.

"See ya in the morning," Najia said.

"See ya at school tomorrow," Maxine added.

AT HOME IN MY ROOM, I really did try to do algebra. But it was so difficult, I just said the heck with it and rode my bike to the library. I returned *Persuasion* and took out *Cujo*. No more love stories for me, —they'd just make me mad.

Usually, I sat out on the front porch to read, but Clinton was calling tonight. And I had no idea when. My room would have to do. Luckily, Mom had bought me my own phone and had it hooked up next to my bed.

When the phone rang around eight fifteen, I was done reading and instead watching *The Greatest American Hero*.

My hand was shaking and I felt queasy. "Hello?"

"Hello?" Even over the phone he sounded hot. "Tia?"

"Hi."

"I closed the shop early. No one was coming in. Now a good time to talk?"

"Yeah. Just watching TV."

"What are you watching?"

I was embarrassed to say, but weakly, I admitted, "*The Greatest American Hero*."

He laughed. Not loudly, but enough to make me slink into my pillow. "There's nothing else on," I lied.

"I'm not judging you," he said with a chuckle.

"Yeah, right."

"I'm not, Tia. So, tell me, do you sing along with the song in the beginning?"

"See. Judging." Yes, I loved singing along to the theme song.

"No judging. I think it's cute."

"As in childish."

"As in cute."

"Ha, ha."

"Anyway, at least I'm not interrupting your homework."

"What? Eh, I didn't even finish."

"Why?"

"'Cause it was algebra. I'm bad at it."

"Algebra? I'm great at it. I can help you if you want."

"Over the phone?"

"Well, no. Not tonight. I can help you at the store."

"You'd do that?"

"For you? Of course. But, Tia, it's just algebra. Please don't go reading anything into this."

That hurt. It really did.

"Tia, you there?"

"Mmm hmm."

"Tia, if my helping you with Algebra is too much, I'll help you find a tutor who'll do it for free. I don't want to lead you on."

After a long inhale, I asked, "So, why did you want to call me tonight?"

"To explain myself."

"So, explain."

I heard him suck in a breath before saying, "I've never had a relationship. And by that, I mean friendships either. As you noticed, I'm a loner. And an introvert. I'd rather be by myself than try to connect with anyone." I heard him suck in air, and then he slowly expelled it. "But that's not the case with you. I can't explain why. Maybe those big green eyes of yours make me feel, I don't know, safe, or maybe comfortable. Maybe something bigger than us made me stop that day to pick you up." He sucked in and let out another breath. "I don't know why. But you are my first friend, Tia. I really feel strongly about being your friend. And protecting you."

"From what?"

"Bad boyfriend choices? I don't know. I just have this protectiveness when it comes to you. It's hard to describe."

He sucked in air again.

"Do you have asthma or something?"

"Asthma? Where'd that come from?"

"You keep breathing loudly."

This time, he guffawed. Him laughing at me seemed to be commonplace in our relationship. "Oh my god, Tia, I'm smoking."

"You smoke?"

"Yeah. But *you* better not. It's bad for you."

"Then why do *you* smoke?"

"I don't really care what happens to me, Tia."

I shot up in bed and, louder than intended, I yelled, "Why the hell not?"

What did Clinton do?

That's right, he laughed.

"Tia, stop. Let's just get back to us." He stopped chuckling, and his tone became serious. "I'd like to be your friend. Real friends. But I don't want to do that with you thinking it's going to lead somewhere."

"Not even when I'm eighteen? You said..."

"I know what I said. Yes. When you're eighteen, maybe we can take things further. But for now, it's gotta be this way."

Curling my finger around the phone cord, I thought about this for a while. If I said yes to being friends, I could be with Clinton. If I said no, I couldn't. Easy decision.

But...

The more I was with Clinton, the more I was going to want to *be* with Clinton. And that would just hurt. Like hell.

"Tia. You there?"

"Yeah."

"I'm being unfair. I'm sorry. I'm thinking of myself and not how hard this may be on you."

I thought about this some more, all the while tightening the cord so tight on my finger that the tip of it was purple.

"Do you want me to let you go? Off the phone, I mean?"

"No." I finally spoke.

"You sure?"

"Yeah."

"You don't sound sure."

"Yeah, okay, I better go." I hung up without saying good-bye. I was so nervous and so confused.

So, I spent the rest of the night sobbing, eventually falling asleep on a soaking wet pillow. But when I woke up in the morning, I decided I was going to let Clinton tutor me in algebra. And I was going to be his friend.

And I was going to try to get him to like me the way I liked him *before* I turned eighteen.

I guess I was a glutton for punishment.

CHAPTER SEVEN

"The Hero"

T IA
My Algebra grade went from an F to a B-minus by the end of the second marking period. *Thank you, Clinton.*

At first, it wasn't easy to be near Clinton and not want to lean over and kiss him. He smelled so good. Like musk, I thought. He would lean over my right arm to explain stupid formulas, and all I would do was close my eyes and inhale. He didn't miss a beat, though. His response was always, "Algebra, Tia. Focus." Once I figured out that I was fighting a losing battle, I stopped smelling him and started learning algebra. Most days, we studied at the shop during its slow time—dinnertime. But some days, when Clinton wasn't scheduled to work, we'd meet at the library. On those days, when we were finished with my math, Clinton would pull out his books and do his college homework while I worked on my other school assignments. If I had none, I'd borrow a book from the library and read. There was no way I was leaving Clinton when I could be spending time with him.

As was the case every time we met at the tiny library, Clinton drove me home, even though I lived right around the corner on the same block. He always took the long way home by driving me around Haledon long enough to listen to one new song. He made it a point to play me something I'd never heard. Tonight's song was a rarely played Tom Petty number called "You Can Still Change Your Mind." It was beautiful.

"I know you're not a big Tom Petty fan," Clinton said when the song was over, "but I knew you'd like this song."

"I do. I love it. And that piano, my goodness, it was beautiful."

"I can teach you how to play it."

"You play piano?" *How did I not know this?*

"Keyboard. I don't have a piano."

"I do. You can play at my house."

"Do you play?"

"A little. I can't read notes, but if I listen to a song, I can play it."

"Wow. You're full of surprises. So, you could probably learn it on your own."

"I'd rather you teach me."

He grinned, and it was so cute.

"Besides, I don't have this song."

"I'll teach it to you, but I can also lend you this tape."

"No. I want you to come over. My mom won't mind. She knows you're tutoring me."

"Okay. Not tonight, though, 'kay? It's after nine, and I have an early class."

"Okay."

Clinton got out and walked me to the door. "See you tomorrow, Tia."

"See you tomorrow, Clinton."

As he usually did now, he kissed me goodbye on my cheek. I wasn't complaining. I would take anything Clinton offered.

He waited for me to go inside, and I locked the door and took my place in the window, pushing back the curtain to watch him drive away.

I walked through the living room to the kitchen to tell my mother I was home, but she wasn't there. *Probably in her room.* When I pushed open her bedroom door, she wasn't there either.

"Mom," I called out.

No answer.

"Mom!" I yelled.

Still no answer.

"Mom." Panic set in as I opened the door to the bathroom and she was thrashing on the floor. "Mommy."

Oh my God.

"Mom." I tried to still her, but she wouldn't stop convulsing.

What do I do? What do I do?

Call the police.

Right.

Call the police.

I ran to the phone in my room and fumbled with the numbers. *Dammit, what's the number? Shit.* Why wasn't Haledon set up with that 9-1-1 number yet?

I pressed zero.

"Operator. Can I help you?"

"I need the police or the ambulance. Somebody." I rushed out the words in a panic.

"I'll connect you with the Haledon Police Department. Hold please."

"Police."

"My mom's convulsing on the bathroom floor. Please. I can't stop her."

"What's your address, miss?"

"433 Belmont."

"First floor or second?"

"Only one floor. Please, hurry."

"We've already sent someone."

"Thank you."

I hadn't hung up more than thirty seconds before they were banging on the front door.

Two stout policemen stood in the door.

"She's in here."

They followed me to the bathroom, where Mom was finally lying still.

"Mom?"

She stared right through me.

"Honey, you need to back up," one of the cops said. "Better yet, can you stand by the front door and let the paramedics in?"

The next half-hour went by in a blur, and the next thing I knew, I was at the hospital—driven there by the policemen.

The room where they brought my mother was cold and dreary. Grey walls. Nothing on them. Not much *in* them, including my mom. They took her for tests. I was all alone with no money to even make a phone call. The bubbly nurse brought me some magazines, but as a fifteen-and-almost-a-half-year-old teenager, *Good Housekeeping* and *Better Homes and Gardens* had nothing in them to interest me. A *People* magazine would have been better. Not that it mattered. I was too worried about my mother to concentrate on anything anyway.

A little over three hours later, a doctor came in and said they were admitting my mother. I followed him to a room on the third floor of the main part of the hospital, where my mother lay sleeping.

"She's on sedatives, but you can come back and see her in the morning. She'll be all right by then."

"Come back? How do I get home?"

"Oh. You're here alone?"

"Yes."

"And you don't drive?"

"I'm fifteen."

"Oh," he said, surprised. "Let me get someone."

He left me alone with my mother. She was ghost-like—pale, greyish, not pretty. I touched her arm. It was cool. "What am I supposed to do?" I asked her, in a vain attempt to get an answer.

"Hello?" A different nurse came in.

"Hi."

"I'm Corinne. Do you have anyone you can call? Your father, grandparent?"

"Father lives in Oklahoma, grandparents are dead."

"Aunt, uncle?"

"None."

"Best friend's parent?"

Najia was my best friend. My best *girl* friend. But lately, I was spending most of my time at the shop or the library with

Clinton. Sometimes, I thought of *him* as my best friend. But in a different way. Not that it mattered right now. I needed someone who could get me home. At one in the morning, I didn't want to call either of them, but since Najia would have to ask her mom for the ride, I decided Clinton was my best bet.

"Yeah," I finally answered. "I can call a friend, but I have no money for the pay phone."

"Oh, honey, you can use our desk phone. Not sure if your mother will be ordering phone service."

She showed me the way to the nurses' desk and I dialed Clinton's number, though I was really nervous about waking him up.

When the ringing stopped, a gravelly voice I didn't recognize said, "Yeah?"

"Um, is, um, Clinton there?"

"Clinton?"

I was afraid I had dialed the wrong number. I had never used the number he'd given me in case of an algebra emergency, so I couldn't be sure. "Um, yes. This is Tia."

"Tia. As in a *girl*?"

"What? Yeah. I'm a friend of his."

"Yo, Dad, get this: a *girl's* calling for Clinton."

"No shit?" A distant, equally raspy voice said. "Clinton's got a *girl*?"

"Looks that way."

"'Scuse me, sir, can I please speak with Clinton?"

"He's sleeping, darlin'. Sleeping beauty needs his rest."

"Um, well, can you wake him up? It's an emergency."

"Emergency, huh? Ya ain't pregnant, are ya?"

I was on the verge of hanging up, but I really needed a ride home. I was certainly understanding why Clinton couldn't stand his family, though. "Sir, I really, really need to talk to Clinton right now. I'm sure he'll understand why I need to wake him up."

"Sure hope I'm not an uncle yet. Daddy's not gonna be too happy with bein' a grandpa either. Hold on, I'll get him." After a slight pause, I heard, "Yo, Clint," and then the receiver must have been thrown to the floor, because I heard a loud thud.

Maybe a minute or so later, he said, "Hello? Tia? What happened? You okay?"

"Clinton." Funny how the sound of his voice made me suddenly want to cry.

"Tia. What? What's the matter?"

"Can you pick me up?" I asked through sudden tears.

"Pick you... Sure, you home?"

"No. General."

"The hospital? What? Tia, explain, please."

"My mom. She had a seizure. They're keeping her overnight. And, and I have no way, no way home."

"Okay. I'm coming for you. Calm down. You'll be outside or should—"

"Outside. Yes. The main entrance..."

"The main entrance is locked, honey," the nurse said. "You need to go through the emergency exit."

"Clinton. The emergency exit."

"I heard her. Be there in ten minutes."

I kissed my mom on her cheek before I left, and the nurse helped me find my way to the emergency room.

"Stay inside until your friend comes," the nurse told me.

"I will. Thank you."

His brown car whipped into the parking lot, stopping short in front of the double glass doors. I ran outside to get to him quickly, and he caught me in his arms as he was coming for me.

"Oh, Clinton."

"Tia." He hugged me as I cried into his chest. "Come on. Let me take you home."

No music came out of Clinton's speakers tonight. No words came out of our mouths. Even when he walked me to the door, Clinton didn't say a word.

"Clinton? Why are you so quiet?"

He shook his head and put his hand on the doorknob. "You have a key?" he finally said.

"It's unlocked. I forgot to lock it."

He shook his head again and turned the knob. Clinton followed me into the kitchen.

"I'm good, Clinton. Thank you for picking me up." I sat down at the table and put my chin in my hands. "I'm really sorry I woke you up."

He pulled out the seat adjacent to mine. "Tia, do you have anyone else in your life?" he asked, frowning.

"Besides who?"

"Besides your mother?"

"Oh. No. You, Najia, my other friends."

"So, you're alone in this house tonight." Not a question.

I shrugged. "It's fine. I'm fifteen. I'm not a child," I said more defensively than I meant to.

"I'll stay."

"What?"

"You're sad. And I don't want you alone."

"My mother leaves me alone a lot."

"Overnight?"

"Well, no. But I'm fine. It's barely overnight. It's almost two in the morning, I'll be up in, like, four hours."

"Yeah, but I don't like the idea of you being alone. And you'll need a ride to the hospital in the morning anyway."

"I can take the bus. You have class in the morning."

"Tia. Stop. I'll stay. I'll run home in the morning to brush my teeth and get jeans and a fresh shirt. I'll grab some things in case she stays one more night."

I dropped my hands from my chin. "Really?"

"Really. Now show me where I'm sleeping. I'm tired."

My room. My *room*. "My room?"

"You got a couch in there?"

"No."

"How 'bout the couch we passed in the living room?"

"I guess. I'll get you some sheets and a blanket." I got up and went through the hallway off the kitchen, nervous and excited that Clinton was staying, but sad because Mom was in the hospital and we had no idea why.

When I turned around, Clinton was standing in my bedroom doorway. "This is your room?"

"Yeah. Mom's is that one." I pointed to the door across from mine.

"So, you like Scott Baio, huh?"

Embarrassed, I said, "That's old. I haven't found anyone to replace him and Shaun Cassidy with."

Clinton just laughed. "They don't make posters of Mr. Darcy?"

"That would be cool. But who knows what he'd look like if he were real?"

"True." Clinton stepped further into my room and picked up one of the cassette tapes he'd made for me that was lying next to my bed. "Did you get to listen to the whole thing?"

"Over and over."

He smiled, but it looked sad. When he put it down, he said, "You should go to sleep. You had a rough night."

"Yeah." Handing him the sheets, I purposely touched his hand.

Again, his smile looked sad.

"See you in a few hours, Tia."

"Goodnight, Clinton. And thank you."

"Anytime."

I quickly changed into my sweatpants and sweatshirt and got under the covers. I'd brush my teeth in the morning. I was beat. I drifted off to sleep with thoughts of my mother and thoughts of Clinton, guilt overcoming me as I realized more of my thinking was about Clinton than Mom. I must have fallen asleep anyway, because my next thoughts were how bright the sun was and *could someone please pull down the shades?*

"Hey, sleepyhead."

The bed squeaked when I sat up. "Clinton." I took a quick look down at my sweats-covered body, then ran my fingers through my hair, hoping the layers would feather into place the way it was cut to.

He walked in and sat at the bottom of my bed, his knee in the direction of where I sat at the top.

"I overslept?" I asked, picking at something in my eye and feeling totally self-conscious.

"No. Not at all. It's only eight thirty." He pointed his chin to the clock on my nightstand.

"Oh. It's too late to call Najia and tell her I'm not going to school."

"You wanted to?"

"I don't know. I feel like *some*one should know where I am."

"You wanna call the school?"

"No. My mom usually writes a note the next day."

"Okay. Then don't worry about it. She'll write you a note for tomorrow."

"I'm really not worried about a note."

"I know you're not."

"You know?"

"Yeah. You're worried about your mother, but you don't want to think about it, so you're worrying about something less important."

"Wow." I removed my covers and got out of bed. I was searching through my dresser drawers when Clinton's hand appeared on my shoulder, and he turned me around. Without saying a word, he pulled me into his arms. His heart beat steady against my ear. It was amazing that I could hear it through his sweatshirt. To me, being held by Clinton felt safe and natural, but I could feel his discomfort.

Pretending to stretch, I casually removed myself from his arms. "Thanks for being here. I hope you know I appreciate it."

"Of course I do. I'll let you get ready."

As he went for my door, I said, "Why don't you go home and do what you need to do?"

"Already did."

"Oh. When?"

"Seven. I couldn't sleep, so once I knew you'd be safe from prowlers, I left."

"Prowlers?" I asked, raising my eyebrows, a smirk crawling across my face.

"You never know, Tia."

"Clinton?"

"Yeah?"

"Please go home."

Striding back into my room and sitting back down on my bed, he dropped his shoulders and asked, "Why?"

"Because. You don't want to be here. And I don't want you to be here if it's out of pity or because you think I can't take care of myself."

"Tia."

"Really, Clinton. My mom keeps emergency funds in the refrigerator drawer. I can take out money for the bus. I'll be sitting there with her all day anyway."

"What makes you think I don't want to be here? Because that's the furthest thing from the truth."

I sat next to him. "Your hug."

"My hug?"

"Yes. It seemed awkward."

"Tia. You're fifteen years old. You're in my arms. We're in your room, standing next to your bed. I was trying to ward off feelings I shouldn't have been having."

"Oh." I felt a blush coming on.

"Get ready, Tia," he said, standing from my bed. "I'll take you to breakfast."

THE KING GEORGE DINER was teeming with old people—men, mostly.

"Feel a little out of place?" Clinton joked.

"Just a little."

We were seated at a booth, which made me happy, because the booths had tabletop jukeboxes on them.

"I love these things," I told Clinton, who was already digging in his pocket for change.

"Here's a quarter."

"I bet these old men won't appreciate the noise."

"Eh. Who cares?"

The waitress came and asked what she could get us.

"Coke, please."

"Same," Clinton said.

The diner's jukebox choices weren't as heavy as they were at Tuffy's, but I supposed that made sense in a dining establishment that served people of all ages.

"Go 'head and pick your AM stuff. I know you're dying to."

Clinton was right. I *was* dying to play the stuff I'd listened to before Clinton came into my life. I played "I'd Really Love to See You Tonight" by England Dan and John Ford

Coley, "Island Girl" by Elton John, and "Shaddap You Face" by Joe Dulce. The latter just because I wanted to see the old men's reactions. It's kind of neat that my song choices played at *every* booth in the diner, whether the other folks liked it or not.

"Island Girl" came on first, and Clinton's eyebrows were suddenly hidden behind his long bangs. "Really, Tia?"

"You don't like Elton John? How can you *not* like him? He's so talented."

"I'm not denying that. I just don't like this kind of music. Too upbeat for me. Plus, it's, like, five years old."

"Is it?"

"Yup."

The waitress was back with our drinks and took our order.

"A tuna melt for breakfast?" Clinton asked after the woman left.

"What? It's protein."

He laughed. *What's new?* "You're different. I like that."

I felt another blush coming on. "I try not to conform *too* much."

"I can tell."

"Speaking of not conforming, did you see Joan Jett's video?"

"'I Love Rock 'n Roll?'"

"Yeah. I love it. I love *her*. I want her hair."

"She's cute. But you're cuter. I like your hair the way it is. It's softer." He paused. "And besides, your hair is bright red. Hers is black."

I shrugged, blushing in the meantime. "I can dye it."

"Don't you dare. Your hair is perfect."

My whole insides tingled with little electric sparks.

"Oh, Tia, by the way," he said, quickly ruining my moment. "Queen's new album is coming out in two months. I was going to get tickets to see their concert at the Garden in July. Do you wanna come with me?"

"Really?" I asked, practically bouncing up and down in my seat. "How do you know they're coming?"

"I read it in my *Circus* magazine."

"Holy crow, I'd love to see Freddie live."

"Okay. I'll get two tickets."

All at once, I felt guilty. "I, I probably shouldn't be happy right now, when my mother's in the hospital."

"I'm sorry. That's my fault."

"Nah. I just forgot there for a minute."

"Hey, check out the old men," Clinton whispered, nodding to the guys in the booth behind me.

They were bobbing their heads up and down. Men at a few booths were doing the same.

"Corny men," I commented.

Clinton laughed. It was a deep, rolling, velvety laugh, and it belied the introvert that he was.

MY MOTHER WAS WIDE awake when I walked into her room.

"Tia," she said, half smiling. "I am so sorry I left you alone."

"It's not like you meant it. What the heck happened?"

"I don't know, Tia, but I feel better now."

"Thank God. You scared me."

She reached for my hand. Hers was warm, the way it always was. "I'm so sorry I scared you. So sorry."

"Mom, it's okay. But do they know *why* you had a seizure?"

She closed her eyes.

"Mom?"

When her eyes opened, they were glossed over. "They're doing more tests, Tia, so they don't know for sure, but..." She shook her head like she was shaking away the tears that were falling down her face. "It may be a *cyst*," she emphasized. "Or a tumor," she whispered. "In my brain."

I didn't think it was possible, but at that precise moment, my world stopped. It didn't spin. It didn't go 'round. I didn't move. I couldn't. *My mother might have a brain tumor*. What if she died?

"Tia. They said it *may* be. It also may *not* be. There was a shadow on one of the scans. It could be just a simple cyst."

All I could do was stare at my mother. Her dark eyes, her long and currently disheveled brown hair, her pale, freckled skin. My mother. My everything.

"Tia, sit. Please. *Please.*" *If I move to sit, I move my world.* Then time would go on.

And then.

And then.

I'd have to face the music.

My mother could die.

She sat up in her bed. "Tia, baby. Sit, please. It looks like you're going to pass out. Mommy's gonna be okay. I promise." Her voice shook as she spoke.

But she promised.

Mom *never* broke a promise.

I sat.

And concentrated on the feel of her warm hand now on my arm.

"It's just routine. They saw a shadow, but lots of times it ends up being nothing. Benign. Please, don't worry, babe. I need you to stay strong."

I nodded, but tiny shards of glass in my throat were keeping me from speaking.

"I'm more upset that they need to keep me overnight again. Tia, were you okay by yourself last night? And were you *here* last night?"

Quietly, I spoke. "I was. I called Clinton to bring me home. He stayed over too. On the couch," I was quick to point out. "I hope you don't mind."

"On the couch?"

"Yes. He really didn't want me to stay in the house by myself."

"Will he stay again?"

"You don't mind?"

"I'm not comfortable with you being alone either. Can I talk with him though? I only met him briefly that one time."

I perked up a little. "Yeah. He's here. He brought me here."

"Oh," my mom said, smiling. "Bring him in."

I went in search of Clinton and found him smoking outside.

"Tia," he said, surprised, tossing his cigarette on the ground.

"How come this is the first time I ever saw you smoking? I almost forgot you smoked."

"I was hoping you'd forget."

"Why?"

"It's not good for you. How's your mother?"

"She's up. Awake. But she says it could be a brain tumor."

"Oh my God, Tia. Cancer?"

"Oh. I don't know. My mom didn't say."

"Tia. I don't, I don't know what to say."

"Say you'll come see her? She wants to talk to you about staying another night."

"Is she mad I stayed last night?"

"No, actually. I think she was happy about that. That's why she wants to see you. Would you mind really much?"

Clinton put his hand on my back and guided me forward through the hospital doors. "Of course not. I'm just glad she's not mad."

We were waiting for the elevator when Clinton said, "So your mother had a seizure and that was caused by a possible tumor?"

"Yeah. Weird, right?"

"Very," he said before saying, "I think it's all gonna be all right, Tia."

"You think?"

"I hope."

My mother was still sitting up in her bed. *The Family Feud* was on the television.

"That Richard Dawson kisses way too many girls, if you ask me," my mother said as we walked in. "You know what

I think? I think he's covering up the fact that he's gay. You know, 'the lady doth protest too much, me thinks.'"

"Quoting Shakespeare, Mom?" I was so embarrassed.

"Sorry. Clinton, right?"

"Yes, ma'am. Nice to meet you again."

"Thank you for staying with my daughter."

"You're welcome." Clinton looked nervous. I'd never seen him like this. He had no idea where to put his hands—in his pocket, on his hips, in his back pocket. It was almost too comical to watch without laughing. But I didn't laugh. That would make him even more self-conscious. I snickered instead.

He rolled his eyes at me.

"Now, I'd like you to stay again, if you're able to," my mother added. "But you'll sleep on the couch again."

"Of *course*, Ms. Mercury," he said as if he wouldn't dream of doing any differently. It kind of insulted me.

"Hopefully, they'll let me out tomorrow. Are you sure your parents won't mind?"

Clinton flinched but said, "No. They won't mind at all."

"Good. Thank you. Now, Tia, I don't want you to miss another day of school, so please go tomorrow. I should be home by the time you get home. Hopefully."

"How will you get home?" I asked.

"I'll call a cab."

"I can pick you up, Ms. Mercury."

"Clinton, call me Tammy. And no, you've done enough. A cab is fine. Don't you have school, anyway?"

"I have some long breaks between classes tomorrow."

"Thank you, but I'll be fine. Tia, I'll call the school and let them know why you weren't in today."

"Okay."

"Now go. Don't waste your time here."

"No, Mom. I wanna stay."

"And what? Watch *The Family Feud*?"

"Yeah. Want me to get you some magazines or something?"

"Well, actually, would you two mind going home and getting my book bag? I have papers I need to grade."

"Mom, shouldn't you be resting?"

"It's so boring here, Tia. Besides, you can grab my Truman Capote book on my nightstand too."

"You read Truman Capote?" Clinton asked.

"I am right now for one of my book clubs. Why? Do *you* read Truman Capote?"

He nodded. "*Other Voices, Other Rooms.*"

Mom raised an eyebrow. "Interesting. We're reading *In Cold Blood.*"

"I'll be happy to take Tia to get your stuff."

"Sure, Mom. We'll go."

"Okay. Thanks."

"Thank you for doing this," I told Clinton in the car.

"No problem."

"What about school? You're going to miss all day?"

"It's fine. I *never* miss."

Clinton was quiet the rest of the ride home. He even forgot to put on his music.

"Help yourself to whatever you want," I said once we were in my house, headed for the kitchen. "I'm just gonna get her stuff out of her room."

He didn't respond.

A few minutes later, I said, "Done," and had put her toothbrush, some toiletries, and her book in a small purse, carrying it and her teacher's bag over my shoulder.

"You okay, Clinton?"

"Yeah, yeah. Let's just stop at Tuffy's. I want to tell Karl I won't be in later."

"You can go to work. Drop me by the hospital, pick me up when you're done."

"Really?"

"Yeah. You'll be bored at the hospital. I'll just grab my book, and I'll read with my mom."

I ran into my room and grabbed *Flowers in the Attic*, my latest read from the library.

Clinton was quiet. He walked me into the hospital and said he'd pick me up at eight fifteen. "I'll just tell Karl I need to close an hour early."

"Thank you, Clinton."

He kissed me on the forehead. "See ya later, babe."

Babe.

"HEY, GOOD-LOOKIN'," Clinton said when he met me at the hospital doors at eight thirty.

"Good-lookin'? Thanks." I giggled inside.

He picked me up, kissed me on the lips, and put me down.

"Whoa."

Then he opened the car door for me and let me in.

"You okay?"

"Couldn't be better."

Odd. "What's that smell?"

"Smell?"

"Like a strong medicinal smell. Like, like alcohol."

He didn't respond.

With AC/DC blaring from his speakers, Clinton looked like he was feeling no pain as he sang along with Bon Scott, Malcolm, and Angus, heading down his own highway to something that I was not quite aware of yet.

Inside my house, I stopped at the kitchen table. "Clinton? Are you okay?"

"Yup. Told ya that already." He went to the laundry closet and took the sheets, blanket, and pillow he'd used last night off the washing machine. "I'll put these back on the couch."

"Clinton," I called after him and followed him into the living room. "Were you drinking tonight?"

"Drinking's not good for you, Tia," he said while pulling the fitted sheet over the couch cushions.

"Yeah. I know that." I grabbed his forearm to demand his attention. "But did you drink tonight?"

He stared me down, eyebrows raised, but he didn't answer.

"You're twenty. You're legally allowed to drink in New Jersey. It's not a big deal. I was just asking, because, well, you're acting weird. And I smell it."

His gaze lasted a few more seconds, and then in the next, his lips were on mine. I reached on my tip-toes and placed my hands on his shoulders. But by the time I leaned in closer to feel his chest against mine, it was over. He'd pulled away.

"I shouldn't have done that. See what drinking does? It makes you do things you wouldn't normally do." He went back to making up the couch.

"Maybe it makes you do things you wouldn't normally have the *courage* to do."

"Courage," he whispered, more to himself than to me. Then louder, he said, "It takes more courage to *not* do what you want to do, Tia."

"But for what reason? I'm fifteen and a half. I'm not *that* young. And who needs to know? I won't tell anyone. I promise."

He sat on the couch, took my hand, and pulled me down on his lap. Clinton made no sense tonight. First a kiss, now I was on his lap. I shouldn't have been complaining.

My lower back was tingling at the touch of his hand, while the veins in my legs shot fireworks at the warmth of his arm draped over my thighs.

"But *I'll* know, Tia." He lifted his right hand and brushed my bangs out of my face. "As much as I want you—" he paused "—I don't think it's right. It feels wrong."

I squiggled in his arms, feeling embarrassed and uncomfortable.

But he held me tighter. "Tia, I really like you. I *want* to be with you. But if we get physical, you're only fifteen. Isn't that too young?"

He asked. Did that mean he wasn't sold on the idea of me being too young? "What if we took the physical part slow?" I suggested, not knowing if my lame idea made any sense.

"Thennnn—" he lingered on his word "—weeee'd beee doin' what we already are. We'd be friends. Who liked each other. A lot."

"A real lot," I said, looking directly into his eyes.

His eyes didn't avert mine—they looked back. "I wish you were older." He said the words while he looked at my mouth.

"I'll be sixteen in seven short months. A junior in high school in September." I was staring at his mouth now.

He laughed before resting his lips back on mine. I watched him close his eyes, and when he did, his mouth opened and his tongue slid inside. The taste of what I can only assume was beer invaded the kiss.

If he hadn't been drinking, he wouldn't have been kissing me. I knew that. But this was Clinton. And for nearly two years, I'd dreamed of this day. The reasons for his kiss mattered very little at the moment.

I loved Clinton.

Beer-tasting kiss and all.

Again, the kiss didn't last long, but this one was real, and when Clinton pulled away, his breathing was labored and in tune with my racing heart.

"You should go to bed, Tia. You have to get up early." He pried me from his lap and stood up. "I have an early class too." He kissed me on the cheek, and when he walked toward the bathroom, he said, "See ya in the morning."

But in the morning...

...he wasn't there.

A yellow piece of lined paper on the kitchen table greeted me instead. A blue Bic pen rested next to it. A knot formed in my stomach as I approached the table, a sixth sense telling me it wasn't a good sign.

Tia,

Left for school.

Figured you'd be okay walking to school.

Call me if your mother needs a ride home.

Clinton

Nothing devastating, but it still didn't sit right with me. Why had he been in such a hurry to leave? It was only six thirty in the morning.

Moving past my disappointment, I showered and got ready for school. I was in no mood to blow-dry and feather my hair, so I went out the door with a wet head and a package of brown-sugar cinnamon Pop-Tarts. Najia was standing outside the Campus Sweet Shoppe, even though I hadn't called her to let her know I was going to school.

"Where were you yesterday, Tee? I tried calling your house a few times after school, but no one answered."

"My mom's in the hospital. I was with her."

"What happened? Is she all right?"

"For now. She had a seizure Wednesday night."

"She gets them?"

"No. That's why it was so scary. I had to call the police and they sent an ambulance. It was all so *Emergency*-like. Minus Randolph Mantooth." I laughed, despite not feeling like it.

"Darn. Why can't there be cute paramedics in real life?"

"Right? They should work on that."

"So, why'd your mom have a seizure? Do they know?"

"They're still running tests. They said it could be caused by a brain tumor."

"No. Your mom's too young for cancer."

"Well, they didn't really say cancer. Just that it *could* be a tumor or a cyst or something like that."

"So, it's *not* cancer?"

"They didn't mention that word."

"Well, that's good news."

"Yeah. Hey, Naj."

"Yeah?"

"Clinton kissed me."

"Whaaaat? No way."

"Way. Last night."

"Last what? Why don't you look happier? I thought you'd be, like, jumping up and down and peeing in your pants and shit."

"Peeing in my pants? Naj, I'm not eighty."

"Why aren't you excited? Does he kiss bad? All wet and sloppy?"

No matter my moods, Najia *always* made me crack up. "No, Naj. He kissed...amazingly," I said with my eyes closed, remembering the taste of him. "Like a man, not like Bobby and Eric, who actually *did* kiss like they were sloppin' up a drippy ice cream cone."

I made Najia laugh too. "So, he's a manly kisser. So *why* are we not happy about it?"

"He left without telling me this morning."

Najia stopped—right in the middle of our crossing the street. "Hold the mayo. He stayed *over*?"

With both my hands, I pushed her from behind to get to the sidewalk. "You wanna get us killed? There's a double yellow line on this street. It's a main street. Holy heavens, Naj."

She looked at me like *I* was crazy. "Let me get this straight. Your mother's in the hospital. Clinton, a *twenty*-year-old man, stayed overnight. And all you did was kiss? A *manly* kiss? You had sex with him, didn't you? And that's why you're upset."

I smacked her in the arm. "God, Naj, whaddya think I am? I wouldn't have sex with him the first time we ever kissed."

"Hey. You've been in love with the guy for two years. I'm surprised you *didn't*. He didn't even *try*?"

I dropped my head. "No. He made me go to my room right after he kissed me."

Najia was no longer by my side. She'd stopped again.

I'd kept walking. "What?" I asked when I finally realized.

She was bent over, hands on her thighs, doubled over in laughter.

"Najia. It's not funny." But I, too, began laughing.

"I think he's confused because he's so much older. 'Do I act like a dad? Do I act like a boyfriend? I should send her to her room for kissing a twenty-year-old.' Hilarious, Tee." Of course, she was still busting a gut while she was teasing me. "'Tia,'" she said in a deep voice. "'Go to your room. You shouldn't be kissing twenty-year-olds.'"

"Are you done?"

She chuckled and then said, "Yeah, I'm done. I'm sorry, Tee. It just struck me funny."

"Yeah, well, if it hadn't happened to me, it would be." I smiled, letting her know I was okay with the joking.

We had just reached the school when she said, seriously, "Why *was* he staying over, anyway?"

"He didn't want me to stay alone in the house. He stayed the night before too."

"Wow. That was nice of him."

"Yeah. He's too nice, I think. He worries more about me than I want him to."

Najia's locker came up before mine. "See ya later, Tee."

"See ya."

MY MOTHER WAS SITTING on the couch by the time I got home from school.

"Mom." I dropped my bag and went to the couch.

"Hey, baby."

I squeezed my mother harder than I think I ever had. It felt good to be so close to her. "Are you gonna be okay, Mom?"

She held me at arms' length and said, "I'm going to try real hard, honey."

"Is it a brain tumor?"

"Well, there is something there. I have to see a neurologist next."

"What's that mean?"

"It means we still don't know. But don't worry. I'll do what needs to be done, so that I'm one hundred percent. I'm going to try my best."

I nodded. "Good. I'm glad you're home. How'd you get home?"

"I called a cab. It was only a ten-minute ride. You have homework?"

"Yeah. Make-up work, too."

"Well, get started on it. Do you mind take-out tonight? I'm not really up for..."

"No, Mom. Don't do anything. I can cook if you want. I'll run to Foodtown."

"No. Chinese is good."

"Okay. I'll call and order in a little while." I got up, grabbed my bag, and went to my room, where I put on MTV and did my homework. My concentration was at a minimum though. All I could think about was Clinton leaving this morning.

So I called him.

No one answered his home phone, so I called Tuffy's.

"Tuffy's," Clinton answered.

My stomach churned. "Clinton."

He paused, which was the first sign that I had not misread what Clinton had written in his note. "Tia." He almost sounded surprised to hear from me. "How's your mother? Does she need a ride? Is she coming home today?"

"She's home."

"Oh. Well, good."

"You wanna come over? After you close? I don't wanna leave my mother tonight to come down..."

"No, Tia. I can't come."

"Okay, well..."

"Gotta go, Tia. Just, please keep me posted on your mom, okay?"

"Keep you posted? What's that supposed to—"

"Bye, Tia."

There was a huge crushing feeling in my chest the second after I heard the click of his phone hanging up on me. The tears came immediately after and intensified my chest pain.

Why would kissing me make him back away? Was *I* a sloppy, immature kisser? What was wrong with me that I couldn't get Clinton Daniels to like me?

Better yet, why couldn't *I* just stop liking *him*?

CHAPTER EIGHT

"The Kiss"

T IA
Two and a half months later, Mom had seen all the necessary doctors, second opinions and all, and each test confirmed the same thing—she had brain cancer. They were going to try to operate, but only *after* they treated her with chemotherapy and radiation in order to shrink the tumor to a more operable size.

Today would start her first cycle. Since I wasn't yet old enough to drive, Mom and I took a car service to get there. Mom suggested I go to school, but I insisted I be with her. At least for the first day. Reluctantly, she agreed.

It was going to be at least a five-hour wait, so I brought a couple of books I had checked out from the library—*The Crystal Cave* by Mary Stewart and *I Know What You Did Last Summer* by Lois Duncan. Plus, I brought my algebra homework along—not that I was doing all that well in it any-more anyway.

Seven hours later, Mom and I were finally back home. She seemed no worse for wear, and that made me feel hope-ful.

That night, after Mom went to bed, there was a knock on the door.

"Clinton." I couldn't believe he was standing at my front door—after all these months of me avoiding Tuffy's and Clinton avoiding me.

"Tia. Lydia called me today. I'm so sorry about your mother. Why didn't you call me?"

I just stood there staring up at him.

"She had her first treatment today?"

I nodded.

"Can you come sit with me out here? Not long. I just wanna talk."

The angry part of me wanted to say, *No, I don't want to come sit with you*, but of course, I would. Of course. "Yeah." I closed the screen door and the two of us sat on my mom's white wicker bench.

"I'm sorry I fell off the face of the earth, Tia. I have no good reason, except to say that I suck."

My eyes met his when I said, "Yeah. You do."

"I know it."

"Why? Why did you leave that morning? It was the kiss, wasn't it?"

He nodded. "Yeah. It was." He closed his eyes and shook his head, then opened them and stared into mine. "I care about you. A lot. And these past couple months without you in my life have been...miserable."

"Were you drinking? I smell something."

"Tia, I'm trying to talk to you here."

"I know, but if you were drinking, then maybe you won't mean what you say. And then I won't believe you."

"Why wouldn't I mean what I say?"

"You didn't mean the kiss when you were drinking."

"Who said I didn't mean the kiss?"

"You did. Just a minute ago."

"Tia, will you let me finish?"

"Were you drinking?"

He stood and sat on the porch railing. "My God. Yes, Tia. I was drinking. I drink *every* night now. Sometimes during the day. I'm barely sober anymore, okay? Does this make you happy? Because it sucks, okay. But regardless of my recent drinking binge, I still know what I'm doing and saying." Clinton was angry. He wasn't yelling, but he was clearly upset. "I don't get plastered. Just drunk enough to dull the pain."

"What pain?"

"I don't know, Tia." He spoke quickly, angrily. "Maybe the fact that I never felt a *thing* about *any*thing until I met you. And now, now all I feel is *every*thing. Everything I shouldn't. Everything I never wanted to feel in the first place."

"Why didn't you ever want to feel anything?"

"Because people suck, Tia. They suck. They leave you. They beat you. They belittle you. They suck."

"Not everybody sucks."

"People in *my* life do."

He sat back down next to me.

"People beat you?"

"Eh. Nothing I can't handle."

"Your father?"

"And brothers. It's fine."

"Why do you stay?"

"Where'm I gonna go? I have a part-time job. I *won't* quit college. It means too much to me."

"Are you gonna disappear again?"

He took my hand and held it on his lap. "I don't want to. It hurts too much. Missing you, I mean."

"Why'd you leave that morning, Clinton?"

He didn't answer right away.

"'Cause I'm too young," I answered instead.

"That's...in a way, yes, but you're right. I did think you were too young. It felt wrong. But you know what else felt wrong?"

I shook my head in lieu of an answer.

"Being apart from you. It made me physically ill."

"Really?"

"Yup. Sick to my stomach. It doesn't make any sense."

"Maybe it does."

His fingers traced mine. His eyes followed his fingers. "How?"

"Because I feel the same way."

His fingers stilled, and he looked at my face. In his eyes, I saw pain. It was written all over his face, too. "I made you feel like that?" His tone contrite, he let go of my hand and touched my cheek. "I am so sorry, Tia. I never wanted to hurt you."

His hand fell back to his lap, but mine was already beneath my thigh.

"Tia?"

"Yeah?"

"Can we start over?" He tried to look me in the eyes. He even pivoted his body so he'd be facing me.

But I wouldn't let him. I didn't want him to see me so vulnerable. The foolish girl in me was willing to start *any*thing with him. But in the past two months, listening to my mother cry behind closed doors, and overhearing phone conversations—thirteen percent mortality rate, inoperable brain tumor, six months to live without therapy. These things kind of knocked the foolish right out of me. I have no tolerance for games anymore. Or people who believe in disposable friendships.

"Tia? Do you *not* want to try again?"

This time, I looked at him, with my vulnerability and all. "What is it you want to try, Clinton? Because anyone I let into my life right now, they have to stay. I can't afford to lose people. Not now. Not when the chance of losing my mother is a whopping eighty-seven percent *if* she continues treatment. Because once she's gone, I've got no one. My friends? I have no time to hang with them anymore. Not when I want to spend all my free time at home." After a mirthless chuckle, I raised my hand and continued. *Don't stop me now.* "Pretty soon, that's gonna change to a need to stay home, not just a want. I could stand to have a friend who's interested in sitting in my dark, dreary, cancer-filled house instead of hanging at the local ice-cream shop, but I want nothing to do with that friend if he or she is just going to drop me anytime his feelings get too intense for him to handle." My heart was racing at the speed of light.

Clinton's jaw hung down.

"So, Clinton, let me ask you. Do *you* want to try again? Or are you just playing games?"

When he finally closed his mouth, he said, "I never played games, Tia," in a whisper.

"Then that's even sadder, 'cause you could just walk out of my life all over again. At your whim."

He was shaking his head. "No, Tia, I won't walk out of your life again. I promise."

I stood up. "And how are you so certain you're able to keep that promise?"

Coming to a stand, and with glassy eyes, he searched my eyes. "Because I know now what it's like to live without you. I don't ever want to go through that again. Ever." He sat down on the railing and took my hands in his as he guided me between his legs. Our eyes level, he said, "I care for you, Tia. No. I *love* you, Tia. So much. I don't want to live without you. I don't know why. I spent many nights asking myself that. How could I love someone so young for me? So unnatural, it seems, but nevertheless, I do. And that's how I know I'll keep my promise, Tia. Because I can't stop thinking about you when you're not with me."

I wanted to believe him. With all my heart, I did. But I couldn't afford to be let down again. Not when I *needed* him so much.

"You don't believe me, do you?" He didn't let go of my hands.

I didn't pull away. "Your track record's not the greatest."

"It's not. Give me one more chance," he pleaded. "I won't let you down again."

He freed a hand and touched my face. "And I'm so sorry about your mother. Is it really inoperable?"

"They're gonna try to operate. She got a second opinion, so..."

"Lydia called for my dad before I went to work this afternoon. I answered. She asked if I had seen you lately. Told her no. That's when she told me about your mom." His fingers traced my jaw. "Nick couldn't cover for me, otherwise, I would have been here right after that phone call. Maybe I should have just come anyway. Closed the store. I'm sorry I didn't."

He stood and pulled me down onto the wicker bench with him.

"I wish I could have been there for you when you first got the news." His hand covered mine on my lap.

I flipped my hand so he could hold it again. "It was the worst day of my life."

Letting go of my hand, he pulled me into his arms and kissed the top of my head. Then we sat there silently for a long time.

So long that I fell asleep.

"Tia. Tia." He squeezed me. "Wake up, babe."

I moaned.

"I think it's really late."

Sitting up straight, I looked out at the street. Not one car was driving by. "Oh my gosh, what time is it?"

"I don't know. I don't have on a watch. But I'm guessing it's sometime after midnight. We fell asleep."

"Oh. Oh wow, I'm sorry."

"No, don't be. I enjoyed having you in my arms. I just better get going now, though."

"'Kay."

We both stood up and stretched.

"I'll stop by after work again tomorrow? Is that okay?"

"Yeah. I'd like that."

"You sure?"

"Positive."

We hugged goodbye and I got another kiss on the forehead.

FIVE HOURS LATER, I kissed my mom goodbye as she headed off with a car service and I headed for school.

Najia was at the campus waiting for me. "How'd it go yesterday?" she asked on the way up Zabriskie Street.

"Long."

"I saw Clinton this morning."

"You did?"

"He was pulling out of his driveway."

"Hmmm." I didn't know how or if to respond to that.

"I'm sorry, Tee."

"What? For what?"

"He told me why you don't hang at Tuffy's or come out after school. And I'm sorry I don't just come over your house. I've been a bad friend. I'm really sorry."

"Stop. It's fine."

"No, it's not. Can I come over today? We can do homework together."

"Really? You want to?"

"If your mother's feeling okay."

"Today's her second treatment. I'm not sure how she's gonna feel, but I'm sure she won't mind if you come over. It's not like we're loud or anything."

"Good. I'll come straight home with you and call my mom from your house."

"Naj, only if you want to. Really. I understand if you like hanging with everyone at Tuffy's."

"Eh. It hasn't been the same without you anyway."

"Thanks."

When we were at the bottom of the hill at school, Najia said, "So, Clinton? When did you guys start talking again?"

"Yesterday." As we walked up the hill and until we reached her locker, I told her what had gone on last night between Clinton and me.

"Wow. How do you feel about that?"

"I don't know. I mean, if he's telling the truth, and he really does like me that much, then I'm really happy about it. But what if he only *thinks* he likes me that much?"

"You think he'd lie?"

"No. Not intentionally." I looked around and saw everyone scrambling to get into their classrooms. "Damn, I better go before I'm late, Naj. See you after school."

I made it inside the classroom just after the bell rang. "Damn," I muttered.

Mr. Ritter gave me one of his chastising looks. "Get a pass, Ms. Mercury."

Darn it.

AT LUNCH, MAXX SAID, "Najia said she's coming over to do homework after school. Want me to come too?"

"What? What did Najia say?" I never told Maxine about my mom.

"She said she couldn't come with me and Chris to Tuffy's 'cause she was going to your house to do homework."

"And you'd rather do homework with me than go to Tuffy's with your boyfriend?" I asked, raising my eyebrows at the absurdity.

"You never come out anymore. I thought if you were asking Naj to come over that you were ready to see friends again."

"Whaddya mean, see friends again?"

"I don't know. You kinda just turned away from us a couple months ago. Najia had said you were upset that Clinton broke up with you, so—" she paused "—we kind of left you alone."

"He didn't break up with me. We were never going out. But, yeah, I *was* upset about Clinton." It was the truth, just not the whole truth. It was hard to just spit out the words, *my mom has cancer*. In time, Maxine would figure it out.

"So, do you want me to come over? I miss hanging with you. I'll bring ice cream."

I laughed. "Yeah. That sounds like fun." Hopefully, Mom wouldn't come home too exhausted from her second treatment. It wasn't supposed to be as long a session as yesterday.

"I'll have my mom drop me off at your house."

"Great."

HOMEWORK WITH NAJIA and Maxine was so needed. We laughed non-stop. And when Mom would come into the kitchen, she'd laugh with us. She even sat down and had ice cream sundaes with us.

"Thanks for the company, girls. I think I'm going to hit the hay." Mom kissed me on the cheek, waved to us all, and went to her room when she'd had enough of us.

"I love your mom," Maxine said. "My mother would never join us for ice cream."

"Yeah, my mom's cool." This realization made me happy and sad at the same time.

Najia caught that and winked. "She's as cool as mothers come."

"Are you going to Jordan again this summer?" Maxine asked her.

"Yup. Leaving on July first."

"What about you, Tee? You going away this summer?"

"Nah. Mom and I are just gonna hang home."

Again, Najia winked at me.

"What about you?" I asked Maxx.

"Cayman Islands for two weeks."

"Nice."

"Can we switch? You go to Jordan with my family, and I'll go to the Caymans with yours?"

We all laughed and then the doorbell rang.

"That's probably my mom." Maxine gathered her books from the table and got up. "Thanks for having me, Tee."

"Thanks for coming. And for the ice cream."

Maxine walked out and Najia said, "I should be going too, Tee. Before it gets too dark and my mom has a conniption."

"Hey." His voice made me jump.

"Clinton."

"Maxine let me in."

"Oh." I looked at the clock. "It's early."

"Closed up shop early. No one was there."

"Oh. Good," I said, pleasantly surprised.

"See ya tomorrow, Tee. Clinton."

"Naj. You need a ride home?"

"Nah. Keep Tee company. It's a nice night for a walk. See ya."

"See ya."

"So, I'm supposed to keep *Tee* company, huh?"

"Well, that *is* what you're here for, isn't it?" I joked.

Clinton wrapped his arms around my waist and kissed the top of my head. Again. I was getting the feeling Clinton wanted a puppy instead of a girlfriend. "How's your mom?" he whispered.

"Good. She's sleeping now, but it was a good day," I said as a matter of fact.

He kissed my nose and let me out of his arms. "Still doing homework?" he asked, lifting up one end of my algebra book.

"Just finished."

"How ya doin' in Algebra?"

"Sucky."

His shoulders dropped. "I'm sorry. That's my fault."

"It's your fault I'm stupid?"

"You're not stupid, Tia. You just get confused with Algebra."

"That's not the only thing that confuses me."

His scrunched up eyebrows made me chuckle. I was in a good mood tonight though. Mom was feeling well, I'd had a fun night with my friends, and Clinton had closed up shop early to come see me. All was right with the world tonight.

"Well, I'll help you with your math if you want."

"Nah. I copied off Maxx. She's got Algebra too."

"You copied? Tia."

"Clinton, it's the end of the school year. Don't worry about it. I'll never have to take Algebra again."

"You need Algebra Two to get into college."

"Algebra Two? I just had Algebra One for the second year in a row. I'm *not* taking Algebra Two."

"What about college?"

"Clinton, I've got junior and senior year to worry about. I'm not thinking 'bout college right now."

"You *always* think about college, Tia. It's important."

"Clinton?"

"Yeah?"

"Ya wanna go watch MTV?"

He drew back his head in laughter. "How 'bout you show me whatchya can do on that piano of yours? If it won't bother your mother."

"I'll tap the keys lightly."

I sat down and played some songs I've been practicing. "Come Sail Away" was the first thing I played for him.

"You *have* to teach me that," he said. "You learned that with no sheet music?"

I nodded. "I don't know how to read music that well."

"That's the *only* way I can play. At least until I have it memorized."

"You took lessons?" I asked while he played that Tom Petty tune on the keys.

"Not officially. My second grade music teacher gave me a couple of starter books to practice on after school when I was young. She knew I was interested but also knew my father wouldn't pay for lessons. He said only *faggots* played piano. When I told my teacher that, she put her arm around me and said not to worry, that she'd teach me after school. She sent a note home to my dad telling him that once a week I'd stay after to help clean erasers." He stopped playing. "His response was that only *faggots* did that too, but he still allowed me to."

"Your father sounds like a prize."

"Oh, he is, Tia. He is. Play something else for me."

I played "Bohemian Rhapsody" for him.

"Holy shit, Tia. That was awesome," he praised when I was finished. "When did you learn that?"

"I've been working on it for a while. Here and there. In between watching MTV and doing homework."

"You're incredible."

"Wanna watch MTV now? I'm kinda getting tired."

"Sure."

I went back to the kitchen table, piled my books, and brought them to my bedroom.

"Wanna watch in here?" Clinton asked behind me, almost fully blocking my doorway with his size.

"Oh. Yeah, I...if...yeah if..." I stammered, unable to get words out with the thought of him standing in my bedroom.

He laughed. "I mean, in case you fall asleep, you're already in bed. Then I can leave without waking you up."

"Oh."

He chuckled and shook his head. "I liked holding you last night, Tia," he said seriously. "I liked having you fall asleep in my arms. So, but, yeah, we can watch in the living room if you..."

"No no," I said quickly. "No." Clinton holding me until I fell asleep? All was *excellent* with the world tonight. "My bedroom's fine," I squeaked.

With a laugh, he went and turned on my TV.

"I'm just going to put on my sweats and brush my teeth."

"I'll be here."

Clinton was sitting, legs long, ankles crossed, looking like a God at the top of my bed when I reentered my room. "You look fresh and clean."

"Yeah, well, I washed my face. Braided my hair."

I pulled down the covers on the side of the bed Clinton wasn't occupying and got in.

"So your mom was really good today? She wasn't sick after her treatment?"

"Nope. She was laughing and everything. Maybe it won't be as bad as I thought."

Clinton put his arm around me and kissed me on the temple.

CHAPTER NINE

"It's a Hard Life"

T IA
It wasn't as bad as I thought.

It was worse.

By the end of the week, and four treatments later, Mom was tired by the time she got home. Fortunately, she didn't need to go back for another two weeks. They were treating her aggressively, but her good cells needed time to regenerate, so she got a two-week reprieve in between cycles. Mom went back to teaching for the last week of the school year, and I enjoyed the end of my sophomore year. Clinton came over every night, sitting at the piano with me some nights, watching MTV videos other nights, and two afternoons, I actually sat with Clinton at Tuffy's—Mom insisted.

It was Mom's second round of treatments that threw us for a loop. They completely wiped her out. So, for the rest of the summer, I picked up where Mom couldn't, and I spent all my time taking care of her and the house.

"I'm sure you can find someone else to go to the concert with you, Clinton," I said at the piano when he told me he wasn't going to use the Queen tickets he bought for us.

"If you can't go, I don't want to."

"But it's Queen. You *love* Queen."

"I love you more," he said quietly. "I bought those tickets for *you*. I'm not going without you. Besides, it's not that important."

"But it's Queen. Besides, we weren't talking when you bought them."

"I never had any intention of *not* taking you. Even if we still weren't talking, I was still gonna pick your ass up to go with me." He paused. "How 'bout you see if Najia's mom could take you and Naj, and I'll stay with your mom?"

"Clinton, no. Just...no. No."

He pulled me into his arms and held me. "It's just a concert. There'll be others."

But I couldn't just let this concert go by without us going to it. So, I devised a plan before Wednesday, July twenty-eighth.

"Clinton," I said groggily to him Sunday, sometime in the middle of the night, when he was getting out of my bed to go home. "Can you take off Wednesday night?"

"Sure. For you, anything." He leaned down and kissed me good-bye. Of course, on the nose. My lips were off limits to him because I was still too young. He told me that one day last month when I asked him why he always kissed me on the head or on the nose. "It'll just be too tempting," he told me. "I'd rather wait until you're at least sixteen to go there."

So, I'm waiting until I'm sixteen, and I'm having a terrible time with it. But at least it's only two and a half months away, even though it feels like forever.

"MOM?" I ASKED QUIETLY on the ride over to one of her long treatments. Clinton took us on the shorter days, but on the longer ones, he wouldn't be back in time for work, so we took a car service on those days. He said he'd drive us there, so we'd only have to get a service for going home, but I wanted him to have a few mornings to sleep in. As it was, he left my house at about three in the morning every night. He'd never stay. I never asked why.

"Yeah?"

"Would you mind if Lydia came over tomorrow night to hang with you?"

"*Hang* with me? Why? Did she call?"

"No. I got her number from your address book. I called her."

"Why?"

I kind of felt selfish now, looking at my mom, her hair gone, her skin gray. I should have never called Lydia. "Never mind."

"Honey. Do you have somewhere you want to go? Did you call Lydia to ask if she'd keep an eye on me?"

I nodded. "I'm sorry. I'll call her back."

"I can take care of myself, baby." She rubbed my arm.

"But what if you need something? Or you're throwing up?"

"Babe. I'll be okay. But I'll call Lydia tonight. If she really wants to come down tomorrow, it'd be nice to see her."

"Really?"

"Yes. Now where is it you want to go?"

"Clinton bought tickets to see Queen at the Garden."

"Queen? Wow. That was nice of him."

"He got them before we knew you were sick. When we weren't talking."

"Well, I'm glad you're talking now."

"He doesn't know we're still going. He wasn't gonna go without me. That's why I called your friend. I hope that was okay."

"Of course it's okay. Thank you for all you've been doing lately, Tia. I really hate that you're giving up your summer for me."

"I don't mind. Is that why you allow Clinton to stay in my room so late? 'Cause...I'm kinda surprised you do."

She chuckled under her breath. "I trust the two of you."

"You do?"

"I do."

"Thank you, Mom."

She leaned over and kissed me on the temple. "Thank *you*, sweetheart."

CLINTON WAS LATE.

I had asked him to be here at five, considering we had to drive into the city, which I had no idea how long it took to get to. But it was already after six and he wasn't here. Lydia was sitting in the living room with my mother, whose spirits were up, because her friend was visiting.

I decided to call him.

"Yeah?" The guy who answered did not sound happy.

"Um, is Clinton there?"

"This that same chick again?"

"What?"

"You know you're wasting your time with my brother, don't you?"

"Shut the hell up," I heard Clinton yell in the background.

Then I heard a thunk and things were breaking. A loud thud came from the phone, and then a bunch of curse words.

I hung up, too embarrassed for Clinton to keep listening.

Twenty minutes later, Clinton was at my front door.

"Oh my God, what happened?" His face was a bloody mess, and his eye was swollen shut.

"Nothing. I'm fine." He took a step inside and said, "Tia, I don't know what you had planned tonight, but maybe..."

"What the hell happened to you?"

"Lydia, what're you doin' here?" he asked when he came upon her standing in front of him.

"Came to sit with Tammy," she said, touching his face and running her hand down his bloody tee shirt. "So you could use those Queen tickets you bought for Tia. Now what the hell hap—"

"Queen?"

Very softly, I whispered, "I thought we could still go."

"Tia," he whispered back.

"Clinton," my mother said from her recliner. "What happened?"

"Your father?" Lydia asked.

"It doesn't matter." Then he looked at me. "Tia, the tickets are in my dresser. I'm not going back there. I don't think—"

"Go wash up, Clinton," Lydia demanded, in a tone not unlike my mother's when she was upset. "I'm going to get your tickets. Which drawer?"

"Lydia, no, he's really drunk and really fowl tonight. They all are."

"Which drawer, Clinton?" she insisted.

"Top right," he said on a sigh.

"Clinton, you can take a shower if you'll feel better," my mother offered.

"I'll grab you a clean shirt too," Lydia said as she walked out the door.

While Clinton showered, I sat with my mother.

"Does this happen to him often?" my mother asked.

"I don't know. He made a reference to it once."

Mom nodded. "That's really sad. His *father?*"

"His brothers too."

My mom shook her head. "What a shame. You know, if it's bad there, I don't mind him staying here."

"Are you kidding? You wouldn't mind?"

"Well, I really don't want him rooming with you, even though I know he stays already until early morning."

I dropped my head, feeling a little shameful.

"But he's welcome to stay on the couch, or...I can set up a cot in your room."

"Really?"

"You guys don't fool around, do you?" she asked on a shrug, as if she already knew we didn't.

I shook my head. "He doesn't even kiss me, except for on the nose or forehead."

Mom smiled and tilted her head. "That's okay. You're young yet. I'm glad he doesn't."

"Not me."

Mom laughed. "Don't grow up too fast, baby. You'll miss out on all the good stuff."

I was already missing out on all the good stuff because I was too young.

Clinton was back in the room, sans bloody tee shirt and his long wavy hair wet on his shoulders. And boy did he look good.

"Feel better, Clinton?" my mom asked, standing from the couch.

"Please, Ms. Mercury, sit. I'm fine."

"Clinton, call me Tammy, come on. And I'm okay standing. But come sit, please." My mom patted the arm of the couch then sat back on her recliner. "Your father did this to you?" she asked, reaching out to touch his cheek.

"It was a collaborated effort," Clinton said with his good eye averted.

"What does that mean?"

"My brothers helped."

"So, you were gang-attacked by your own family?"

"I fought back. We were all involved."

"What triggered it?"

Clinton fell silent.

"Clinton, this is important. You need to be safe in your own home."

"Ms...Tammy, I am safe. I'm partly to blame. It's fine."

At this point, Lydia walked back in holding out the tickets in one hand, a paper bag in the other. "A whole new outfit," she said, handing Clinton both.

"Thanks. Be right back."

"How is he?" Lydia asked after Clinton shut the bathroom door.

"Pretty collected. I'm surprised."

"This isn't the first time." She sat on the couch where Clinton had been sitting. "I hated moving away from them. My husband wanted to get away from the negativity though. I didn't blame him. I couldn't raise my kids and be at those boys' beck and call too. I wanted to take Clinton with us, but Bill wouldn't hear of it. He said he'd shoot us all if I even attempted."

"Shoot you? Geez. And does he just do this to Clinton or to all of them?" my mom asked.

"Just Clinton. Don't really know why, though. He *is* the baby. And he must look like his mother, since he looks nothing like Bill. Plus, Clinton is, how shall I say, different. When he was younger, he was so weak and frail. Sickly. I remember when they first moved back here from wherever Bill's family moved when he was twelve. I felt so bad for Bill and those boys. He came back because his wife left him. Cheated on him. I never even met her. But I promised I'd always take care of them. But then, I never knew Bill had grown to be so violent. When he was younger, he was volatile and all, drinking at such a young age, but I don't know. He just became this monster. Especially to Clinton."

"But why? I don't understand. Clinton seems so kind."

"Like I said." She paused. "Clinton's different. An introvert, and a genius, which probably intimidates him and the other boys. The other three have that drinking gene. And a screw or two loose. Even though Clinton grew to be bigger than them, they still pick on him. They know his weaknesses, I guess."

"He's such a nice boy. By the way—" my mother leaned into her "—did you know he read *Other Voices, Other Rooms*?"

"Truman Capote? I told you, he's a genius. He reads what others don't."

"Mmmm." My mother looked like she had more to say, but she didn't.

When Clinton walked back into the living room, he asked, "So, why were my ears ringing?" He was smirking, but I could tell he was uncomfortable.

"You kids get going. I'm sure you're going to miss the opening act," Lydia said.

"Long as we see Queen," Clinton responded, then put his hand on my lower back. "I'll have her back as soon as the concert's over."

"No speeding. And Clinton...stay here tonight."

He dropped his hand from my back and stared at my mother. Just stared.

"You can stay every night, Clinton. Rent-free."

Clinton looked like he was going to pass out.

Or cry.

Or both.

And he still kept staring at my mom.

"Clinton?" I asked, grabbing and hanging on to his arm. "You okay?"

Lydia came over and hugged him. "There *are* good people in this world, baby. They're not all assholes."

My hand was still on his arm while Lydia embraced him. He was shaking. Then I heard his breath hitch.

"Clinton, go enjoy yourself." Lydia squeezed him tight then let him go.

His hand was back on my back. "Thank you," he said, looking at my mother.

"Have fun, Clinton."

I was proud of my mom. She was sick, but she was still kind. And she made the boy I loved feel okay.

In the car, I was quiet. It seemed obvious that Clinton was preoccupied in thought, so I didn't want to disturb him. But once we parked at Port Authority, he was all kinds of excited and talking non-stop.

"Did you know Freddie Mercury had *four* extra teeth in his mouth?"

"Nope."

"Yup. And he can sing almost four whole octaves. I always wondered if his teeth had anything to do with that."

"What?"

"I studied music in high school. Resonant Embouchure, I think it's called."

"Never heard of it."

"Eh. His teeth could have helped."

I laughed. He was so darn talkative.

"I told you his real name was Farrokh Bulsara?"

"Yeah, you did." I laughed. "His name sounds like the F-word."

"You're silly. But yeah. Farrokh. Some name. Thank God someone nick-named him Freddie in high school."

"That was fortunate. You know a lot about him."

"Yeah. I read a lot of music magazines."

"Like I know a lot about Marie Osmond."

"What?"

"Like we share the same birthday."

"October 13th."

"You remembered."

"How could I forget?"

"Thanks." I blushed, hoping he was just as anxious for me to turn sixteen as I was.

"What else you like about her?"

"Marie? Her voice. I wish I could sing like her."

"I can honestly say I've never heard her sing."

"She's good. She's also beautiful. I want to look like her too."

"Tia. You're beautiful as *you*. You don't need to look like anyone else."

I was blushing big-time now.

"We're here," he said, all excited, prompting me to forget about Marie Osmond and her beauty in the wake of the presence of Queen in the same building as we.

Madison Square Garden was packed. People everywhere. Music was coming from the arena, but it wasn't Queen.

"Good. We didn't miss anything," Clinton mimicked my thoughts.

He handed the guard our tickets, and he led us through the stadium. The bass of the music being performed equaled the intensity of my heartbeat as we followed the man closer and closer to the stage.

Third-row center.

"Holy shit, Clinton, *third row*? How did you get these?"

"I stood in line at the ticket center overnight."

"Oh my God. I *never* ever had seats this close to the stage."

"What concerts have you been to?" he yelled above the music.

"Shaun Cassidy. Billy Joel."

We stopped talking, because it was just getting too difficult to hear each other.

Freddie came out dressed like an angel in skin-tight white and singing like only someone sent from Heaven could. Freddie Mercury was even more amazing live than I could have ever imagined. The sound of his voice made me cry. Literal tears. It didn't matter that I was embarrassing myself in front of Clinton. This man and his voice *moved* me. His band was riveting too, but it was Freddie who stole the stage, the show, the whole gosh-darn arena.

"Bohemian Rhapsody" was, of course, a grand production, as was "We Will Rock You" and "We are the Champions," but my favorites were when he sang "Somebody to Love" and "Save Me." My tears did not end until Clinton and I were well on our way through the Lincoln Tunnel.

"Thank you again, Clinton, for getting those tickets. This was the best night of my life. Best. Thank you." I couldn't sit still in my seat.

"Well, thank you for making it happen tonight. It was nice of you to call Lydia."

"Clinton?"

"Yeeees?" He knew what I was going to ask.

"What happened at home?"

As expected, he didn't answer right away. But I waited, and he spoke. "I told you, I don't get along with my family. *This*—" he pointed to his face "—is physical proof." He laughed, but it wasn't funny.

He must have noticed the frown on my face when he looked at me out of the corner of his eye.

"It is what it is, Tia. I can't change things until I can support myself. And I won't drop out of school."

"Then live with us. Mom said you can."

He glanced my way again. "She's sick, Tia. I'd feel uncomfortable."

I sighed. "I know you think I'm immature and only want you to live with us for my own selfish reasons, but that's not it. One, I *hate* that you came to my house looking like you were in a street fight. I mean look at you. Your eye looks like you were fighting with Rocky Balboa." He laughed, I continued. "And two, you've been driving my mother to her chemo treatments every week, and maybe she wants to pay you back."

Clinton laughed again. "Payment for taking someone on a ten-minute drive is a free dinner or a couple bucks toward gas. Not a free place to live." He was still laughing.

"I'm not a silly kid, Clinton. Stop laughing at me."

He immediately stopped laughing and sighed. "I'm not laughing at you, Tia. I'm sorry. I just feel it's a big commitment to take someone else in."

"You're an adult. It's not like we have to take care of you."

"I'll stay tonight, okay? But I need to go back home. I don't want to be a burden."

"You're not. But...whatever you want."

Clinton stayed that night.

But not the next.

On the third day, he came over with a new shiner covering the old one, and he smelled like alcohol again. He stayed all night.

It went on like this for a while—he'd come over half drunk and newly beaten and he'd stay. The nights he was sober, he'd leave at two in the morning.

The nights he'd been drinking, he'd kiss my lips and rub my arm or my back. Sometimes, he'd actually make out with me in my bed.

But the nights he was sober, he'd just hold me in the crook of his arm.

I wasn't complaining about the extra affection he'd give me when he was drunk.

But I *was* worried.

CHAPTER TEN

"Hammer to Fall"

S eptember, 1982
TIA

Mom's tumor didn't shrink enough. In fact, her newest neurosurgeon deemed it advanced and inoperable. Her old doctor, after looking at her new scans, concurred.

Mom had less than six months to live.

How was I supposed to go on?

I didn't think I could.

"You can't quit school, Tia. You just can't."

I didn't even respond to Clinton's absurdity. Like I was going to leave my mother for *any* period of time.

She got to the point where she was on so much morphine that she was sleeping almost constantly.

That didn't stop me from sitting at her side for nearly twenty-four hours each day. If I slept, it was in her bed with her. Clinton stayed in my room in my bed by himself. Considering my mom's state, and the fact I wouldn't leave her side, Clinton moved in. He, of course, went to class. Hospice took care of Mom throughout the day, so there was no reason for Clinton to stay in with me. Plus, he had work four nights a week. He always closed early, and Karl didn't seem to care—kids just hung around for the arcade games. By eight, no one was buying sodas or ice cream, he'd said.

On the infrequent occasions Mom was awake and coherent, she apologized. And cried. I cried along with her.

One day, Clinton heard us from the kitchen and came in. "How 'bout I bring in a couple cups of tea and a deck of cards? I already have the water on."

I looked at Clinton like he had two heads. "Clinton," I whispered, almost chastising in my tone.

Mom's hand covered mine. "Tea and cards sound perfect. Make it three cups of tea."

"Three?" he asked.

"Join us. Please," my mother said.

He nodded and disappeared.

"Cards?" I asked my mom.

"We can play Go Fish. It's a good idea."

"But you're so tired."

Her eyes filled with tears, but she smiled anyway. "Let's play. Clinton's a smart boy."

I hugged my mother with both arms, cuddling up close to her in her bed. "I love you, Mom. So much."

"Oh, baby, I love you so much." Her tears fell. "Baby, I have to tell you some—"

"Here ya go." Clinton walked in with a tray topped with three mugs, Social Tea cookies, and my mother's deck of cards. I laughed thinking about this six foot three grown man carrying tea and Social Tea cookies. But for some reason, it made my mom happy.

Clinton shuffled the deck and passed out seven cards to each of us.

"I haven't played Go Fish since you were in first or second grade," my mother said, leaning her head back against the headboard. "We used to play this all the time."

"That's right. Out on the front porch."

"Summer mornings out on the veranda." Mom's voice was weak, but I could still hear the smile coming through.

"The veranda?" Clinton asked.

"Mom's fancy word for porch."

Mom's eyes were closing, but she said, "Tia, you go first."

"Okay." I looked at my cards. "Mom, do you have any threes?"

"Sorry, honey, go fish."

The game was lame, but I understood why Clinton had suggested it and why it made my mother happy—for the while we played the game, no one was focusing solely on the death that was facing us. So, we played as many rounds as my mother's strength allowed.

When my mother was finally succumbing to her pain and exhaustion, we cleared the cards, the tea, and the cookies, and brought them into the kitchen. Clinton went back to bring my mother her requested glass of water. From my spot at the kitchen sink, I heard her whispering. Since I was still my fifteen- almost sixteen-year-old self, I moved surreptitiously closer to listen to what she could possibly be whispering to Clinton.

"...honest with her. When you figure it out," my mother said to him.

What the heck did that mean?

"And...stay in her life. When she leaves...just...keep her in your life. Figure out how. She'll need you."

I didn't hear a word from Clinton. Was my mother on the phone? I had to know, but when I looked in the room, Mom was sleeping and Clinton was walking out.

"Shh," he whispered, his finger to his lips. "She finally fell asleep."

"What was she saying?"

Clinton took the box of cookies and put them back into the cabinet. "She was mumbling stuff. I really couldn't understand her."

"Mumbling?"

"Yeah. Like saying words that made no sense."

"What did she mean about me leaving?"

Clinton looked at me. "Honestly, Tia, I don't know what she meant. Like I said, she wasn't making sense."

On my way back to my mother's room, I was stopped by Clinton's hand around my arm. "Let her sleep."

"I know. I'm gonna sleep with her."

"Give me a few minutes?"

"Okay."

"Can we sit on the porch?"

"Sure."

But before we stepped outside, my mother screamed.

"Mom," I yelled as I ran to her.

She continued to scream, holding her head in her hands.

"You need more morphine? Oh my God. Hospice won't be here 'til tomorrow."

"My end table," she screamed.

"But they said..."

"Tia, she's in pain. Just give her one."

I looked at Clinton.

He nodded.

My hand was shaking as I opened the bottle and took out the pill. Clinton put the straw to my mother's mouth as I placed the pill on her tongue. As I slipped under the covers, Clinton slipped out of the room, but I heard him pull out one of the kitchen chairs. He was staying nearby but out of sight—I'm sure to help secure my mother's dignity.

I held my mother as she continued to scream, and once the morphine kicked in, I held her still. Letting go was not an option. If I just held her forever, she couldn't die. Mothers didn't die in their daughters' arms. That would just be too cruel. The world didn't work that way.

The only time I left my mother's bed was to go the bathroom. Clinton brought me food, but I never ate it. He made me drink my milk though. "At least drink your milk," he said. "What good will you be to your mother if you can't even hold her because you're too weak?" So, I drank my milk.

Hospice hooked my mother up to IV so the increased strength morphine could drip into her veins. The pain had become too much.

On October thirteenth, my mother barely opened her eyes. But I didn't want to leave her side. All I wanted for my sixteenth birthday was to be by my mother. If I still believed in wishes, I'd wish for her tumor to just disappear.

But I didn't believe in wishes.

Not anymore.

Clinton brought in my glass of milk, like he usually did first thing in the morning, but this time, he held a gift-wrapped package in his other hand. He sat down next to me, keeping his legs crossed on top of the bedspread.

"Happy Birthday, Tia," he said quietly.

"Thank you." I barely smiled.

He handed me my milk and stared at me until I finished it. He took my glass and replaced it with my gift. "I know you don't feel like celebrating, but I couldn't just let your day go by without acknowledging it."

Slowly, I unpeeled the red wrapping paper. I couldn't even get excited that Clinton had gotten me a present. I wasn't even excited that today was the day Clinton had deemed me old enough to kiss.

"Hellooo." The female voice came from the front door.

Clinton hopped up and went to see who it was.

The hospice nurse walked into the bedroom with Clinton. "Good morning," she said, smiling. Like there was anything to smile about.

"How is she today?" she asked after my silent response.

"The same," Clinton answered.

She put down her bag and asked us to leave the room for fifteen minutes while she cleaned up my mother, changed her bags, and whatever else they didn't want me to watch.

"Come on, Tia," Clinton said, helping me out of bed. "My God. You weigh practically nothing." Then he full-on picked me up and carried me into the living room, lowering me to the couch, his gift still nestled between my stomach and my lap.

The doorbell rang just as Clinton was placing me on the couch.

"Yes?" I heard Clinton say.

I heard a man say both my name and my mother's name. Then Clinton stepped outside and closed the door.

The gift still sat on my lap, and I looked at it, deciding whether or not I should open it. Opting against it, I stretched my legs out on the couch and curled up in the fetal position holding the half-open package in my hands.

When I woke up, it was dark outside. "Oh my God." I jumped off the couch and ran into my mother's room, barely registering that Clinton was sitting at the kitchen table.

She was still breathing.

"Why'd you let me sleep all day?" I asked Clinton, who had half a dozen books open and strewn across the table.

"You needed it. You barely sleep when you're in there with her."

"Because I don't want to sleep," I screamed. "That's time I lose—" a loud sob escaped "—that I'm not with my mother."

Clinton reached for me and took me in his arms, where I soaked his black tee shirt until there was not a dry spot left on the front of it.

He didn't talk. Or shush me. He just held me while I cried.

And when I was done, he picked me up, carried me to my mother's bed, and tucked me in.

FOUR DAYS LATER, SHE died.

I don't think I could explain how that felt. To wake up with her cold hand covering mine. I was the last thing she touched. And I wasn't even awake to appreciate it.

Clinton knew as soon as he walked in with my milk. I knew he knew, too, because the glass shattered on my mother's hardwood bedroom floor. I heard the splash of the milk before it weeped across the floor. I concentrated on every sound that was made on October seventeenth, nineteen eighty-two.

What I couldn't focus on, even though I tried and tried, was my mother's warm body and how it felt to be near it. Not one good memory popped into my mind that day or many days after. All I could seem to think about was how cold my mother felt. How hard and dead and unalive she was. My mother. My protector. The only person to know me every single day of my sixteen years, was gone. And I'd never see her or touch her or hear her voice ever. Again.

CHAPTER ELEVEN

"Nevermore"

TIA

Hospice took care of transporting my mother to the funeral home. But I didn't want a funeral. I didn't know where to get the money, and I didn't think anyone would come—certainly not family. We had none. Maybe the teachers at her school. But I still decided that I couldn't spend money I didn't have.

Lydia came to help us after Clinton called her, and Najia came to see me. She'd stayed away when my mom got too sick for company, but Clinton called her and asked her to come over.

So, while Clinton and Lydia went through my mother's stuff to find paperwork—anything to let us know what to do—Najia sat in my room with me.

"What's this?" Najia picked up my half-opened birthday present.

"My present from Clinton."

"How come you didn't open it?"

"I started to, but then, I don't know, just never got around to it."

"So." Najia paused, looking uncomfortable. "What are you gonna do? You going back to school?"

"I guess. Clinton told me a truant officer came by one day with papers. They were going to arrest my mom."

"What?"

"He said he explained everything, and they'd talk to the school. But Clinton called the school for me. They told him they'd work it out with me and the Board when things *settled*. Their words, not mine."

"You missed a whole month and a half. You think you'll have to repeat the year?"

"Who knows? Who cares?"

"Yeah. I guess it'd be hard to care right now."

"I just want to quit."

"And do what?"

"Work. Get a job. Who's gonna support me now?" I lay on my stomach and plopped my face in my pillow.

Najia rubbed my back.

"I can ask my mom if you could stay with us."

I flipped over. "You think my mom would have had this taken care of, you know, before she... I mean, she knew she was... Oh my God, Naj." I flipped back over, face-first into my pillow again.

"Maybe Lydia and Clinton will find a will or something."

I groaned.

"Why don't you open Clinton's present? Maybe it'll put a smile on your face."

It took me a few moments to turn over and sit up.

Najia handed me the gift.

"I should probably open it in front of Clinton. Maybe he wants to watch me open it."

"You're not even curious?"

I fingered the box, corner to corner. "It makes me sad."

"Oh."

Still looking at the box, I continued. "My mother didn't even know it was my birthday, Naj."

I didn't expect Najia to say anything, and she didn't.

"She didn't even know I turned sixteen." I pulled the box to my chest. "How can I acknowledge my birthday when she couldn't?" I looked at the stupid red wrapping paper again, and I knew right then I didn't ever want to see it again. Without another thought, I threw the box into the mirror on my dresser. It crashed, then thunked.

Clinton barged in two seconds later. "Tia? You okay?"

My heart ached so much, I could almost feel it shattering into tiny pieces—sharp shards of it cutting into my chest. Clutching it, I stopped breathing.

Clinton sat next to me and held me until I caught my breath. And then he held me some more.

"Tia? You want me to go?" Najia said after a while.

I shook my head.

Najia stayed another hour, and I'm sure I made her too uncomfortable to stay any longer. I wasn't the greatest of company, and I barely spoke after throwing Clinton's present across the room.

"Tia, Clinton, food's here." Lydia was in the doorway.

"Thanks, Lyd." To me, Clinton said, "Lydia got Chinese."

"I'm not hungry."

"Come on, Tia. Just a few bites. 'Kay?"

At the table, Lydia looked grim, and she kept passing glances between Clinton and me.

"What is it, Lydia?" Clinton asked.

Her eyes darted back and forth between us again, and then she slid a packet of papers toward us.

CHAPTER TWELVE

"Spread Your Wings"

T IA

"He can't just take me away. I'm sixteen. I'm old enough to live on my own."

"No. You're not. Not until you're eighteen or you become emancipated."

"What's emancipated?"

"You're capable of taking care of yourself."

"You can take care of me then, Clinton. Please?"

We were sitting on my floor against the bottom of my bed. Clinton kissed the top of my head. "I can't even take care of myself, Tia. As it is, I have to move back in with my father and brothers. I can't have you living there. They're brutal. I won't put you in that situation."

"Please? I'd rather. Please, Clinton? I can't leave you." In the midst of hyperventilating, I cried. "My mother's already gone. I can't lose you too. Please please please." I got to my knees and grabbed hold of him. "Don't let me go, Clinton. Don't let me go." I was sobbing so hard, I didn't know if what I said was even comprehensible.

When I opened my eyes, Clinton's face was soaking wet from his own tears.

"See. You don't want me to go either. So why can't I stay?"

He pressed his lips to my forehead as I straddled his lap. "Of course I don't want you to go," he said, still crying, sniffing up his tears like a small boy. "But besides not wanting to subject you to the violence in my house, it's the law, Tia. It's written in your mom's will. You have to go with him. Until you're eighteen, there's nothing we can do."

"But, but I don't even know him. I was five. Why would she do this to me? Why would she make me go with my father?"

"Maybe there was no one else? You don't have other family, right?"

"Why couldn't she let me stay with you?"

"Tia. I'm not even twenty-one yet. I'm sure she didn't think that would be appropriate."

"But you will be twenty-one in less than two months."

"Tia, I'm not a caregiver."

"But you are. You've done nothing but care for me and take care of my mom and me."

"I'm your boyfriend, Tia. I'm not your father."

That was the first time Clinton had ever acknowledged that he was my boyfriend, and I couldn't even revel in it.

"What about Lydia? Why couldn't she give me to her?"

"Lydia's a coworker, not a close friend. Look, I don't know why your mother chose your father, but it's only for two years. When you're eighteen, you can legally leave."

"In two years, you'll forget all about me."

"I could *never* forget all about you. Never." He kissed my nose again.

"Come to Oklahoma with me."

After a long silence, he said, "I can't afford to live on my own. Not without quitting school."

"Go to school in Oklahoma."

"I'd still have to live on my own. I'd have no way to pay rent."

"Live in a dorm."

"That's thousands more dollars to add to my loans."

"Aren't I worth it?"

He pulled me tight, and over my shoulder, he said, "Of course you are, but I'll barely be able to pay the loans I have." He held me for a few silent minutes then said, "Let me look into colleges in Oklahoma. I won't be able to transfer this year, but maybe next year."

I pulled back and looked at him. "Really?"

He smiled, his mouth still wet from tears. "Really."

"Oh, thank you, Clinton. Thank you." I hugged him with all my strength. I never wanted to let him go. A year was going to be way too long, but it was better than two.

"Here." He handed me a Sam Goody's bag, so I lifted myself off his lap and sat back next to him.

"What's this?" I asked, taking the bag from him.

"It's the replacement to that gift you threw across the room."

"My birthday present?"

"No. No. Nothing to celebrate that day. I know that was a difficult day for you. No, this is a gift to keep you abreast of all new music out there."

I opened the bag and took out the box inside. "A Sony Walkman?"

"Yup. And I have these for you, too." He reached behind him and handed me three cassette tapes. "I recorded a bunch of songs for you."

"Oh, Clinton. Thank you."

"I'll mail you a new cassette each week too."

"Really?"

"Really. Now open the box."

I pulled out a shiny red Walkman. "Red? I didn't know they made red."

"New this year."

"I love it, Clinton. Thank you." Once again, I embraced him and didn't want to let him go.

"Now you'll always have a part of me with you. Through my tapes."

"And in my heart."

"And in your heart."

CLINTON BROUGHT ME to the airport two days later. My father arranged for one of the stewardesses to keep watch over me during the flight. The lawyer was arranging the estate sale of all my and my mother's stuff that I couldn't take with me. He'd mail me the check when everything was sold.

Clinton had to peel me off of him when it was time to board the flight. I didn't even care that people were watching.

"It's okay, Tia. We'll talk on the phone every day. The year will go by quickly. Please, don't make this harder than it already is."

"This was supposed to be the year. I turned sixteen. We were gonna try to be a couple. Now we can't."

Clinton peered into my eyes and sighed. "I love you, Tia. I'm so sorry it has to be this way."

"I love you so much. I don't know how I'm gonna live without you."

"You don't have to, sweetheart. I'm only a phone call away. It's not forever."

I could contain my sobs no longer.

"Miss, you really have to board the plane now," the woman who was bringing me onto the plane said behind me.

Clinton ran his thumbs across my tears before he leaned in and crushed his lips against mine. I clutched him again, and his hands cupped the back of my neck and head. I opened my mouth to welcome his tongue, and I tasted salt. I couldn't tell if it was from my tears or his, but when he broke the kiss, his face was glistening with as many tears as I felt on my face.

"Please call me when you get there so you can give me your number."

I didn't even have my father's phone number. The lawyer took care of all the phone calls to him.

"And your address, so I can write to you."

I only nodded.

"Call Tuffy's if I'm not home. Don't assume my dad or my brothers will give me any messages. But Nick or Karl will, so call there too."

Again, I nodded. I couldn't speak.

He pressed his lips to mine and said, "Be safe, Tia."

But I wouldn't be safe. I was leaving my home. Not my house, but my home—Clinton. Now that my mother was gone, *he* was all I had. And I was being ripped away from him. Stripped bare of the only thing that mattered to me.

CHAPTER THIRTEEN

"Liar"

TIA

I was the first to get off the plane in Amarillo, Texas. The stewardess walked me out, and I was greeted by another airline employee and a man with dark blond hair, bright blue eyes, and crow's feet out of place on a boyish face.

"Tia?"

My father. I remembered the eyes.

"Oh, Tia." He awkwardly hugged me.

I let my arms hang at my sides.

He let go. "I'm really glad you're here."

Really? He's glad my mom died?

"I mean, I'm not happy for the reason you have to be here, but I'm, I'm glad to be in your company again." His voice cracked. "Thank you," he said to the airline employee as he took me farther into the airport and farther from my other life. Because it already felt like I had died and been transported into someone else's life.

He lived on a nice-size ranch with his wife and two sons, ages eight and six. That's how he phrased it in the car. Then he offered their names. "Scott is the eight-year-old and David is the six. My wife's name is Melanie. We call her Mel. She's excited that you're here."

Everyone is excited my mom died. Yay.

I still hadn't said one word yet. This didn't seem to phase Tommy Mercury. He just continued chatting away until we got to his house in some really small town in the panhandle of Oklahoma. Tommy Mercury said it's called Texhoma. Texas, Oklahoma. Good Lord.

Melanie—Mel—was a cute little blonde with similar blue eyes to my dad's. Scott and David were her spitting image.

"Hello, Tia," Mel said with a huge smile, not insincere at all—to my dismay; I'd rather she was an unpleasant witch of a woman.

"Hi." I had no beef with her; she hadn't abandoned me when I was five. Unless of course, she was the reason for my father's abandonment. In which case, maybe I *should* have given her attitude.

"The boys are so excited to meet their big sister."

Thing One and Thing Two were all smiles. "You should see your bedroom," the older boy said.

"Yeah. Purple," the little one added.

My favorite color?

"Go 'head, boys," Tommy said. "Show Tia to her room."

Though the boys dashed down the hall, I moved slowly, unexcited to see my prison cell.

"Daddy said you like music, so he put up those posters," Scott said.

My duffel bag fell to the floor. Hanging on my purple walls were posters of Freddie Mercury—one with no shirt and the white pants he wore at his concert, and one of all four of the members of Queen.

"Your mother said you liked Queen." It was my father behind me.

I didn't turn to see him, because he'd see the tears falling out of my eyes. My feet were planted to the lavender shag rug and my heart was racing.

"She called me two months ago. To let me know what was going on."

Two months ago? And she couldn't bother to say one word about it to me?

"Judging by your silence, she hadn't told you?"

I needed to talk to Clinton. I needed to hear his voice. Scanning the room, I saw a white donut phone sitting on the nightstand. "What's the phone number here?" I asked, still not turning around.

The boys were butt-jumping on my bed.

"Scott. David. Tia will hang with you guys later. Go see what Mommy's making for dinner."

They ran out, leaving me alone with my father.

"You have your own phone number. It's listed on the sticker on the phone."

I went right to it and picked up the receiver.

"I'll leave you to your privacy." My father left the room and closed the door.

Clinton was probably at work, so I called Tuffy's. As soon as I heard his voice, I broke down. "Clin...ton."

"Tia?"

"Mmm. Clin..."

"Tia, hold on." In the background, I heard Clinton say, "Karl, you mind if I take this in the back?"

"No. Go 'head."

"Okay, Karl. Thanks." I heard the click of Karl hanging up the front phone. "Tia, you made it?"

"Mm hmm."

"Is your father nasty?"

"No," I squeaked out. "He's, he's trying to be nice. But, but I'm not."

"You're not what? Being nice?"

"No."

"Well, he left you. I don't blame you."

"I miss you, Clinton. Really bad."

"I know you do, honey. But look. Try to make the best of it. I went to the library after I left the airport and researched some colleges in Oklahoma. But Tia, Oklahoma's big. What town are you in?"

"A stupid town. Texhoma."

Clinton laughed. "Like Texas and Oklahoma?"

"I guess."

"I'll go to the library again tomorrow and check where that is and if there are any colleges nearby. But, sweetheart, you're gonna be okay."

"No, I'm not," I whimpered.

"Tia. What's your number? I'll call you when I get home."

I read him the number off my phone.

"You're two hours behind, right?"

"I think. It's five forty-five."

"Oh. You're an hour behind. It's quarter to seven here."

"Oh."

"Is eight-thirty your time okay?"

"Yeah."

"Chin up, babe. I'll talk to you later."

"Okay. Bye," I said, choking on a sob and tossing a yellow daisy pillow across the room.

There was a knock on the door about fifteen minutes later.

"Yeah?"

"Tia, dinner's on the table." It was Melanie.

"Not hungry."

"Please, Tia. I need you to come to the table."

Part of me wanted to rebel, but I was too sad to make the effort. "Yeah. 'Kay."

Macaroni and cheese, broccoli, and Pillsbury croissants. My favorite meal.

"Your father said he remembered this being your favorite meal."

"I know you were only five," Tommy said, "but it's one of the things I remember."

"My favorite food is hot dogs," David said.

"I like hot dogs too," I told him.

"I like cheeseburgers," said Scott.

"Yeah, they're pretty yummy, too," I said.

"So, Tia," Tommy said, "your mother mentioned that you have a boyfriend. Would you like me to pay for him to visit soon?"

I snapped my head in his direction. "What?"

"I'll pay for a round-trip ticket for Clayton to come out."

"Clinton. Really?"

"If his parents approve."

My mother must not have mentioned Clinton's age. "Um. He, he's, like, twenty-one. Well, in December."

"Your mother let you date a twenty-one-year-old?" Tommy didn't sound mad, just concerned. But he did put his fork down when he asked.

"Well, he's not twenty-one *yet.*"

"Maybe that's why she emphasized the word boyfriend when she said you had one."

"What? What's that mean?"

"I don't know, Tia. She said you had a *boyfriend* and it'd be hard for you to be away from him. She said you guys were always together. But the way she said boyfriend...maybe 'cause she thought he was too old. Is he good to you?"

I nodded. "Very." But now I was wondering if my mother didn't really consider Clinton my boyfriend. Was she being, what's that word? Condescending? "May I be excused? I'd like to go to my room."

"Sure," Tommy said.

In my room, face down on my new bed, I cried. And for no *one* specific reason—I sobbed for *many.* The loss of my mother, the loss of Clinton, this stupid, hick state I now lived in, my stupid purple room. And why my mother hadn't really considered Clinton my boyfriend. Clinton said he was, so why hadn't my mother believed it?

Did Clinton tell my mother he really didn't love me? Is that what she meant when I overheard her telling him to be honest with me?

Then why is he with me to begin with?

What isn't he telling me?

My phone rang at seven forty-five. I picked it up before the first ring ended. "Hello?"

"Hi, Tia," he said with a sigh.

"Hi, Clinton."

"Rough day?"

"Yeah."

"I'm sorry I couldn't be there with you."

"I wish I could be *there* with you instead."

"The rest of the night went bad?"

"Yeah. Well. I don't know. I haven't talked to anyone since dinner."

"Why?"

I took the Walkman from my nightstand and set it between my pretzeled legs. "I listened to the tape you made me."

"Yeah? You like it?"

"I do. I listened to it on the plane. The whole time."

"The whole time? You didn't bring any others with you?"

"Of course I did. But I liked the songs on this one."

"Which were your favorites?" Clinton sounded like he was drinking something.

"'The Waiting.'"

"Tom Petty. He's good." Clinton sucked in a breath. When he let it out, he said, "How 'bout 'Open Arms'? That was Journey."

"Mmm. That one made me cry. So did 'The Best of Times.' Was that your intent? To make me more sad?" I laughed, but just a little one.

"Of course not, Tia. I picked songs that made me think of you."

"Really?"

"Really."

"Clinton?"

"Yeah?"

"Are you smoking right now?"

After a brief pause, he said, "Yeah."

"You're drinking too."

"Yeah."

"You hate being back home, don't you?"

"It's okay, Tia. I'm fine. You worry about yourself. This is a big change for you."

"I hate it. I wanna run away. Come back home."

"Don't, Tia," he said, his voice louder. "You have no money to get here. Give it a year, darlin'. Give your father a chance."

"I don't want to."

After another puff of his cigarette, he said, "Look, babe, make the best of the situation right now. And, and I'll see what I can do about coming for you."

"You'll come for me?"

I heard him swallow his drink. "Give me time to apply to colleges. I'll save some money and come see you during Christmas break. You think your father will mind?"

"Oh my God, no, he won't mind at all. He even offered to pay to fly you out here. Round trip."

"What? When?"

"At dinner tonight. He said my mother told him I, I had a, well, a boy, a boyfriend, and he said he'd pay to fly you out to visit."

"Oh. Well, that would make it easier for me. And I can visit colleges while I'm there."

"Oh, Clinton, really?" For the first time in a long while, I felt hopeful.

"Really. See. In just under two months, I can hold you again."

"Thank you." I was smiling ear to ear and bouncing my heels on the bed.

"So, are you going to get your ass back in school soon?"

"On the way home from the airport, Tommy said he already registered me."

"Do you get to continue as a junior?"

My heels stopped their bouncing. "I didn't ask him. But, but he did say my old school sent my transcripts."

"Well, I hope you don't have any problems." Clinton sucked in that air again.

"Why is school so important to you?" I fussed with a string that was hanging off my shirt.

"What kind of question is that? School's important."

"But to you, it's, like, everything."

"It *is* everything. How are you going to do what you want if you aren't educated?"

I shrugged, not that he could see me.

"My family. They never finished high school. My dad let them drop out. Said they can work with him at the factory. But they complain daily about the working conditions. If they'd finished school or continued their educations, they could get out of there." After another drag of his cigarette, he said, "Maybe they wouldn't be so angry either."

"Are they always angry?" I lay down on the bed now. My eyes were closing because I was so tired, even though it was only after eight.

"For as long as I can remember."

"How come you're not?"

"Have no idea. Listening to music helps. I always loved hearing it. Always wished I could play an instrument well. As you know, my piano lessons were brief. Besides that elementary teacher, I also briefly paid for my own lessons a few years ago, but then my father found out. He said if I had money for piano lessons, I had money to start paying rent. So I had to quit and pay rent."

"I'm sorry, Clinton."

"You're sorry my father's an asshole?"

"Yeah," I said with a small smile on my face.

"Clinton?" My eyes were staying closed, but I didn't want to hang up with him.

"Yeah?"

I was too tired to answer.

"Tia, I hear you breathing. Are you falling asleep?"

"Mmm."

"Want me to let you go?"

"No," I forced out. "Stay."

"'Kay. You go to sleep, and I'll lie here on my bed listening to you breathe. When you're totally out, I'll hang up. I can't stay on all night. I'll run the phone bill too high, and Billy-boy will take a fit. Tia...I love you."

"Love...too."

I WOKE UP ON MY STOMACH with the phone under my neck. After I hung it up, I reluctantly got out of bed. My morning pee was not going to wait just because I didn't want to face my new life. And my new family.

Melanie caught me as I was coming out of the bathroom. "Did you sleep okay, Tia?"

I nodded. "Yeah. Thanks."

"Your dad wanted to come in and see you, but I thought you needed time by yourself last night."

Again, I nodded, then went into my room.

She followed.

I went through my bag and started putting my clothes in the light oak dressers they had set up for me.

"I know this is hard on you, Tia. It can't be easy. Hopefully, you'll adjust soon to being here."

Continuing to take clothes out of my bag and transfer them to my new dressers, I ignored her.

"He really is a good guy, your dad. Just give him a chance."

Really? I abruptly turned to look at her. No words came out of my mouth, but I'm sure my eyes told her she was full of shit.

"He is, Tia. You may not see it now, but he is a stand-up guy."

A stand-up guy? Since when had a father who abandoned his child become a stand-up guy? "You got a bridge to sell me? I just may buy that too."

"He took on my boys when he didn't have to. He loves them like they're his own."

"What?"

"He adopted Scott and David. Their fathers wanted nothing to do with them, so Tommy adopted them as his own."

Whoa. I slammed the dresser drawer. "So my *daddy* felt bad for two bastard children, so he adopted them? But he didn't think twice about leaving his *own* daughter. Nice. I'm outta here." I grabbed the Walkman off my bed and ran out of the room and out of the house. Melanie was calling after me. And then after Tommy.

I ran down the street to the end of the block, but Tommy was a faster runner than me, because he got there barely seconds after I did.

"Tia. Stop."

"Go away." I put my headphones over my ears and pressed play on the Walkman before I broke out into a slower jog.

Tommy jogged up next to me but didn't stop me. He simply ran alongside me while I ignored him.

After several minutes, I found it quite comical that he was running in jeans and work boots. I, at least, had sweats and sneakers on. Since my only attempt at running had been in gym class—and I'd barely run a lap without stopping—I had to stop because of cramps and lack of air. Tommy obviously was in better shape.

He lifted my earphones off my ears and hung them around my neck. "I wish you'd let me explain."

When I caught my breath, I said, "What's there to explain? I wasn't worth your love. End of story."

"*Wrong* story. Very *different* story."

I just stared at him and shook my head.

"Please come back to the house. Get a glass of water, catch your breath. Please?"

Because I needed water, big time, I walked with him back home.

He took out a glass, took out the ice tray, filled the glass with ice, then went to the sink and filled my glass. "Here," he said, handing me the water and pulling out the seat adjacent to me.

I guzzled the water then looked at him. "You're not thirsty?"

He shook his head. "Tia, I want you to understand why I left you and your mother. Your mother never wanted you to know, but on our last phone call, she agreed that in order for you and me to have a relationship, you needed to know."

"Why would *Mom* not want me to know why you left me and never even bothered to contact me ever again?"

"Well...a couple of times, I tried, but because I was still so angry, she wouldn't put you on the phone."

"*You* were so angry? Shouldn't mom have been the one angry?"

"Tia." Tommy looked over my shoulder.

Melanie was behind me. "You need me?" she asked her husband.

"No, I'm good."

I got up and ran more water into my glass.

Tommy waited for me to sit before he spoke again. "You were about three when your mother and I started trying to have another baby." Tommy paused and gazed into my eyes. "You're eyes are so green."

"And?" I said, annoyed that he had broken topic.

"And...after about a year of trying, we decided to see a doctor." Tommy looked down and sighed. When he returned his eyes to me, he said, "Found out...*I* was infertile. Something about a drug my mother took when she was pregnant with me." He looked like he was waiting for me to respond.

I didn't.

"I was infertile, Tia."

"Right. So—" I shook my head "—I was okay being an only child, just not a *fatherless* one."

"Tia, I was *always* infertile," he said slowly.

"Wait. What?"

"I *never* could have children. But I hadn't always known that."

"Then how..."

"That was *my* question too."

"I don't understand." My heart was racing. I was scared.

"Your mother had an affair. I'm not your biological father."

Now I couldn't breathe. "Oh my..." I was hyperventilating. He had to be lying, because my mom would never. She'd never lie to me, and she'd never have an affair.

I hadn't even realized Tommy had left the table, but he must have, because he was handing me a brown paper lunch bag. "Breathe into this, Tia."

After several quick breaths into the bag, I removed it from my mouth. "You're lying."

"I'm not."

"You are. My mother wouldn't do that. And she definitely wouldn't lie to me. You're a, you're a, you're... Go to Hell."

I pushed back the chair so hard it fell over, and I ran into my room and locked the door.

Picking up the phone, I started dialing Clinton. *Please be home. Please be home.*

"Hello?" It was him.

"Clinton, Clinton, please come out here please or take me back home please."

"Tia. Calm down. Talk slowly. I can't understand you."

"I wanna come home."

"Did something happen?"

"He's a liar. I don't want to live with him."

"What did he lie about?"

"He said my mother had an affair."

"That's why they divorced?"

I paced the floor with the entire phone in my hand. "You're on *his* side?"

"No, Tia. I'm just trying to figure out what you're so worked up about."

"He's saying I'm not his kid and my mom had an affair."

"What? Does he have proof?"

"I don't know. I didn't ask."

"Well, ask. Make him prove it to you."

"Why would he say that?"

"Two reasons. One, he wants you to forgive him for leaving you, so he's making it up. Or two, he's telling the truth, so you'll forgive him for leaving."

"He's lying."

"Maybe. Maybe not. Ask him for proof."

"What kind of proof?"

"I don't know. Ask him to give you the name of the person he says is your biological father."

"Oh my God, Clinton. I have red hair and green eyes."

"Uh, yeah. So?"

"My mother had brown hair and brown eyes, my dad has blond hair and blue eyes. Oh my God. Please just come and get me, Clinton," I cried.

"You want me to kidnap you?"

"No. Maybe I can take a credit card out of his wallet and get a flight back."

"Tia, you can't do that."

"Why not?"

"You know why. You'll be considered a runaway. The police will be looking for you."

I plopped backwards on the bed and sighed.

"Ask him questions, Tia. I'm sure you'll be able to tell by the way he answers if he's lying or not."

HE HADN'T BEEN LYING. Tommy's story never wavered, no matter how many ways I rephrased a question, and days later, he took us for paternity tests. Up until the doctor had informed my parents of my father's infertility, my mother had had no reason to believe I couldn't have been Tommy's. Until I wasn't. Then she had to finally confess to her brief—she'd said at the time—affair with a fellow teacher (she also claimed). My mother never did tell Tommy who the man was, for fear of my *father* confronting him and possibly hurting him. Tommy believed it was more to keep my mother's and the other teacher's honor and reputations intact. Tommy tried to stick around after that, but he couldn't. He took off and went back to Oklahoma where he grew up. He and my mother had met in college, and because they had fallen in love shortly after, Tommy stayed in New Jersey to be with her. They'd rented a house in Wayne.

According to him, he had attempted to contact me several times, but my mother wouldn't put me on the phone—she had been afraid Tommy would tell me the truth. After my mother had changed our phone number and moved us out of Wayne, Tommy tried sending cards and letters, but they had come back return to sender. That pile of cards and letters was in my nightstand now. Tommy had kept them.

He wasn't the enemy anymore.

But I was finding it hard to forgive my mother. She had not only lied to me, and I couldn't care less about her affair anymore, but she had kept me from the only father I knew. And she'd made me think he'd deserted me.

THE HALLS OF TEXHOMA High School looked like the halls of Manchester Regional High School, only the kids walking through them here were complete strangers. Being the new girl in the middle of junior year sucked. No one talked to me. Not one wicked teenager.

But they did stare.

Lunchtime? Sucked balls. I slid *The Game* cassette into my Walkman and covered my ears with my headphones. I spent the hour listening to Queen and reading *Tiger Eyes* by Judy Blume. Like Davey, Ms. Blume's protagonist, my anxiety was so high I thought I'd pass out on my first day. Thank God I didn't.

I was so depressed about the day that I ate my dinner in my room. Mel told Tommy that sometimes teenagers needed to be alone to absorb their day. I just didn't want to talk to anyone. *Tiger Eyes* wasn't doing it for me either, because its premise hit too close to home. I didn't want to read how some other fifteen-year-old was dealing with the death of a parent when I had barely dealt with my own mother's loss.

After homework, I put on my favorite channel—MTV—and drowned out my sadness with some Toto, Bananarama, The Cars, and of course, Queen. "Body Language" wasn't my favorite Queen song, but at least it was a video on MTV. I bided my time with music videos until Clinton called at nine fifteen.

"Hey."

"Hey, Tia. How was your first day?"

"Sucked."

"Really? There wasn't any part of it you liked?"

"Nope. No one talked to me."

"No one? At all?" He sounded shocked.

"Not if you don't count the teachers."

"I'm sorry, Tia. That does suck."

"At least I don't have Algebra this year."

"They didn't make you take Algebra Two?"

"No."

"You need it to go to college."

"*You* need it to go to college. I'm not going."

"Then what are you gonna do with your life, Tia?"

"I don't know, *Dad*, be a secretary?"

"Then go to secretarial school. Do *something*."

"I got a typing class."

"Okay, good. You have to have plans, Tia."

"I do have plans. To be with you. When I turn eighteen, I'm coming home. Or going wherever you are."

He sighed. That didn't sound promising.

"You're still applying to colleges out here, aren't you?"

I heard him suck in a breath. Another cigarette. After he exhaled, he said, "I am. I actually sent in one application. To the one closest to you, believe it or not. Oklahoma Panhandle State University."

"Really? Oh thank you."

"It's an agricultural college, but oddly enough, they have a good computer programming program."

"Oh, I hope you get in. How far is it from my house?"

"I looked at a map when I was at the library. It's about ten miles."

"Oh, Clinton, I'm gonna pray so hard."

"Don't get your hopes too high, Tia. I'm still not sure about it all. There are costs involved. I may not get the same scholarships. So, let's just enjoy this time on the phone. Please?"

My mood quickly plummeted. "Okay," I said, my throat hurting from keeping back tears.

"Now, Tia, come on. That's not fair."

"I said okay."

"Tia, look, I'm doing my best to come out there, but I'm still financially dependent on my father. I need to make sure I can afford this."

The tears came despite my attempt at holding them back, but I didn't want Clinton to know.

"Tia, say something."

"I'm kinda tired. I gotta go."

"Really, Tia?"

"Call me tomorrow." I had to keep my sentences short, or else he'd know I was crying.

"Tia." He said my name in exasperation. "You realize this is one of the things that concerns me about our age difference, don't you?"

"What?" Oh my God. He was mad at *me?*

"You're being immature about this."

I couldn't respond. My chest hurt. He was crushing it from two thousand miles away.

"I gotta go." I hung up.

My hopes for Clinton coming here crashed. *What if he never does? What if he doesn't want me to come home when I'm eighteen?*

I had swaddled myself in the hope that one day soon, Clinton and I would be together. But now there was doubt. And, wow, did that hurt.

Cold and afraid, I balled myself under the covers and cried myself to sleep. A really bad day was finally coming to an end.

CHAPTER FOURTEEN

"I Want to Break Free"

TIA

Grudgingly, I dressed for my second day of school, so not wanting to endure another day of stares and silence. I should have just quit school when I turned sixteen. It was probably a long shot to expect Tommy to entertain that idea if I asked him.

History and English periods were nearly identical to yesterday. But Chemistry was different. First of all, I didn't have to sit alone at my lab table—Kelly Burke was sitting on the stool next to me. Second of all, Kelly was awesome. Her smile lit up when I sat down next to her, and right away, she introduced herself. A tiny thing dressed in pink, all the way down to her ballet slippers, she looked more like she was from Jersey than I did. I liked the fact that she stood out in this land of corduroys and overalls. Kelly was funny too.

"Are you a dancer?" I asked, nodding to her little feet.

"Me? Yeah, right. As much a dancer as Fred Flintstone."

I laughed. "Fred dances?"

"Not gracefully."

We both laughed.

"Was yesterday your first day? I had a project due, and I wasn't done, so my mom let me take the day off."

"Cool mom. Yeah, yesterday was my first day. It sucked."

"My first day sucked too."

"You're new?"

"Moved here in August. No one here wants to initiate conversation. You gotta say hi first. But once you do, they're real friendly. I think because we look a little different, we intimidate them or something. Out here in Oklahoma, they think Jersey's like New York City."

"You're kiddin'. You're from Jersey too?"

"Yup. Montclair. Far cry from Texhoma. My dad got a new job. He's a professor at the Panhandle University."

I slapped the bench, louder than I'd meant to. Some of the others in the class turned to stare at me. I cowered a little, but I whispered, "Oh my God. The Panhandle University? Really?"

"You've heard of it?"

"Well, yeah. I have a...friend who applied there."

"Really? From New Jersey? Here? Why?" she asked, stunned that anyone would want to apply here.

"Well, he's applying to a few here in Oklahoma."

"He? You got an older boyfriend, Tia?" she asked, raising her eyebrows.

Yesterday, I would have said yes. Today, I wasn't so sure. "Kinda. We're mostly just friends."

"Friends with a college boy? How'd you manage that?"

"What, you think I can't *get* a college boy?" I joked.

Laughing, she said, "Nah. I just wondered how one went about that. I mean, even with my dad being a professor and me visiting all the time, I still couldn't get a college boy to look at me."

"Probably 'cause you look like you're ten." I laughed, hoping she could take the joke.

"You're probably right." She laughed back.

Kelly and I hit it off as if she and I had been long-time friends. We sat together at lunch, and after school, we sat with each other on the bus. Because she'd had her bulky project, her father had brought her to school. I was ecstatic to know she was on my bus. And even more thrilled to learn we got off at the same bus stop.

"I had no idea someone new moved into the neighborhood," Kelly said when we stepped off the bus.

"Well, just me. My...father...he's lived here for a while."

"Who's your father?"

"Tommy Mercury."

"Mercury Electricians?"

"Yeah. You know him?"

"I know they did some work on our house when we first moved in. I remember the trucks in the driveway. You live down the road, then."

"Yup."

"So cool. We're like a quarter mile from each other. You got a bike?"

"Oh. I left it in Jersey."

"Who with? Are your parents divorced?"

I looked down at the ground and kicked some gravel while I answered. "They were. Years ago. But my mom just died. That's why I'm here."

"Oh. I'm sorry. That sucks, Tia."

"Yeah. You're not kidding."

"I have an extra bike. We can go bike riding later. You up for it?"

"Yeah, okay."

"I just have to wait until my mom comes home from work. I get my little brother off the bus in half an hour, and I gotta watch him 'til she comes home."

"Okay. I'll do my homework and come back down. What time?"

"Four-thirty? Unless you eat dinner then."

"No. We eat about seven, I think."

"Oh. Us too. Good. See ya later, Tia."

"See ya."

Today was a much better day. And don't think it went unnoticed by Mel.

"Your smile lights up your face," she said when I was doing my homework at the kitchen table. I heard her words because the tape in my Walkman was in between songs.

I didn't even realize I was smiling. I suppose it could have been because I was happy to have a new friend, but I was also excited because the tape I was listening to came in the mail today. Clinton sent me new songs. I realized he had sent them days before our phone call last night, but it made me happy to hear his song choices. "Best Friend" by Queen was first. *I was his best friend and I was all he sees.* The second song on the tape was 38 Special's "Caught Up in You," which I loved. The third song, the one I had been listening to before Mel made her comment, was "I Wouldn't Have Missed it for the World" by Ronnie Milsap—which I found odd, because that was definitely a song that would have been played on AM radio. But it made me smile because in the lyrics, the singer said the girl made his whole life worthwhile.

"You're happier today?" Mel asked, still trying to engender a response.

"I'm sorry." I pressed stop and took off my headphones. I hadn't meant to ignore her, but my thoughts had taken over.

"I didn't mean to bother you. You just look so happy."

"Yeah. I met a friend today." Mel was nice. I kind of wanted to open up to her, but only a little at a time.

"I'm so glad. It's important to have at least one friend you enjoy seeing at school."

"Yeah. Is it okay if I go ride bikes with her at four thirty? She has an extra bike."

"Of course. Wow. We need to get you a bike."

"It's okay. I had one at home, but, well..." I trailed off. She knew.

"Just be home when it starts to get dark, which, this time of year, is about six. There are no lights on the roads here."

I left for Kelly's at four twenty-five. She was already in her garage when I got there.

"Hey, Tee," she sang.

"Hey, Kell. I gotta be back before six."

"Me too. It gets daaaark up here. So different than Montclair."

"Different from Haledon too. There are so many lights coming from Paterson that even if Haledon had no lights, it'd still be kinda bright."

"Unless there's a full moon here, you can't even see your hand in front of you."

We rode our bikes several miles down the road to a cute little ice cream shack called The Ice Cream Shack, and it was not too unlike Tuffy's. But not fifties style—it was more wooden and rustic.

And it made me miss Clinton.

Kelly got off her bike and slipped it into the bike rack next to a bunch of other bikes.

"Oh. I didn't bring any money."

"It's okay, we can share a milkshake. I'm not supposed to eat before dinner anyway, but I do." She laughed.

"Thanks." I parked my bike next to Kelly's.

"Besides, I like one of the boys who works here."

"Oh my God. Back home, I liked the boy who worked at *our* ice cream place."

"The older boy?"

I dropped my head. "Yeah."

Inside the store, about a dozen kids sat at the little tables scattered throughout. A girl with hair so blond it was a pale yellow jumped out of her seat when she saw Kelly.

"Kell. Hey." She hugged her so tight I thought Kelly couldn't breathe.

"Mar. Hey." Kelly hugged her back. "Marilyn, this is my new friend Tia. Tia, this is my friend Marilyn. The only girl to give me the time of day my first week of school."

"Hi," we said to each other before we all sat at Marilyn's table.

"So, you're new here?"

"Yeah. Just got here last Thursday."

"Rough couple o' days?"

"Just yesterday. Today was good."

"Marilyn's a year older than we are, but she took the bus in the beginning of the year."

"Until I got my car two weeks ago."

"Lucky," I told her.

"I'll be driving in starting January," Kelly said. "I can drive you in then. No more bus."

"How old are you?"

"Sixteen. But my parents didn't sign me up for the written test here right away, so I've only had my permit for four months."

"You can drive here at sixteen?"

"Yup. Beats Jersey, right?"

"Yeah." Though I wasn't ready for driving. The whole idea scared me.

"Get your dad to sign you up for the written test. You need to have your permit for six months before you can get your license."

"Well, it's not like I'd have a car to drive."

"Eh. You can drive my car. My dad got me an old Pinto. It's a piece of crap, but he said my first car shouldn't be a good one, since I'll probably bang it up anyway."

And that's why I was afraid to drive.

"I'll go get us a milkshake. You like a black and white?"

"Sure."

"Where are you from?" Marilyn asked while Kelly went up to the counter.

"New Jersey. Like Kelly."

"Did you guys know each other before?"

"No. She lived in a different town. But it's kinda neat."

"Yeah. It's cool."

Kelly came back with the milkshake and two straws, and we sat with Marilyn and some of her friends that came in a bit later. Marilyn and I even exchanged phone numbers, since she said it always helped to have more friends to rely on. We had a nice time, and I thought that maybe it wouldn't be so bad here.

But then Clinton never called that night.

Nor did he call the next.

Or the next.

By Saturday morning, I was well into losing hope that Clinton would join me out here, and though I was enjoying spending the afternoons with Kelly, Marilyn, and a few other seniors, I was getting depressed and mourning the loss of not only my mother, but of Clinton and our friendship.

At least Najia and I got to talk with each other every other night or so. But I was sure Tommy and Mel weren't going to like the charges on the phone bill once it came.

I stayed in my room most of Saturday. It was raining, and it was chilly, and I had no motivation to venture outside my bedroom. Besides, I needed to catch up on my MTV time.

And I really wanted to cut my hair short like that new chick Madonna in her "Everybody" video. I'd have to ask Kelly and Marilyn where I could get a good haircut.

Sometime in the late afternoon, right in the middle of "Our Lips are Sealed," my phone rang. Instantly, I felt excited and sick to my stomach at the same time.

"Hello?"

"Hey. It's me."

"Clinton? Are you okay? You sound funny." I sat down on my bed.

"Yeah. I'm, uh, well, I'm in the hospital."

"What? Oh my God, what happened?" I stood up, taking the phone with me, and started pacing.

"My father happened."

"Oh my goodness. He hit you?"

"That's an understatement. He's in jail."

"Oh my God, Clinton."

"That's why I haven't called you. I felt bad. I know you were probably worried that it was because of our last conversation, but I promise, Tia, it wasn't."

"It's okay. Are you okay?" I stopped pacing and sat back on my bed.

"I will be. I'm gonna live with Lydia when I get out. I can't go back there. My brothers are no better."

"Why the hell are they like that?"

"I'm guessing no female influence. I don't know."

"So what happened? How could he hurt you so badly that he put you in the hospital?"

"No. I can't."

"You can't what? Tell me?"

"Yeah. I just... No. I'll be okay. That's all you need to know, sweetheart. I..."

"Clinton," I cried. Or screamed. Or something like that to make my voice unrecognizable, even to me. "You're scaring me. Please. Please just tell me."

He let out a big breath. "He threw me through my bedroom window."

"What?" I slid my backside down the side of the bed and dropped to the floor. "Oh my God," I whispered. "Your bedroom. It's on the second floor."

"Yup."

"Oh my God. How... You could have died." Now I was full-on crying.

"Yeah. Fortunately, I bounced on my car first and then fell to the ground. I broke my leg and shattered my elbow. Broken nose, broken teeth, and that's after he broke my jaw."

I was out of words. How could his father do that to him? He broke my Clinton.

"Tia," he called from the other end of the phone. "Tia. I'm gonna be fine." He exhaled. "See, this is why I shouldn't have told you. I knew it'd be too much for you."

After another few silent seconds, he said again, "Tia? You there?"

"Yeah. I'm here." Then it occurred to me. "Why didn't Najia tell me this? I'm sure she knew."

"It happened in the middle of the night. My bedroom is in the back of the house. They probably didn't hear the ruckus. My father didn't even call the ambulance. Neither'd my brothers."

"Clinton. Please move here. You can't live with them anymore."

"I'm not. I'm moving in with Lydia."

"But..."

"Tia. One day at a time. As it is, I'll have to drop out of school until I heal."

"Oh my God. I'm sorry...Clinton?"

"Yeah?"

"What if they *find* you at Lydia's?"

"They won't even bother looking." Clinton sounded so dejected. And I felt dejected *for* him.

"How can you be so sure?"

He paused. For a long time. "'Cause I'm an embarrassment to them. As long as I'm out of the house, they won't bother with me."

I couldn't believe my ears. "How are *you* an embarrassment to *them*? You're so smart and kind and..."

"That's why. I'm not a goddamned barbarian like they are, Tia. I'm not a tough factory worker. Or a merciless animal killer. And I take pride in my education."

"They're thugs."

"Lydia's paying for the phone in my room. I told her I needed to call you. I miss you, Tia."

"I miss you too," I choked on the words. I was going to start sobbing again.

"Listen. I'm getting tired. I'll call you a little later. But take my number in case you need to call me."

I took his number, and we said goodbye. And now I was even more depressed than I had been before. *Why did I have to be two thousand miles away from him?*

Unable to just sit in my room, I went searching for Tommy. I found him doing paperwork in his office.

"Hey, kiddo." He greeted me with a smile until he saw my face and all the tears running down it. "Tia, what's wrong?" He put down his pen, took off his glasses, and stood up.

My knees were buckling as I walked toward him.

He grabbed a chair and sat me in it. "Oh, Tia. Is this about your mother?"

I shook my head.

He leaned against his desk. "School?"

"Clinton."

"The boy from home?"

I nodded. "He was in an... His father threw him out a second-story window."

Tommy stood up again. "Tia, that's awful." He kneeled down and put his hand on my knee. "Did he...did he...?"

"He didn't die. No. He's in..." I stopped to catch my breath.

"The hospital?"

"Yeah."

"How hurt is he?"

"Bad. Broken leg, broken nose, broken teeth...shattered elbow. Oh, and a broken jaw."

"What?" Tommy stood up. "What the hell?"

"His father broke his jaw *before* he threw him out the window. Tommy, I really want to go see him."

"Has his father always been abusive?" he said, leaning back into his desk.

While wiping my face with my sleeve, I nodded. After a sniff, I said, "I think so."

"Oh dear. Now, he's twenty-one, right? Why does he stay there?"

"He'll be twenty-one next month. The twenty-first. He can't afford to live on his own."

"Does he have a job?"

"Part time. He goes to college. Tommy," I said impatiently. "I want to go see him. Please?"

"Go see him? Tia, you have school."

"Please? Just a few days? You said you were gonna fly him out. Well, he can't come out now. So, I can go there."

"You just started school. And where would you stay? Your mom's house is probably rented by now. And you can't stay alone anyway. And there is no way you'll be going to *his* house."

"Can you come *with* me? We can stay at a hotel."

"Tia, I can't just cancel appointments. I'm sorry, hun."

"It's fine," I lied.

In my bedroom again, I called Najia and hoped she was home.

"Hello?"

"Naj?"

"Tee. Hey. What's up? I was supposed to call *you* next. Tomorrow. Did I mess up?"

"No. No. Hey. Have you heard from Clinton?"

"Clinton? No. I haven't been to Tuffy's though, and...I can't recall seeing him outside."

"He's in the hospital. His father threw him out his bedroom window."

"What? His bedroom? Upstairs?"

"Yeah. How is that possible? Clinton's so big."

"Oh my God. Wow. Their windows are those long, low, old-fashioned kind, like on my house. But geez, what happened?"

"I don't know. I mean, I don't know."

"How's that man get away with this stuff?"

"Clinton said he's in jail. How could you not know? He lives right next door."

"We don't pay them any mind, Tee. Except for Clinton, that is one evil family. It's very rare for them to even talk to us. Rarely happens."

"Would I be able to stay with you if I came out there?"

"You're coming here? Sure. Your dad don't mind?"

"I told you, he's not my dad."

"Well, you know what I mean."

"Yeah."

"So, he's letting you?"

"Well, he hasn't said yes yet. But I have to see him, Naj. He sounded terrible when he called. He's got no one. I have to show him he's got me."

"Yeah, well, of course you can stay here. Let me know when you're coming."

"That's another thing. You think your mom would, like, wanna pick me up from the airport?"

"Oh, Tee, I don't know. She never drives farther than the Wayne Hills Mall."

"I'll figure something out."

"I'm sorry."

"It's fine, Naj. At least I can stay with you. Thank you."

"When you coming?"

"I don't know. I have to check."

"Okay. Let me know."

"I'll call you tomorrow."

"See ya, Tee."

"Bye."

I hung up and sprawled out on my bed. I had to figure out how to get Tommy to agree to let me go to Jersey. I had to have a plan.

"HEY, MEL," I SAID, faking glee and putting into place phase one of my plan.

"Good morning, Tia. You feeling better this morning?"

"A little." Feigning too much joy would be obvious. She had already heard me sobbing all night, and I was sure Tommy had filled her in on Clinton. "He called me last night."

"Is he feeling okay?"

"Kinda."

"Hang in there. I'm sure he's in good hands."

"No. Not with his father in the same state."

She put a plate of pancakes in front of me and sat down. "That man is terrible." She turned around to reprimand David, who was throwing Scott's Matchbox cars across the kitchen floor.

"What's he going to do when he gets out of the hospital?"

"He has a cousin he's gonna move in with."

"Is she good? She's not violent like his father, is she?"

"No. She worked with my mom. I met her. She's a nice lady."

"Good."

I heard the shower go on in Mel and Tommy's room. Here goes nothing. "Hey, Mel. I was gonna ride bikes with Kelly, and she usually stops at The Ice Cream Shack. Does Tommy have a few dollars I can have? Just to get a cone?"

She stood from her chair, so I did too. "Oh, Mel, I can get it. Sit. Relax. I don't mind."

She sat back down. Good. She took the bait. "He usually keeps his wallet on his dresser. I'll let him know you took a couple dollars."

"Yeah, just, like two, if that's okay?"

"Of course."

Tommy's wallet was on top of his dresser, just like Mel said. And like I told her, I took out two dollars.

Phase Two. *Ready*.

Bedroom door locked. *Check*.

Phone moved to far corner of my room. *Check*.

Airline reservation number I got from Information last night on my lap. *Check*.

"People Express Airlines, this is Monica, how can I help you?"

I can do this. I can do this. "Yeah, hi. This is Melanie Mercury. I'd like to purchase a one-way ticket to Newark, New Jersey from Liberal Mid-America airport for tomorrow."

"Okay, Ms. Mercury. Tomorrow is not possible, unless there's a death in the..."

"There has been," I cut in, not needing to fake the panic in my voice. "My mother." No need to lie there. Adults have mothers who pass too.

"Okay. I'm sorry to hear that. Let me check."

I waited impatiently while she checked for a flight.

"Ms. Mercury, I have a 1:15 p.m. going straight through."

"Okay. I'll take it."

She took down my credit card information and told me where to pick up my flight pass.

I stuck the credit card in the waistband of my sweats and went back to the kitchen, where Tommy was eating breakfast.

"Hey, kiddo. Ya good?"

"Better," I said. "Mel said it was okay if I rode bikes with Kelly."

"She told me. Sure. Be back for dinner. We eat at five on Sundays."

"Okay. Thanks. Just going to grab my coat."

I quietly went into Tommy's room and prayed his wallet was still there. It was. I slipped the card back in his wallet, left the room, and went to mine to get my coat.

"Okay. Leaving. Bye." I walked out the door and headed for Kelly's, whom I had actually made plans with before I left my room the first time.

And as I told Mel, we rode our bikes to The Ice Cream Shack, where we met up with Marilyn, whom I had also called.

"So, what's this about?" Kelly asked after we ordered a few black and whites—the best milkshakes ever—and sat down. "Why the big rush to meet us?"

"I need a ride to the airport tomorrow morning."

"What?"

Speaking directly to Marilyn, I said, "My father won't let me go see my boyfriend, who's been in an accident and is in the hospital. But I have to see him. I have to. And, well," I sighed, looking from her to Kelly and back, "I was wondering if you could drive me in the morning."

"And skip school?" Kelly asked.

I don't know if she was worried about me or Marilyn skipping school, but I nodded.

"I don't mind," Marilyn said.

"Really?" Kelly and I were both shocked by her immediate positive response.

"Why not? It's not like I've never cut school before."

I looked at Kelly.

"What? You want *me* to come too?"

"Please?"

"You'll keep me company on the ride back."

"Oh, why not?"

"Oh, thank you, thank you, thank you. I really appreciate it."

"Now, tell me. How are you getting a ticket back to Jersey?" Marilyn wondered.

"Got it already. Used Tommy's credit card and called the airline this morning."

"Tommy? Is that your father?" Marilyn asked.

"Yeah." (For all intents and purposes.)

"He doesn't know?"

"Of course not."

"He's gonna know you're missing, you know?" Marilyn pointed out.

"Hopefully not until I'm already on the plane."

"You're gonna be so grounded," Kelly said.

"If I come back."

"What? You can't just run away."

"Why not? Tommy's known me all of one week. What's he gonna care?"

"A week?" Marilyn asked.

"Yeah. He left me when I was five. Hadn't seen him again until ten days ago."

"Whoa."

"Yeah."

"You gonna move in with your boyfriend, then?"

"I have no idea. But I have a friend I can stay with for a few days until I figure out what to do."

"You're brave, Tia," Kelly said with admiration in her voice.

"Not really. I just love Clinton *that* much."

Phase Three: *complete.*

Tomorrow morning, 6:00 a.m., I put into play the final phase—leaving Texhoma. Maybe, hopefully, for good.

CHAPTER FIFTEEN

"Don't Stop Me Now"

TIA

I left for "school" my usual time, since the bus picked us up at 6:20 a.m. But right before the bus came to get us, Marilyn was waiting at the stop.

"Thank you again, so much," I said after I hopped in the back seat with some clothes stuffed into my book bag.

"What if I never see you again?" Kelly whined.

"I'll call you. I promise."

"It's not the same. I just met you."

My mind drew a blank on a response to that, so all I said was, "I'm sorry."

Marilyn had one of her father's big yellow maps, but we still managed to get lost a few times. Luckily, we got to the airport in the nick of time. Hopefully. I still had to pick up my boarding pass.

After a quick hug over the seats to Marilyn and Kelly, I thanked them and told them I'd call when I got to the hospital, if I could manage some change for a pay phone. Kelly got out to let me out and then hugged me again. "I hope you come back," she told me. "But good luck."

"Thanks."

Once I got inside, I grabbed an elastic band out of my purse and put my hair up in a makeshift bun, hoping to add a few more years to my appearance.

Up at the desk, I gave Mel's name and flight information, and the woman gave me a big smile. "Okay, Ms. Mercury, I'll just need to see some I.D."

"I.D."

"Yes. Driver's license. Passport. Identification."

"Oh. Okay. Um. Hold on a second." I fumbled in my purse, stalling for time. *Oh my God, what am I going to do?*

"I have identification, but I'll need to purchase a second ticket."

I spun around in search of the deep voice behind me.

"We'll talk on the plane."

Tommy. And he didn't look happy. At all.

I stepped aside to let him take over with the attendant while I ran through excuses in my head. He may have only been my "father" for the past ten days, but I already felt like I was in for the grounding of my life.

Since we were late, the passengers were already boarding the plane, so Tommy had no time to reprimand me. He simply took my hand and hurried us through the gate and to the boarding area. I noticed he had a small duffel bag in his other hand. *How did he know where I was?*

He was dead silent until the plane was safely in the air. "When we get back home, you're grounded. No phone. No television. No going out after school with your friends. *Or* on the weekends. I will let you know when you can have your life back." His tone was even. Quiet. Serious. Tommy was angry with me, and I guess I couldn't blame him.

I just nodded.

He closed his eyes and shook his head. Then he took a deep breath and looked me in the eyes. "You must *really* love this kid for you to travel cross country without adult supervision or money in your pocket."

"I do." My voice was squeaky. Scared.

"I guess I didn't realize how much he really meant to you. Your mother didn't make that clear enough, I guess."

"She might not have known."

"Does he feel the same about you?"

Does he? The last time we'd talked, before his accident, I'd had my doubts. But I couldn't think about that. "I think so," I told my father, convincing myself in the meantime. "He applied to colleges out here so he could be close to me."

"Really?" my dad asked with raised brows.

"Yeah."

"And he's older than you," he said more to himself than to me.

"Yeah."

"I don't understand how your mother allowed that. I mean you're only sixteen." He sighed. "Then again, I guess I never really *knew* your mother to understand her."

"Why'd you leave *me*? I had nothing to do with what she did." The words came out before I had the chance to stop them.

"Oh, honey. I know you didn't." He took my hand in his and looked at it. "I tried to stay. I did. But...every day, I'd see your face, then go to work and try to put your face and your red hair and green eyes with one of the other teachers. I became so obsessed that I even accused my best friend Sam of having an affair with Tammy. That's when I knew I had to get out of there. Out of New Jersey."

"You were a teacher?"

"Yeah." He squeezed my hand then let it go. It was starting to get uncomfortable for me too. "When I moved back to Oklahoma, I started all over again. Wanted a job where I could work alone."

"But you have people working for you."

"Yeah. Now. But running electricity is pretty much a solo job. I don't have to hold conversation with people."

"I'm sorry I made you take off work."

"I'm sorry I didn't see how important this was to you. And I'm sorry I left you eleven years ago. There's no excuse. You're right. Did you go through the letters I gave you?"

"Not yet." (Eventually, I would go through them. Yes, Tommy had loved me. He'd missed me, and he'd sent me a check for every birthday and holiday...until he'd realized I wasn't even receiving them.)

"Read them. If you do, I promise, you'll know I never stopped loving you. I'm sorry I didn't work harder to find you. I prayed every night we'd be reunited." He clicked his tongue. "I guess I'm sorry about that too."

"Would God do that?" I cried, my voice louder than I intended.

He shook his head. "No. No. He wouldn't."

"I wish she were here."

"I know you do, sweetheart."

I couldn't help but cry now.

"This is such a mess." I continued talking louder than I should. "Why'd this year have to be so bad, Daddy?" As soon as I said it, I covered my mouth with my hand.

Tommy wrapped an arm around me and let me cry on his shoulder. Eventually, I fell asleep.

"WAKE UP, SUGAR PLUM." I'd already been coming to when I heard him say it.

"That's what you used to call me."

"How could I forget?"

Tommy was a good guy. I wished he'd made more of an effort to stay in my life, but he wasn't the heartless monster I'd made him out to be.

We rented a car and headed up the New Jersey Turnpike toward Haledon.

"Tommy?" I asked somewhere near Rutherford.

"Yeah?"

"How'd you know I was at the airport?"

"Mel. She sent me down to the bus stop. You'd forgotten your lunch. The bus came, but you weren't at the stop. When I got back home and told her, she said, 'Check your wallet. Tia needed money yesterday.' But when I checked, only two dollars was missing." He glanced in my direction. "But my credit card was backwards. I never put my credit card backwards."

"Oh."

"Mel knew right away what you did. I guess being a lot younger than me, she *gets* you better. Or because she's female. Anyway, she made me pack a bag and go with you. She called the airports while I got my stuff together to see which flight you booked."

"Wow."

"She's good, right? Anyhow, I wanted to see if you'd actually go through with it, so I watched you go up to the attendant."

"Wait. You were *waiting* for me."

"Yeah. Somehow, I got there before you. I saw Professor Burke's daughter get out of the car with you."

"Kelly. Yeah. Don't tell her parents. Please."

"Who drove you?"

"My friend Marilyn. I begged them. I swear. They didn't encourage me. I'm the one who set the whole thing up. I..."

"Tia. I got it. I get it. I won't say anything to their parents."

"Thank you."

"Do you want to go straight to the hospital, and I'll see about renting a hotel after?"

"I guess."

"So, tell me. Where were you going to stay had Mel not figured it out in time?"

"Najia's house. She's my best friend."

"And was Najia going to pick you up from the airport?"

"No."

"Who was?"

"Um. I didn't really know."

"You do realize the danger you were putting yourself into, don't you? I mean, you had no money, no way of getting out of the airport. Tia, there are bad people in the world."

"I know, Da—I know."

"I don't mind."

"What?"

"You calling me Dad. I'd like it actually. When you're ready. *If* you're ready. No pressure."

I nodded. I'm not sure what possessed me to call him Dad. I mean, it had been over ten years.

"Okay. This is Route 3. I may need help from here. It's been so long since I've been here."

"I don't even know where we are."

Tommy laughed. "Don't think that irony is lost on me."

"Ha ha."

Once we got on Route 46, Tommy said he remembered where he was. He took the roads as if no time at all had passed since he'd been on them.

"See that house there?" He pointed to the big castle up on the hill behind the florist in my hometown. "Your mother and I used to go to poetry readings up there. One of our professors used to hold them while we were in college. It was our big date night. Of course, we had no money back then, so we had to do the free stuff. Sam and his girl used to come with us. We had some good times back then."

"So, you didn't always hate Mom?"

"Hate her? God no. Never. She was the love of my life. I *hated* that I may not have been hers."

I didn't know what to say, but I was grateful he'd loved my mother. That had to count for something, right?

We made it to the hospital five minutes later. Clinton was on the third floor. Tommy stayed in the waiting room.

I walked into room 311 and nearly fell to the floor, catching myself on the edge of the bed before my knees made contact with the floor.

"Tia. Oh my God. Be careful."

"Oh my God. You, you, what happened?"

Clinton tried to smile, but since half his face was covered in gauze, I couldn't tell if it was really a smile or a grimace.

"I told you. I went through a window." He tried to make light of it, but I knew he was faking it.

The side of his face that wasn't covered in gauze was covered in black, blue, purple, yellow, and green. His left arm and left leg were in casts that went past the joints, and his head was wrapped in more white gauze. Band-Aids covered different sections of his right arm, and an IV needle invaded the top of his right hand.

"You downplayed it."

"A little." He patted the right side of his bed. "Sit."

I sat.

"What are you doing here, Tia?" His mouth barely opened as he spoke.

"Is that metal in your mouth?"

"Told you, he broke my jaw."

"Oh my God."

"Tia. What are you doing here?" he repeated.

"I came to see you."

He lifted my hand and held it with his good hand. "Did you run away from home?"

"Yes. But Tommy caught me. And let me come anyway."

"Really?"

"Uh huh. He even came with me. He's in the waiting room. He's, he's different than I expected. Nice."

"I'm glad." Clinton squeezed my hand. "I miss you."

"I miss you, too. So much."

"I know you do. I made a decision."

"About?"

"Coming out to Oklahoma."

Please please please please please please please. "Yeah?"

"I'm coming."

My whole body sagged with relief, and I broke down in tears. Then I lay gently across his chest. His fingers found my curls.

"This was supposed to make you happy."

"I *am* happy," I mumbled into his chest.

"Tia. You gotta get up. My chest is bruised and..."

I jumped up. "Clinton, I'm so sorry. I'm sor—"

"Stop. Stop apologizing. Stop. I'm glad you were hugging me. It just hurt after a while. That's all." He took my hand again. "I spoke with Lydia. She's going to help me get through this. Take care of me until my casts come off. And then I'm gonna fly out. Even if I don't get accepted into a college right away, I'll find a YMCA or something. Lydia's gonna help make calls for me."

"Oh, I'm so glad. Thank you."

"It's sad, Tia, but you're the only one I consider my family. I mean, Lydia is great. She's like an aunt to me, but as far as immediate family...you're it. You're my heart, Tia. When you left, I felt lost."

More tears slipped down my face. "Then how come you told me not to get my hopes up? You made it sound like you weren't sure about us."

"Oh, Tia. I'm always sure that I love you. I just, there are things. I don't want to get into it now, but the cost was also an issue. If I don't get a full ride or even enough of a scholarship, it puts a wrench in my plans. But Lydia is going to help where she can. I don't like taking help from people, but I need to get away from my father. *Before* he's let out of jail."

"Why'd he do this to you?"

Clinton shook his head. "It's not important, Tia. I just gotta get away from him. *And* my brothers. Ronnie did some of this before my dad got to me."

"I just don't understand."

"Don't try to. They're not worth it."

"I'm glad you're coming to Oklahoma. Maybe Tommy will know where you can stay. Wanna meet him?"

"Of course I do."

CHAPTER SIXTEEN

"Jealousy"

S eptember, 1983
    TIA

Clinton moved into his apartment off campus today. As I expected, Tommy, who I now called Dad, helped him find the place by requesting the assistance of Kelly's professor father.

It had taken Clinton three months to recover at Lydia's, during which time his father had been found guilty of assault, or something like that, and was serving a five-year prison sentence. In February, Lydia had helped my father move Clinton into our back sunroom, where he was staying until this morning. Clinton had introduced Lydia to Najia, so when Lydia came with Clinton over the winter break, she'd brought Najia with them. It had been so nice to hang with her again. Najia's mom had said she could skip going to Jordan next summer and come stay with me instead. I couldn't wait.

Today, however, I was going to miss Clinton. Miss sitting in the sunroom with him watching MTV. Miss going to the new video rental store to rent movies we'd watch at night. Miss falling asleep on his lap while we watched them. Tommy had his rules, but I didn't mind. I was still *living* with Clinton, and it was wonderful.

"I promise, Tia. Nothing's gonna change," Clinton said outside his apartment, where he would be engaging in co-ed living. Professor Burke's professor friend owned the house and rented out both floors to deserving college students. And now Clinton.

On the second floor, Clinton lived with two guys, Billy and Henry. Downstairs lived three girls, Lindy, Trisha, and Rita. So, though it wasn't exactly co-ed living, it still didn't sit well with me. It was like he was going to live in his own version of *Three's Company*. And that bothered me. A lot.

"Are you kidding? Everything's going to change."

Tommy was sitting in his truck waiting for me.

"Tia, I'm ten miles away. You can ride your *bike* that far." My new bike that Tommy had bought me in the beginning of the summer, since I still hadn't gotten my license.

I was trying to hold back my little-girl tears. Next month, I'd be turning seventeen, but I still felt too young where Clinton was concerned. It was his big-brother attitude that made me feel that way.

"Right. It won't be that bad," I lied, my feeble attempt at being mature. "Call me."

When I turned to walk away, Clinton grabbed my arm and spun me around. "Hey. I love you."

"I know." He always told me he loved me. That I didn't doubt.

Then his lips came crashing down on mine. I melted into his arms and parted my lips to invite in his tongue. Clinton didn't kiss me often, but when he did, I could barely breathe.

My chest pounded. My limbs turned to jelly. And my mind went blank, thinking of nothing but Clinton's tongue in my mouth, his hand on my hip, and his arm wrapped around my back.

It never went much further than that, because Clinton insisted on waiting until I was eighteen. He said if we went any further, he'd never be able to stop, so we made out on occasion, but that was it. *Much* to my disappointment.

"I'll call you tomorrow," he said after ending the kiss. "And I'll come by Friday night. 'Kay?"

"Yeah."

"Love you."

"Love you, too."

FRIDAY NIGHT, CLINTON called. He wasn't coming by.

"I'm really sorry, Tia. There's a party going on at one of the frat houses, and...I'd really like to go."

"Oh."

"Please don't be mad. This is the first time I've actually made friends...besides you of course."

"Sure. Kelly wanted to go to the movies tonight anyway, so it works out." But I'd rather Clinton came over.

"Good." I could actually *hear* his smile. "I'll come by tomorrow."

"Sure. See ya then."

That was the beginning of the end. I had myself convinced of it. Clinton was going to thrive in college. I had a strong feeling I wasn't going to be part of it.

My senior year started yesterday. Marilyn had gone off to college—not far, The University of Oklahoma—and Kelly and I felt her loss. We had been the three musketeers all summer long. Even though I'd had Clinton in the evenings, he had been busy working on campus setting up the library computers during the day. Professor Burke had gotten him a job working at the university library. So, I'd spent my days swimming in Kelly's pool, and on rainy days, we'd watch our favorite channel, and our current favorite videos: Duran Duran and Hall and Oates. When I'd told Clinton I enjoyed them, he'd thrown a pillow at me. "All that work I did teaching you good music gone to waste. Those two are a bad influence on you."

I'd laughed. "Duran Duran's good."

"Yeah...if you listen to AM radio," he'd joked.

THE RELIEF I FELT WHEN Clinton walked through our door Saturday morning surprised me. Until I saw him, I guess I'd really thought he wouldn't show up.

"Clint." My father greeted him with a slap on the back. "How was your first week?"

"Hey, Tommy. It was great." Clinton was forced to call my father Tommy, instead of Mr. Mercury, when he first moved in, or else he wouldn't be allowed to live here. "My classes are terrific and I like my professors."

"Good. I'm glad to hear it. You adjusting to your new living quarters?"

"I am. I got a good bunch of roommates."

"Good. Sit. Mel made French Toast."

"Thanks."

Clinton finally made it over to me. "Hey, beautiful," he said as he kissed me.

"How was the party?"

Clinton pulled out a chair for me to sit.

"Thanks."

As he sat down next to me, he said, "I had a good time."

He deserved it. It seemed without his family to harass him, Clinton's confidence had grown stronger. "Good. You deserve a good time." As jealous as it made me.

Mel set two plates of French toast in front of us, and Clinton dug in. With his mouth full, he said, "So, you wanna come over today?"

Of course! "I guess. Is that okay, Dad?"

"Can you bring her home tonight?" Tommy asked.

"Of course. I'll even let her drive my car," he teased. Clinton had sold his Grand Prix back in Jersey and bought a black 1978 280Z. It was five speed, which he knew I was reluctant to drive. Tommy had promised to buy me my own car, but I had to pass the driving test. I kept failing it. Parallel parking and three-point turns were stupid, especially because I'd just park in a normal parking lot anyway. And who cares if it took me more than three points to turn around? But Clinton and Tommy kept trying to teach me, usually in Mel's Granada.

"I don't wanna drive stick."

"Looks like you don't wanna drive anything," Clinton joked. "I think you're failing on purpose."

I wasn't. Though I *did* like Clinton driving me everywhere.

Although Clinton didn't live with us anymore, we still had a couch and television in the back sunroom, so after breakfast, he and I went back there.

"Here." He handed me a tape. "I made you another one."

"You had time?" I asked, turning the tape over in my hand. It made me feel good to know he still had time to think of me even though he had his college life to contend with.

"I made time."

Aw. I felt my cheeks warm to his words. "Thank you."

"You can listen to it later or tomorrow."

"Okay." I turned on the TV and sat down next to Clinton. "My father's friend from a long time ago is coming to visit next week."

"Yeah? What's the occasion?" he asked, wrapping his arm around me and pulling me in to his side.

"He retired from teaching and wanted to see him." Rubbing my hand up and down his thigh, I was still so thankful that Clinton had shown up this morning. "He's bringing the stuff left from my mother's estate."

Clinton leaned his head against the couch and closed his eyes as he spoke. "I hadn't realized it wasn't closed."

"With no one doing anything, it just sat there. Tommy made some calls and Lydia told him about Sam retiring. Tommy called him."

"Good. I guess that piano isn't headed your way?" He turned towards me and opened one eye.

"I think it got sold," I told him, disappointed to know he may have wanted it.

"I should've taken my keyboard when I left."

"You miss playing, huh?" I asked, still running my palm up and down his thigh, inciting little goose bumps in my arms because I was touching him.

"A lot. It helps me unwind...without drinking." He was conversing, but his eyelids must have been really heavy, because he couldn't keep them open.

"Did you drink last night?"

After a pause. "Does a bear shit in the woods?"

"You get drunk?" I asked with more exasperation than I'd intended.

"Does a dog bark?"

"Clinton," I said harshly. "Stop joking. I found a bunch of bottles behind the couch last night."

He finally opened his eyes and lifted his head from the back of the couch, then took his arm out from around me and slapped his thigh. "Oh. Jeez. I forgot about them. Did your Dad see them?"

"No." I sat forward and inched away, turning to face him and say, "He wouldn't care. You're almost twenty-two."

Shaking his head back and forth, he sighed. "Still. I don't want him to know how much I drink."

"Why *do* you drink so much?" I asked, twisting my fingers in an attempt to placate increasing nervousness.

"I don't know, Tia. It makes me forget."

"Forget what?" Clinton and I hadn't broached this subject in a while, and I was hoping it was okay for me to question him so much.

"My privileged past?" he joked.

"Stop. You still smoking?"

"Not around you." With a raise of his eyebrows, he looked like a kid who'd just fibbed about pulling the pigtails of the girl he liked.

I shook my head, saying, "Then you should always be with me."

"Okay. I'll quit school so I can be with you twenty-four hours a day. You'll have to quit too." He was joking. I knew it. But it wasn't funny.

"Can you quit teasing? You're giving me a headache."

"Oh yeah? Will this help your headache?" He tickled me. In the stomach. Under the armpits. On my side. Then he plopped on top of me and devoured my mouth. His tongue probed my mouth like this was the last time he'd ever kiss me. Or the first time.

He then withdrew his tongue and wildly started kissing my neck. And the area above my breasts. His hand came up and cupped one of them.

That's when it hit me. "You're drunk." I slid out from under him and sat up. "You taste like maple syrup, but I smell it. Were you drinking already?"

He was still on his knees on the couch when he dropped to his heels and sighed. "I never slept. I've been drinking all night."

"But...if you didn't just kiss me... How do you hide it? I can never tell you've been drinking, unless... Like now."

"Built up a tolerance, I guess," he said, shrugging it off and sitting his ass back down on the couch.

I stood up and shut the television off. I didn't feel like hearing about little red corvettes. "Were you drinking *every* time we made out?"

"I don't know, Tia. I can't really remember."

"You can't remember if you ever kissed me sober?"

He shrugged and leaned back against the couch.

"Clinton," I clipped, my hands on my hips, trying hard not to stomp my foot like a child.

"I'm not sober often," he whispered.

I sat and slunked back down on the couch. "How did I not know this?"

"I'm good at hiding it," he said just as softly.

"Are you an alcoholic?"

Shaking his head, he swallowed. "I don't think so."

"You have to be."

"I've tried stopping. I can." I watched as he ran his hand through his thick hair and bit his lip.

"Then why do you start again?"

"Ironically," he said, taking my hand, "it keeps me focused. When I'm sober, I think too much, and I can't get work done."

"What do you think about?"

Abruptly letting go of my hand, he stood. "Tia, I really don't want to talk about this anymore. Okay. Can we drop it?"

"But..."

Both his hands flew through his hair when he said, "Tia, if we're gonna continue this, I'm leaving."

On a sigh, I said, "Fine. I'll drop it. But you drive while you're drunk?"

"Tia," he yelled through gritted teeth. "Enough."

The rise in his tone pierced my soul and punctured my heart. Clinton had never yelled at me before. I was quickly losing oxygen as I held my breath to keep from crying. I was too old to cry. I wouldn't cry.

I nodded to let him know I would not bring it up again, but I walked out of the room and into my bedroom, closing the door behind me to let him know, in my way, that I was finished with this conversation as well. A mature person's solution.

In the privacy of my room, though, I let a few tears fall. Until I got mad at myself for acting like such a child. Maybe that was why Clinton *saw* me as a child. *Treated* me as such. Maybe, maybe, I needed to change my tune.

So, I changed from my pajamas to my shorts, slid on a tank top and my hot pink cut-off sweatshirt, put on my Wigwam socks, and tied up my Reeboks. I was going to act like I couldn't care less.

But when I reentered the sunroom, Clinton's head was in his hands. Staring at him for a few seconds, I decided to drop my resolve and sit on the couch next to him. "Clinton," I whispered, rubbing his back. "I'm sorry."

He shook his head but didn't look up. "Don't."

With a start, I removed my hand from his back. "Okay."

Sighing, I leaned back on the couch. Truthfully, I didn't know what a more mature person would do in this situation, but all I wanted to do was make the crushing pain in my chest go away.

I picked up the cassette tape that was lying on the edge of the couch. What would be on it this time? The last few tapes from Clinton hadn't been about anything specific. Just some bands he thought I'd like: Def Leppard, The Police, The

Clash, U2, John Cougar. I liked them, but I wondered now if this tape held any clue to the mystery that was Clinton Daniels. As long as I'd known him, and as close as we were, there was still too much I didn't know about him.

It made me sad.

As I was turning the tape over to open and see the list of songs Clinton chose, his hand clasped my wrist.

I put down the cassette.

"I don't want to argue with you, Tia. You're the only one I can count on. The only person in this world that matters to me." He pulled me closer and rested his chin on my head. "But I can't. I don't want to discuss my drinking right now. Not today."

"Okay," I whispered.

"I love you, Tia. More than anything. But there are some things...." He closed his eyes, struggling to say something. Then, his lashes flickered up, "Not today."

"Not today," I repeated. He loved me more than anything. That *had* to be enough. "I love you, too."

He lifted his chin from my head, ran a thumb over an errant tear on my cheek, and searched my eyes. "I'm sober now." He pressed his lips to mine and rested his hand behind my neck, his thumb grazing beneath my ear as his tongue begged for entrance into my mouth. I parted my lips and let him in. Without disrupting the kiss, Clinton lifted me onto his lap and slid his hand to my hip. He moved his lips from my mouth, to my jaw, to my neck, to my ear. "Oh, Tia," he breathed into my ear.

"I don't want to wait anymore," I breathed back.

"Your parents are in the next room." He continued kissing down my neck, beneath my chin, back to my lips. His hand slipped beneath my shirts.

When his hand reached my breast, he gasped and stopped kissing me. "No bra?"

I kissed *him*, shaking my head in answer to his rhetorical question. It's not like I actually *needed* a bra; I was pretty flat-chested. My breathing stopped when his thumb circled my nipple. When he pressed it gently, he caused an unfamiliar, pleasurable pain. I gasped when I caught my breath at the same time he cupped my breast and squeezed.

When I groaned out loud, Clinton pulled his hand out from under my shirts and removed his lips from mine. "We can't do this here," he rasped then kissed me on the forehead.

"Then let's go to your place," I practically begged.

"I have roommates."

Both of us sighed and leaned back against the couch. Was he sighing for the same reason I was? I *really* wanted to be with Clinton, in the biblical way, as the saying went. Or was he sighing for a different reason?

"How 'bout we go to the record store? I need some new music," Clinton suggested.

"Okay," I murmured, realizing, again, that he didn't want that biblical knowledge of me like I wanted of him. The record store was the last place I wanted to go. But after a brief—but to me, significant—argument, I just wanted to be with Clinton. In *any* capacity. Biblical or not.

We had to drive to Texas to reach the nearest record store, but we didn't mind. Clinton blasted Journey's *Frontiers* album, and when that ended and we still weren't there, he put on some new band that I wasn't familiar with called R.E.M. I loved it. It was different from what Clinton usually listened to, and I asked him to make me a copy.

When we got to the store, Clinton knew exactly what he was looking for—the new Mötley Crüe and the new Kiss albums, both released this month. I, of course, lingered in the pop section where I picked up Bryan Adams' album, *Cuts Like a Knife,* and Clinton bought it for me.

We listened to Mötley Crüe on the way home, but I couldn't tell you if I enjoyed it or not, because I fell asleep and didn't wake up until we got to Clinton's apartment.

"Come on, sleepyhead. You can call your dad from inside."

"Okay," I said, still groggy, my neck cramping from leaning against the window.

"He said you can come over, right?"

"Yeah. You heard him. But, Clinton, I'm gonna be seventeen. And he's not that strict."

I followed Clinton up the stairs, but before he got the chance to unlock his door, Lindy called up to him. "Clint. We're all down here. We ordered pizzas and we got Jack."

"'Kay, Lin. We'll be right down."

He unlocked his door and led us in.

"Your roommates are downstairs?"

"Yeah," Clinton said, bringing his bag into his room.

I followed him in, hoping to pick up where we had left off in my sunroom. With the back of my foot, I slowly closed his door.

"Tia? What're you doing?"

"Nothing." I sat down at the edge of his bed.

"You hungry? There's pizza downstairs."

He slipped his cassettes in alphabetical order on his shelf then tossed the bag in the garbage.

"Not really." I was more interested in kissing Clinton.

"You haven't eaten since breakfast," he pointed out.

"I know." Were all guys this dense?

"Well, I'm starving. Plus, I can go for a beer."

"Great," I muttered. "Okay."

He shook his head and took my hand. "C'mon, we'll have fun. You'll get to know everybody."

"Sure," I said, faking a smile and squeezing his hand.

Downstairs, Clinton's roommates, Billy and Henry, were on the couch eating pizza, while the three girls who lived there were sitting on the floor around the coffee table. *Three girls. Three guys. This did not sit well with me at all.*

"Hey, Clint," Lindy welcomed him, patting the floor next to her. "Dig in."

"Guys, this is Tia. Tia, you met Billy and Henry. This, of course, is Lindy and her roommates, Trisha and Rita."

"Hey," we all said in unison.

"Sit. Eat," Rita said. "Beer and Jack are in the kitchen."

Following Clinton into the kitchen, I could sense eyes on me. I couldn't tell whose, but I sensed they were Lindy's.

"I'll get you a Coke," Clinton said, opening the refrigerator.

"I'll have a beer," I told him.

He pushed the red can into my hands. "You'll have a Coke."

"You're not my father," I whispered.

"But I have to bring you *home* to your father. You'll have the Coke."

"Tommy won't care."

"*I* care." His tone said he was done discussing this further. I took the Coke.

He and I sat on the floor next to Lindy. Well, *he* sat next to Lindy. I sat at the corner of the table.

"So, where do you go to school?" Rita asked me.

"She's in high school, remember?" Lindy answered instead. "Professor Burke's daughter's friend."

"Oh. Senior?"

"Yes," I answered before Lindy had a chance.

"Cool."

"You coming here next year?" Trisha asked.

"I don't know. I didn't apply to any colleges yet."

"What?" Lindy gasped.

"She's going to college," Clinton said. "She's just late to apply."

I nudged him in the side. Truth was, I hated school. Reading was the only thing educational I liked. Why put myself through four more years of school? Clinton didn't agree with me. To him, an education represented freedom. Needless to say, he wasn't thrilled with my decision to find a job right after high school. "You need an education," he'd kept telling me. *Maybe I don't.*

The rest of the night, I watched as all the roommates drank, laughed, and shared in stories I knew nothing about. Psych classes? I didn't even know there *was* such a thing. No wonder Clinton thought I was immature. Next to people his age, I guess I was.

"So, Clint, man," Henry said. "You have to come with us to The Lounge next weekend. I'll tell my cousin Michael to add you to the list."

"The Lounge?" I asked Clinton.

"It's a club."

"Exclusive," Lindy added. "It's invite-only. Twenty-one and over," she made sure to point out.

I wasn't liking Lindy too much.

"Ya in?" Henry asked.

"Sure," Clinton said gladly, not even glancing in my direction to see if I'd mind.

"Great. Saturday night. I'll call Michael."

At about midnight, Clinton said, "I better get Tia home."

Inwardly, I cringed.

"Make sure you come back," Lindy cooed.

"Maybe. I'm kinda beat. Never slept last night."

"You can crash here if you get too tired."

Oh, shut up, Lindy. Just shut the hell up.

"I don't have to go home yet," I told Clinton outside.

"I'm beat, Tia. I'm gonna bring you home and come right back to go to sleep."

He opened his car door to let me in. When he got in on his side, I said, "You can sleep at my house."

"Not tonight."

"Okay." My instincts told me not to push the subject.

He put the music on but kept it low. "You're not too drunk to drive?" I asked, trying like heck to keep my voice light and carefree.

"I'm not drunk at all."

"You had six beers." Damn. I just couldn't keep my mouth shut.

"I'm fine." His words came out a little on the curt side, so I didn't continue my interrogation.

But he wasn't fine. I noticed him swerving onto the other side of the road a couple times. They were empty, dusty roads, but still, I knew he shouldn't be driving.

When I looked over at him, I saw his eyes were closed, and there was no way I was keeping my mouth shut now. "Clinton," I yelled.

He startled. "What?"

"You're falling asleep."

"Sorry."

"Sorry my ass. You're gonna get us killed. You know, if you're not gonna let me drink, you might as well teach me to drive."

"Mmm." He was too tired to even respond.

Luckily, we made it to my house, but when he got out to walk me to the door, I turned off his car and took his keys.

"Tia, what're ya doin'?"

"You're not going home. You're tired and you've been drinking."

"I'm fine. Give me my keys."

I stuck them down my shorts, inside my underwear. "No."

"Tia. Stop. You just don't want me going back there. I saw you were jealous the whole night."

"Go to Hell, *Clint*." Isn't that what Lindy had called him?

"See. I told you. Jealous. Now give me my keys."

"Come and get them."

He picked me up and put me on the hood of his car. "Give me my keys."

I shifted my hips up toward him. "Get them."

He closed his eyes, breathed, and opened them, daggers shooting from his eyes. "Is that what you want, Tia? You want me to undo your pants so I can get my keys. You want it that way, Tia? Is that what you want?"

"What?" I was confused.

"You want me to screw you right here? Waiting until you're eighteen isn't good enough for you? You want me to take your virginity right here over a set of keys?"

"What are you talking about?" He was talking crazy.

"You put your keys down your pants. Your shorts are quite short, so I assume you stuck them in your panties. Just like you decided to go braless today." He turned and walked away from me. "Stop trying to seduce me, Tia. I don't want to be seduced."

I cannot tell you what those words did to me. My chest constricted. My head pounded. My body went numb. I couldn't even slide off his car.

"Give me my keys, Tia."

I heard his words but didn't move. *Couldn't* move.

But I did feel his hands on my button, when several seconds later, he unbuttoned my shorts, slid down my zipper, and stuck his hands down my underwear. His hand stilled on my curls. When I looked up at him, we were both crying.

"This is *not* how I wanted the first time I touched you to be," he whispered, moving his hand to my hips.

Reaching down my own pants, I pulled out his keys. "I just didn't want you getting in an accident on your way home." I was embarrassed at how choppy my sentence came out, but I couldn't contain the tears.

He pulled his hand out of my pants, zipped and buttoned me back up, and pulled me against his chest.

"Something's different," I said into his chest.

"I know," he whispered. "And I'm sorry."

I think I stopped breathing. I wanted to ask him. I wanted to say something. But I couldn't find the courage.

"I know we never *defined* our relationship," he said over my head, "but we need to break up."

No.

No.

"No," I finally managed—a half-cry, a half-whispered scream.

"I'm so sorry." He ran his fingers through my hair but kept his chin on top of my head. I didn't think he could look me in the eye.

"You want what I can't give you right now."

Why did he have to keep talking?

"I love you more than anything in this world, Tia. You are everything to me. But...I can't give you a physical relationship right now. And I know that's what you want, but...I don't. Not now. Not when there are so many differences in our lives."

I pulled back.

"What differences?"

"I don't know. College. My studies. Our age difference. Like next week. I *want* to go out with Henry and Lindy and them. But I can't bring you, 'cause you're too young. Tonight, we were all drinking... You couldn't."

"I could have," I interrupted.

"But I didn't *want* you to."

"Why? Why do you act like you're my father and not my boyfriend?"

"'Cause maybe that's how I see myself in your life." He said it quickly then sighed.

"You don't think of me as your girlfriend?"

Slowly, he shook his head. "I tried," he whispered.

Oh, how that hurt. Deep down into my soul, that hurt.

"I think as you get older, that will change. But right now...I'm sorry."

I DON'T KNOW HOW I got into bed that night. Nor do I remember how many days I stayed in bed. Mel called me out sick from school because there was no way I could walk a straight line or focus, or anything. I cried, I slept, I cried, I slept, and I didn't know it then, but this wouldn't be the only break-up Clinton and I had that would leave me near comatose.

Sometime, a week or two later, I put that cassette Clinton had made me into my Walkman: "A Change is Gonna Come" by Sam Cooke, "Changes" by David Bowie, "Have you Ever Seen the Rain" by Creedence Clearwater Revival, "Bridge Over Troubled Water" by Simon and Garfunkel, "Times They are a Changin'" by Bob Dylan. This wasn't even music Clinton listened to. He was definitely trying to tell me something, so his breaking up with me *hadn't* been impulsive. It had been premeditated. And then, a Boston song came on, "A Man I'll Never Be," about a man trying to love a girl who thought he loved her back. It made me wonder just how long Clinton didn't see me the same way I saw him.

It broke my soul.

CHAPTER SEVENTEEN

"Who Needs You"

S eptember, 1984

TIA

Senior year had sucked, every bit of it, all the way to, and including, graduation. I was glad it was over. For me, it had been pure hell. I'd tried hanging out with Kelly, and when Marilyn had come back on weekends, I'd tried to be happy.

But I couldn't.

This past summer, instead of Najia coming to me, I'd decided to go out there.

Bad move.

Aside from seeing Clinton's old house up for sale, I also saw Bobby. Not a very good idea, being in the tangled state of mind I was in.

"What are you doing?" Najia said one night. One very significant night. "Do you even like Bobby anymore?"

"He's cuter than I remember."

"But do you like him?"

"He's bigger. Muscly. Hot."

"Tee. Stop. You're talking about giving away your virginity to him. You sure that's what you want?"

"Positive." No, I wasn't positive at all. But I wanted to punish Clinton, who thought it'd still be okay to send me mix-tapes with songs about how much he missed me. And how I was his best friend. And how he tried to be the man I wanted him to be but couldn't. Not yet, his accompanying letters would indicate. And that song. That damn Boston song. It showed up on every mix-tape he sent me. "A Man I'll Never Be." Over and over. I get it. You don't love me the way I love you.

Screw you, Clinton Daniels. *My new mantra.*

Every time I lit a cigarette that summer—Screw you, Clinton Daniels.

Every time I took a drink that summer—Screw you, Clinton Daniels.

When I gave Bobby Bennett my virginity the night before I headed back to Oklahoma—Screw you, Clinton Daniels.

And that estate of my mom's that had been closed? Yeah, I got a pretty nice sum from her life insurance, but it came with a telling letter from my mother, which I crumpled up and threw into the back of my closet. Not quite ready to throw away. Not quite ready to have Tommy find it.

I deposited the money I received into an account that Tommy opened up for me, keeping a thousand dollars cash out for car emergencies. Yes, Tommy bought me a car, because I finally passed my test.

To top things off, one night about a week ago, Mel had called me into the living room to show me something on the television. Clinton was being interviewed and recognized for his computer work at the university. Apparently, computers were becoming a big thing for colleges, and Clinton had helped execute a new graphic design program unique to the university's agricultural program. I guessed Clinton hadn't only been working in the library anymore. Good for him, I guess, but it had made me bitter. I'd left the room without saying a word, grabbed a cigarette from the pack I hid in my room, and went out back where I couldn't be caught to smoke it. *Screw you, Clinton Daniels.*

But today.

When Kelly was starting college in Los Angeles, and Clinton was busy being a genius at college, I was starting my first day of work—as an electrician's apprentice. Tommy said if I couldn't make up my mind about what I wanted to do for a living, I could work with him for a year while I thought about it. Like Clinton, he agreed that an education equaled freedom. Freedom to choose your path in life. But I had the feeling Clinton used it to free himself from his father's brutality.

Being an electrician's apprentice? Not fun.

I hated it so much that I dreaded getting out of bed each morning. Day in, day out, I'd grab a cup of coffee to go, get in the truck with my dad, drive to whatever job he had going that day, and help him run wires. Every night, I went to bed wondering if I should just choose college now as an undecided major.

At the end of the month, with my cup of coffee in hand, I begged Tommy to let me apply to college instead of going into work. He laughed, saying his plan had worked out quicker than he'd thought. So that day, and the weeks following, I spent all my energy on getting into college.

I applied to every college in Oklahoma and Texas, but I didn't really want to live away, so I hoped Oklahoma Panhandle State University would accept me. I worked extra hard on *that* essay, for sure. Tommy also talked to Professor Burke, and he was going to see what he could do about getting me in for the spring semester. He also advised me to take a non-matriculated class or two in January if I didn't.

It was that essay I was working on at the kitchen table with Mel when the doorbell rang. I thought nothing of it while Mel went to answer it, until a musky scent invaded the room. I didn't turn around, and I didn't move. Too scared to do anything, I stared at the blurring words on the paper, trying hard to calm my racing heart.

"I'll leave you two alone," I heard Mel say before leaving the room.

"Tia."

I closed my eyes, letting the sound of his voice linger in my head for a moment. I'd missed that voice. So much.

"Tia?" he said again.

Clinton. I couldn't speak.

A wet spot appeared on my paper, smudging the ink. A tear? *Why must I always cry? For God's sake, I was going to be eighteen in three days.*

"I miss you," he said, still standing somewhere behind me. "So much. So much it hurts."

More tears stained my essay. Still unable to move, I let them fall.

"I need you. I do. I don't want to live without you anymore."

These words.

They made me angry.

Angry enough to finally speak.

"Then you should have thought of that when you broke up with me."

He pulled my chair out from the table and spun it around. "I broke off the physical relationship you wanted. Not our friendship. You're the one who stopped answering my phone calls, locking yourself in your room every time I came to see you. I wrote you a goddamn letter every week. You never answered. *You* ended our friendship, Tia. Not me." He stood there looking down at me.

My gaze was on the floor when I responded, speaking slowly, quietly, still unable to meet his eyes. See that face. "How can we be friends when I'm so in love with you it hurts?"

He didn't answer right away, but he knelt down and lifted my chin with his fingers. "Look at me, Tia."

I did. That face. I missed that face so much. The pain in my chest increased tenfold. I clutched at it to try to ease the hurt.

"You don't think I'm in love with you, too?"

I shook my head. "Not the same way."

Clinton took my hand in his, and I clutched my chest harder with my other fist. "I love you in *my* way, Tia. I wish that were enough for you."

The hand that was pressing into my chest was now at my head. "I need aspirin." It suddenly felt like my brain was on fire. This was too much for me.

He stood up. "Still in the cabinet by the sink?" He went and got it without waiting for a response.

"Here."

I took the two pills and the glass of water from him and swallowed. "Thank you."

"Come sit outside with me?" he asked, taking my hand and leading me off the chair and out the door.

"You're gonna be eighteen in three days. I thought maybe we could try again. Like I promised you years ago."

When I didn't respond, he continued, "Now that you're legally an adult, and I won't feel like a creepy child molester, I thought we could try again...with the kind of relationship *you* want."

Afraid to meet his eyes, I did anyway. "Really?"

He smiled. "Really." After a long pause, he said, "Now can I hug you? Because it's killing me not to."

CLINTON PICKED ME UP three days later dressed in blue jeans, a white button-down, and a black leather blazer. My heart and brain turned to mush at the sight of him.

"You are so beautiful," he said to me at the door, a small bouquet of wild flowers in his hand.

He took me to a fancyish restaurant in Texas, about an hour away. And though I was so happy to finally be with Clinton again, something seemed off. We didn't easily pick up where we had left off, as was usually the case. The dynamics had changed, but I chalked that up to us finally defining our relationship.

Conversation during dinner was stilted at first, but once I told him I was applying to colleges, he got so excited and started talking about school, and classes, and how I was going to love learning new things.

"Yeah, right," I said. "How long have you known me? I haven't changed. I still hate school."

He laughed. I'd missed that laugh.

"Before I forget, Happy Birthday." He handed me two small packages wrapped in green. "Like your eyes. Got the wrapping paper to match."

"Thank you. But dinner's my present."

"This is just something small. Don't worry."

I opened the larger of the small packages first. Queen's *The Works*. Their latest album. "Oh, Clinton, thank you."

"I figured I'd buy you your own instead of recording one from mine."

"Thank you."

"Open the other one."

This one made me nervous. It was a box made for jewelry. I could tell. Slowly, I unwrapped it to reveal a silver box underneath. With a shaky hand, I lifted the lid.

"Oh my God, Clinton, they're beautiful." Two perfect diamond solitaires stared up at me from the box. "This is too much," I said, looking up at him.

"They're not *nearly* enough. I wanted to get you bigger ones, so you could see them through all your hair, but...well..."

"No. Clinton. I just feel like this is so much."

"Believe me, they're not enough." He took the box from my hands, took out the earrings, and kneeled beside me to put them in.

I kept bringing my hands up to touch my ears the rest of the night.

He dropped me off at my door and said, "I want to do this right, Tia. I wanna start from scratch. So, can I take you out again tomorrow night?"

I nodded. "Sure."

He brought his hand to my face and let his thumb graze my cheek, my temple, the outline of my ear. He quirked his mouth then leaned in and kissed me. A soft peck goodnight. I wanted so much more.

THE FOLLOWING NIGHT, Clinton came to my door with another cassette tape in his hands and took me to the movies. In the car, he put the tape in. "I'm not sure if you bought this while we were apart, but it's a band I thought you'd really like."

The first notes played, and I knew exactly who it was. "Oh my God, Bon Jovi. That guy is hot."

"Yeah, I had a feeling you'd think so. Do you have it?"

"No. I've been wanting it, but I don't drive too far from home, so..."

"That's right, Tommy told me you got your license. And how many times did it take you to pass the test?"

"Five. I must be part stupid, right?"

"Tia, you're not stupid."

"My brain gets confused. Sometimes, I feel like my perception's off. But at least I passed, right?"

"And Tommy got you that cool Camaro."

"Yeah. '79. And it's automatic. No stick for me."

"Wuss. Your red curls probably look great in that white car."

"Thanks." I blushed. He still had that power over me.

"I like your perm, by the way."

"Thanks. Again. So, where we going?"

"A movie good?"

"Sure." Anything was good, as long as I was with Clinton.

Irreconcilable Differences was playing, so we bought two tickets and took a seat in the last row. For some reason, I was too nervous to eat, so I turned down Clinton's offer of buying me popcorn. Clinton didn't want any either.

It was odd being so nervous around each other. Before, even though I had always wanted to be physical with Clinton and he hadn't, I had never been uncomfortable. I didn't like this feeling.

During the previews, Clinton held my hand and didn't let it go until we were back in his car after the movie. "Do you want to go home? Or...you want to come to my place? My roommates are at an all-night party, so...if you want."

My stomach swirled. "Okay."

"Okay, you want to come over, or okay, you want to go home?"

"Come over?" I asked, but I knew without a doubt I wanted to go back to Clinton's. No question about it.

Clinton was quiet all the way back. He even forgot to raise the volume of his stereo, which was unlike him. But when we got home, he took my hand as soon as I got out of the car. "Thank you for coming over."

Clinton was nervous. It was cute.

Inside, he tossed his keys on the credenza, closed the door, and picked me up, cradling me in his arms *An Officer and a Gentleman*-style. "I'm kinda nervous," he finally said as he carried me into his room.

"Me too." *I can't believe we're finally doing this.*

He kissed my lips, closed his door with his foot, and laid me on his bed. "Let me lock it."

After turning the lock on his door, he went to his stereo and pressed a button. When he returned, he lay down on his side next to me and pushed some hair out of my eyes. "You sure about this?" he asked quietly, as "Love" by John Lennon played through the speakers.

"More than anything."

He leaned down and kissed me softly on the lips. A few pecks before he slid his tongue across them, parting them gently. He timidly stroked my skin, the tremble of his touch an erotic tickle. When his hand reached the hem of my shirt, he lifted it up, breaking our kiss just to raise it up over my head. His lips found mine again before they found my neck. Then the space between my breasts. Pulling back to look into my eyes, he let his finger trace the outlines of my bra. "You okay?" he whispered.

My nod, most likely imperceptible, was accompanied by a deep intake of breath.

Kissing my lips again, he then proceeded to unclasp my bra and cast it aside. His hand quivered again as he cupped my breast and his thumb found my nipple. I felt my eyes roll behind my head as he made tiny circles around my hardened skin. His other hand traveled down my stomach until he reached the button of my jeans, and as he unzipped them, I stuck my foot behind the other to kick off my pink pumps.

Slowly, he slid off my jeans, leaving me bare, with only my white lace panties covering me. Clinton kneeled before me as he took off his tee shirt and unzipped his Levi's. "Your Song" by Elton John now played through the speakers. Clinton hopped off his bed, pulled down both his pants and underwear, and crawled back between my legs, kissing my stomach just above my panty line. Again, a trembling finger traced the outline of what was left of my clothes, fingering not only the top of my panties, but all the way around until he found the edge between my legs.

I was wet. Really wet. Embarrassed by my obvious arousal, I closed my legs as much as I could, considering he was between them.

He wrapped a hand around my thigh and met my lips with his. "Open your eyes, Tia," he whispered into my mouth.

When I did, he asked, "Is this too much?"

I shook my head. *So not too much. Perfect.* But I was embarrassed. I felt like I was more aroused than he was, and this made me self-conscious.

I didn't know how to touch him though. With Bobby, the act had been done in, like, three minutes. It had taken more time for him to put on the rubber than it had for us to have sex.

This. This was different. This was real. And I was too self-conscious having Clinton touch me like this.

"I can stop if you want." Out of the speakers came "I'll Be There" by the Jackson Five.

"No," I rasped. "Please don't." Self-consciousness aside, there was nothing I wanted more than Clinton inside of me.

He slipped the lace down my legs and tossed them to the floor.

His hands splayed on the tops of my feet, and he tenderly ran them up my shins, past my knees, and around my thighs. When his lips met mine again, one of his hands slipped into the space between my legs, and his fingers traced the area. As I became more wet, he slipped a finger inside, and I grabbed his hair, clutching it between my fingers as I pulled him tighter to deepen our kiss.

His tongue probed.

His fingers prodded.

My heart pounded.

I felt the need to explode.

Thoroughly wet now from his touch, my body started to thrash involuntarily. He released his fingers from inside me and removed his lips from mine.

"Open your eyes, Tia," he demanded again.

I did.

"Are you positive?"

"Yes. Are you?" I had to ask, even though I barely had a breath to speak.

He smiled and kissed my nose. Then, while I thrashed about, he reached into his nightstand, pulled out a foil packet, and tore it open. Slipping it over his erection, he then hovered over me and *bit* my nose.

I giggled.

"Positive?"

"Positive."

In the next instant, and as Foreigner's "I Want to Know What Love Is" came through the speakers, he slid inside me. Slowly. Carefully. Lovingly.

"You okay?"

"Yes," I breathed. "Yes." He felt so good inside me. So big.

As my hips bucked up, he pushed forward, until we fell into a slow but steady rhythm that coordinated with the climax of the Foreigner song.

My heart was racing too fast, and my breathing was too quick to keep up with the slow pace. But as I pushed up, Clinton thrust faster and, when he knew I could take it, harder, until the song disappeared around us and all that could be heard were Clinton's grunts and his name escaping my lips.

As if Clinton had timed it himself, he fell to my side as Lionel Richie began professing his endless love to Diana Ross. The exact words to express how I felt about Clinton.

He kissed my temple and then held me until our heartbeats returned to normal. Once they did, he grabbed his tee shirt and removed the rubber, wrapping it inside the shirt and carefully placing it on the floor next to the bed.

"Tia?" he asked, bringing his hand to my face.

"Yeah?" I asked, still euphoric.

"I thought there was supposed to be...blood...the first time."

Oh my God. Oh crap.

"Tia?" His hand abruptly left my face.

Tucking in my lips, I closed my eyes.

The air next to me became cool. He was sitting at the edge of the bed when I opened my eyes.

I sat up and covered myself with the crumpled sheets.

"I'm not your first." I could barely hear him.

"No."

His back was to me, but I swear, I heard his heart breaking into tiny pieces. Or maybe...I *felt* it.

"I'm sorry," I said, already forming tears and a knot in my throat.

Taking the sheets with me, I moved behind Clinton and put my hand on his back.

He shrugged it away. "Don't."

"Clinton." My throat wanted to close up, but I forced out words despite it. "That's not fair."

His shoulders rose and fell. Up. Down. Up. Down.

Up.

Down.

"I purposely..." Up. Down. "Held back." Up. Down. "Until you were eighteen."

"I know," I whispered.

"I was trying to protect you."

"From what?"

Finally, he turned around. "From yourself."

"Nobody asked you to."

This was getting really upsetting. Our first time together was supposed to be special. Now he was just making me feel dirty.

"You don't get it, Tia."

I made sure I was totally covered by the sheet before I got out of bed and started picking up my clothes and putting them on. "Open Arms" was finishing up over the speakers. "What don't I get, Clinton? Tell me. Because Heaven knows, you're *so* much smarter than me, and you're *so* much wiser, be-cause you're *so* much older."

"Stop it, Tia."

"You started it. You started it." I was half crying, half screaming.

And then I heard it. That song. That goddamn Boston song. "And what's *this* all about?" I yelled, pointing to his stereo. If you'll never love me like I love you, why the hell make love to me tonight?" I couldn't keep my voice down. "Why the hell be mad at me because I'm not a virgin? And why the hell put this goddamn song on the tape you made for having sex with me? Why, Clinton? Why...all those things...why?"

I stopped. I couldn't listen to the song any longer. Eject-ing the tape with a forceful finger, I tore it out of the player, ripped the tape right out of the cassette, and threw it at him.

"Tia, calm down."

I ran over to him, kicking him in the shins just like the little girl I was.

"Stop it."

Then I punched him in his chest. Right fist. Left fist. Right.

I was punching the man I loved.

Just like his father had.

Just like his brothers had.

I was no better than them.

He grabbed the tops of my arms and pushed me against the door to stop me from thrashing. "Tia, get a hold of your-self," he yelled.

"Everything okay in there?" an unfamiliar male voice asked from the other side of the door.

"Yeah," Clinton said, calm as anything. "We're good."

"Ooh," I said in frustration. I pulled away from his grasp and unlocked his door.

Showing myself to a room full of people—Lindy, Rita, Trisha, Henry, and some guy I'd never seen before.

Oh my God. Great.

All five of them were staring at us.

"Clinton," Lindy said. "Clothes."

Clinton was still naked. "Shit," he said and slammed the door.

Rita and Trisha said they'd be downstairs and left. Henry said he was right behind them. Lindy and the other one busied themselves around the apartment, pretending to ignore Clinton's infuriated, jilted lover.

When he came out of his room, Clinton had on only his Levi's. Nothing else. Not even underwear, because his button was unbuttoned and his zipper was barely zipped, showing his dark curls for all the world to see.

"You okay, Clinton?" Lindy asked, all sweet and caring.

The guy I didn't know eyed Clinton, then me, then Lindy.

It suddenly clicked. "Why'd you have sex with me tonight, Clinton?"

The other two sucked in a breath. When I turned to look at them, Lindy was looking at Clinton. The nameless guy made himself scarce by going into the kitchen.

"Let's go back in my room, Tia."

"No. I wanna know. Why? When it's obvious you're already fooling around with someone else."

Lindy quickly followed the other guy into the kitchen. "Michael, let's go downstairs. C'mon." Lindy and the guy she called Michael rushed out of the apartment like bats out of hell.

"Tia. Please. Calm down."

"You're seeing her, aren't you?"

"Who?"

"Lindy. I saw the way she was looking at you."

"No, Tia, I'm not seeing Lindy."

"Stop being so condescending. Why did you have sex with me tonight?"

"Because."

"Because why?"

"Because I, I wanted..." His shoulders dropped. "I wanted to see..." He didn't finish.

"Wanted to see what?"

"When, Tia? When did you...lose it?"

"Lose what?"

"Your virginity."

I paced the room, not knowing where the hell to go or what the hell to do. "That's not answering my question."

"I'll answer yours after you answer mine."

"I asked first."

"Tia." He raised his voice again. "Was it this past year when we weren't together?"

I didn't mean to, but I nodded.

He clutched his chest and sunk to the floor, leaning his back against the TV stand. "It was my fault."

"What was?" I asked, stopping mid-pace.

"Because I wasn't around, you gave yourself to a stranger," he said so low I could hardly hear him.

"It wasn't a stranger, Clinton, jeez. I'm not a whore. It was one time."

"Who with?"

I rolled my eyes. "Why do you care?"

He banged the back of his head against the TV screen. "Goddammit, Tia. I *always* care. *I* was supposed to be your first. Just like *you* were my first."

It was good the back of the couch was in front of me, because I needed it for support. "What?"

"You were *my* first."

"Ever?"

"Ever."

I bowed my head and walked around to the couch to sit.

"Who were you with, Tia?" His eyes were closed.

"Bobby...Bennett."

Clinton's face contorted in pain. "No," he mouthed, sound not escaping his lips.

"I went back to Jersey this summer. Stayed with Najia."

His eyes still closed, he brought his fist to his mouth. "Why couldn't you answer my calls?"

When I didn't answer, he opened his eyes to look at me. They were as red and teary as mine felt. "Did you not love me anymore?"

"My God, Clinton," I answered right away. "I never *stopped* loving you. How can you even ask that?"

"Because you let him have you... You gave away something I was saving..."

"It wasn't yours to save. It was mine, remember?"

With a mirthless laugh, he said, "But...it makes me sad."

"Why?"

"Because. It's something I wanted to share with you. If I couldn't give you anything else, I wanted to give you that. I waited for you."

"Did you, like, have a choice? Like, a chance, to be with someone else?"

He nodded. "Yes."

"Like, were you *seeing* someone else this year?"

"Yes," he said honestly. A matter of fact.

"Lindy?"

He shook his head. "No, Tia. Not Lindy."

"One of the other girls downstairs?" Not that I saw chemistry there at all.

"No."

"Do I know this person or is it someone you just met or are you going to let me ask twenty questions before you tell me?" I asked in one breath. "Are you in love?" I asked in the next.

"No. I love only you. That's the honest truth."

"So, it's not serious?"

"We don't know yet."

"Yet?" I stood up.

So did he.

"Yet? You had sex with me knowing you were still in a relationship with someone else? How could you do that? And who? Who, Clinton? I spilled my guts. Now *you* need to tell me who *she* is."

"Sit back down, Tia."

"No."

"Sit."

"Why? She's someone I know, isn't she? It *is* Lindy. I knew it."

He sighed.

"It *is*."

"No. It's not."

"Then who?"

He took me by the shoulders and guided me down onto the couch. Then he sat down on the coffee table in front of me.

"Stop evading the question, Clinton. Who the hell are you going out with?"

He stared at me for what seemed like forever before he said, "Michael."

CHAPTER EIGHTEEN

"The Great Pretender"

T IA

"Wait. What? Who's... Oh my God. That..." There was no way I could form a coherent sentence.

"Henry's cousin. The club bouncer. My new roommate. I'm gay, Tia."

My one hand covered my mouth. The other, my heart. My stomach was rebelling against the news. I got up and darted to the bathroom, where I threw up yellow bile, along with my dreams of marrying Clinton.

Hugging the bowl, mid-puke, my hair disappeared from my face. Clinton was holding it back. "I've been trying to find a way to tell you for years."

I sat back on my heels, and Clinton pulled toilet paper off the roll and wiped the vomit off my mouth. "For *years*?"

He pulled out a brush from the drawer and started brushing my hair while he sat behind me on the tub. Pulling out my legs from underneath me, I sat cross-legged between his legs.

"I've been so confused for many years," he began, stroking my hair slowly with the brush. "I didn't think I *could* be, you know. I don't fit the stereotype. Well, I don't think I do anyway."

If he did, *I* didn't know it.

He continued stroking the brush through my hair. "And I love *you* so much. That's another part of what has me so confused." He paused in speaking, not in brushing. "I want to be around you all the time. This past year has been so...just terrible without you. I was walking around with half my heart, 'cause you were holding the other half. I couldn't understand why, then, I was...*feeling* certain things when I'd be around certain, certain...*people*...of my same sex.

"My father knew it. My brothers too. They'd been calling me a faggot since I can remember. Anytime my father even *thought* about me being a fag, as he called me, he'd hit me. The night he threw me out the window? He found me looking at a magazine. One that had men in it."

My stomach rumbled again, the nausea building up through my esophagus. I lunged for the toilet, and Clinton pulled back my hair as I threw up again.

"I spent a lot of time doing the same thing, Tia," he admitted quietly as I continued to dry heave over the toilet.

The man I dreamed about spending my entire life with would never feel the same way about me.

Oh my God.

I sat back, this time turning to look at him. "That song. You were trying to tell me..."

He nodded.

I sighed and leaned my head on his thigh. He replaced the brush-stroking with his hand.

"I'm sorry, Tia. I tried. I tried not to be."

Lifting my head, I asked. "Wait. Then why'd you have sex with me tonight?"

"Don't say it like that. We made love. I *loved* being with you tonight."

"You *loved* it? Isn't that a contradiction? Are you bisexual?"

"I don't think so, Tia. I don't get those *feelings* for girls. Except..."

"Then, why?" I interrupted. "Why tonight? You said the other day you wanted to try a physical relationship with me. Why?"

"Because." He sighed. "I told Michael I couldn't *be* with him until you and I...until I at least *tried* with you."

"Tried?"

"To see if those sexual feelings would surface. I mean, sometimes, I feel so close to you that..."

"Wait," I interjected again. "You *used* me?"

"No, Tia. I didn't use you. I..."

"You used me." I stood and dry heaved again. Nothing was coming out, so I stormed out of the room.

"Tia, please." He followed. "I need you to talk about this with me. I've been dying to get this out. Please."

"I'm sure you've talked about it with Michael."

"Not like I need to. Not the things I need to say to you. Tia..."

"No. No. You had sex with me just to *see* if you were or were not gay. That's using me. And that's worse than letting Bobby *screw* me for three whole minutes."

His fist went to his mouth again, his other hand to his stomach.

So, that's it—he had been nauseated when I talked about losing my virginity to Bobby. "Good. Now you know how it feels to hear the person you love has been with someone else. Oh. Wait. You don't. Because you don't love me the same way I love you."

"Tia, I *do* love you. More than anything."

"You love me like a father loves a child. That explains everything. Ew. So you just had sex with someone you think of as a daughter. Gross."

"I *don't* think of you like that, Tia. At all. I'm protective of you, but I don't..." He stopped. He remembered.

"'Because maybe that's how I see myself in your life.' Remember, Clinton? Those were *your* words last year. Not mine."

He stood there, hands at his side, beautiful chest exposed, his jeans still unzipped. Even his bare feet were sexy as hell. "Tia, you didn't even let me tell you what making love to you tonight did for me."

My heart couldn't take anymore. "I can't handle the truth. I don't want to hear it." I opened his door to leave.

"You can't leave, Tia."

"Watch me." I walked out and down the stairs.

I was about sixty seconds down the road when Clinton, now dressed in a blue tee shirt, his pants buttoned and zipped, still barefoot, stopped me. "I'm driving you home."

"No. I'd rather walk."

"No. It's late. It's dark..."

"You're not my father. Leave me alone."

"Then let me call your father. You can sit on the front steps while you wait."

"You'll stay inside?"

He nodded.

"Go 'head." I really didn't want to walk ten miles in the dark. I just didn't want to be around Clinton.

Fifteen minutes later, Dad pulled into Clinton's driveway. "What happened?" he asked when I got in his truck.

"I don't wanna talk about it."

"Tia. What hap—"

"Dad. No."

Dad never asked me again what happened that night, but my guess is Clinton told him. I heard my father on the phone with him a few days later. My phone had been torn out of my wall. By me. And when Clinton came to visit me, I locked myself in my room after begging Mel and Tommy not to let him see me.

After I'd spent days in my room again, not unlike last year, I wrote him a letter telling him how much he'd hurt me, and I told him I never wanted to see him again. And if he ever tried to contact me, I'd tell my father that he'd raped me against my will. That's what I wrote. It was mean, but I had to make it clear how adamant I was about him contacting me—via phone call, letter, or physical visit. And I also made him my own mix-tape. The first song I put on it was "Goodbye to You" by Scandal. Then I had a ball adding "Separate Ways," "Missing You," "Tainted Love," "I Will Survive," "Go Your Own Way," "Dancing with Myself," and then of course, I added "The Breakup Song" as my last screw you to Clinton, since I had a feeling he'd remember me playing it on the jukebox for Eric. Before I sealed the package, I took out my earrings and stuck them in. Yes, I was a baby. An eighteen-year-old, scorned, bitch of a baby. And then I mailed it.

Two days later, and way too soon for him to have been responding to my nasty letter, I think, I received a cassette tape, sans any written correspondence. I stuck it in the stereo in my room that Dad and Mel had bought me for Christmas.

Brian May's twelve-string guitar graced the speakers.

No.

He was not going to make me hate Queen.

"Love of My Life." One of my favorite songs, and Clinton had to send it to me. Now anytime I heard it, I'd think of him. And *hate* the song.

Love of his life? Yeah, right.

I'd hurt him? Wrong. He'd hurt me.

I'd broken *his* heart? No. He'd broken *mine*.

I dropped to the floor, put myself in the fetal position, and cried. Again. My body must have held a ton of water, because *The Love Boat* could have sailed to Puerta Vallarta on my recent tears alone.

When the song ended, it started again. Three minutes and thirty-one seconds later, it replayed. Then again. When it played a fifth time, I let out a scream so loud, my throat burned afterward.

"Tia." My father came barging into my room. "Oh, baby," he said, kneeling next to me. "This has to stop. It's been two weeks, honey."

"Tia?" Mel came in and sat on my bed. "Tia, sweetheart. Come on. Get off the floor. Get on the bed, please."

Dad continued rubbing my arm. "This is crazy, Tia. That boy loves you so hard."

I shrugged my arm away from my traitor father.

"He's right though, Tee," Mel said cautiously. "Clinton loves you so much."

I sat up and leaned against the bed. "You can both leave my room now."

"Is this Queen?" Dad asked.

"Yeah. He thought it'd be funny to send a tape with the same song playing on it over and over." I wiped my eyes with the back of my already soaked hand.

My dad laughed. "He doesn't think it's funny, Tia. He's begging you to come back. Listen to the words. He's saying you left him. Deserted him."

"What?" I yelled. "*He* deserted *me*." I brought my hand to my face and covered it. "I can't take this anymore. It's making my head hurt."

"Let me get you some aspirin," Mel said.

When she left, my father said, "He's heartbroken, Tia. I feel his pain. I do."

I just stared up at my dad through my fingers that were still holding my face.

"Your mother was the love of my life too. I told you that. And even though I left her, she's the one who broke my heart. I was lost for so many years after that. It's like she took my home right out from under me. She was my home, Tia. And she left me homeless, figuratively." He paused. "But this isn't about me. It's about you."

"I'm sorry that she did that to you." Especially after knowing now what I read in that letter I got from the lawyer. After hearing how much she meant to him, I could never let him find out the truth.

"It's water under the bridge. But listen to me, honey. Clinton told me about his being gay. But he also told me how much he loves you."

"But...I love him differently. I can't see him, knowing I can never have him. Like, as my boyfriend. I wanted to spend the rest of my life with him."

Mel knocked on the door.

Tommy told her to come in.

"Thanks," I said when she handed me water and the aspirin.

"Tee," my father said. "You'd rather have Clinton out of your life completely than love him as he is?"

"Well." I don't know. When he put it that way.

"Unconditional love doesn't put conditions on relationships."

Mel sat on the bed behind me and stroked my hair.

"But...I'm *in* love with him, Daddy. How can I see him with someone else?"

"I suppose that would be difficult, but he came to me in tears, sugar plum. It took a lot of courage for him to tell me he was a homosexual, you know." My dad waited for a response from me, but when he didn't get one, he said, "You know what I think?"

I shook my head.

"You're being selfish."

"Tommy," Mel scolded.

"I'm not saying you don't have a right to feel like you're feeling, but this boy, gay or not, moved across the country to be with you. Some husbands and wives wouldn't even be that flexible. He uprooted his life to be with you. He even promised you the relationship *you* wanted when you turned eighteen, and he kept that promise."

"How much did he tell you?"

"Everything? I'm not really sure. There may have been stuff he left out, I wouldn't know, but I met him last week at the diner. He never wanted to stop seeing you."

"What about Michael?"

"I'm sure he wants to talk to you about this himself, but Michael was his turning point. Maybe there was some passion there."

"He said that?"

Tommy nodded. "But there wasn't love, sweetheart. You need to talk with him about this. I made the mistake of running and not talking things over with your mother." He looked at Mel. "I'm sorry."

"Don't apologize," she said. *Did I ever mention how much I adore Mel?*

"Don't run, Tia. It's one of my biggest regrets."

"I think I need to sleep." I hadn't in two weeks, and I was really feeling it now. My head was foggy because of it.

"Sure."

They helped me up, and Mel tucked me into bed. Just like my mom did when I was a kid.

"Thank you," I told her, grateful for her love.

As soon as my head hit the pillow, I knew tonight would be a restful night. Because tomorrow...

I would hear Clinton out.

Thank you, Dad, for helping me see straight.

I SHOWED UP AT HIS apartment 8:00 a.m. sharp, figuring if he'd already left for class, I'd just sit on his front step and wait. His car was not in the driveway. So I waited.

Not fifteen minutes went by before Lindy walked out the front door.

"Tia?"

"Hey." I stood to greet her.

"What's going on?" she asked, her expression one of genuine confusion.

I didn't trust her, but I said, "Waiting for Clinton to come back from class."

She scoffed. "Guess you haven't heard. Clinton left."

"What?"

At that moment, Michael walked out, his books in hand. I felt my hands shake, so I stuck them in the too-tight front pockets of my jeans to still them.

"Tia," he said, surprised. "Is Clinton all right?" He sounded worried.

"She came here *looking* for Clinton."

"Oh." He paused. "Tia, come inside, okay?"

"What's going on?"

"I'll leave you to her, Mike. Gotta get to class."

Michael led me up the stairs. "Coffee?"

"No. Please, just tell me where he is."

Michael pulled out a chair for me to sit, then sat across from me at the kitchen table. "He wouldn't say where he was going. He's so close-lipped. But he got a letter in the mail two days ago, then packed a bag and took off."

"Letter? I don't understand."

"He was really distraught when he read it. He folded it up, slipped it in his pocket, and said he had to get outta here. I've been upset since."

I sat back in my chair and sighed. "Oh my God."

"Do you have any idea, Tia? I'm really worried. He was so...beside himself." Michael was soft-spoken. Kind, it seemed. His face was pleasant and exuded goodness. His dimple was deep, even as he frowned.

"I sent him a letter three days ago. He probably got it the next day."

"What did it say?"

I wanted to die, right there and then. "It said I hated him." Choking back a lump of guilt, I continued. "I told him I never wanted to see him again, and he hurt me so bad. Oh my God. Where could he have gone?"

Michael reached out, placing his hand over mine. "You said what you needed to say because you were hurt. I think he knows you don't hate him. Tia, something tells me it wasn't your letter that sent him over the edge."

"Then what?"

"I don't know. I'm hoping he calls to tell us he's okay. That's all we can do."

I dropped my head in my hand. "This can't be happening." I felt like I would go crazy, but I didn't know this person, and I didn't want him to think I was a lunatic. But I really wanted to scream. Or throw something. Or take off running because my insides were trying so hard to jump out of my body. My head was pounding, and I suddenly felt like I needed to throw up, or pass out, so this night could end already.

"Hey, Tia. You look green. Why don't you lie down."

"I'm okay." I wasn't. My insides were going to implode any minute.

"If anything were to happen to you here, and Clinton found out, he'd kick my ass." Michael got up and helped me to the couch. "You look like you're gonna pass out."

"I'm fine. Can I just have some water?"

He was back in a flash with my water, and then he sat next to me and watched me drink the water.

"I'm good now," I said, putting my glass down on the coffee table and standing.

"Tia, please sit."

Why? What did I possibly have to say to him?

"Please. Maybe the two of us together can figure out where he went."

"Why? So you and he can get back together?" I don't know where that came from, because I *did* want to figure out where Clinton had gone. I wanted to know he was okay. I wanted him to know I didn't hate him. And I wanted to apologize to him over and over for turning my back on him when he'd needed me most—to understand, to love him...with no conditions.

I sat down despite my snide remark.

"We're not getting back together, Tia. He ended things before they ever really began."

I turned my head to face him.

"When he went to see you, before your eighteenth birthday, he'd stopped what we had started." Michael shrugged.

"Did you guys, like, you know?" I know Clinton said I was his first, but maybe that didn't include having sex with a guy.

He shook his head. "No, Tia." His tone was so much like Clinton's. His blonde hair and fair complexion was a stark contrast to Clinton's dark hair and olive tone, but his kind and noble and mature demeanor was nearly identical. "Clinton's...not ready for that. He's just figuring all this out. I wouldn't take advantage of him like that."

"You...you've been..." I swallowed back my words.

"I've known I was gay since I was twelve. Never even looked at a girl."

"Do you think Clinton's...not?"

"He's confused. About how he can be gay but in love with you."

"So, maybe he's not gay, then." I was hopeful.

"Does it matter? If he loves *you*, then does it matter what his sexual preference is?"

"Is he really in love with me?"

"Yes. Without a doubt, darlin'. He's been walking around here like a man's who's lost his will to live. Even before that letter, all he did was lie in bed. Skipped so many classes. And drinking. That boy drinks way too much."

Standing up, my back straight, I declared, "We gotta find him."

He stood as well and pulled me close. "We will."

CHAPTER NINETEEN

"Sleeping on the Sidewalk"

T IA

We didn't.

"I went to see Cal Burke today," my father mentioned when I came to the dinner table.

It was December twenty-first. Clinton's twenty-third birthday. He and I never seemed to be together on his birthday.

"Clinton officially withdrew from his classes," my father continued.

"Did he call?" I asked quickly. This was the first anyone had mentioned Clinton in a month.

Tommy shook his head. "No. He mailed Cal a copy of the letter he sent to the university. He pulled out of school completely."

"Was there a return address?"

"No, honey, I'm sorry. I even went to the Dean of his department. They're *all* concerned. Do you know he had a flawless GPA? Never scored anything less than perfect."

No, I didn't know. Clinton never bragged, but I kind of figured.

"Sugar plum, I'm trying my best to find him. There's not much I can do. He's not considered a missing person, because he left his roommates of his own accord. I've given his license plate number to the authorities, but sweetheart, he's not a priority to them."

"Tommy," Mel said. "Don't." To me, she said, "Tia, eat. You need to keep up your strength."

My father's expression changed. Without the topic of Clinton being allowed, Tommy now had no choice but to face my other reality—I was gearing up for my first chemotherapy treatment. To start the day after Christmas. This coming Wednesday.

My mother's fate was quickly becoming mine.

I had brain cancer.

Just like my mom.

And according to my father, just like *her* mom. Another thing my mother had decided not to tell me. Evidently, my grandmother had died in her late twenties, when my mother was only seven years old, leaving her father to raise her alone. *My* mother had been fortunate, I suppose, to live to her late thirties. *Big deal, right?*

Well, I was probably not even going to get as lucky as either of them. According to my doctor, this type of brain cancer had been found hereditary in some families. Unfortunately, in my family, it seemed the females were the lucky victors.

That night at Clinton's, after Michael promised we'd find Clinton, I had passed out for real. That had led to some routine tests—just to rule out the improbable. The improbable had turned into a biopsy on a tumor they'd found sitting in the same exact place as my mother's. Only mine wasn't as large. *Chemo should shrink it enough to make surgery a fairly simple brain procedure.* That was what I was told.

But I knew the risks.

I had *lived* through the risks with Mom.

I hoped she was ready to have some company up there, because without Clinton in my life, I didn't even *want* to fight this thing.

Dad and Mel were *making* me.

However, I was eighteen now. I wasn't sure if they could *make* me do anything.

"I just need you to know, Tee, I contacted Lydia. She's putting in phone calls too. So, if he returns to New Jersey, she'll find out. I'm sure."

"Tommy. Really. It's upsetting her," Mel said, referring to my head resting on my folded arms on the table.

"She needs to know we're gonna bring Clinton back," he said, almost desperately.

Mel just sighed.

I lifted my head. Through my snot and tears, I said, "He isn't coming back. I told him I hated him and I never want to see him again. Don't you get it? He's gone for good. He left after he got a letter in the mail, Michael said. *My* letter," I screamed, repeating what I'd told them a thousand times.

"He's just cooling off," he continued.

"*Dad.*" I pushed back the chair, making a loud screech against Mel's new wood floor. "Just stop. He hates me. And I'm gonna die without him."

I went to my room and locked the door. It killed me to hurt Dad like that. He was always so good to me. But I couldn't take it anymore. I wanted to be alone and wallow in my bad luck by myself.

My room and the bathroom were the only walls I saw until Christmas morning. Mel asked me to please join them by the tree, since it would be confusing to Scott and David why I wouldn't want to see what Santa brought me. Mel never asked for much, and she was always so kind, so I complied.

Christmas Day was a nice day. Mel always went overboard with the gifts, so there was a total mess when we got through opening presents. Santa could follow a wrapping paper path across all of Oklahoma and Texas with what was splayed across our living room floor.

It was seven in the evening Christmas night when our doorbell rang. From my bedroom, I heard my father mumbling. A part of me got excited, hoping Clinton had decided to come home and make me whole again. I crept open my door to listen.

But it was Kelly's voice.

It wasn't Clinton, but I was happy to see my friend whom I hadn't seen since the summer.

When I walked out to greet her, she gave me the tightest hug. "I've missed you, Tee."

"Missed you too, Kell."

In my room, we sat on my bed chatting, just like we had on the rainy days when we were younger.

"So, your dad told my dad about your...you."

"My cancer?"

She nodded.

"When did you find out?"

"Well, essentially, two days before Thanksgiving. That's when it was confirmed. When they started running tests, though, I kinda figured. My mom had the same thing, and my father told me that her mom had it too."

"Oh man. Can they cure it?"

"They couldn't for them."

"I'm sorry, Tee. That sucks."

"Yeah. Not as much as Clinton leaving."

"My dad told me about that too. Were you guys talking again though? Last summer, you were broken up."

"Yeah. Well, he came back into my life four days before he left it again."

"Oh, Tee. What the hell? What happened?"

I couldn't tell her he was gay. I don't know why, but I just couldn't. "He was mad at me, because...I had sex with Bobby Bennett when I went out to New Jersey."

"But you weren't seeing Clinton then."

"I know. He wanted me to wait for him."

"You waited since you were what, fourteen?"

I laughed. "Yeah. Right? Screwy."

"I'm sorry, Tee."

"Eh. It is what it is." Covering up the mess I was inside exhausted me as much as the headaches my tumor gave me. "Listen, Kell, it's been a long day. Can you come back tomorrow?"

"Sure." She hugged me tight and said, "See ya tomorrow, girl. Love you."

TOMORROW NEVER CAME.

At least not the way it was supposed to.

In the middle of the night, tossing and turning, and fighting tears and headaches, and my fears of being sick like my mother, and losing my hair, I decided that, no, this wasn't happening.

I grabbed underwear, a few shirts, and two pairs of jeans and stuck them in my duffel bag. I dumped every mix-tape Clinton had ever made me into the bag and threw on the new Queen sweatshirt that Mel had specially made for me for Christmas. I took my keys, grabbed the envelope where I kept what was left of my thousand dollars, and quietly went out the side door.

I left home.

To go where?

I had no idea.

I headed out to the highway and went east. The drive would be longer that way. Plus, I think New Jersey was east. And even though Lydia had told Tommy she hadn't heard from him, who was to say she wasn't lying? If Clinton had asked her not to say anything, I knew she wouldn't. So, maybe I'd see for myself.

Luckily, Dad had installed the new stereo I bought back in the summer. I definitely needed it for this trip. Once, not too long ago, I had been so mad at Clinton Daniels that I never wanted to see him or hear from him again. Now *all* I could do was think about him. Think about finding him. Think about loving him. Think about the feel of my body clothed in just him. Without him, I was naked and bare, a lost soul without a place to call home.

I followed I-54 for a couple hours until my eyes couldn't take it anymore. Besides the throbbing headache behind them, I was quickly fading. At the next rest stop, I parked my car and slept, waking only when the sunlight broke through my front windshield. With what felt like a live Ozzy concert, "Crazy Train" the only song on the set list, going on inside my brain, I dragged myself out of the car and into the welcome area to go relieve myself. And hopefully find some aspirin.

"I'm sorry," the fifty-something-looking woman said when I asked about the aspirin. "We only have vending machines here. You'd have to take one of the exits to find a store that sells that."

"Okay, thank you. By the way, you wouldn't know how to get to New Jersey, would you?"

"Oh, no, dear. You're a long ways away."

"Yeah. I realize that. Thank you, though."

I was halfway to my car when the woman called out to me. "Miss, miss."

On a turn, I said, "Yes?"

"Here's a map of the United States. All the major highways are listed. Hopefully, it helps."

"Oh my goodness," I said with a tired smile. "Yes, it helps a great deal. Thank you."

From my rearview mirror, I saw her watching me leave the rest stop. I did a little finger wave then put in the Queen CD that Clinton had bought me for my birthday. "Radio Ga Ga," the perfect screw you to "Video Killed the Radio Star," came on first. When both sides of the tape were finished, I let it play through again, if only to hear "It's a Hard Life" again.

I lost myself in Freddie Mercury's voice as he took me east until my bladder wouldn't hold any longer.

Once it got dark again, and I couldn't handle the pain behind my eyes anymore, I pulled into a rest stop and slept again, but only until a banging on the window woke me up.

Startled, I grabbed my chest, ineffectively trying to calm it, then noticed it was a police officer.

"Miss?" he said as I rolled down the window. "Insurance, license, registration, please."

"Yeah, sure. Okay." I tried focusing to pull out what he needed.

"You're not supposed to use this rest area as an overnight stop. You need to find a motel or something."

I handed him my credentials. "Oh. I, uh, didn't know." The burning in my head reminded me of why I was here in the first place. "I had a really bad headache and was falling asleep at the wheel. This map—" I held it up for him to see "—doesn't tell me where hotels are."

"I understand. If you take a right at the next exit, there are a bunch on that highway. If you still need to rest before driving to one, go 'head, but you really need to leave as soon as possible."

"Okay. Thank you." He handed me back my stuff and sauntered away.

Though my head was pounding, I felt too uneasy now to sleep here, so I pushed up my seat and headed out to the highway again. But I took the cop's advice and found a motel off the next exit. Forty dollars for the night. It wasn't the fanciest, but it was clean, and the bed was comfy.

It was, however, the first time I've ever been alone, and it did kind of spook me a bit. After taking a long warm shower, which helped my headache some, I found sleep on this foreign mattress.

Ten in the morning, I headed back out, grabbing a cup of coffee and a roll with butter from the deli next door.

About five o'clock that night, I found another motel to stay in, because I was way too beat to continue on. Even with the more upbeat mix-tapes playing, I still had trouble keeping my eyes open.

After about a fourteen-hour nap, I got moving again and found myself in my old hometown sometime in the late afternoon. On my way towards Najia's house, the first person I'd stop to see—maybe she'd give me moral support and come find Clinton with me—I had an impulse. Making the next right, I went around the block to change directions. Back on the main road, though, I didn't see a street to get to where I wanted to go. I went around the block again, parked my car on the side street, and started the trek up the hill.

I couldn't tell where the entrance was, but I could see where I needed to be—way up on top of that hill.

Trespassing on property I did not belong, I cut through every path I could follow, stopping every now and then to catch my breath, until I was standing in front of the massive architecture. Like something from another time, it did not belong in Haledon, New Jersey.

I drew in a deep breath, exhaled courage, and stepped up the stone steps that led to the huge double doors. The sound of the doorbell chimes were as imposing as the building it was meant to welcome.

A boy a little older than me answered the door. "Hello," he said, happily enough.

"Hi." I stood there like a jackass, not knowing what to say. It wasn't like I had planned this. Nor had I contemplated this moment while climbing through the woods.

"Can I help you? Are you lost or something?" the green-eyed boy, *guy*, asked, his demeanor still pleasant.

I shook my head as I closed my eyes, wincing on a sudden shooting pain in my head.

"Miss, are you okay? Do you need..."

I nearly dropped to the ground, my knees buckling beneath me, but he caught me around the waist in time.

"Whoa, lady." He held my up and looked into my face. "When was the last time you ate anything?"

"Um." Trying to focus, I said, "Yeah, yesterday. Morning."

"Yesterday morning? Shit. No wonder you're passing out over here." He looked me up and down. "You don't look like an ax murderer or anything, so why don't you come in. I'll feed you."

Too stunned to say anything, I let him guide me inside. As we passed a huge sitting room, a shiny black grand piano sat mocking me, reminding me that I still needed to find Clinton, and it had probably been a mistake coming here.

The brown-haired, green-eyed boy led me to the kitchen, where he sat me at the table in his old-fashioned yet modernized kitchen. "Peanut butter and jelly good?" he asked as he retrieved the peanut butter out of a ceiling-high cabinet.

"Yes, thank you," I said quietly, anxious about sitting in this stranger's house.

While he was making the sandwich, he continued talking. "So, lady, what's your name, or should I just keep referring to you as lady?"

"My name's Tia."

"Nice to meet you, Tia. I'm Landon." He put a plate in front of me, the sandwich cut into two triangles.

"Thanks," I said before taking a bite. I'd never had a better tasting peanut butter and jelly sandwich.

He then put a tall glass of milk in front of me.

"Thanks," I mumbled again, the peanut butter sticking to the roof of my mouth.

Landon pulled out the chair across from me and sat. And stared.

I averted my eyes, and before I took another bite, I asked, "So, who plays the piano?"

"My dad. He's like a piano savant. Can hear a song and then immediately play it."

I nodded.

"So, why you here, Tia? Certainly not to ask about my piano."

I was about to tell him when the back door to the kitchen swung open. "Hello," a honey-brown brunette sang. "Landon?"

"Mom. Hey. Uh, this is—" Landon looked at me "—my friend. Tia." He kept looking at me. Into my eyes.

Even when his mother spoke, "Well, Tia, it's nice to meet you," he still stared at me. "Would you like to stay for dinner?"

I broke eye contact with Landon to answer his mother. "Uh, no. No, thank you. I, I need to get going anyway."

After bringing my plate and empty glass to the sink, I thanked Landon and let myself out the way I had come in.

Landon followed me.

"Yo, Tia."

Not turning around to face him, I kept walking down the hill. "It was a mistake coming here. I'm sorry."

"Tia." He cupped my shoulder and spun me around. "Sit with me."

"I'm sorry. This was a mistake."

"Says the girl who has my father's emerald-green eyes and bright red hair."

"Oh."

"Yeah. Now will you just sit with me a few minutes?" Once we made it back to the stone steps, he asked me, "So, are you or are you not my half-sister?"

"Do I really have your father's eyes?"

"And hair. I mean, thank goodness I was spared the red hair." He winked. "But yeah. You do. So, wanna tell me what you know?"

With my focus on the view of Haledon and Paterson below me, I said, "My mother died a couple years ago, and she never told me that my father was not my father." I sighed quite audibly. "She led me to believe he just walked out of my life for the hell of it."

"Wow."

"Yeah." I nodded. "Crazy shit, right?"

"Oh yeah."

"Anyway, she wrote a letter that I only got after her estate was closed...this past summer. In the letter, she named *your* father as my biological father. She said she couldn't let anyone know because your father was...esteemed and all that, and it would crush *my* father—the one who *thought* I was his daughter. He believed I was his for almost five years...until he was told he was sterile and always had been."

"Ouch."

"Yeah. I kinda felt betrayed, ya know? First, by Tommy, my dad. Then by my mom." I looked at Landon. "She knew she was dying. Why couldn't she tell me herself? Before she died?"

"You found out in the letter?"

I turned my attention back to the view, which was breathtaking when I noticed the New York skyline lit up across the river twenty miles out. I hugged my knees to my chest.

"Are you getting cold? You should come inside."

"No, I'm good. If you're cold, go on in. I'll go back to my car." I jutted my chin in the direction of the street where I had parked my car.

"No. If a girl can handle the cold, *I* certainly can," he joked. "Anyway. She told you in the letter?"

"Yes, but that's how I found out *who* my biological father was. She left it up to poor Tommy to tell me I wasn't his when he took over custody."

"Oh. Poor Tommy. I gather you're in good graces with him now?"

I nodded, my chin dipping into the space between my knees. "Though I'm not sure he's so happy with *me* at the moment."

"Why?"

"I ran away."

"From where?"

"Um." I shook my head, suddenly feeling an odd sensation. "Oklahoma. Texhoma."

"Texhoma? Where the hell is that?"

There was an emptiness in my head. An empty, dizzying feeling. I put my head in my hands.

"Tia? You okay?"

"Yeah. I better go."

The last thing I remembered was stepping down one step.

THE PAIN IN MY FACE was excruciating. When I touched my cheek, I cringed. Then I felt gauze. Padding my fingers across my face, I realized that the entire region below my eyes was covered with it.

"You took quite a fall. I'm sorry I couldn't stop you."

Landon. As a sharp pain radiated in my temple, I winced then asked him what had happened.

"You said you had to go, then fell face first off the steps."

"Oh, God. Well, *that's* embarrassing."

"So, you're a clutz. Big deal. Sorry you broke your nose though."

"I did?"

"Mm hmm. At least you didn't knock your teeth out."

"How'd I get here?"

"Ambulance. You were unconscious. My mom followed it up."

"Oh, God. Does she know?"

"No. She's still under the impression you're my friend...from school. But they *have* contacted your family through your driver's license. Someone named Melanie?"

"My step-mom. Oh jeez. Now Tommy's gonna find out."

"Sooner than you think. She told them he was already *in* New Jersey. Took the red-eye two nights ago."

"Oh, God."

"He called the hospital from a friend's house in Greenwood Lake. He's on his way."

"Shit."

"So's my dad."

"What? Why? We can't tell him now."

Landon laughed. "Nah. He's just coming to pick up my mom. She's gonna leave me her car. I took the ambulance with you."

"Whew. Okay. Please don't let them run into each other. He'll wonder why I was at your house, and then...oh, please. He'll definitely figure it out."

"Hopefully, they won't run into each other in the lobby."

"Shit shit shit."

"Tia?" an older-looking man in a white coat walked in. "I'm Doctor Dolan." He greeted both Landon and me and shook our hands. "We did an MRI when you came in. Are you aware you have a mass in—"

"Yes," I said quickly, interrupting his question.

"A mass?" Landon asked.

"So, you're taking care of this?" the doctor asked, obviously realizing I didn't want to discuss this in front of Landon.

"In the process."

"Okay. Because it's the reason you fell."

"Oh." I didn't realize that could happen.

"You're under the care of an oncologist in Oklahoma?"

"Texas. Yes."

"Miss, I know you're eighteen, but do you have a guardian with you? Or are you dealing with this alone?"

I flitted my eyes toward Landon then back to the doctor. "I believe my father's on his way."

"Okay. Because I can't release you until I've spoken with your doctors in Texas."

Shit. The pillow crunched when I sagged deeper into it. *A crunchy pillow. How comfy.*

"Can you give me a list of your doctors in Texas?"

"No. I'm sure my father could. He's been scheduling all my appointments."

"All right. I'll be back."

Dammit.

"What's going on, Tia?" Landon asked.

"Nothing. Just headache stuff."

"Yeah. A *mass* in your brain will do that."

"How do you know it's my brain?"

"When they were taking you in, they told me they were doing an MRI on your brain."

"Well, it's nothing."

"How'd your mother die?"

I stared at him. No need to answer.

"Shit, Tia. Are you dying?"

It took a few seconds to respond, but I did. "Probably."

"She's right in here, Mr. Mercury," a female's voice uttered from the hall.

Landon's eyes grew as large as mine felt.

"Tia." Dad ran to my side and gathered me into his arms. I felt him crying on my shoulder. "I'm sorry, Dad."

Squeezing the back of my neck, he said, "All you had to do was ask. I would have flown out here with you."

"I'm...I know."

He unwrapped his arms from me and looked at my face. "Holy hell, Tia. What did you do?"

"Fell down a step."

"*A* step? As in *one*?"

"She fell down a huge stone step, which kinda sloped downward," Landon spoke. Darn him.

"Hello."

"I'm her friend."

"Oh." To me, Dad said, "I can't believe you came out here looking for Clinton. When did you get here? And how could you drive so far in that car? You know, thank goodness there are some curious cops out there. I had two of 'em contact me."

"How?"

"Rest stops. One state got a call from a welcome center. Another caught you sleeping in your car. They both said something seemed off about the situation."

"Oh."

"Yeah. Oh. Never mind you skipped out on your chemo treatments. It's dangerous for a girl your age to travel this far alone. Tia, I wish you could see this from my point of view. No boy is worth risking your life."

"Clinton is," I disagreed.

Dad looked at Landon again. "Can you give us some privacy?"

"Oh, sure. I'm sorry."

"Be nice to him, Dad."

"I am nice. I'm pissed at you."

"I'm sorry."

"Clinton's not here, Tia. I went straight to Lydia's from the airport. She hasn't heard from him."

"Is she covering for him?"

"I don't think so. She let me spend the night. She helped me make phone calls. No one's seen him. Not even his father."

"You saw his father?"

"No. Lydia went to see him in jail. He hasn't been by. He even gave her the number to the boys' trailer out in New York state. They hadn't heard either."

"They live in a trailer?"

"According to Lydia, they all lost their jobs at the factory. They had a hunting trailer up there. Sold their house, moved into it."

"Where could he be, Dad?"

"I don't know, honey. But we have to worry about *you* first. Your health. So that when he does come around again, you'll be here." He shook his head and sighed. "I'm gonna go call Mel. Let her know I'm here."

"Okay. Oh. The doctor needs to contact my doctors in Texas."

"Yeah. I spoke to the nurse outside."

Landon came in after Dad walked out.

"Did your mom leave yet?"

"No. My dad hasn't come yet."

"I hope they don't run into each other."

"Tia," he said slowly. "I was thinking."

"Hope it didn't hurt."

"Ha ha. Seriously. If you're...this sick...maybe my father has a right to know about you."

"No," I said with gritted teeth, which killed my jaw.

"Tia, he should know. And you must have wanted him to. I mean, you rang our doorbell, for goodness' sake."

"Landon?" I did not recognize that voice.

A second later, a tall, greyish-red-haired man walked around the curtain.

"Dad," Landon said, surprised.

"Yeah. Hey. I came to get Mom. I just wanted you to know." The man looked at me and smiled. "Hi. I'm so sorry you fell on our steps. We'll pay your medical bills. It's the least we can do."

"Oh, no. It was. It...it...it was my fault." I did not know how to talk to this man. This...stranger...who was my biological father.

"My wife said your name's Tia."

"Yes, sir." I tried not to look directly at him, keeping my gaze on my hands on my lap, for fear he'd see his own eyes in mine. If Landon could recognize them, he may too.

"That's an uncommon name. I've heard it only once before."

I nodded, wondering if my mother had ever mentioned me to him.

"Professor Cavill?" My father had entered the room, but since my head was down, I hadn't even realized it.

"Yes?" Landon's father tilted his head when he saw him.

"Tommy Mercury." I saw Professor Cavill's eyes widen. "I used to take your classes. Attended those poetry sessions of yours up at your castle with my girlfriend, Tammy Longo." As my father spoke, he reached out his hand in greeting.

"Yes. Yes. Of course I remember you," Professor Cavill responded in kind. "How are you?"

"I'm good. Good. Um, Professor Cavill..."

"Landon, please." I guess my half-brother was a junior.

"Landon, this is my daughter, Tia. Tia, you remember I mentioned going to those poetry readings up at that castle I showed you?"

After a swallow, I smiled a tight smile. "Yeah, I remember."

"How *is* Tammy?" Professor Cavill asked with a longing smile.

"Oh, she passed a couple years ago. We had been divorced already."

My stomach was hurting now as much as my head and my face.

"I'm sorry to hear that. She was the most beautiful creature."

"Yeah...she was," my father said warily.

"Wow." The professor looked like he was enjoying a nice memory or two.

"Uh, Tia," my father said, looking from me to Landon Jr. "Your friend?"

Young Landon said, "My name's Landon also, sir."

With narrowed eyes, Dad addressed the professor and spoke slowly, as if he was speaking the words as he thought them. "So, you already know my daughter?"

"No, son, not at all. My wife said she'd been at the house when she got home."

"You were at Professor Cavill's house?" my father asked me, his brows knitting while his eyes narrowed.

I nodded, my heart traveling my esophagus up to my throat. I felt it lodge right in the center of it, stopping my breaths from flowing freely.

"Uh, Dad," Landon Jr. Said. "Mom's waiting and all." Landon sensed my extreme discomfort, I'm sure.

"Sure," his father responded, clueless to the change in Dad's demeanor.

I sure wasn't.

"Wait." My father held up his hand for them to stay put. "Tia, why were you at their house?" he asked, though I was pretty sure he'd caught on by now.

"Um..."

"Tia," he said louder.

"That letter Mom left me?"

"Yeah?"

"*He's* the one."

My father found the nearest chair and sat, his head in his hand.

I remember Dad saying my mother had been the love of his life, so I'm sure his heart was breaking, at least a little, with the news of late.

"Thomas?" The professor was now concerned.

"You had an affair with my wife?"

Landon's father found the other empty chair in the room and plopped into it. "Tia?"

I nodded.

"Why didn't she ever tell me? She just stopped taking my calls."

"You bastard." My father stood.

The professor did too. "I'm sorry, Thomas. I am. Oh wow. Oh, Landon."

"Don't worry, Dad. I already knew," Landon said, smiling at me.

"Mom?" the professor asked his son.

"No. She doesn't have a clue."

"Oh my. She's waiting for me." He shifted from foot to foot, looking as if he was a mere innocent in this whole mess.

"Go to your wife, Cavill," Dad told him. "It's not like this changes anything."

"I loved her, Tia," Professor Cavill said to me. "I did. She wasn't even married yet. But I was."

"How long were you *screwing* her?" I had never heard my father say that word before.

"I remember the night she met you," the professor told my father. "The baseball game. She came to me that night. Asked me if I'd leave Debra. I couldn't. And not 'cause I didn't love your mother, Tia. I couldn't ruin my career. She was so much younger than me. Plus, Debra was pregnant with Landon by then."

Dad's face was bright red. On a growl, he asked, "How long did this continue?"

"Until she stopped taking my calls."

"You son of a bitch." *Wow, Dad was really mad.*

"Landon?" I asked. "Can you get him to leave?"

"Sure. C'mon, Dad."

The professor had tears in his eyes. "I'm sorry, Tia. Had I known, I would have been there. I'd like to still."

"Please leave. I already have a father." There was no way I was breaking my father's heart again.

"Dad, c'mon," Landon demanded again.

When the room was empty, I looked at my father. "I'm sorry, Dad. I shouldn't have gone there."

"No, Tia," my father said more calmly. "You were curious. That's natural. I'm just really pissed at your mother right now."

"Yeah. I kinda am too."

He sat on the bed, scooted close to me, and took my hand. "I'm not happy your mother died, but I'm glad it gave us the chance to reconnect. I'm sorry I was so stupid and lost that precious time with you. I can't lose you again."

"I love you, Dad."

"I love you, too, kid."

BECAUSE THE DOCTOR couldn't contact my Texas doctors at that time of night, he took my dad's word for it and released me, though Dad said they had no right keeping me anyway. He brought me to Lydia's to spend the night, telling me we'd worry about my car in the morning.

"Look at you, Tee," Lydia said when I walked into her house. "What did you do? You look almost as bad as Clinton did *last* year."

At that, I sighed.

"She fell," Tommy answered instead. "She needs her chemo. That tumor caused her to black out."

"You don't want the treatment, Tia?" Lydia asked, pulling out a chair at the dining room table. "Is that why you ran away?"

I sat. So did she and my dad.

"No, I don't want the chemo. But I also wanted to find Clinton. If I have the treatment, I'll be too sick to look for him. What if I never see him again?"

Lydia's hand covered mine. "I don't think he'd stay gone forever, Tee. Maybe he just had to figure things out."

"For almost three months?"

"Your father told me what happened."

"That he told me he was gay and I told him I never wanted to see him again?" I dropped my head into my hands—carefully, though; my face was killing me. "How could I do that? He's never coming back."

"He'll come back," Lydia assured. "Give him time."

"I don't have time," I whispered.

"Tia, don't say that," my father insisted. "I think it's time you get some sleep."

"Let me show you where you can sleep."

DAD AND LYDIA TOOK me to get my car the next morning. He didn't want me to drive anymore, not if there was a chance I'd black out again, so he was driving my car back to Oklahoma with me and returning his rental. But we wouldn't leave until the day after New Year's. This way, I could spend time with Najia. Mel didn't mind.

On my windshield was a note.

Tia,

I sure hope this is your car. I left one on every car from my house down Oxford Street. If this is you, here is my phone number. Use it. If it's not you, please throw it out, I don't need random callers.

Landon Matthew Cavill, Jr.

His number was at the bottom.

I already loved this half-brother of mine. *Crazy shit, right?*

"MAN, TEE, I CAN'T BELIEVE you drove your ass across the country by yourself. That takes balls," Najia said to me from the beanbag chair in the corner of her room.

Tasha was cuddled up next to me on Najia's bed. "It was stupid. It didn't take balls. I was scared. But I really thought Clinton would be here. Where could he have gone?"

"Could he have gone back to his family?"

"His dad's in jail."

"I mean his brothers. Maybe he went back to them."

"No, Lydia called them."

"Maybe they're lying. They're not the most trustworthy guys on the planet."

"Shit. Maybe. That would suck."

"Yeah, it would."

"I don't think he would though." My heart *knew* he wouldn't go back to them.

"Let's take Tasha for a walk. She likes the cold."

Outside, we walked past Clinton's old house. I felt a palpable sadness that I couldn't hide from Najia. The sight of the house brought back the conjured image of Clinton being thrown out his bedroom window like a bag of garbage—lying there, bleeding, until he could crawl into the house and call for help. I hadn't been there that night, but from two thousand miles away, I could practically feel his pain.

"He'll be back, Tee." Najia touched my back. "He can't stay out on his own forever."

That's when it hit me. "He *can*. Oh my God, Naj. Before me, Clinton said he couldn't stand people. Had no use for them. He's never coming back, Naj. Never."

She pulled me into her arms and hugged me. She was much shorter than me, but her hug was enormous. She didn't let me go until Tasha started barking at a passing car. "Okay, Tash. Cool your jets. I'm just hugging my girl here." Naj let go to take care of Tasha.

"Hey. That's *my* car," I said as the white Camaro pulled to the curb.

Dad got out.

"I thought I was sleeping at Naj's house tonight, Dad."

"Hi, Naj," he said.

"Hi, Mr. Mercury."

"You can if you want, sugar plum, but I got a call from Mel. Clinton came back."

"What? Oh my God. Where is he?"

"Probably his apartment. He came to the house to see you. Mel told him you were in Jersey. She told him to stay put, you'd be back after New Year's. She didn't tell him about the cancer."

I looked at Najia then at Dad. He shrugged. Then at Naj.

"Go. Get outta here," she said.

"I love you, Naj, but..."

"But it's Clinton. Go."

"Ya sure?"

"Go, Tee. Maybe you can get to him by New Year's Eve."

"Can we, Dad?"

"We'll be cutting it close, but I'll try."

"Oh my God, Naj. He's back." I shook her shoulders.

"Go get your stuff upstairs," Najia said.

"I got the stuff from Lydia's," Dad said.

Naj and I went up and were back in two minutes. At the car, I gave her a ginormous hug. "You're the best friend ever, Naj. I love you so much. I just want you to remember that always. Forever."

"Will you stop? You act like you're dying." Then I saw it in her expression. I *was* dying. Maybe she *wouldn't* ever see me again. Or I her. I had to be grown-up about this and not cry. No. I don't do that anymore.

But sometimes...the tears come all of their own accord.

CHAPTER TWENTY

"Good Old Fashioned Lover Boy"

TIA

Tommy dropped me off at Clinton's apartment at 8:26 p.m. New Year's Eve. We'd made it. He walked me to the door to make sure Clinton was actually there. Mel had called Clinton to tell him to expect me, but my father wanted to see for himself.

Of course, the girls were having a party downstairs, so there were hundreds (or less) of people hanging around.

Nerd alert: teenager crashing college party with her dad.

Part of me cringed, but the other part couldn't care less. I was reuniting with my best friend. The love of *my* life. Like the love of my father's life, Clinton may not have reciprocated the feelings, but I wasn't living the rest of my life, whatever was left of it, without him. I'd take him in any capacity he wanted me. Because I knew he loved me with all his heart, even if it wasn't romantically.

I heard the footsteps galloping down the stairs before the door flung open and Clinton gathered me up in his arms, lifting me so my legs wrapped around his waist, and he hugged me tighter than I'd ever been hugged. At least, in his large arms, it felt that way.

I wasn't sure how long we stayed like that, but when Clinton lowered me to the ground, my father was gone. As was my car.

My veins fired when Clinton took my hand and led me upstairs. It was quiet on his floor. Everyone must have been downstairs.

The memory of my last visit with Clinton came rushing back. Then the words I had written in his letter entered my mind. "Clinton, I am so sorry about what I said. I could never hate you. Ever." The words tumbled out non-stop. "You're the most important thing in my life, and if you're gay, then I'm just gonna have to deal with it. You're too important to not be in my life. I was so wrong to treat you like that when..."

"Whoa. Tia. Stop." He hugged me again. "I never for a minute thought you hated me. When I read your letter, I knew you were just angry and upset." He pulled back so he could see my face. "I knew you wouldn't stop loving me, just as I could never stop loving you. It's an impossibility. Like the sun never shining again. Or the Earth never again rotating. *We*, my darling, will always *be*. No matter how our relationship unfolds."

Always be.

I didn't want to ruin this moment with the truth. I couldn't. I wouldn't.

Brushing my fingers down his arms, I asked, "If you knew I didn't hate you, why'd you leave?"

He grabbed my ass cheeks with both his hands and lifted me onto his waist. Then he brought me into his room, shut his bedroom door and sat at the top of his bed, me, still straddling his lap. He swept my hair off my face and cupped my head in his hands. "Oh how I've missed you."

"I missed you, too, but that doesn't answer my question."

He laughed. *Oh how I'd missed that rolling, boyish laugh.* "I went to see my mother, Tia. If you can believe it." His hands dropped to my hips.

"How, when, how?"

He chuckled again.

I reached behind him and pulled off my Reeboks. His feet were already bare...and sexy.

"The day I received your lovely letter, I got another letter from a woman by the name of Shawna Bates. My mother. She'd legally changed her name so my rotten father couldn't find her. She showed me her birth certificate though. Diana Hughes. And her marriage license. Diana Daniels."

"What did the letter say?"

Clinton leaned his head back against the headboard but kept me on his lap and kept his eyes on mine. "She saw me on that news segment." Clinton the computer genius. "I guess it was a big deal."

"You *know* it was a big deal."

"Anyway, she heard my name, and when she saw my face, she just knew I was her son." He smiled. "It's crazy, Tia. I look exactly like her."

"She must be beautiful."

With the backs of his fingers, he brushed my cheek. "In the letter, she explained why she left. I mean, it sounded feasible, but I had to *see* and *hear* her say it to believe it, you know."

"What? Why?"

"Get this," he said on a snicker. "She told my father she was having feelings for a friend. She said she tried to talk rationally about it with him, but...Bill Daniels does not do rational. Shawna didn't cheat. She said she wouldn't have. But things were horrible with my father, and she turned to her friend and, I guess, she started shifting her feelings."

"Wow. Why would she leave *you*, though? If she wanted to divorce your dad, couldn't she have still taken her kids? At least her baby?" I was kind of mad at this lady at the moment.

"Well, according to her, she didn't want a divorce. She just wanted to be truthful with my father."

"So, she expected him to say, 'Oh, you like another man, no problem'?"

"No. I think she expected him to say, 'Oh, you're attracted to women? Well, maybe we should discuss this.'"

"Wait. What?"

"My mother's gay."

"Oh."

"And seeing how you reacted to *my* coming out, I'm sure you could guess Bill Daniels' reaction."

"What did he do?"

"He pulled a rifle on her."

"What?"

Clinton nodded. "When she threatened to take the kids, *he* threatened to kill us. Starting with me."

"Oh my God. Why didn't she go to the police?"

"Scared, I guess. He said if the cops ever did show up, he'd know it was her that called, and he'd shoot us and then himself before the cops got to the door."

"Really?"

"You know, Tia. I know she should have done what she could to save us from him. If I had children, I'd risk my own life for them. But who knows how some people react when confronted with their biggest fear. Fight or flight, right? She chose to run. I don't agree with her choice, especially knowing how dangerous that man was, but I forgive her. I don't want her in my life, but I do forgive her."

"Wow. Did she ever try coming back for you?"

"She said she did, but we weren't there. I had no idea we lived in Florida. I thought we always lived in New Jersey. But she didn't know where he'd gone. She thought he always lived in Florida, too. When I spoke to Lydia yesterday, she said Bill lived in Jersey until he was twelve. He didn't return until he brought us back."

"Do you believe she really looked for you?"

"I don't know. I'd like to think so, but, truthfully, it doesn't even matter to me anymore. *You* do."

"Why were you gone so long?"

"She lives in Manhattan. I stayed in the city for a while."

"*That's* where you were? New York City?"

"Yeah. Actually applied for some internships."

"Really? In New York?"

He nodded. "For next summer. I talked to Professor Burke earlier. He's gonna pull some strings to get me back into school for this semester."

"Well, that's good. I was sad when I heard you quit."

"I needed time to figure myself out. I didn't want to fail out of my classes; that would look horrible on my transcripts. So, I withdrew completely. I like New York though. Lots of opportunity there." He ran a hand around my neck, thumbing my nose as he did. "Do you think you'd mind New York? I could see myself living there, but not without you."

"I see myself wherever you are." I just hoped I'd live long enough to accompany him to New York. Maybe I shouldn't have skipped out on my chemo treatments. I needed to look at this differently. Fight for my life. Because Clinton was part of it, and he was worth fighting for.

"What's on your mind, Tia? You okay?"

"Yeah." I nodded. "More than okay." I reigned in the tears that were threatening to escape. "You know what though? I really have to pee."

"Well, go 'head," he said, laughing.

When I returned to his bedroom, we resumed the same position—my legs wrapped around him, his legs extended behind me.

"So, why were you in New Jersey?"

"Uh, looking for you." *Duh*.

"What? Mel didn't tell me that."

"No. Mel wouldn't say anything unless it was necessary."

"Good quality."

"Yeah. She's cool like that."

"I'm sorry, Tia. You two flew out there, and I wasn't even there. I feel so bad."

"Oh. You should. *I* didn't fly. I drove. By myself."

"What?"

I filled him in on my little runaway stint, and how Tommy had flown out to find me. And then the whole biological father, half-brother, me in the hospital bit. Of course, I omitted the whole *reason* I'd fallen in the first place.

"Tia, oh my God. That sounds crazy. I'm so sorry I made you run away from home. And so far. You should *not* have traveled that far alone."

"Whaaaat? *You* did."

"Yeah, well. I worry about *you*. Not me."

"Well, don't. I got there just fine."

"Not fine. You ended up in the hospital."

"*That* was irrelevant. I fell down a set of stairs." *A set of two. Technically, I fell down only* one *of the two steps. Shh.* "Nothing to do with traveling."

"Maybe it was because you were so tired from traveling."

"No. Nuh-uh."

"You want something to drink or eat, Tia? I have stuff, since I knew you were coming."

"Like what?"

"Oh. Oh." He lifted me up, and we went into the kitchen. "Look what I found during my ride back from New York," he said from behind the open refrigerator door.

He closed the door and handed me a can of soda. "Strawberry. I had no idea it existed. I bought you a case."

"Holy crow. Nehi Strawberry soda," I read from the can. "Thank you, Clinton," I said, cracking the can open and taking a sip.

"You hungry?"

"Not really."

Clinton opened a beer and grabbed a bag of chips. "Just in case."

"You still drink?"

Holding up his beer, he said, "Whadda *you* think?"

On a head tilt, I frowned.

"But nowhere near as much, Tia."

"Good," I said honestly.

"Let's go back in my room. Ya never know who's gonna pop in from downstairs."

"How come you're not down there?"

"'Cause you're here, silly."

"We can go if you—"

"No way." He put his beer on his nightstand, took my soda from me, and placed it down, then sat me between his legs, my back against his chest. "I only want to be with you tonight. It's been way too many months."

"Did you and...uh, Michael talk?"

"About?"

"About...you and Michael?"

He took my chin in his fingers and turned my face toward his. "That conversation happened before I came to see you in October. I told you that."

"You and he never..."

"No. I have *never* been with anyone but you. I told you that too."

"And you didn't meet anyone on your trip?"

"No, Tia. I didn't. After the day I spent with my mother, I was alone. Just me and my thoughts."

"And...what did you figure out? You said you needed to figure yourself out," I asked, leaning back against his chest, afraid to hear the answer.

"I had a very productive figuring-myself-out trip."

"And?"

"And." He leaned down and kissed the top of my ear. "If we're going to label it, I'm a gay man in love with a straight woman."

My heart swelled.

He adjusted our bodies so we were face to face. Cross-legged. "But I don't think we should be labeled. Yeah, so I'm attracted to men, but I love a girl." He covered my knees with his hands. "That doesn't mean I'm bisexual, right? 'Cause you can put a hundred girls in front of me, and I probably wouldn't look twice. A hundred guys? I'm sure I would. But out of those two hundred people, I could never feel what I feel for you. My heart found the heart it was searching for. Whether it sits inside a female body or a male body is secondary to me. I love *you*, whatever gender you are." He reached in and touched my face. "Let me ask you, Tia. Can you love a man who's naturally attracted to men but fell in love with *you*?"

Without hesitation, I said, "I love *you*. I don't care what label anyone sticks on you."

He swiped my nose. "I was hoping you'd say that."

"I'm ashamed of how I reacted when you told me."

"Don't be. You were being honest at the moment. It wasn't a small admission on my part. Truthfully, it was *my* reaction to you being with Bobby that was wrong."

I covered my face with my hands. "Don't bring that up. Being with Bobby was a huge mistake."

"You know what I learned these past few months? We don't make mistakes. We act on things to help us get to the next step in our lives. Like my short fling with Michael, which didn't go beyond kissing," he emphasized. "If it hadn't happened, I wouldn't have figured out that the heart plays a role in a sexual relationship. My heart wasn't in it, and though lots of people can separate the two, I learned I can't. I need to be in love if I'm gonna take things further. And maybe you being with Bobby led you to your next step."

"Yeah, it led me to realize I shouldn't do things out of spite."

"Out of spite?"

"*To* spite? I did it to spite you. Because I was mad at you."

He shook his head and moved to pick me up and place me on his lap again, my legs once again wrapped around him. "I'm sorry, Tia. For making you feel that you needed to spite me."

"Eh. I should control my own actions. I can't blame you."

"So...whaddya say?"

"About?"

"About us. And our love for each other."

"So even though I'm not a boy, you love me anyway?"

With a huge grin, he nodded. "I love you anyway...and any way...with all my heart, all my soul. With everything I am. I hope you can love me any way I am. Gay, straight...pink."

"Pink. I'd definitely love you if you were pink."

My boyfriend chuckled. "Hey...it's almost midnight. Wanna watch the ball drop?"

"Yeah." I hopped up and turned on his television. "Dick Clark?"

"Yep."

When I jumped back down on the bed, Clinton's phone rang on his nightstand.

"Hello?" he answered, all smiles and patting the spot next to him.

"Hey, Tommy. Thank you for bringing her here tonight." Clinton laughed. "Yeah, sorry about that. Sure. I was hoping she could stay. I was going to have her call you in a bit," he said, still smiling, his eyes on my while he talked. "Ok, sure."

His smile dropped. "Um, repeat that."

Clinton's eyes grew wide as his frown deepened. "Oh. Um." He shook his head and blinked. Repeatedly. Until he closed his eyes and sighed. "Yes. I'll let her know," he choked out. "Yeah, bye."

He tossed the receiver to the floor, not even bothering to hang it up. When he opened his eyes, they were already glossing over. "Your dad...wanted me to tell you. Mel...scheduled your chemo treatments. But...uh, couldn't, get it earlier than two weeks from Wednesday. The sixteenth," he said way too slowly.

"Oh."

"Chemo treatments?" He wiped his face with his hand.

"Guess you're not the only one to inherit something from your mother," I tried to joke, patting his thigh with the flat of my palm.

"When were you gonna tell me?" He stilled my hand by taking my wrist.

"I didn't want to ruin the night."

"Tia, even your father probably thought you'd tell me by now."

"Not tonight, Clinton, please."

His hand ran over his face again. "Is it brain?"

I nodded. "Like Mom."

He closed his eyes and took a deep breath. "Is it as bad?"

I shrugged. "I don't think. But please, Clinton. Please not tonight." I climbed back on top of him, slipping my wrist from his grasp. "Clinton." I hesitated. "Make love to me."

"I can't believe you're sick, Tia."

"Not tonight. Please. I'm begging you." I grabbed his face in my hands. "Make love to me, Clinton. Please." I kissed his lips. Once. Twice. Then I lifted his shirt. He let me pull it over his head. I kissed him again, this time with my lips parted.

His hands traveled up my back, beneath my shirt. I pulled back so he could lift it over my head. When his thumb skimmed the edges of my bra, I gasped. Clinton's touch consumed me, firing little firecrackers of pleasure throughout my veins.

"Tia," he whispered, tugging at the center of my bra but looking into my eyes. "How sick are you?"

"Sick enough to know I need this right now. I promise. I'll talk about it tomorrow." I took his hand and brought it behind me, stopping at the back closure of my floral bra. "Please," I mouthed. "I don't wanna talk about it."

He nodded once, unclasped my bra, and slid it off. I know he was holding back tears. I could see them pooling at his lower lids. But he kept his gaze on my face as he lowered his hands down my torso. "I love you," he said, sadness staining his words.

"I love you, too." I smiled, reassuring him that I was okay. For now, I was.

His mouth turned up before it was joined with mine. Instead of a fiery twirling of tongues, though, it was a bittersweet dance of reconciliation and melancholy.

Unlocking my lips from his, I begged. Again. "Please, Clinton. Stop being sad." I waved the back of my hand and hit his bare chest then climbed off his lap.

"I'm sorry, Tia, but how do you expect me to be? I know how it ended with your mother. This... You spring this on me and then expect me *not* to feel the rug pulled out from beneath me? *Not* to feel my heart shatter into a million pieces?"

I grabbed my bra and stepped onto the floor to put it back on.

"You expect me *not* to feel like my world is coming to an end?" He got off the bed and stood in front of me while I fumbled with the straps on my bra.

Dick Clark, behind us, was counting down the last ten seconds of 1984.

Ten.

"You expect me...

Nine.

"*not* to hear...

Eight.

"the sound...

Seven.

"of my heart...

Six.

"screaming...

Five.

"in pain...

Four.

"because the...

Three.

"only person...

Two.

"I ever loved...

One.

"is facing death?"

Happy New Year!

He took my bra from my hands and threw it aside.

"Do you really think..." He pressed up against me and looked down into my eyes. "...I could..." And enveloped my face with his large hands. "...just ignore this..." He kissed my nose, wetting my cheeks with his tears. "...devastating..." He pressed his lips to mine. "I can't live..." He breathed into my mouth. "...without you." He choked, our faces drenched in his tears.

I latched my hands to the front of his jeans, the backs of my fingers brushing the curls on his lower stomach, the tips of my fingers grazing his velvet tip, which was already peeking out from the waistband of his underwear.

My eyes rolled back behind my lids, and I moaned into his mouth.

His lips still on mine, he took his hands off my face and ran them down my torso, stopping at my hips.

When Clinton deepened the kiss, his fingers found the button on my jeans with one hand, while his other cupped the back of my neck.

I took this to mean he was okay with me unbuttoning *his* pants. So I did. We unzipped each other's jeans at the same time. Though tears remained on Clinton's cheeks, his eyes stopped spilling them, and he looked at me intently.

Slowly, he slid my jeans and panties down and off, leaving me in just my Wigwam socks—which I really wished he'd taken off. Then he ran his finger down the center of my body, from my neck all the way down, causing me to shutter involuntarily.

He then slipped off his jeans and underwear, kicking them aside and taking me by the hips. Jamming my body against his, he plunged his tongue deep inside my mouth as his erection stood hard against my stomach and his hands went wild exploring my body. It had been too long since his hands had touched me like this. Since his body was held naked against mine. I never wanted it to end.

When his hands stopped their journey up and down my body, he cupped my butt in his hands and positioned me around his waist again. This time, he took two slow steps backwards, sat at the edge of his bed, and with gentle movements, lowered me on top of him, moving beneath me with slow, even thrusts.

I followed his lead and moved with him, until in one smooth move, he lifted me, pushed back on the bed, and flipped me onto my back, never disconnecting from each other. Lifting my hips, I matched his rhythm, picking up speed and intensity, until I screamed out his name right before he grunted mine. He collapsed on top of me and kissed me beneath my ear.

His body on top of mine comforted me. I felt safe—like nothing on earth could harm me. Not even cancer.

Pushing up on his elbows, he swept some errant hairs off my cheeks. "I'm sorry that went so quickly," he said, embarrassed, his voice raspy. "I've been thinking about you too much these past couple months." He smiled. "All the time, actually."

Closing my eyes, I smiled back.

His warm body rolled off of me, leaving me chilled, but when I opened my eyes, he was pulling down the covers and covering us with his sheets. I nestled in beneath the crook of his arm as he held me until we fell asleep. Not another word was said until the sun broke through the blinds in the morning.

That's when things got heavy.

He wanted to talk about the cancer. The size of the tumor. The prognosis. The treatment plan.

And I was still naked under his sheets.

But I answered him as best as I could, and on January sixteenth, he came with Dad and me to my first chemotherapy treatment. Clinton insisted on coming with us. He looked more nervous than my father and me—bouncing his knee while we sat waiting for blood results, biting his lip, getting up and down out of his seat.

"Clinton, sit down," Dad demanded. "You're making me nervous."

"I'm sorry, Tom. I just...I can't bear the thought of her going through this." But he sat.

"Well, she is. So calm down and accept it. You being a basket case isn't going to help her."

"No. You're right. You're right." Clinton took my hand and squeezed it hard.

I realized, though, his nervousness actually calmed me. It had the opposite effect it had on my dad. So, I didn't mind that he was stopping the circulation in my hand. It didn't bother me at all.

When the nurse came in, Clinton flew out of the seat, my hand still attached.

"Whoa," she said on a laugh.

Tommy stood up gracefully, yet his face showed anxiety.

"Tia," the nurse said, holding out a urine sample cup, "the doctor just needs a urine sample. Do you think you can give us one?"

I shrugged. "Yeah. Sure."

I took the cup, went into the bathroom, and peed into it, not missing my hand as I did. "Oh, yuck," I murmured to myself as I put the cup on the tank behind the toilet and grabbed some toilet paper to wipe my hand. "Jeez. They need to make a bigger cup." Mumbling to myself again, I washed my hands and brought the cup back to the nurse. She came back into the waiting area about ten minutes later. "Okay, Tia, the doctor would like to talk with you now in his office."

"Oh." I looked to my dad.

"We can call in your father afterward. He'd like to speak with you first," she said through a tight smile.

"I know she's eighteen," Tommy said, "but she's still a kid. I need to be present for whatever the doctor needs to say to her."

"I understand. That's going to have to be your daughter's call."

I shrugged. "Sure. Can Clinton come too?"

Dad sighed.

The nurse raised an eyebrow and said, "Sure, why not."

Dr. Baldwin, sitting behind his desk, raised his eyebrows when we walked into his office.

"She and her father insist," the nurse told him.

He waved us in and had us sit, while the nurse left us to business.

"We have a problem, Tia. Mr. Mercury." He looked at Clinton.

"This is my daughter's...this is Clinton," my father said. He really didn't know *what* to call him, since we hadn't told him our relationship had recently changed. He still thought Clinton was *safe*, because he was gay, which meant he was allowing me to stay over at Clinton's every other night. "She'd like him here too."

"Is this true, Tia? You want them both here?"

"Yes. They'll understand better than me, anyway. Clinton's really smart."

Dr. Baldwin scoffed under his breath.

What was that all about?

"Alright then. The routine blood results came back positive, so we ran a urine test just to be sure...."

"Positive for what?" Tommy asked, not giving Dr. Baldwin time to finish his sentence.

"Positive for pregnancy, Mr. Mercury. Chemotherapy is not an option while your daughter is pregnant."

I didn't know if the world stopped or started slowing down, but everything I was seeing and hearing was in slow motion. My father pinching the bridge of his nose. Clinton covering his mouth with his hand. Dr. Baldwin's lips...moving, but me...hearing nonsense spouting from them. Like the adults in Charlie Brown's life, he spoke in garbled-ese.

The next thing I knew, Dad's hand was wrapped around my wrist, and he was pulling me from my chair.

"What?" I asked, oblivious to the past several minutes' discussion.

"We're going home," he clipped.

Clinton held my hand all the way to the car. I let him sit in the front of Mel's Granada while I sat in the back behind Clinton. That way, I wouldn't catch my father's scowl from the rearview mirror.

Pregnant. It had to have been New Year's Eve. We didn't use protection that night. Over the past two weeks, when we fooled around, Clinton made sure to put on a rubber before he entered me. But New Year's Eve was only a little over two weeks ago. How could I be pregnant already?

But all of a sudden, I felt my body relax, and I couldn't stop the smile that was forming on my face.

I was pregnant.

With Clinton's baby.

I couldn't even express how happy that made me. How complete my heart felt.

Evidently, I was the only one happy about it. My father slammed the door behind him, leaving Clinton and me on the other side of it. We opened it and went into the kitchen, where Mel was standing, her eyebrows dipped in confusion. "What happened? You were supposed to be gone for hours and—" she looked at Tommy "—why do you look pissed?"

Dad glared at me but answered Mel. "Oh, I'm more than pissed. I'm livid," he spat.

I sat down at the kitchen table. "I'm sorry, Dad. I had no idea."

"Whose is it?"

"What are you talking about?" Mel said at the same time I said, "You're kidding me, right?"

He looked at Clinton, who just walked up behind me and placed his hands on my shoulders. "It's mine, sir," Clinton eeked out.

My father shook his head like he was shaking out fleas.

"You're pregnant?" Mel whispered.

I nodded.

"Wait a minute," Dad growled, majorly annoyed. "What happened to being gay?"

"Well...I am, sir, but..."

"You have AIDS?"

Clinton sighed and pulled out the seat next to me and sat. "Not everyone who is gay has AIDS." Now Clinton was annoyed.

"You were tested?"

"No, sir, I was not," Clinton clipped. "I have no need to be. The only person I've ever even been with was your daughter."

Dad jumped over the table and grabbed Clinton's collar. I'd never seen him so angry. "What the hell kind of homosexual are you, anyway?"

"Not a very good one, sir." Clinton tried to remain calm.

My father dropped Clinton's collar and paced, stopping only to punch the refrigerator with the front of his bare fist.

"You're gay, Clinton. This wasn't supposed to happen."

"Truthfully, I love your daughter, and she's the only thing in my life I care about. That being said, I'm trying to stay away from the whole gay label thing right now."

My father side-punched the refrigerator door this time. Fortunately, Scott and David were at school, so they couldn't see their father like this.

"Gay label? What the hell, Clinton? Three months ago, you broke up with her because you were in a relationship with your roommate."

Clinton looked at me confused.

"I was crying a lot. I don't remember what I said."

"It wasn't much of a relationship, sir."

Tommy paced the floor again before finally sitting. Mel put a cup of coffee in front of him then sat with us. "So my daughter *wasn't* the only—"

"She was, sir." Clinton wouldn't allow my father to finish that sentence.

"What's with the goddamn sir-calling all of a sudden?"

"It just seems like the situation calls for the formality, sir."

Mel chuckled.

Dad certainly did not. "Well, stop. It's annoying."

"Sorry."

"Dad. Can we get back on topic, please? This isn't about Clinton's sexual preference. It's about our baby." *Our baby.* Holy shit.

Clinton's skin paled. Like, immediately.

"Well, his confused *lack* of sexual preference is evidently what *caused* this."

"Tommy," Mel scolded.

"That's enough," Clinton scowled, finally standing up for himself. "Tia's right. We should be discussing where we go from here."

"We abort it. That's what we do," my dad commanded.

"Excuse me?" I said, snapping my head in his direction. "I am *not* aborting this baby. No way."

"You'll die if you don't, Tia. Didn't you hear the doctor?"

"No. He kinda lost me after he said I was pregnant."

Clinton covered my hand with his. "If you don't have treatments for nine months, the tumor is going to grow. The cells are advancing aggressively," Clinton explained. "By the time this baby would be born, your cancer would be too advanced to treat effectively." I guess Clinton had been paying attention.

"So, you see why you need to have an abortion as quickly as possible," Dad pointed out, his voice gruff with anger. "Clinton agrees."

Clinton pushed his chair back. "I did not say that."

"I'm not getting rid of our baby. I'm not. I won't."

Dad's fist landed hard on the table. "I'm not going to let my daughter die."

"And I'm not going to let *my* child die either."

Mel laid her hand on my father's arm but stayed silent. I saw her gears turning in her head though. She's a mom. She gets it.

"You agree with this, Clinton?" my dad yelled. "You're gonna let her do this?"

"I didn't say I agreed. But I would like to discuss this with her...privately."

"Privately? This doesn't just concern the two of you. It concerns us, too."

"I'm sorry, sir...Tommy, but it really doesn't."

"Like hell. Who's going to take care of you all? You guys don't work. So this goddamn *does* involve us. One hundred percent. I can't just watch you die, Tia."

"What makes your feelings more important than mine?"

"I'm your father."

"And now I'm a mother."

"You're what, a week pregnant? It's not even a baby yet."

"I'm *two* weeks pregnant, and who says it's not a baby yet?"

"Melanie, help me here," my dad said desperately, his voice cracking.

"Tommy," she breathed. "I can't help you. As much as I don't want Tia to make her cancer worse, the minute she became pregnant, this became her decision."

"So you all don't see it my way at all?"

After several seconds of silence, Clinton spoke. "I do."

I jerked my head around. "You just said—"

"I didn't *say* anything. I'm trying to see every angle here. But...ultimately...I'd rather lose the baby than lose you."

I felt my eyes grow wide, stinging with new tears. My face grew hot, my body tense. I pushed my chair out from the table, stood, and looked Clinton right in the eyes. "You did *not* just say that."

"I did, Tia," he said, challenging my stare.

When he didn't back down, I shook my head and said "Don't talk to me right now." I went to my room to calm down.

Then I took my Walkman and put on whatever was already inside. I needed to close my eyes and forget for a moment. Allow the music to distract my thoughts.

About twenty minutes later, there was a hard rap on my door.

I took off my headphones and on a sigh said, "What?"

"Let me in, Tia."

"It's not locked."

"It is locked. Now stop being immature and let me in."

Oops. I hadn't realized I had locked it. Must've been out of habit. "I don't feel like getting up."

"Then I'll stick a bobby pin into the knob and unlock it myself."

"Whatever. Good luck finding a bobby pin."

Five minutes later, he was in, holding up a bobby pin. "Bathroom drawer."

I rolled my eyes.

He sat at the top of my bed and pulled me up in front of him. At first, I resisted, but this was Clinton. I didn't have that kind of willpower. So I let him hold me.

"I wasn't saying I *wanted* you to get rid of the baby. I just wanted you to know that I'd rather take care of you first. We can always have a baby after the cancer's gone."

"How can you say that, though?" I asked, forcing myself to stay calm. "This baby's here now. Maybe God has a plan for him. Or her."

"And He doesn't have a plan for *you*? Except to die?"

"His plan is for me to have this baby. This baby is bigger than my cancer. Can't you see? Maybe *this* is why we're together, Clinton. Maybe you fell in love with me, even though you're gay, because this baby is meant to be. Maybe I stuck around so long, waiting for you to *decide* if you even wanted me, because this baby is meant to be born. Maybe God has plans for this baby, and it's the reason you and I are here together. This baby, Clinton, is supposed to grow up and do *great* things. I just know it. I feel it. It's the reason for *us*. It all makes sense now—God has a plan for our little baby."

After a minute or so of absorbing what I'd said, Clinton spoke. "Tia. Why all of a sudden is this God's plan? You never preached what He wanted before. And secondly, maybe the plan was that I should have taken the fifteen seconds to get a rubber out of my nightstand and put it on. This is all because of carelessness, Tia. *My* carelessness. I take full responsibility. But don't go saying this happened because God wanted it to."

I tried to untangle myself from Clinton's grip, but he wouldn't let me. "We're going to talk about this, Tia. You're not squirming away."

"I'm not getting an abortion," I insisted.

"Okay. I'm not gonna force you to. I couldn't if I wanted to. I just want you to really think about it. Please."

"I did."

"Tia. Go over everything in your head. Think this through. That's all I'm asking."

"Okay. I'll think about killing my baby. Hmm. That's gonna be a difficult decision." I yanked myself from his grip so I could look at him. "Because yeah, killing is always the right thing to do. Is that right, Clinton? I can murder my baby to save my own life? Is that what the mothers of the year do these days?"

Clinton got off the bed. "Okay, Tia. That's enough," he commanded, much like my father had in the kitchen.

"What you're asking me to do is the very antithesis of the definition of a mother. My heart is telling me to keep my baby. Our baby. Maybe he's only two weeks in my stomach, but I love him like I've known him forever. Already. And if you all are asking me to give up this little person so that I can live longer, then I don't want to live at all."

I didn't cry. Because I knew they couldn't make me abort my baby.

But Clinton did cry. "Then we keep this baby," he choked out, and I wasn't sure it was from happiness or disappointment until he continued. "And I'll try not to resent it for taking you away from me."

"You have to love this child, Clinton. You're the one that has to raise him once I die."

With daggers shooting out of his eyes and fire coming out of his ears, he said, "Then why the *hell* aren't you letting me have any say in this decision?"

CHAPTER TWENTY-ONE

"Coming Soon"

TIA

T   In the weeks following, no one talked about it anymore.

We barely talked at all.

Clinton still came over daily to see me and make sure I was feeling all right, but he didn't talk about the baby. Not after that first night. And we hadn't had sex since before then either. Clinton never seemed in the mood to even hold me anymore.

As for Dad, he wouldn't even look at me. He went so far as seeking legal advice to see if he could take me to court to get Power of Attorney over my medical decisions. But the lawyer advised him against it, saying by the time it'd get to trial, my pregnancy would be too far along to get an abortion. And so far, this type of case was unprecedented. The fact that I was eighteen really made the case moot. Mel told me this. She was on my side but wanted me to see my father's and Clinton's. I understood it, but I'd never agree with it.

Today was Valentine's Day. Clinton said he'd come over after work. He got his job at the library back, and Professor Burke gave him a job as his teaching assistant, even though

Clinton was a semester behind. But because he was picking up extra credits, and then again in the summer, Professor Burke made an exception.

But tonight, we were going out. I was nervous because we hadn't talked much this past month—just general questions and answers back and forth. It was Clinton's idea to go out, though, so I was hopeful.

"So, where we going?" I asked when we got in his 280Z that night.

"I thought we'd go to the movies. A new one just came out."

"Oh." I guess we weren't going to be talking much if we'd be sitting and watching a movie. "Which one?"

"*Breakfast Club.*"

I nodded. I missed Clinton. He was sitting right next to me, yet it felt like he was two thousand miles away again.

He bought my ticket. Bought my popcorn. But he didn't hold my hand. It was as if I repulsed him or something.

The movie was funny though, and I was glad Clinton had taken me to see it.

After the movie, Clinton took me home, walked me to the door, kissed me quick on the lips, and said goodbye.

I couldn't hold back tears when I said, "I love you, Clinton."

"Love you, too." Then he ducked his head and walked away.

"Clinton."

He stopped but didn't turn around.

"Mel's taking me to the doctor tomorrow. Do you wanna come with us?"

After a moment, he said, "Can't. Got class." He picked up walking again, got in his car, and drove away.

Happy Valentine's Day, Clinton.

In my room, I held my stomach and prayed to God to give me back my Clinton.

"CLINTON HARDLY TALKS to me," I told Mel on the way to the doctor.

"This has to be hard on him too, honey. Give him time to work through this."

"How *much* time? It's been, like, a month already."

"I don't know. Your dad's not coming around much either."

"I'm sorry about that, Mel. I noticed Dad doesn't talk to you much either."

She shook her head. "He wants me to talk you out of this, but I told him how I felt. This can only come from you. I get that." She glanced my way. "You know, Tee, once that baby is in their arms, they'll love him or her to death."

"And maybe my tumor won't have grown out of control. Can we set up chemo for right after I give birth?"

She smiled. "I hope so."

Yeah, me too. Because I really, really wanted to live. Especially now that I had a baby growing inside of me.

MEL TOOK ME TO THE cancer doctor the next week, but there wasn't much he could do to check the growth since all the tests could be dangerous for the baby. So he just asked me questions about headache frequency, blacking out—which I would still do on occasion—and changes that he'd monitor each month throughout my pregnancy. It was hitting me now that my tumor was probably going to get worse. Apparently, Mel must have been worried about the same thing.

"Tia?" Mel asked on our way home from the doctor's.

"Yeah?"

"You should have a will done."

"A will?"

She hesitated but then said, "A Last Will and Testament. It's a legal document where you state who will receive your possessions."

"I don't have any possessions."

"Your baby, Tia. God forbid... Well...you need to talk to Clinton about it, but...if he chooses not to...care for your baby after you, if you don't...make it..." Mel was obviously uncomfortable. I couldn't blame her. She was making me nervous now. "Well," she continued, "you need to name someone else to become his or her guardian. And then, even if Clinton does want the baby...you need to name a guardian in case something happens to him."

Talk about a heavy heart. Suddenly, I felt overwhelmed. Beyond that. I couldn't breathe. Drowning. That's what I think it felt like. In a panic, I yelled, "Oh my God, Mel. Oh my God."

"Tia." She patted my leg. "I just want you to talk to Clinton. That's—"

"My baby's gonna be all alone. Clinton's not gonna want him. Daddy's not gonna want him. Oh my God, Mel. What's gonna happen to him? Who's gonna love him?" I cried. I yelled. I kicked. And screamed. "No. Mel. My baby's gonna be all alone. Just like I was. Only, only, he's not even gonna know better. He's just a baby. Oh my God..."

Mel pulled off to the side of the road and took me in her arms. "*I* love your baby, Tia. I love your baby already. And once your daddy gets over this, he will too. And...I can't see how Clinton won't fall madly in love with him or her the minute that baby's in his arms." She pulled back and looked at me. "This baby is part of *you,* and Clinton loves *you.* There is no way he is not going to love it. My only concern is, well, because he's so young, Clinton may not be able to raise the baby on his own."

"Will you be my baby's guardian?" I asked after several minutes of sobbing and hyperventilation.

"I damn sure will." She hugged me again and kissed me on the head. "I know I'm only eleven years older than you, Tia, but I love you as if you were my own daughter. Please know that."

As I wiped the snot and tears off my face with my sleeve, I nodded.

"Let's get home."

Silently, I continued to cry all the way home. Clinton's car was parked in the driveway when we pulled in.

"You can do this, Tia," Mel encouraged. "Just be honest and calm."

I nodded. If I spoke, I would have broken down again. As it was, I'm sure my face was swollen from breaking down in the car.

He was in the kitchen having a beer. When Clinton saw me, he surged to his feet. "Tia. What happened?" he asked with emotion I hadn't seen in more than a month.

That did it. I ran to him and melted. I hugged him with all my might, that if he'd tried to pull away, he probably couldn't. He grabbed my butt cheeks, lifted me up, and carried me to the sunroom, kicking the door shut behind us.

He sat down on the couch, me on his lap facing him, and he pressed his cheek to mine. "What happened, Tia?"

"I don't wanna die," I cried.

"I don't want you to die either," he said on an exhale.

"But I can't kill our baby." I cried louder.

"I know that too," he whispered.

Pulling back at arm's length to look at his face, I pleaded with him. "Please tell me what to do. Please. I don't want our baby to be alone." I hiccupped. I sobbed. "I want him to be loved."

"Shh. Tia. He will be." He smoothed down my hair and said, "I'll love him enough for both of us if... I can't say it, Tia. But I will." He was crying now. "I will love him enough for both of us," he said again, before breaking down himself.

He repositioned me so that I was now cradled in his arms. Nothing was said between us for a long time, but I knew we were no longer on separate sides of this bittersweet nightmare. My heart was feeling just a teensy bit lighter now.

Clinton stayed over that night. He held me in my bed all night long. It was the most solid sleep I'd had since before I found out I was pregnant.

In the morning, Mel called us out to the kitchen for breakfast. She made my Dad call in one of his workers to fill in for him at work, and Scott and David had already left for school.

"Tia, I take it, since Clinton stayed, you spoke with him?" Mel started right after serving us some blueberry pancakes.

I shook my head. "Not about what you and I spoke about."

"Okay. Well, good. It's better coming from me anyway."

"What's this about, Mel? I have a business to run," Dad said, clearly annoyed.

He was always so good to me. It hurt to see this change in him.

"Family comes first, Tom. You know that."

He issued a light tap with his fist to the table before he resigned himself to listening.

"Tia is keeping this baby..." She held up her hand when Tommy leaned forward, ready to speak. "Whether we like it or not, we have to accept this, and quickly, because she needs us. Her baby needs us."

Tommy's jaw tightened, but otherwise, he continued hearing Mel out.

"We have to talk about what's going to happen..." Mel stopped, to change course, I presumed. "Tia's going to need caring for while she's pregnant. Who knows if her headaches and the blacking out are going to get worse?"

Clinton took my hand.

"And she needs our support. No more shunning her because we may not agree with her decision. Because this *is* her decision. Accept it."

My father wouldn't look at her or me. He kept his gaze down at his balled fist on the table.

"And though we're going to get her treated as soon as she has her baby, we need to talk about...what happens...in case."

In case I die. More like when *I die.*

Dad squeezed his eyes shut.

"The baby's mine too," Clinton said.

I looked at him and smiled.

He squeezed my hand. "I won't abandon our baby."

Thank God.

Mel smiled. Nodded. "Good. And we're here to help. And—" she looked at Tommy "—I think I speak for both of us when I say you always have a home here. All three of you."

Tommy didn't move. He still wouldn't look up.

I had to say something. "Dad?"

"Tommy." Mel nudged him when he didn't respond.

Finally, he looked.

"I need you to love our baby."

While his eyes were still on mine, his Adam's apple bobbed up and down, but he didn't speak.

Instead, he stood up.

And walked out the door.

"I'm sorry, Tia," Mel apologized.

I shrugged.

"Mel?" Clinton asked. "Would it be okay if I moved in when the baby's born?"

With a warm smile, she said, "You can move in now if you want."

"I don't want to upset Tommy."

"Don't worry about it. He'll get over it."

"Well, no. I won't move in until he's okay with this. But I have a feeling once the baby's born, he will be."

Mel continued to smile. "Me too."

DAD WAS OKAY WITH THINGS the day Mel made him take me to the doctor in April. She and Clinton had come in March, and they got to hear the baby's heartbeat with me. Mel was sure that once Dad heard the heartbeat too, he wouldn't be able to help but fall in love with his grandchild.

She was right. Once he heard the beat of the little life inside me, he changed his tune. Dad was still quiet, but I saw how his face lit up when the nurse hooked me up to the monitor. But how did I know for sure he was accepting my baby? When we got home, before we walked up to the front door, my father took my hand and pulled me into a hug. "I am so sorry, Tia," he said over my shoulder. "I never *didn't* want your baby. I just don't want to lose you."

"Thank you, Dad. I'm gonna fight this. I'm still gonna fight it. I just have to wait a little, that's all."

He kissed the top of my head. "I love you, sugar plum. A whole bunch. And I'll love your baby just the same."

I broke the embrace first. "I know you will, Dad. Thank you."

LIFE AROUND THE HOUSE was pretty much back to normal after that. But my headaches grew worse. And I was vomiting like crazy. The doctors said it could be from morning sickness *or* the tumor's growth causing pressure on my brain. Or it could be a combination of both. Whatever the cause, I was dropping weight instead of gaining it, so I didn't do much more that summer than sit around and watch television. My head hurt too much to even read. Clinton continued taking classes through the summer so he could be finished with his undergraduate credits before the baby was born. He said he wanted to put off getting his Master's until the timing was better. He'd look for a full-time job in the meantime.

On July thirteenth, Clinton and I set our alarms to wake up early and watch the Live-Aid event we couldn't wait to see. It was one of my favorite memories—Clinton and me sitting in the sunroom all day long watching some of our favorite bands performing from London and Philadelphia. "We are the World." One of my favorite performances.

The next day, I was rushed to the hospital for dehydration. They fed me IV fluids for twenty-four hours and sent me home. But I was never well after that. My headaches were non-stop, and I couldn't take anything to ease the pain. Mel fed me chamomile tea to calm me enough to hopefully fall asleep, the only relief I got from the torture that was my brain.

Clinton sat by my side nearly twenty-four hours a day after his summer sessions ended, his pile of newspapers and trade magazines in front of him. While Clinton searched the want ads for a job, I forced myself to sleep. Until one morning in September, I woke up with unfamiliar stomach pain.

I was in labor.

CHAPTER TWENTY-TWO

"Now I'm Here"

T IA
        "Oh my God, Clinton. Wake up." I shook his arm. "Wake up." My head was pounding, but I tried to ignore it.

"Hmmm? What?" He pried open his eyes and shook free his groggy head. "What's the matter?"

"I think I'm in labor."

He popped up. "Now?"

"Yes. I think." I held on to my stomach. "It feels weird."

"Okay." Clinton got out of bed and pulled on his jeans. He was living here now, moved in permanently on September first. Today was the twenty-second. "Where's the doctor's number? He said to call him."

"It's on the fridge."

I put on my sweatpants and my tee shirt and sneakers, grabbed my prepared duffel bag, and met Clinton in the kitchen.

"Go wake up your father. Let him know," Clinton instructed after he hung up the phone.

I did. Dad got right up. Mel too, but she stayed home with the boys while Dad drove us to the hospital.

A nervous wreck didn't come close to describing my emotions at the moment.

In the car ride over, Clinton, who was sitting in the back seat with me, took my hand. "Tia. I've been wanting to do this for a while, but you never had a good day. I kept waiting. So, I'm sorry it's in the back seat of your father's car." He slid down to the floor of the car, balancing himself on one knee. In his hand, he held up a small diamond ring. "I love you so much, Tia. Will you make me your husband?"

My feelings were mixed. I really wanted to say yes, but if I weren't having his baby, would he even be asking me?

"Tia?" he asked, lifting off his knee and sitting back on the seat.

In the rearview mirror, Tommy was sneaking glances.

"Is that a no?" Clinton asked, sounding disappointed.

I shook my head. "It's not a no," I said quietly. "But it's not a yes either."

He rolled in his full lips and took a deep calming breath in through his nose. Then he exhaled slowly through his mouth.

"Are you just asking me because we're having a baby?"

"Well, I'm asking *now* because we're having a baby, but I'd ask you anyway, regardless. I thought you would know that by now."

Just then, I had another contraction, interrupting the conversation. We didn't get back to it before arriving at the hospital.

Things went fairly quickly once we got there, since when I'd reached ten centimeters, I was told the baby was breech. They had to do an emergency C-section, so I was out of it until the anesthesia wore off and they handed me my baby wrapped up in a blanket. I wouldn't let them unwrap the blanket until they brought Clinton into the room, but it didn't matter what sex our baby was, because I loved it more than anything. When I held this little perfect angel in my arms, I felt my heart leave my body and enter his...or hers. I was no longer me. I was this little baby's mother. I never knew my heart could swell as big as it did. And I never knew it could hold as much love for this one little person as it did.

"Well?" Clinton asked, all smiles when he entered my room.

Looking down at our baby, I said, "I waited for you before I looked."

Clinton sat next to me and ran his hand up my forearm while I held this keeper of my heart.

"Go 'head," I said, trembling. "You open the blanket."

"No, Tia. You."

"I want you to, Clinton."

One quick nod and he fingered the blanket, slowly unwrapping it from the baby.

I sucked in a breath when he dipped the diaper down.

"Oh, Tia," Clinton cried.

"He's beautiful."

"He sure is."

Clinton swaddled our baby boy in his blanket, and I handed him to his father. Then I looked at the nurse. "Can I breast feed him?"

"Um. I was told you'll be receiving chemo."

"But not yet."

"Oh. Well, you had a general anesthetic, so you really can't until tomorrow. How 'bout we try tomorrow afternoon? Your baby will get some colostrum, and it'll be a nice time to bond before getting your treatment."

I nodded, but I was sad. Then the nurse walked out.

"You okay, Tia? You look sad."

I shrugged.

Clinton handed me back our son. "Here. He'll make you smile."

After I took the baby in my arms, Clinton took *me* in his.

"So, what are we gonna call our little fella?" Clinton asked, holding me under his right arm and brushing the baby's cheek with the back of his left hand.

I leaned into Clinton's shoulder. "I was thinking Freddie."

"Freddie?"

"As in Freddie Mercury. It was his music that brought us together. Plus...he was phenomenal. I think our baby should have a phenomenal name too. Because he's gonna be somebody great."

Clinton smiled, but I wondered if he was restraining a laugh due to my silliness. "So, you want to name our son Freddie Mercury?"

"No. Freddie Daniels."

Clinton's face went slack. "You're giving him *my* last name?"

"You *are* his father."

"But what about you? Don't you want him to have *your* name?"

"Uh, well, I was hoping your name *would* be my name."

"Does that mean you'll be my wife?"

"Yes, please."

He reached into his pocket and took out the ring. "I left the box at home so you wouldn't see it in my pants," he whispered. "Okay. First, I need to ask our son. Freddie," he said to our baby boy, "would you mind too much if I asked your mommy here to marry me?"

Freddie didn't respond.

But I did. By crying.

"He said yes," Clinton fibbed. "Tia Joy Mercury, will you allow me the honor of being your husband?" he asked from his spot next to me on the bed.

"Yes. If I can be your wife."

Clinton took my left hand and slid the ring onto my finger. Then he kissed my nose. "I love you, Tia."

"I love you, too."

"So, if Freddie needs a phenomenal name, I think he needs your name too."

"'Cause it's Mercury?"

"'Cause it's *your* name. We'll give him Mercury as his middle name. How's that?"

I looked at my baby. "He's gonna hate us when he gets older," I joked half-heartedly. I wasn't going to be around when he got older. It was killing me to think about it, yet I couldn't stop myself.

"Tia," Clinton whispered, wiping my cheek with his sleeve.

Bending down to kiss my now sleeping baby, I found it hard to breathe.

Clinton rubbed my back. "We're gonna fight this, sweetheart. You're gonna be fine." Clinton's words were more wishful thinking than true belief, but it felt nice to hear the words...even though I didn't believe him.

But right now, I had no choice but to try to believe him. Otherwise, I wouldn't be able to enjoy my Freddie now. For however long I had left.

CHAPTER TWENTY-THREE

"If You Can't Beat Them"

September 22, 2015
CLINTON

"Okay, wait. When did Uncle Landon come back into the picture?"

"Freddie, you just interrupted your mother."

"Oh. I'm sorry. I just..." Freddie shrugged. "I don't think I ever heard how. I assumed he was always in the picture."

"Oh. Okay. My turn. I'll tell it." I smiled, happy to talk about the past some more.

"You were almost a year old. As much as Mom—" I looked over at my beautiful wife and beamed "—loved her brother when she met him, her headaches and her morning sickness kept her from reaching out to him."

"So, I reached out to her," Landon piped up.

"Ohhh...kaaaay...*your* turn, Land," I said to my wife's CFO of the largest toy store in New York City of a half-brother.

"Don't mind if I do." Landon inched forward, positioning himself at the edge of the couch. "It'd been almost two years since Tee and I met. I thought maybe she hadn't gotten the note I left on every car within a one-mile radius of my house. So I searched for her. Remember, the Internet wasn't common yet, so I had to rely on Information, four-one-one, to go through all the Mercurys in Texhoma, Oklahoma. One. An unlisted number. Fortunately, though, Grandpa Mercury owned his own business. Once I figured out that Mercury Electricians in Texhoma was the same Tommy Mercury as the one I'd met nearly two years prior, and since there was only one Thomas Mercury in all of Texhoma, it wasn't too hard." Landon took a sip of his white wine, probably for dramatic effect, since that's how Landon rolled, and continued. "Of course, convincing Tommy I had no other ulterior motive besides connecting with my long-lost half-sister—he didn't want my father contacting her—was a little more difficult. But he finally gave me her number."

"Okay," I interrupted. "Mind if I finish telling the story?" I asked, annoyed that Landon chimed in in the first place.

"Be my guest, Clint."

CHAPTER TWENTY-FOUR

"Sail Away Sweet Sister"

S eptember, 1986
CLINTON

"I raced to the phone ringing on the nightstand, not wanting it to wake up Tia and Freddie, who were napping together on the bed. "Hello?"

"Um. I'm looking for Tia Mercury. Is this the right number?"

"Who the hell is this?" I wasn't accustomed to anyone calling Tia, let alone a guy.

"This is her brother, Landon."

Brother? "Oh...that professor's kid?"

"Yeah. That one. Is she there?"

"Well, she's sleeping at the moment."

"At one o'clock in the afternoon?"

I took the phone, and its long cord, into the hallway and shut the bedroom door. "She's...uh...not feeling well today."

"Is she still dying?"

I cringed. "Boy, you don't pull any punches, do you?"

"I thought when she didn't contact me, she might have, you know, croaked, but then I thought, maybe she just never got the note I left on the car."

"Well, she didn't *croak*." I was getting annoyed with this kid's cavalier attitude.

"Good. I should have looked for her sooner, but I got involved in my schoolwork and preparing for my GMATs. Lately, though, she's been on my mind. So, tell me...you the boy she came looking for here in Jersey two years ago?"

"Yes."

"Clinton, I think I heard her say."

"That's right."

"So, how is she, man? Is she getting any better?"

I hesitated to answer, not because I was worried about how this clown would take it, but because I hated hearing myself say it out loud. "No. The tumor grew. They're trying to shrink it with a second round of chemo and radiation treatments, but as it stands now, it's inoperable."

The boy went silent.

For a second.

"Shiiiit. I'd love to come see her. Won't get a break 'til Christmastime. Think she'll be up for it?"

I remember Tia telling me how much she liked Landon, so I wouldn't hurt her by telling him not to come just because the guy grated on every single one of my last nerves. "Sure."

LANDON DID COME OUT. Two days before Christmas. The day before my and Tia's one-year wedding anniversary. As a Christmas present to each other, and to our baby boy, Tia and I got married in front of the mayor of Texhoma, a friend of Tommy's who came to our house on Christmas Eve last year to perform the ceremony.

"Oh my God, Landon." Tia jumped into his arms with the most energy I'd seen from her in months.

"Look at you, girl. Married with a kid. Shit. You're younger than me."

She tapped him on the arm when he put her down. "I can't believe you're here. Did you know?" she asked me.

"We wanted to surprise you," I said, walking in from the airport and kissing my son in his high chair.

"You didn't even give it away on the phone," she said to Landon.

"Then it wouldn't have been a surprise." Walking toward Freddie, Landon said, "So, this is the kid?"

"Yup."

"Hey, kid. Good luck in life with a name like Freddie Mercury. You'd-a been better off with the name Bono."

"Hey." What an ass. What the hell did my wife see in him?

"So, Tia. You're really looking wonderful „\you know..."

Tia's hand flew to the bandanna wrapped around her bald head. "I look like crap, but thanks."

"You're beautiful," he said with a brush of his fingers against her cheek. "Flawless."

He finally said something I could agree with.

For an hour, before Mel came home with the boys and Tommy came home from work, the four of us—Freddie included—sat around the kitchen table catching up. Well, Tia and Landon caught up. Freddie and I did a puzzle together.

Christmas morning, before anyone else got up, I gave Tia a video camera. This way, she could tape Freddie's second Christmas, from start to finish. Which, of course, she did.

Thank God I bought her several blank VHS tapes to go along with it.

At the end of the night, after Freddie, Scott, and David went to sleep, we replayed the videos on Tommy's VCR in the main living room.

Landon's visit was surprisingly pleasant. It only took me half a day to warm up to his *friendly* sarcasm, as he called it. It took Tommy a *whole* day, but only because he was working out some father issues within himself before he could embrace Tia's biological half-brother.

All in all, we were all going to miss Landon. Even Freddie, who cracked up at anything Landon said to him.

He left on the second, but I had work—I got a job last November doing programming for a company in Texas—so Tommy took him to the airport.

LANDON CAME BACK THE following summer.

When Tia was at her worst.

"Who's taking care of her and the baby while you're at work?" Landon asked on our way home from the airport.

"Mel's been doing everything. They've been good at work with letting me work from home twice a week."

"How do you manage that?"

"They gave me a computer to take home."

"Good deal. So...Tia. Not good?"

I shook my head and rolled my wedding band around my finger. "No."

"I'm sorry, Clint. That's just...just terrible."

I wanted to say thanks, but my throat was constricting.

"You know, my father'd like to come out and see her. I know she doesn't want to see him, but I feel bad for the guy. He wasn't even given the option of being her father."

I held up my hand. "Not now," I managed.

"'Kay. Is she up for seeing me?"

"Oh yeah." I swallowed, trying not to cry at the thought of my wife on her deathbed. She was too young for this. She had a son to raise. Surely, God could manage one of His miracles right about now. *Couldn't He?*

CHAPTER TWENTY-FIVE

"Keep Yourself Alive"

September, 22, 2015
CLINTON

"Okay, so, Uncle Landon, you came back in the picture in eighty-six?"

"That's right. And each year after until you guys moved here."

"When was that, Dad? When did we move to Manhattan? I don't really remember."

I paused, not because I couldn't remember but because I remember being unsure about moving in the first place.

It was a huge decision—moving back across the country without the safety net that Tommy and Mel had provided us for so long. My company had offered me a transfer to their corporate headquarters. It meant a lot more money and opportunity, but it also meant we'd be on our own. In the busiest city in the nation. It took me a month of deliberating and talking over the pros and cons, but we finally made the move in April of 1992. Freddie was only six and a half years old.

Landon was there to meet us at JFK Airport.

"Oh my goodness, it's so great to see you." Landon took Freddie in his arms right away. *"Hey, big guy. Look how big you are. Come on. Let me show you all where you'll be living,"* he'd said.

His apartment was bigger than I'd expected when we walked in. He had two floors, which was pretty impressive at the time, considering he was only twenty-nine. I was thirty-one and making a good salary, but I didn't think I could have afforded that place on my own back then.

But Landon could, and he was gracious enough to take us in with him.

"Nineteen ninety-two," I finally shook myself free from my reveries and responded to my son's original question. "We moved here in nineteen ninety-two."

"Oh. Okay. Now can we get back to Mom telling us our story?"

"Sure."

CHAPTER TWENTY-SIX

"Save Me"

September 22, 1987

TIA

"Mommy, Mommy." Freddie came running into our room holding a vanilla cupcake. "Look. Gama made."

"Oh, Freddie," I said weakly.

He hopped up on my bed and snuggled close to me, sticking the cupcake in my face. "Wanna share?"

Wrapping my arm around him and kissing him on the head, I said, "Of course. But we have to both take a bite at the same time."

"Okay. One. Two. Fwee. Bite."

We bit. Our noses touched. "Mmm," I moaned, more because I loved these moments with my son than I loved the cupcake. *All* food made me sick now, not just cupcakes.

"Mmm mmm good, wight, Mommy?"

"Mmm mmm, little man."

"Where'd that birthday boy go?" Clinton called from the hallway.

"Wight heya, Daddy, by Mommy."

Clinton's beautiful form appeared in the doorway. "My two favorite people in the whole wide world sitting in one place."

"Thanks for staying home today, Clinton."

"And miss my boy's second birthday? Wouldn't dream of it."

Clinton sat on my other side, extending his long, strong legs in front of him. Leaning in to me, he said, "Took the day off, so I don't even have to do any computer work. The whole day is yours."

I dropped my hand to his thigh. "Thank you."

"You want me to get you tea or anything?"

"No." I leaned my head back against the headboard. Just sitting up exhausted me.

"Mommy, pwesents now?"

"Of course, Freddie. We can open presents now."

Clinton got out the presents from the closet. *He* shopped for them, but *I* wrapped them—well, the small ones. Such a simple exercise, yet it took me so long to finish. But I did. And I was determined to stay awake and participate in my son's birthday celebration—as small and lame as it was. I would not sleep through any part of his day.

By evening, when Tommy got home, Clinton helped me to the kitchen table, where I stayed through dinner and birthday cake. Freddie's smile was a mile wide. "I'm big boy now. Wight, Mommy?"

"Right, sweetheart."

"I love my piano, Mommy."

"I know you do, honey." Besides the common two-year-old toys—big Legos, some more puzzles, a Tonka truck—Clinton had gone out and found a used piano. An inexpensive but well-kept baby grand piano. It'd been a long time since either one of us had played, and Clinton hoped it would give us some bonding time with Freddie. I expected it would be useful to Clinton and Freddie, but I couldn't see how I could sit there. I wouldn't mind listening to them play though.

Clinton got up from the table and took me by the arms. "Come on, Tia. Let's go play something."

"What?" I looked at him like he was high.

"Come on." He lifted me up and walked me to the piano.

Tommy brought over a chair with a back and slid the bench to the side. I closed my eyes and tried to think of a song.

The first one to come to mind: "Save Me" by Queen.

With my eyes still closed, I hummed the song in my head then slowly brought my fingers to the keys. It was one of my favorite Queen songs, if not my very favorite. Listening to the tune in my head, I found the G chord and hammered out the song. I may not have had much physical energy, but my fingers didn't know that.

When I ended the song, Freddie was to my right, sitting on Clinton's lap. "Wow, Mommy, you weally good."

Clinton put Freddie on my lap, and I kissed his head. "Me pay now."

His fingers pressed the keys, and my fingers followed. We played ourselves a little off-key tune together. It was the most beautiful sound I had ever heard.

After we put Freddie to sleep, Clinton sat next to me on the bed. "It was a nice day today, wasn't it?" Clinton wrapped his arm around me.

"It was." And I couldn't stand the thought of my son never having another birthday that included me. And that's when my big idea came to me. "Clinton?"

"Yes?"

"Can you do me a favor?"

"Of course. I'd do *anything* for the love of my life."

CHAPTER TWENTY-SEVEN

"My Life Has Been Saved"

S eptember 22, 2015
CLINTON

"Freddie," Tia said, wiping a tear from her eye. "I hope you enjoyed our little family's story." She tried to laugh, but it was strained, so my wife sucked in as big a breath as she could and said, "I hope I made it clear to you just how much you mean to me. That I love you more than my own life."

"I know, Ma," my son whispered.

"I just need to remind you of that. That I will always. Always. Be right here—" she tapped her heart "—in your heart. Because the day you were born, little man, I gave my heart to you." Tia wiped at her tears again.

I watched as our thirty-year-old son did the same.

"Your father helps protect it too. He's the best, Freddie. Your dad. Stuck with me through it all. Went against his nature to be with me too."

"I had no choice, baby. You stole my heart," I strained to speak. I don't even think Freddie heard me.

"But I'm so grateful he did," she continued, "because God meant for you to be here. He meant for you to be phenomenal. How else could you explain your daddy falling for me?" Tia smiled, her face struggling to do so. She took in a few ragged breaths and promised, "I am so proud to be your mother, Freddie. And so proud to be your daddy's wife. My two biggest accomplishments. I may not have gone to college or got some high-powered job, but I was able to love you two with all that I have. We may not have had a lot of time together—" she gasped "—but I cherished every second. There's a song, Freddie, sung by your namesake. 'One Year of Love.' Listen to it. It may not be forever that we have together, but it beats having no time at all. I love you, Freddie. Eternally. Happy Birthday, little man."

"Mom," Freddie cried.

And I did the same.

Pressing the pause button on the old VCR we kept for just these occasions, I left Tia's image up on the screen—not having the heart to turn it off and have her disappear from the screen just yet.

"I wish I'd had more time with her, Dad."

Drying my eyes with the tissues I'd set on the coffee table before we sat down to our annual tradition, I agreed. "I wish you did too, son." Spending time with Tia once a year via the VHS tape she had the idea of making for Freddie the month before she died just didn't seem adequate. Sure, I'd burned several copies on DVD and downloaded it to my computer and phone. And sure, I watched any chance I got. But every year, on Freddie's birthday, we'd pull out the old VHS tape that she actually held in her hands, and played it on the old VCR. I did appreciate, though, that she'd taken the time to tell our story on tape. And I know our son cherished it as well.

On October twenty-ninth, 1987, Tia Joy Mercury ended her struggle with brain cancer and went up to Heaven, where, hopefully, she was spending a pain-free eternity. That was my only solace—that she would be free of the agony and suffering her cancer caused. But the pain, for me, was beyond tolerable. It still hurt as much today as it did the day I lay next to her in our bed and waited for her to take her last breath. My throat still constricted with the thought, and my heart still wrenched with misery every single day. But I tried, still, to live each day with happiness and *joy*, because that's how Tia should be remembered.

And she may have had some type of insight when she said God had a plan, as much as I wanted to disagree with her on that at every turn.

"You know, I wish I had more time with my sister, too," Landon said, responding to our wishing for more time with the woman we all loved in different ways. "I fell in love with her the minute she sat down in my kitchen all those years ago—scared but gutsy."

I chuckled at Landon's on-point explanation of Tia. Situations *did* scare her, but never enough to stop her from going after what she wanted. Thank God what she wanted was me, and that she'd kept after me...and didn't see what I believe her mother had seen when she asked me to be honest with her daughter, once I was honest with myself. Because had Tia seen the signs of my homosexuality, which weren't all that clear, even to me, she may not have kept our relationship going. And I may not have realized I loved her despite her being the opposite sexual preference.

But besides giving me her unconditional love and the best son any man could ever wish for, she indirectly led me to the man I'd spend the rest of my life with.

The man that would become my husband four days from now.

EPILOGUE

"Made in Heaven"

September 26, 2015
FREDDIE

I know this should have been a big day for me, but really, it was just a piece of paper. I'm not sure why it meant so much to them. I guess I could understand it though. Finally, no one could stop their love from being real. Accepted. But it *was* real. It *had* been all these years, regardless that they weren't married legally.

Though I loved my mother, I didn't remember her—just the woman I watched on TV once a year. I knew she was a good woman, a *girl* really. I mean, she died when she was only twenty-one. I knew she loved me with everything she could, and I loved her...because I felt loved. Dad's stories, Mom's tape, even Uncle Landon's brief stories about her showed me she loved being my mom.

But it was Dad and Uncle Landon who raised me. They were my parents. And they. Loved. Fiercely. Not just me, but each other. Dad said my mother was the love of his life, that he could never love as deeply anyone else the way he loved my mother. Unconditional love, he'd called it. But Uncle Landon was the *passion* of my father's life. I saw it in his

344

eyes—the way they sparkled when he looked at him. I saw it in his actions—the way he embraced Uncle L after a long day at work.

I realized my father saw my mother in my uncle, but he also saw more. My mom was right in surmising that God had a plan in putting Tia Mercury and Clinton Daniels in each other's lives—but I don't think it was only to bear me. Mom gave my father safety, devotion, true unconditional love—my father, being born into a loveless, abusive, and neglectful family, never had that. Mom was God's gift to him, so he would know that kind of dedication from someone. And someone he could offer that to as well.

But I believed God's plan in putting Mom in Dad's life was also to bring Landon Cavill Jr. and Clinton Daniels together—so my father could experience what it felt like to crave someone. Desire them in the most intimate way. My father could know the mother of all emotions—sexual, amorous, romantic love.

But they didn't need a piece of freaking paper for that. I know *I* wouldn't. If I even ever found that kind of love. But love was love. It wasn't something one needed permission for.

It was important to my dad and Uncle L, though, so I would support them.

"How do I look?" my dad asked, straightening his tie.

"Gorgeous," I told him. "Stop being so nervous. You guys have been living together for twenty-three years."

"Still. This is a big day. I didn't get a day like this with your mother. I know she would have wanted one." My father tugged on his cuffs and adjusted the links.

"I think Mom was just happy to be with you."

"I wanted to give her everything, Fred." I cringed at the shortening of my name. Freddie was even ridiculous. My friends called me Merc. But I digress.

"You did, Dad. You gave her a home in your heart."

"On the contrary, she gave that to *me*. And even though Landon and I live in a penthouse now, part of me still feels homeless. I know it's silly, but...today makes me feel a little guilty."

"Dad, Mom would be happy for you. You know it." I flattened his lapels. "Plus, everyone's already at the park waiting. Grandpa and Grandma Mercury. Uncle Scott and Uncle David. Aunt Lydia. Even Grandma and Grandpa Cavill. And Grandpa Merc is even pretending to *like* him this weekend."

Smiling on a sigh, I said, "Well, that's a relief."

"I've never seen you this nervous." I pulled out a chair to sit, but the box Grandpa Mercury brought was in the way. "Oh, I forgot, Grandpa Merc brought that in late last night," I said, pointing to the box.

"Hmm." My father crouched down in front of the box and ripped the tape open. "Oh my God. The tapes I made Tia," he muttered more to himself than to me.

I moved to sit on the other side of the dining room table.

"Wow. I didn't realize I hadn't taken these with us during the move." My father picked up each tape, reverently touching them as if my mother's soul was attached to them.

"Hey, Dad. Maybe we can look at these later, since, like, everyone is waiting in Central Park for you and Uncle Landon to get married."

He pulled out one of the tapes and sat back on his haunches. Unwrapping the piece of paper that sheathed the cassette tape, Dad's face paled. "Oh my God, I never saw this," he whispered so low, his voice crackling as he spoke.

"Dad?"

He shook his head, tears beginning to crawl down his face.

"Dad?" I took the paper from my suddenly distraught father and skimmed it. His eyes drowned now in tears, I asked, "Dad? Do you want me to read this to you?"

He simply nodded, plopping himself on his ass where he was.

I began to read the letter that my mother wrote to my father on October seventeenth, 1987.

"To the man who stole my heart and gave it a home. To my Clinton. Today is five years since the day my mother died, and it got me thinking... You've been with me through it all. You didn't have to be. But I appreciate that you were. Maybe I was too young when we first met, and maybe you saw me as just an annoying girl who had a crush on you, but I knew from the minute my eyes set upon you that you would be the one to save me. The one to make me whole. And I know that in my own way, I have done the same for you. I think we can both safely say that we saved each other. But now, *our* time is over. It's coming to an end. I know we've only had seven short years of knowing each other, but for me, those seven years were a *lifetime*. For you, they'll just be a blip in your existence. I know you will remember these past seven years as a special time in your life. But, Clinton, don't let these years hinder you from moving forward. You have our child to raise, and you have *your* life to live. Live it for me. Live

it so I can live vicariously through you...from my ghost-perch on Freddie's shoulder (cause you know I'm not leaving this world to go to Heaven when I can watch my only son grow up. I'll have time enough for Heaven when you guys show up). So, make me smile, Clinton. And you can only do that by going through life with your own smile. Find that man that you are supposed to be with. Give him what you have to offer. Show our son that love comes in all shapes and sizes, colors and genders, and is as important as the air we breathe. And for God's sake, raise him with a grand appreciation for music. Because sometimes, we can't find the words that are deep within our soul, but we can certainly find a song that speaks them. And in that regard, my love, I made *you* a mix-tape...to make up for the vengeful one I should never had made you three years ago. I love you, Clinton. Enjoy your life and make Freddie and me proud. Love, Tia."

It was almost as if my mother knew my father would need to read this letter today. As if she knew his guilt would keep him from enjoying this day, she sent him this letter to give him permission to do so. I said nothing after reading the letter, so that my father could let her words sink in, our waiting guests be damned.

After I'm not sure how much time went by, my father finally stood and said, "We better get a move on."

And I wasn't about to stop him from attending his wedding now, no matter how late he was.

IN MY CAR, ON THE WAY to Central Park, Dad put in the mix-tape that Mom had made him. "Seasons in the Sun" was the first song to flow from my Kicker speakers. At the end of the song, Dad lowered the volume and said, "Thank you for loving me."

I glanced at him from the corner of my eye. He was lighting a cigarette, even though he knew I hated that he smoked. But I looked past my annoyance for the moment and said, "Dad. Of course."

My father had been so broken for so long in his younger years that even after all these years of being loved by Mom, by me, by Uncle Landon...he was still grateful for every bit he received. And he never stopped giving out his love as well.

Clinton Daniels was a wonderful, honorable, well-loved man. A man who defied the odds and rose above the hand he was dealt. He may have only had seven short years with Tia Mercury in his life, but I knew he had *her* to thank for it.

The End

BEFORE YOU GO...WOULD you mind leaving a review of Love Me Anyway on whichever site you purchased this book? Reviews, no matter how short, are the next best thing to word-of-mouth in helping a writer's book to get read. I would truly appreciate it. Please and thank you very much.

<u>**Sign up here to receive my newsletter and a free ebook.**</u>[1]

<<<<>>>

ACKNOWLEDGEMENTS

"Was it All Worth It"

I wish to personally thank the following people for their time, effort, contributions, and support in helping me to get this book out into the world.

Murphy Rae of Indie Solutions by Murphy Rae for her fantastic and talented cover design skills. And for helping me with the title change. I LOVE my new cover.

Murphy Rae of Indie Solutions by Murphy Rae for her superb editing eye.

Marilyn Scmidlin, Renée Napolitano, and Lois Riga for doing me a huge favor and beta-reading this book.

Kathleen Ball, Amber Dane, and Stefan Ellery for encouraging my writing journey.

My husband and children for putting up with my lack of domestic participation while I'm writing.

My little doggie Auggie who snuggles up next to my lap while I sit on my couch and write. xo

And you...for reading my book. Because if you weren't reading, I'd be writing only for myself. And what fun is that?

When Glass Shatters
(Read the first five chapters here)
CHAPTER ONE

Lorraine was home with the twelve-year-olds when the officer showed up at the door. "Your parents were killed in a car crash on the interstate. They were pronounced dead on the scene." Or something like that. Lorraine couldn't remember if the news was actually presented so unsympathetically or not, but that was the gist. "Your parents are dead. Deal with it."

Her parents were dead.

Dead!

She didn't know whether to scream. Or cry. Or scold the officer for involving himself in such a cruel prank. The battle to keep the contents in her stomach down pretty much signified he was telling the truth, but a hopeful heart and irrational brain were keeping her suspended in an erroneous reality. To get the three on the same page would be a test she was afraid to pass.

And then came the challenge of telling her siblings that their parents had died, and they would never see them again. How could she do that? How would she find the words to tell the kids that their worlds were about to shatter?

The officer spoke again. "We need you to come down to identify the bodies."

The bodies. The bodies? As in her parents' *dead* bodies? No. No. No. No. No. She couldn't do that. How could she do that? What kind of person could look at her own mother's dead body? No. Just...no.

But when she went to speak, all that came out was, "What would you like me to do with the kids?"—the only question out of the hundreds of questions racing through her mind that slipped out of her mouth.

The officer shrugged. "Whatever you want, miss, just come in as soon as you find a sitter." That was all. Business as usual. Was he really that callous to not see the devastation in front of him, or was Lorraine unable to process his empathy? Really? *Just come in as soon as you find a sitter?* Who would watch the kids? Did she really *need* someone to watch them? No. No, they were nearly thirteen years old. Lorraine was just not ready to go look at dead corpses of her mom and new stepfather. No. She wasn't ready, but she agreed to come down anyway just to say something. Anything. At least she thought she'd said something, her brain wasn't really registering what the heck her mouth was spewing.

Where was her mother right now?

Where was her mother to tell her what to believe?

Where was her mother to tell her how to get through this?

If this was all true, and not some haunting nightmare, how on earth was she going to live without her mother?

How on earth was she going to live without her mother?

How on earth—

The pain in her chest, almost unbearable, brought her down, her butt hitting the bottom step of the staircase. Lorraine was eighteen, but her mother was always her rock. Her strength. Her guidance when Lorraine was clueless. The only person who made her life...right. The only one who could ever take away her pain.

"*Oh, Mom,*" Lorraine recalled from a time not long ago. "*What if I don't graduate high school? I'm failing almost every class.*"

"You're not going to fail out of school, Lorraine. I'm going to help you get through it."

"You must be so disappointed in me. A teacher whose daughter can't even pull Cs in school."

Tatum brushed her daughter's cheek with the back of her fingers. "You can never disappoint me, Rainy-Girl. You are the kindest, most considerate girl I know. You love with all your heart and have the most beautiful soul."

"But I'm stupid."

"You are not *stupid, Lorraine Marie Mattina. You have a learning disability. That means you have trouble learning, it doesn't mean you lack intelligence."*

"I feel like I do."

"Well, you don't." Lorraine's mother took her daughter in her arms and reassured her that she would not fail out of school. "Your teachers know how hard you try. They aren't going to fail you."

"But I'm not going to get into college. I can't even take the SATs, because I can't sit still long enough."

"There's nothing wrong with going to community college, Lorraine. You'll just have to work doubly hard to get through it. But you can. I know you can."

"Thanks, Mom." Lorraine smiled on her mother's shoulder. "You always make me feel better."

Who was going to make Lorraine feel better now?

Lorraine put aside her self-pity in an effort to face her immediate reality. Her parents were dead. Her world was going to change dramatically.

As she paced the parlor floor while figuring out how to go about identifying her parents' dead bodies, she spotted the new picture above the fireplace—Noah in his wrestling get-up and his hand held high in the air by a referee. The reason he couldn't come home for Christmas; it was wrestling season, or so he claimed. Lorraine knew he'd used that excuse just so he didn't have to face his new family.

Noah.

Should she call him?

He had a right to know; it was *his* father after all. But she'd never even had a conversation with him; she'd only met him once, and she was too busy playing Maid of Honor to her mother to worry about saying hello to Brick's oldest son. He wasn't the epitome of friendly and welcoming anyway when Brick did try to introduce him.

"Noah. Noah, come here." Brick called to his son to join them—Lorraine's mom Tatum, Brick's daughter Norah, and Lorraine, all celebrating the soon-to-be marriage of Brick and Tatum. A marriage that would take place the very next day.

"Yeah?" Noah said when he sauntered over many moments later.

"I want you to meet Tatum's daughter Lorraine. She's about your—"

"Yeah. Right. Okay. Brick, Tatum. I'm gonna head on out now. Sofia and I are heading to the city. The dress-rehearsal was fun." The end of his sentence was spoken over his shoulder, because he wasted no time in getting away from his father and his soon-to-be new family.

"Don't take it personally," Norah whispered into Lorraine's ear. "His problem is with my dad, not you."

"She's right, Lorraine," Brick agreed, overhearing his daughter's explanation. "His problem has been with me for a

while now. Don't take it personally at all." Brick smiled at his new wife. "I told your mother the same thing." To all of them, Brick said, "Noah's never gotten over his mother's death. And he blames me. Though, I don't know how Keri's getting cancer was my fault. But to a fifteen year old boy, I guess anything is possible."

The wedding went on without Brick's oldest child, because he'd decided last minute not to show up. But he wasn't missed. Not by Lorraine, and by the genuine smiles on Brick and Tatum's faces, certainly not by them either.

After that wedding weekend, Lorraine recalled that her mother, accompanied by her new husband, took off for Aruba, and Noah headed back to Duke, while Lorraine spent the week at home with her brother Carter, her new stepsister Norah, and her maternal grandmother, whom she called Mimi.

Mimi. That's who she'd call.

With trembling hands and a heart beating so fast she thought it would explode, Lorraine dialed her grandmother's number.

"Lorraine, what's going on?" her grandmother asked when she heard her granddaughter's shaky voice over the phone. "It's late. Is everything all right?"

"No, Mimi, it's not." She broke down. The next words, choking her as she spoke them, came out garbled.

"Rainy, darling, calm down. I can't understand what you're trying to say."

Lorraine coughed up the strangled words after several breaths. "Mom and Brick were killed in an accident."

Mimi's response was not unexpected. "Oh my God." It was breathy, her larynx untouched by the words.

"Mimi. I have to go identify them."

When Lorraine's grandmother finally spoke, she told her she'd take the first flight out. "Hang tight, and don't go until I get there." Mimi lived in Florida; Lorraine would wait.

In the meantime, Lorraine once again struggled with her next move. Does she go up to the kids' rooms and tell them? It was closing in on midnight, maybe they were sleeping. Not likely; they were night owls—teenagers in the making. Still pacing the floor, Lorraine pulled out her cell and texted them to come down. She heard the door knobs from both bedroom doors click, and seconds later, four feet trampled down the staircase.

"What's up, Rainy?" Carter asked.

Norah kept silent and stood on the bottom step.

"Guys." Lorraine didn't know where to go from there. Oh my God, she'd rather be pulling out her fingernails one by one. She hadn't even had time to digest the news herself, how could she comfort them if she had no comfort to give yet?

"What is it, Rainy?" Norah asked quietly, seeing her stepsister squirm. Norah was shy. The kind of shy that was painful. A prepubescent girl who answered a question in the form of a question. To the question, "How old are you, Norah?" "Twelve?" would be her response. Lorraine liked Norah, but she wished she'd show more self-confidence. Entering the teenage world, it was eat or be eaten, and Lorraine was afraid Norah would be eaten alive if she didn't find some inner strength soon.

"Um, this is, well—" Oh my God, she can't do this. Lorraine was feeling dizzy, so she sat on the couch and put her head in her hands.

"Rain?" her brother asked, sidling up next to her, his hand resting compassionately on her shoulder. "What?"

No. No. Her head began to pound, the pressure of changing these kids' lives too great. *Someone help her through this. Someone. Help.* Her brother's hand squeezed her shoulder. In a minute, *he'd* need the comforting. In the background, she heard Norah shuffle over. Another young life she'd be devastating. How could life be so cruel? How could these kids lose both parents in their lifetime? Wasn't it bad enough that they both lost a parent before they'd had a chance to even know them? Carter's dad died before he was even born; Norah's mother, when she was only eight. Now, at the most impressionable times of their lives, they had to lose their only remaining parent too? Oh my God, how would she tell them?

"Okay, Rain, you're scaring me. Tell us what's going on?" Carter insisted, his hand lifting from his sister's shoulder.

She lifted her head from her hand and looked at Carter, then at Norah, who crinkled her brow. "You're crying? Why are you crying?"

Swallowing her apprehensions, she said, "Norah, do you have your brother's phone number?"

"Noah? Why? What happened to Noah?" Norah plopped down on the side of the couch where Carter wasn't.

Her hand now on Norah's knee, Lorraine said, "No. No. Nothing's happened to Noah. I just, well, he should hear this too."

"Oh my God," Norah cried. "It's my Dad?"

Carter must have seen Lorraine's expression, because he gasped.

Norah lifted her cellphone, which, being the age she was, was naturally glued to her hand at all times, and began pressing buttons.

"Norah, wait," Lorraine said, unsure if she should have Norah call her older brother.

"You said he needed to hear this, right?" Norah's eyes were already spilling tears.

Lorraine nodded. "Yeah," she mumbled.

"What happened to Brick?" Carter asked.

Not just Brick, little brother. "Um, well—" but she heard Noah answer his phone.

"Hey, little sis, what's up?" Norah's phone was set so loudly that Lorraine could hear him loud and clear.

A few sniffles later, Norah so quietly said, "Noah? Rainy said something happened to Daddy."

"What happened to Dad?" he shouted, so completely unlike his soft-spoken sister.

"I don't know, she was just about—"

"Put her on the phone, Nor."

Norah held her hand out as Lorraine pulled the phone from her hand.

"Hi, Noah." Lorraine was shaky, because one, she had to deliver the news, two, Noah was intimidating, and three, she'd only met the guy once.

"What happened?"

"May I put you on speaker phone?" Give her courage give her courage give her courage.

"Yeah, whatever, just tell me what the hell happened?"

Lorraine put Noah on speaker and laid the phone on the coffee table. She took a deep breath, grabbed her siblings' hands, then blurted, "My mom and your dad were killed in a car accident tonight."

"Oh my God," one or all of them said. "Oh my God," she heard again. "Lorraine," Noah said slowly, calmly. "Please take me off speaker."

Carter and Noah were in shock, their hands covering their mouths, their other hands gripping Lorraine's hands until her hands hurt. "In a minute, Noah, I'm comforting Norah and Carter." *More like they were comforting her.*

"Off speaker. Now."

She didn't know why, but she obeyed and picked up the phone. "You're off."

"What the hell kind of thing is that to say in front of my sister?"

"I—" Lorraine got up and crossed the room.

"You should have called me first so I could have told her. You had no right—"

"I had no right, what? Telling my *sister* that her father died? She—"

"She is my sister, not yours. And this is something she should have heard from me, not from some teenager she barely knows."

"I'm not some kid she knows from school. I share a toilet with her. And if you're so concerned about her, you should be speaking with her right now. Consoling her; not arguing with me. Or, you could hang up and let me console the two of them. God." Lorraine hung up and went back to her siblings. She took her place between the two stunned preteens, and tossed the phone back on the table.

Norah was sobbing, while Carter was trying not to. "Mimi is flying in to stay with us." She didn't know how to begin making this better, so she took their hands again. Carter yanked away from her and went upstairs. Lorraine wanted to follow him, she did, but Norah was sitting here crying. She needed to split herself in two, but had no idea how to do that.

Norah's phone rang, and on her screen, Lorraine saw the name Noah flashing in white. "Noah?" Norah answered, but this time, Norah got up and walked away. Lorraine heard a lot of "yeahs" and "okays" and then she heard Norah rattling off Lorraine's cell phone number. Oh dear God, she had to talk to him again?

Just as Norah hung up and said, "My brother's gonna call you," Lorraine's cell rang.

"Yeah?" she answered unwillingly.

"Tell me what happened?"

Trying to fight her emotions, she told him what she knew. Her mother and Brick were coming home from their Valentine's Day anniversary dinner and slid right into or underneath, she couldn't remember, a semi-tractor-trailer truck on Route Eighty. They'd died on impact. Lorraine really tried to keep from crying, Lord knew she didn't want to cry while talking to Noah, but her emotions took over and made a weeping idiot of her. "I guess I better come up," he said. *Ya think?*

After she finished with Noah, Lorraine went up to check on Carter. His door was locked and his music was on. "Carter, let me in, please," she pleaded.

"Leave me alone, Rain. I just...I need to be alone right now, 'kay?" He didn't sound like he was crying, just sad.

"Will you talk to me in the morning?"

"Yeah."

She left him and went back down to see Norah. "You okay, Nor?"

Norah was still sitting on the couch. Still crying. "What are we gonna do, Rainy? What's gonna happen to us?"

Lorraine hadn't even thought about that. What *were* they going to do? "Well, my gram is coming up as soon as she can. She'll know what to do."

"Noah said he's coming up to see me, but when I asked him what was gonna happen to us, he said he hadn't had time to think about that yet."

"It's true. We have to just get through tomorrow first." Lorraine was dreading tomorrow. Right now, she could fool herself into thinking it was all just a bad dream, or a big, nasty mistake. Once she identified the bodies, saw for herself that it was real, she didn't know what was going to come next. How could she look at her dead mother anyway? And what if it wasn't even her? Maybe the whole thing *was* just a huge mistake. Maybe the officer got the wrong information. Maybe, just maybe—

CHAPTER TWO

Lorraine woke up with Norah sprawled out across her lap. Norah had cried herself to sleep in Lorraine's arms, and only after she knew she couldn't be heard, did Lorraine let herself cry again. She knew it was going to hit her soon that her mother died, but right then, she was crying because she was scared of how she should act in front of Carter and Norah. Did she have to be strong? Did she have to act like everything was going to be all right, even though she had no idea how it could be? Was it okay if she let them know she was more scared than she ever was in her life? Even more scared than when she was six and she watched her father drop dead on the floor in front of her. *Daddy wake up; stop teasing me. Daddy. Wake up. Why won't Daddy wake up? What's a brain aneurysm, Mommy?*

MIMI ARRIVED BY NOON that day, which surprisingly, relieved a lot of the tension Lorraine carried until then. But now, the next challenge needed to be met—identifying the bodies. The same officer that came to the door last night visited right after Lorraine's grandmother showed up with a small suitcase and a huge hug for her oldest grandchild. "Hello, Officer, I'm Corrinne Blanchett. Tatum Mattina's mother. Excuse me, Tatum Mack." Mimi shook the officer's hand.

"Ma'am, I'm so sorry about your daughter, as I explained to—" the officer looked at Lorraine, then continued, "your granddaughter?" he asked, unsure of the relationship. "Richard and Tatum Mack were in a car crash on Route Eighty late last night. An eighteen wheeler was involved. I'm sorry, they didn't make it."

Mimi nodded. "Yes, my granddaughter told me." Mimi's bottom lip quivered, but she remained composed. "You need someone to identify the bodies she said?"

"Yes, ma'am. I'm sorry. If you can come down," the officer hesitated, but Mimi jumped right in.

"Of course. I will come. Can I follow you, I'm not sure of the way?"

"Sure. We can bring you if you'd like." Only then did Lorraine notice that there was a second officer standing a few feet behind the first. Was he there last night? She couldn't even remember.

Mimi turned to Lorraine and said, "Rainy. I'll be back. Let me do this. You take care of the children, okay?"

Lorraine was more than happy to abide. "Thank you, Mimi," she said, before plopping herself back onto the couch, where Norah took her hand. "I'm sorry about your dad," Lorraine said.

"I'm sorry about your mom."

They sat there in silence, their heads resting on each other, until Carter finally came out of his room. Lorraine jumped up. "Carter." She moved to hug him, but he shoved her away and said, "I'm hungry."

"Sure. I'll make you some lunch, or breakfast, or whatever." Lorraine got up and searched the kitchen for something comforting to make, before she remembered—she can't cook. She never had. Her mother always did the cooking, and now Lorraine felt so inadequate, because she'd never even learned to make a grilled cheese sandwich or a scrambled egg. In the cabinet was a box of Kraft Macaroni and Cheese. She could make that; that was her go-to snack when her mom had a late meeting at school and Lorraine got hungry. Lorraine never thought about how fortunate she was to have a mother who had school hours and summers off—a mother who was pretty much at her children's beck and call whenever they'd needed her. Not that Lorraine or Carter took advantage of her, but their mother was always there when she was needed. For everything. Who would relight the flame beneath the water-heater? Who would change the batteries in the smoke alarms? When did they even need to be changed? What grade was Carter in? Oh my goodness, who would help him with Algebra? Or Chemistry? Carter was smart. Lorraine, not so much. She went to community college because she couldn't get into other schools. Her Auditory Processing Disorder kept her from doing well. Her grades were pretty much below average, except for gym class, where she was able to pull an A. So, she was going to community college to get her Associate's Degree in Exercise Science, where hopefully, she'd pull good enough grades to transfer to a four-year school to get her Teacher Education and Physical Education Degree. But who paid for college? Did her mother? Did her mother need to take out a loan to pay for school? She didn't even know. With the Kraft Macaroni and Cheese box in her hand, Lorraine sat down on the nearest chair and cried. Where was her mother? Who was going to take care of everything? Lorraine was frightened. More frightened than she'd ever been in her life. Come to think of it, except for her father dying in front of her—and one other devastating moment she chose not to think about right now—Lorraine had never been frightened in her life—her mother must have gotten to her children's fears before they even knew they were supposed to be afraid.

"Rain?" Carter was standing in the kitchen doorway.

Lorraine looked up at him and smiled and held up the box of Kraft. "This is all I know how to make, Car." She shook her head and tucked in her lips, her tongue tasting the salt from her dripping tears. "This is all I know how to make," she repeated.

Carter stared at her a few seconds. Lorraine saw his eyes tear up, but then Carter side-fisted the door jam and turned and left. The front door slammed soon after.

That's when Norah came into the kitchen. "What happened?"

Still holding that Kraft box, "This is all I know how to make, Norah? This is it."

Norah's shoulders dropped, and she sighed. "It's okay, Rainy. We'll figure it out." Lorraine kicked out the chair in front of her, and Norah sat. Patting her big sister's knee, Norah said, "Rain? We'll figure it all out, right? You and me?"

Lorraine smiled through her tears and nodded, saying, "Yeah. We'll figure it out."

Norah took the box from Lorraine, got up, and said, "Will you show me how to make it, so then we'll both know?"

And so, together, they made a box of Kraft Macaroni and Cheese. But they didn't eat it; they covered it and put it aside for Carter. "So, would you like me to make you a cup of tea, Norah? I know how to make that, too." Lorraine was more grateful than she'd ever been to have Norah as her sister. Norah said she knew how to boil water too, and she'd be happy to have a cup of hot chocolate while Lorraine had her tea. Lorraine dumped some cocoa in one mug, a tea bag in another, and they both sat and watched the tea kettle until it started to whistle.

Lorraine and Norah didn't know what to talk about, since small talk seemed inappropriate, and the big stuff seemed too heavy, so they drank their hot beverages in silence, both of them focused on what would become of their family.

CHAPTER THREE

Mimi returned to the house red-eyed and sad, dashing Lorraine's very tiny hope that her mother was still alive. "I'm sorry, girls," she said when she saw them at the kitchen table. "I'm so sorry."

Norah got up and made Mimi a cup of tea and then the three of them solemnly mourned over their mugs filled with hot comfort. Mimi explained to them what to expect over the next few days. She'd take care of the funeral arrange-ments and go through paperwork to find Brick's and Tatum's Wills—hopefully, they each had one. And Mimi would call the lawyer, or find one to use if they didn't. All she wanted the kids to do was process the deaths of their parents. Lor-raine was once again grateful today, and that made her laugh. How could she be grateful for anything, when her mother just passed away?

"So, where's Carter?" Mimi asked, when she finally real-ized she hadn't seen him.

"He ran out right after you left. I think he doesn't know how to feel. Or how to," Lorraine shrugged, "act. I don't know what to do for him."

"He needs time to accept this." Mimi patted Lorraine's hand. "He'll be okay. Give him time. And you two," she nod-ded to both Lorraine and Norah, "need time as well. Let yourselves cry it out. Don't think you have to be strong through this. It's important to cry." She patted Lorraine's hand again. "Both of you, go take a nap. I'm sure you barely slept last night."

"No. Not well."

"Go. Get on," Mimi insisted. "I'll look through the kitchen; see if I can't throw something together for dinner."

Norah thanked Mimi and went up to her room. Lorraine kissed her grandmother's delicate cheek. "Thanks, Mimi." As Lorraine turned to walk out, she stopped. "Is Grandpa coming up?"

"Yes. He's flying in after he gets some things in order."

Lorraine nodded and went to her room, where she fell asleep pretty much right away. But she didn't sleep peacefully. *She had no arms. And she was floating, trying to reach the boy, but she couldn't. And she was unable to get her feet to stay firmly on the ground. And unable to grab the boy, because she had no arms. Was she in space? Was she on Earth? As much as she tried to reach him in the black room, she couldn't. She screamed for help, but no one heard. Where were her arms? If she had arms, she could take hold of him. Save him.*

Lorraine woke from her nightmare to the sound of a loud engine beneath her bedroom window. As she got up, her foot stuck in the tucked-in sheet and she tumbled off the bed face first, her nose touching ground while her arms were somehow caught behind her, wrapped up in the comforter. How in the world? And then, OUCH. When she brought her hand to her nose, she felt slime. Red slime to be exact, because when she took her hand away, it was covered in blood. *Great.* Thank you very much, you loud-engine-car driving person. Lorraine got herself to her feet, found the box of tissues on her dresser, and went to the window, a load of Kleenex jammed up against her face. A white Harley Davidson sat in the driveway. A motorcycle? She didn't know anyone who owned one.

After she exchanged her bloody tissues for a few new ones, Lorraine headed downstairs and saw Mimi standing at the opened front door, a deep voice rumbling from its other side. "Noah, right? Come in."

When Lorraine heard his name, she stopped mid-staircase. Noah was here? Lorraine gripped the handrail, using her hand that held the tissues, forgetting that her nose was probably still dripping with blood. "Honey, I'm so sorry about your father," Mimi said as she pulled Noah in for a hug. Noah patted her back and separated himself right away.

"Where's Norah?" His voice was strained, like he was trying to either keep from crying or keep from sounding irritated. Lorraine couldn't decide.

"She's napping. Can I make you a cup of coffee or something? A piece of cake? I just made—" Mimi stopped talking, because Noah wasn't paying attention to her. He was looking over her shoulder at Lorraine. Mimi followed his gaze and gasped. "Lorraine! What did you do?"

Lorraine's tissue-filled hand flew back to her face. "I fell out of bed," she mumbled into the tissues.

As Mimi said, "Oh, Rainy, come on, let's go get you cleaned up," Noah snickered, causing Lorraine to flush. "Come on," Mimi repeated.

With as much dignity as she could reclaim, Lorraine glided down the steps, hoping Noah would stop staring and wipe the smirk off his face. So, she had a bloody nose. Didn't wrestlers get bloody noses? It can't be the first time he's seen one. Lorraine swept past him, finally taking her eyes off him, and followed her grandmother into the kitchen.

"Come on, child," Mimi said, making Lorraine feel even more ridiculous. "Here's a wet cloth. Clean up your face, and I'll get you an ice pack." Mimi kept talking—about hoping her nose wasn't broken, and praying her eyes didn't sport two huge black-and-blues—but Lorraine found that her attention was once again on Noah. Come on, Rainy, he's a jerk. He laughed at your bloody face. As she dabbed at her face, she flinched. There probably *would* be two black eyes, but Lorraine couldn't think about that right now; it was trivial compared to everything else going on.

"So, Noah," Mimi said, placing a mug of coffee in front of him after tending to Lorraine. "Was the drive up okay? You go to Duke, right?"

Noah nodded. "Yeah." And Lorraine realized they barely knew him, and he, them. Had Brick told Noah anything about Tatum's family? Brick talked about Noah's accomplishments—two-time New Jersey State Champion in high school, Valedictorian for his high school class in 2014, National Champion his Freshman year at Duke, 4.0 GPA, or higher, or whatever, because Lorraine could never keep track—but he never spoke of anything beyond Noah's scholastic accomplishments. Even Norah hardly talked about him. Was he kind? Was he popular? Lorraine assumed he was, since he was both an athlete and a scholar. Was he shy? Or angry? Was he carefree or did he get uptight about things? Who *was* Noah Mack behind the All-American? Lorraine felt she needed to know.

And with him sitting right here in front of her, she had this overwhelming urge to find out a lot more than what she probably ought to.

CHAPTER FOUR

Noah drank his coffee anxiously. Where the hell was Norah? He didn't know these people, and making small-talk was painful. For all he'd accomplished in his nineteen years, Noah was still uncomfortable talking with people. He was quiet. A loner. Some called him an introvert, but he disagreed. There was nothing shy about him; he just hated socializing. And the word introvert made it sound like he was introspective, which couldn't be further from the truth. For Noah, stuff was just stuff. There was no deeper meaning to life, and everything did not happen for a reason. What possible reason could there be for his mother dying of cervical cancer when she was only thirty-six years old? No. For Noah, life was what it was, and he didn't overthink it. He did what was expected of him, he enjoyed wrestling, and he did well in school, because, for some reason, his brain found nothing a challenge. Noah wasn't what anyone would call a happy person, but he was fine with that. Happiness was overrated.

"I'm sorry about your father," Lorraine said after some time. Her nose had stopped bleeding, and she was now holding an icepack to it. "And I'm sorry you had to hear it the way you did." Her voice was on the high-pitched side, like a girl who hadn't reached puberty yet. Noah kind of liked it.

"Yeah. It's fine." With his foot, Noah was tapping the floor, repeatedly, beneath the table, and now he found his finger doing the same thing against the coffee mug. When the hell was Norah going to wake up?

"Noah," the grandmother said. "I know I asked you this already, but are you sure you don't want something to eat? I made a cake. It's warm. I have pot roast simmering on the stove, but it won't be ready for another hour."

"No. I'm good. When do you think Norah is going to wake up? I really wanted to be able to talk with her."

"I'll go check," Lorraine said, putting down her ice pack.

"If you tell me where her bedroom is, I can check on her myself." Noah was annoyed; he was sure they noticed the irritation in his voice, but he didn't care. Norah was *his* sister, and he had more right than any of them to go check on her.

"Okay. I'll show you."

Noah got up and followed Lorraine.

Norah was snoring when Noah opened the door to her bedroom, so he sat on the purple corduroy chair next to the window and watched her. She didn't even look like Norah anymore. How could a year change someone so much? She didn't look like a little girl anymore. She was a teenager. Well, soon, anyway. But she looked more like the teenager she was becoming, then the little girl Noah had last seen. When was the last time he saw Norah? That's right. The wedding. More like the wedding weekend, because Noah never showed up at the wedding. The last thing he'd wanted to do was watch his father marry Tatum. Instead, he took off with his then on-again off-again girlfriend Sofia. It had not even been four years then since his mother died. After two, his father was already dating Tatum. It's not that Tatum was a bitch or anything. On the contrary, she'd always been sweet to Noah—well, the few times they'd come in contact with each other. Even when Noah walked out in the middle of a Sunday dinner that Tatum went to the trouble of preparing, and before he did, he'd slammed his fist so hard on the table that his soup and his sister's soup went flying. On his way out the door, he'd heard Tatum stop his father from going after

Noah. Her words, specifically, were, "No, Brick. He's hurting. Give him time to warm up to me. He'll be okay." Noah's been sitting on those words all this time. Would he warm up to her? He'd never know now. Would he be okay? He still had no idea.

Noah's eyes were closed when a soft young voice broke through his thoughts. He immediately thought it was Lorraine again, but when he opened his eyes, Norah was scooting to the edge of the bed. "Noah. You're here?" she said in question, as she got off the bed to hug him.

"Hey, kiddo," Noah responded in monotone, but embraced her with a hug as intense as hers. He missed his sister. He should have kept in contact with her more often, but calling her reminded him too much of what he didn't have anymore—his mother. And that was something Noah wasn't quite able to get over yet. Unlike his father, Noah was not able to get over the death of Keri Mack. Even if it had been well over four years now since she'd died.

Norah pulled away and sat at the edge of the bed. "I'm so glad you're here, Noah. I'm so scared. Lorraine says everything will be okay, but—" Norah trailed off.

It'll be okay. Where had he heard that before? Lorraine must have learned from her mother. Everything will *not* be okay. They had no parents now. Noah was an adult, he could take care of himself, but Norah was now an orphan. Who would be her guardian? Would *he* have to care of her? What did that mean in regards to his studies? To wrestling? Why was he even thinking like this? He wasn't a thinker. Not when it came to situations. His parents took care of those things—his mom until she died, his dad ever since. Noah just took care of Noah. Always had. Now did he have to take care of Norah, too?

"Noah," his sister said softly. "Will everything be okay? Is Lorraine right?"

Her eyes were wide and questioning. How did he answer that? "I guess," was all he could think of. He shook his head and sighed. "You wanna go get a bite?"

Norah shrugged, and a frown took over her face. He could tell she'd wanted him to confirm Lorraine's sentiment that everything would be okay, but he couldn't bring himself to say it. He knew all too well that it wouldn't. Her life was about to change in ways she couldn't fathom, and he didn't want to think about that right now.

"How 'bout it, kid? Is there a McDonald's around here?" Noah needed to get out of this house.

"I think Mimi is making dinner." The frown stayed on Norah's face as she took a hair band off her dresser and tied her hair up in a ponytail.

"So," he said with a shrug. "Lorraine and her brother can eat it." Noah stood and headed for the door. "Come with me. You can wear my helmet; I'll just risk going without one."

"A helmet?"

"I got a Harley. I'll take you for a ride."

Norah shook her head. "I just wanna stay home."

Greeaat. "Fine."

"Noah?" Norah stopped midway down the hall before descending the stairs.

"Yeah?"

"Why did it take you this long to come home?"

"I left a few hours after I heard. I didn't even call my coach, Nor."

"No. I mean, why did you have to wait for them to die before you came home?"

"This isn't my home." He heard the clip in his own voice, but it was the truth. This was Brick and Tatum's house; they'd bought it and moved in before they'd gotten married. He'd taken Norah from her home three huge towns away, to live in a new house, leaving their childhood home up for sale so strangers could live in it.

"It *would* be if you left college once in a while," she muttered as she walked away from him. *Norah's gotten snippy lately.*

Just as Noah made it down the stairs, the brother walked through the front door.

"Oh. Hey," Carter said.

"Hey. Sorry about your mom." Noah really was sorry for Carter. The boy lost his mom; Noah knew all too well what that loss did to a teenage boy. Not that he knew if Carter was a teenager yet. He only recalled that he was somewhere close to Norah's age.

"Thanks. Sorry 'bout your dad."

"Thanks."

Both boys moped into the kitchen, where they were greeted with a warm hello by the grandmother, but a "Where have you been, Carter? We were worried sick about you," by the swollen-eyed Lorraine. Even though she pretty much screamed at her brother, and even though her face shouted "I'm in a fighting mood," Lorraine was not intimidating. Her brother responded with an exaggerated roll of his eyes and said nothing else.

The grandmother, on the other hand, ignored her granddaughter's outburst and said, "Sit down, boys, I made pot roast." She put two plates and sodas in front of them, and all five now sat down to a delicious but somber meal. Noah hadn't had a home-cooked meal since...since...since, well, forever.

Lorraine's lips were pursed before she blurted again, "Really, Carter. I wish you'd just have called. You didn't even answer my texts."

"Yeah, well, sorry there, Rain. I just happened to lose my mother today and had other things on my mind than worrying about you."

Great. A family feud. "You know what?" Noah said, standing from his chair. "I have to leave. Norah. I'm going for a ride. I'll be back later."

Norah jumped up. "No, Noah. Please stay."

"I didn't come here to play happy family," Noah glanced at Lorraine, "or Family Feud."

"Nobody asked you to come." Lorraine sneered.

The grandmother slammed her hands on the table. "Stop it now. All of you. Noah, sit down."

Noah wanted to say, "You're not my grandmother," but he didn't think he should be disrespectful to an old lady, so he sat back down. "Now, this is hard on all of you," she said. "You're all on edge, and you're all very sad. Instead of fighting, you should be comforting each other. We have a long road ahead of us; we're going to need to stick together." Lorraine's grandmother's eyes welled up, but she continued. "I'm here to make things as easy as possible, but there are still decisions to be made. We still have to figure where—" She stopped. Why'd she stop?

"Where what?" Lorraine asked what Noah was wondering.

"Nothing. We just have to pull together."

"Where what, Mimi?" Lorraine asked again. "Where we're gonna live?" Lorraine looked at her grandmother, then at Noah, then back at her grandmother. "We're not staying here? Then where? Where will we live?"

Shit. Where will they live? Noah was going back to school. He was right in the middle of wrestling season. He had classes. What was he going to do about Norah? Did his dad name a guardian for her?

"One day at a time, Rainy. Okay?" her grandmother said.

Lorraine didn't take another bite. Noah glanced her way every so often. Her chest was rising too much. Her lips quivered, and her eyes were glassy. The dinner table? It was so quiet you could almost hear the hearts of five people breaking. Noah's included.

CHAPTER FIVE

Lorraine couldn't take the silence or the unknown any longer. All she wanted to do was mourn the loss of her mother, not worry about where she, Norah, and Carter would end up. If her grandmother went back to Florida, would the kids have to go? Lorraine was old enough not to have to, but Carter and Norah—would they have to? Lorraine couldn't take care of two twelve-year-olds. She could barely take care of herself with her part-time fitness instructor job and full-time college schedule. She took her uneaten dinner and threw it away, leaving the kitchen to be alone.

In her room, unable to get comfortable, she slid on a pair of leggings and her sneakers, grabbed her fleece, and went out for a run. Her mind was too busy racing for her to enjoy her iPod, so she took to the sidewalk without her music, in an attempt to outrun her thoughts. It was stupid, really, because it was pitch-black outside, and it kept her from venturing too far. At the end of her development, she turned around and ran home.

When she got there, under the garage light, Noah was sitting on his bike. "Got far," he mocked, referring to her short five-second run.

Lorraine looked at him and said nothing. His eyes looked grey out in the dark. She wondered what color they actually were, since she couldn't recall noticing before.

"Not much of a runner?" he asked.

She continued her staring. "I run. It's too dark right now."

"Afraid of the dark?"

"Afraid I'll fall."

"Don't wanna bust up your nose?"

Lorraine ignored his side-splitting joke.

"Wanna go for a ride?"

"What?"

"A ride. On my bike. This thing I'm sitting on."

Lorraine thought about it for a minute. She didn't even know if she liked him. So far, he'd seemed rude and aloof. To her surprise, though, when she opened her mouth, she said, "You got another helmet?"

"No. You can use mine."

"You can't ride without a helmet."

"Who says?"

"The law."

"I'm not too concerned about it. Would you like to go or not?" He was rude about it, but she was rude at dinner. Carter was rude to her. Didn't they all deserve to be rude right now?

"Sure." She took his helmet and straddled behind him, knowing she was running away, even if for the moment, just like Carter had. Here she was, six years older than her brother and doing exactly what she'd yelled at him for.

But as soon as Noah took off down the road, Lorraine's busted nose pressing into the brisk air, she felt unburdened. She closed her eyes and let the wind wash away her worries. Noah's bike produced the effect she'd attempted to achieve through running. As Noah picked up speed, Lorraine was afraid to fall backwards off the bike, so clutching him tighter, she rested her chin against his leather shoulder. Her heart raced with the dangerous thrill. Why hadn't she ever thought of owning a motorcycle? It was so much better than running.

Miles passed by before she felt the bike come to a stop. "Where are we?" she asked when she opened her eyes.

Noah turned down the engine and said, "My old home."

A large colonial-style house sat across the street from the field where Noah parked.

"Wow. Nice house." Lorraine unwrapped her arms from around Noah and got off the bike, but Noah remained put. He stared at the house for so long that Lorraine became uncomfortable. She didn't know if she should get back on the bike or stay standing behind it, so she did neither and sat on the frozen grass.

It took Noah a few beats before he realized what she'd done. "What the hell are you doing down there?"

"Waiting."

"For what?"

Lorraine frowned. "For you."

Noah shook his head and got off the bike. He pulled a green knapsack out of his luggage trunk and took out a sweatshirt. "Here. At least sit on this," he said as he tossed Lorraine the shirt.

"Thanks." She took it and spread it beneath her.

He took out another shirt and laid it down before he sat.

"You miss it?" she asked him.

With his eyes still on the house, he nodded. "Yeah."

"Sorry."

He nodded again.

At first, Lorraine didn't know what to say, but then she decided to ask, "Why haven't you come back?"

The look she received from him made her feel stupid. "Because he sold it," he said in a tone that *confirmed* he thought she was stupid.

"I mean to *our* house. Your father built an apartment for you."

"What are you talking about?"

Lorraine leaned forward over her pretzeled legs and rubbed at her hands. "He had an addition put on the back of the house. It's called a mother-daughter, but he added it so you'd have a place to stay during the summer and Christmas break and whatever."

By the baffled look on Noah's face, Lorraine assumed he'd had no idea about the apartment.

"Why didn't *you* take it?"

"Because. Brick said it was yours."

After a pause, Noah said, "Even though I told him I rented an apartment with some teammates?"

"Even though." Lorraine didn't know he'd said that to Brick, but she went with it.

They sat there for several more silent minutes. Lorraine was uncomfortable with his silence. Maybe because he never smiled. Obviously, he wouldn't be smiling now, but even the first time she met him, all he did was scowl. But Lorraine couldn't help herself, she had to break the silence. "So, you never answered me. Why haven't you come back? Like, even before they got married, you never came home."

He eyed Lorraine from the corner of his eye. "There was no home to come back to."

"What?"

"Brick sold our home." Noah pointed across the street at the house that no longer belonged to him. "That's my home. And I'll never be able to go back again."

"But—"

"Rain? Is that what they call you?"

"Or Rainy."

"Well, Rainy. I don't want to talk about it anymore." His words were crisp and articulate. He stood, picked up his shirt and put it in the trunk, and straddled the bike.

Lorraine got up and held the damp sweatshirt in her hands. "Is your trunk locked?"

"No."

Noah was a moody thing. But since his dad just died, she'd cut him some slack. She was pretty moody herself today.

Despite Noah's moodiness, Lorraine enjoyed the ride back home just as much as the ride to Noah's old house. She just avoided leaning her chin on his shoulder. But she did stay as close as possible for fear that she'd fall backward off the bike.

When they pulled up, Mimi was standing on the front porch in her nightgown, winter coat, and a glower that could rival the one Noah was sporting at the moment.

"Lorraine," she said cooly. "Did you not just do the exact same thing you accused your brother of? And at almost midnight?"

"Midnight?" Lorraine hadn't realized it had been so late. Yes, dinner was eaten later than usual, but...wow. It had been over twenty-four hours that she'd lost her mother and Brick. And it hadn't even sunk in yet.

If the first five chapters of When Glass Shatters grabbed your attention, you can purchase it on most online outlets where books are sold. Thank you for reading!

Don't miss out!

Click the button below and you can sign up to receive emails whenever J.P. Grider publishes a new book. There's no charge and no obligation.

https://books2read.com/r/B-A-BXUE-VWOQ

Connecting independent readers to independent writers.

About the Author

J.P. Grider is a New Adult and Young Adult author who is a sucker for a good love story - whether it's reading one or writing one. And when she's not reading or writing a fairy tale, she's living one with her husband, four children, and her beloved Auggie Doggie.

Read more at https://www.jpgrider.com/.